The Secrets of Avigdor

Redemption Pirates
Book One

Chaney Hobson

Paperback isbn 979-8-9865961-0-5

Hardback isbn 979-8-9865961-1-2

Ebook isbn 979-8-9865961-2-9

Cover art done by Janelle Hovde

Cover formatting done by Chaney Hobson

Editing done by lili_writes, Holly Leth and Michelle Emanuelli

Formatting by Chaney Hobson

CONTENTS

I'd like to thank my family. Without them this would not have been possible. Thank you, Mom, for listening to my dreams and encouraging me.
Also, I would not have had the confidence to get this book published without my brother, Caleb.

PROLOGUE

Rain began to fall at a gentle pace, a cool distraction from the island heat. Gabriel Hoffman lifted his sweat-drenched face to the heavens, relishing the cool relief. Lightning flashed across the sky and was soon followed by a loud crack of thunder.

How long had he been here? It had to be almost two weeks and probably more than three since he had left the shores of his homeland. Not that he was in the frame of mind to count the days. It seemed easier to keep his mind elsewhere and to not think of the present. Unfortunately, the only place his mind seemed to visit was the day that led to this island and to the present company that he kept.

Gabriel sat down on a rock and closed his eyes, memories from that day assaulting his mind. Years at sea, away from his homeland, his king, to return to.... His stomach churned at the memories.

The fight for his home, the kingdom of Lookonia, had been going on for years and it had been wearing the army thin. The king had personally asked—almost begged—him to join the army as lead navigator and strategist. He had been a final resort. Not because he wasn't trusted with the task. Quite the opposite in fact.

King Joel and he were close friends, more like brothers. Gabriel's father had been the royal family's teacher and advisor, a highly prestigious job. And ever since the day they met, Joel and Gabriel were inseparable.

Warm memories of his childhood were a welcome distraction from his current situation. He remembered rainy days sitting around the fire with Joel, reading books and playing games. Even the memories of school and hours of tedious studying were now some of his favorite memories. They had spent much of their youth studying mathematics, politics, and the scriptures. He couldn't put a number on the many hours they had spent especially studying scripture and, when they got old enough, debating on the meaning of certain passages.

As they grew, they were there for one another during many joys and through the hardest of sorrows. Within a few short years they both lost their fathers. Joel was crowned king at the young age of eighteen and Gabriel became his advisor, just as his father had been before him.

Joel eventually married a wonderful woman who helped to ease the grief in his heart. Shortly after, they were blessed with two sons. This new family openly and honestly accepted Gabriel into their fold. Even with no blood family of his own, he felt like he belonged.

They all grew quite close, and he taught Joel's boys, taking pride in the role his father had passed down. Both boys were quite smart, though he slightly favored the adventurous streak of the eldest.

The kingdom had lived in peace and flourished until the kingdom of Narine fell and its new king lusted after their prosperity. That's when the fighting began and Gabriel had been asked to join. Goodbye had been bittersweet, but he had known he was fighting for his family's freedom, for the future of his kingdom.

After a year at sea, he had heard of the queen's passing and it grieved him that he could not be there with them. It took a while, but he eventually got someone trained well enough to replace him and he hurried home. Finally, three years later, he would be able to see his family. He hadn't realized how far from the truth that had been.

Gabriel opened his eyes, begging the memories to stop though it was to no avail. The castle had been engulfed in flames when he arrived and screams had filled the night air. The castle was under attack.

Everything after that had happened so quickly. He'd run in to find his home aflame, pirates and guards in bloody battle. He'd been captured, attacked by a group of men and bound, forced to watch as these pirates looted and pillaged through his father's old belongings.

In amongst all the chaos he had not forgotten about his king but was helpless. There was nothing he could do as the enemy ruined his home and his family.

The dreaded call went up among the guards, "The king is dead. King Joel is dead."

Gabriel had screamed in anguish, not caring what threats his captors had thrown at him. Nothing could quell the anguish that had torn a gaping hole in his heart. Finally, the pirates had knocked him unconscious, and he had awoken aboard their ship.

Amongst his father's belongings they had found an old map. Unfortunately, he was one of the few people who could read his father's writing. So here he was now, heartbroken, hands tied, trying to find an imaginary treasure.

Yelling broke through his reflections and pulled him to the present. The pirates he was begrudgingly with were up to their usual bickering and fighting. Hardly a day went by when Captain Steele Eye didn't have to threaten someone with a pistol or a sword to the throat.

Miraculously, despite his dangerous companions, Gabriel had felt calm since arriving on the island. Perhaps that was because of shock, but something told him it was deeper than that. It had to be Elohim. The only times he felt peace from his thoughts and the situation he was in was when he prayed.

A man with rotten teeth and an equally bad attitude walked past and kicked Gabriel off the rock and into the mud. He laughed as if that was the only entertainment he had experienced in a while.

The bickering had turned into outright yelling now, drawing Gabriel's full attention. Captain Steele Eye drew his gun and aimed it at several men, which was his go-to form of discipline it seemed. This time, however, several men drew their own guns and aimed back.

The captain's eyes grew dark with fury. Before anyone could react, he shot the first man who had talked back, then drew his sword and stabbed the man next to him. Shouts rang out over the thunder, and screams erupted as everyone began to attack their own neighbor.

Suddenly afraid, Gabriel rolled behind a large rock and kept his head down. This was bad, even for this group. Somehow, this night felt different. Something dark and forbidding seemed to weigh the air.

A movement out of the corner of his eye caught his attention. His eyes scanned the forest as shots rang out and screams erupted amidst the storm's fury. He had just about decided he had been mistaken when he locked eyes with the most beautiful brown eyes he had ever seen. Thirty feet away a young woman was partially hidden behind a palm tree. Only her dazzling eyes and delicate nose were visible.

Those eyes...he had thought he had glimpsed those same brown eyes days prior but only for a moment. He had convinced himself that it was just his imagination. Now, he hoped and prayed he wasn't imagining things.

Her lips tilted into a charming smile. In that moment his pain and grief melted a little, making room for something new. Something warm and inviting.

Suddenly her face grew fearful, and she ran towards him amidst the gun fire. What had caused her fearless jump into the battlefield? As she neared, a noise caught his attention near the water. He looked over and a scream caught in his throat. So much blood. So many teeth.

CHAPTER ONE

Annika looked into the early morning sky and smiled at the colors that were beginning to appear. A beautiful display of purple and orange was streaking across the grey sky. Early morning was a special time for her. A time of peace and reflection before a hard day's work of teaching at the orphanage.

It was the time of day that she felt the most calm. Each color that spread around the sky was a testament to the handy work of her Creator, reminding her that Elohim was very much in control. He so expertly and effortlessly could take an empty sky and turn it into a masterpiece that not even the most accomplished of painters could create.

Not long from now the other children in the orphanage would awaken, and she would not have another moment of rest. For these brief few moments, she could breathe easy and not worry about the future.

Annika looked over her shoulder at the tall and rundown building she called home. Her room was at the top of the central tower, three stories up. She had started off as an orphan looking for a home and now stayed as a teacher and friend.

Even though she wished for a different life, she couldn't deny the happiness she felt at bringing joy to these children. She turned back to her task at hand, determined to actually stay focused for a few minutes. She shifted her grip on her bow, pulling an arrow from her quiver and drawing the bowstring back, feeling the resistance from the flexible wood. The shaft of the arrow pressed into her cheek as her eyes focused on the target at the other end of the courtyard.

Annika took a deep breath and released the arrow. It hit its mark on the tree with a satisfying thump. She smiled widely, thankful that her aim had improved this much. She took out another arrow and shot a target even further out. Upon closer inspection she discovered it was a perfect shot as well. Father would have been proud.

Annika leaned against the tree, with the notch that doubled as her target, and looked out over the valley. The sky was quickly changing and the surrounding clouds were turning red and were a dazzling contrast to the orange sky. The light cast shadows on the surrounding hills. Nearby she could spot several farmers out in the land beginning the day's work. Nearest was a grove of orange trees where a man stood checking his harvest for the year, and a bit further was an apple orchard where several workers were tending to the trees.

It was a joyous and difficult time for the people of the kingdom. Crops were going to be harvested soon, but that meant the yearly taxes would be upon them. After the king taxed them for their land and whatever else he could leech, there was not much to go around.

Despite the difficult taxes and the injustices in their system, the people had a cheerful attitude. They still had harvest parties and festivals. All of the ones the king let them have, at least. He had set up festivals only to the gods he deemed real and parties to honor them.

She shook her head in sadness and walked back down the hill. That was one thing she was thankful for about living in the orphanage. They were protected here and kept away from the godlessness that was developing elsewhere.

She put down her bow and unsheathed her sword. The welcome feel of it in her hand was like having an old friend. The weight was perfectly balanced, and it sliced easily through the air. She began some simple routines, her sword moving flawlessly in her grasp. Before she could advance to some harder moves, a voice called to her.

"Annika!"

She paused for a moment and looked over her shoulder. Her best friend Carter was running towards her. His sword was attached to his belt, and the sheath bumped his legs as he ran. He was smiling from ear to ear. He often joined her for sword practice in the mornings, if he was able to wake up early enough.

"You made it."

He stopped at the base of the hill and huffed from his run. His blond hair spilled over his eyes before he swept it back.

"I told you I was coming." He grinned. He was fifteen years old, almost four years younger than her. They got along great, despite their age difference. He was like a brother to her.

"You're just in time. I was just getting started." She held her sword aloft and he drew his by instinct. He was getting very good. When she knew he was ready, she began some simple routines. He blocked and dodged and even swung some of his own blows.

Soon, they were both huffing from the exertion and doing more advanced moves. Carter was definitely improving, and the smile on his face said that he knew it as well. Even though he was improving, he wasn't to her level yet. She dodged his sword and whirled behind him. Before he knew it, her sword was pointed at his back.

He held his arms in the air. "Ok, you got me."

She laughed and returned her sword to its sheath. "You're improving."

"Thanks, I have a great teacher." His eyes opened wide. "I forgot! I found this letter for you by the front door. You know Mr. Colburn doesn't tell us when the mail arrives."

Annika accepted the letter and read the return address. It was from her brother! It had been months since his last letter, and she had been getting worried.

Forgetting about their swordplay, she plopped on the grassy hill and used the growing sunlight to read the short letter. She had barely started reading when she noticed Carter hovering close by, equally as curious about its contents.

Annika laughed. "Sit down. I'll read it to you." Carter sat down next to her and began to listen intently.

Annika, my dear sister,

So much time has passed since we last saw one another. I miss you more than I ever thought possible. Your smile was enough to brighten even the dreariest of days.

I finally have secured a place to teach in a small community, although it has taken a little while for the people to warm up to me. Now that a few months have passed, it seems they have at long last accepted me. Now we all feel like family. If ever you need something, there is always someone to help. Why, just the other day, my horse and I got in a bit of a bind, and everyone came out to help. I had been on my way to visit a family in my congregation and the poor horse got stuck in the mud up to her chest. Upon hearing of it, the entire congregation got together and hoisted her out. Do not worry, for she is fine as can be now. I must say, though, it was quite a lengthy chore to clean her.

The children here are so sweet but are lacking a fine role model. Someone to teach them on the Sabbath. Since you are now nineteen, I had hoped, if you are willing, that you could join me and be their teacher? I could use your help throughout the rest of the week as well. If your answer is yes, I have a ticket enclosed in this letter. The captain of this ship is a good and honorable man. We first met on my journey here and have been good friends since. The journey is two weeks if the weather cooperates. The choice is yours. I will not sway you. Hopefully, I shall see you soon, but if not, I will await your next letter.

All the information is on the ticket.

I love you my dear sister. Safety and blessings to you always. May Elohim bless you and keep you.

Mathew

Annika looked up from the letter with tears in her eyes. There was no debate in her mind. Of course she would go. She would see her brother soon! She noticed that Carter had tears in his eyes as well but for a completely different reason.

"Do you really have to go?" he asked, his voice hitching a little. His brown eyes, so full of excitement a moment ago, looked at her in dread.

"Oh, Carter, I don't wish to leave you by any means. I have to go, though," Annika said softly. She glanced down at the ticket in the letter. It was not large, but she felt like it held her whole future. She turned it over and looked in the fine print.

"Carter!" Annika fairly shouted in excitement. "This says for an adult and attendant. I know I'm not your blood relative, but you are as close to me as anyone could be. How would you like to come with me?"

The tears vanished from his eyes and were instead replaced by a look of utter disbelief. His mouth gaped open, and for a second he struggled to put a sentence together.

"M-m-me? Go with you? Are you serious?"

"Oh, if you would rather stay here…" Perhaps she had read him wrong, and he really did enjoy this place more than she had thought.

He snorted. "Are you kidding? Of course I will go! No way I'd let you go without me." He jumped forward and gave her a fierce embrace. After a minute, Annika pulled back, smiling. Her eyes drifted to the horizon once more. Elohim's masterpiece was at its brightest in the sky. To Annika, it seemed to speak of hope, love, and maybe a bit of adventure.

The time to leave was fast approaching, and Annika couldn't help but be a little nervous. The relationship between her home, the kingdom of Narine, and the kingdom of Lookonia had been shaky for years. Her earliest memories of the two countries were filled with war. After Narine's royal family had been dethroned when she was a baby, trade had stopped, as did any sort of travel. Years passed by with little contact, unless it was violent. Their new king desired to overthrow Lookonia as well. It seemed he would stop at nothing, even at the expense of his own kingdom. Sadly, King Joel of Lookonia had been killed. After a new king had taken the throne, a shaky treaty had been drawn and now trade resumed and travel continued.

One year after the new king took the throne in Lookonia, Mathew had decided to go into ministry. He had left with big dreams of being a leader to his own congregation. Before he could do that, he decided to study scriptures under the wise Orelious. Orelious was a renowned expert in the scriptures, as he had been deep in the word for most of his life. Once Mathew had learned that Orelious was accepting students, he had even more reason to leave for the kingdom of Lookonia.

Since Mathew had left to learn, he was unable to take Annika with him, but he had promised to call for her one day. Once he was settled in his own church, he would be able to support her.

He had such a kind heart, and Annika had no doubt he would light a spark in everyone he touched.

Annika and her brother had been taught about Elohim at a young age, though they hid their faith. The king was already putting his new laws in place. Despite that, their father had instilled in them a deep love for Elohim. She could remember countless days reading scriptures at the table with her father, mother, and brother but sadly those days could not last forever. Her mother had died suddenly, taking a bright light from their home.

Her father had been a traveling businessman, often on the road for weeks at a time, but that changed with her mother's death. He stayed home with them, teaching them all he knew and making many happy memories.

One day, something had changed in their father. His happy face had become worried and his actions became sporadic. With no warning, he had abandoned them on the front step of the orphanage and hadn't even looked back. Her memories of him had always been pleasant up until that day. Even though the memory was hazy at best, in her mind she remembered one thing for certain. The pain she felt as she watched his tall form leave, and the piece of her heart that she knew would never return. That was five years ago now.

Annika jolted out of her musing and determined not to think about her father. It was now the day before they would forever leave the orphanage. Thank goodness for that.

"I can only say it's about time for you to leave," the head of the orphanage, Monty Colburn, had said with a huff when Annika had told him of her plans to leave. When he had heard Carter would be going with her, he had laughed. "Figures you'd take that sorry child. He follows you around like a sick puppy. It'll take a strain off of this orphanage to have you both gone. You two have been here so long, it's obvious no one will adopt you. Your absence will make it easier for the other children to be adopted."

It had taken everything in Annika to not speak out at the injustices the man had said about them. She was used to hearing them said about her, but to hear it said of Carter was almost unbearable. If only Mr. Colburn had taken time with the children to see how special they all were. If he had taken time to speak with Carter, he would see the bright and intelligent young man he was.

Carter was excellent with pen and pencil. He could draw things that were so lifelike you felt as if you could touch them. Another strength of his was book knowledge. Give him a topic, and he could study it and know it better than you in no time. He already had no need for Annika's daily lessons to the children. In fact, he could teach the classes all on his own.

Annika had turned from Mr. Colburn with clenched fists, her teeth gritted. How happy she would be when she was free of this place. Her only regret would be not being able to take the rest of the children. Thankfully, they were young and Mr. Colburn found value in their presence. Young children were much more likely to be adopted.

The day before their departure, the children put together a small going away party for them. They presented hand-drawn pictures as going away gifts with teary goodbyes. It would be hard to leave the children she had grown to care about so much, but it was time for her to leave. It was past time actually. Not many of nineteen years were still in orphanages. The only reason she had been allowed to stay was her skills in teaching the children, which had been free.

She had spent endless days teaching them all and took great pride in their progress. Most could now read and write, and they even knew a bit of math.

She had also taught the children some swordplay. That was admittedly their favorite class. Annika's father had left her and her brother a sword each. The steel swords were not worth much, and in exchange for her teaching the children, she had been allowed to keep them.

When Mathew had decided to go into ministry, he had left behind his sword to Carter, who had been ecstatic about the gift.

After the short party, Annika and Carter packed what few possessions they owned. In her case was a few blouses and skirts. Carter had even fewer articles of clothing than she. They would have to buy a few things when they arrived in Lookonia. Hopefully, her brother would help them out with that.

Annika lay down in her little bed for the last time and looked out at the stars. The stars seemed a bit brighter tonight. With the crickets chirping she fell asleep, dreaming of sailing the high seas.

Ethan stood at the bow of his ship, his piercing dark brown eyes looking out to the horizon. He scanned for anything that was not the normal calm sea he had grown accustomed to. His perceptive gaze had found many a ship or storm on the horizon far more often than many of his men. But nighttime was quickly approaching, and soon there would be no use in even looking.

His crew rested and relaxed for the evening below deck, but Ethan found it hard to calm his mind. His memories and dark thoughts were too overwhelming for him to find any bit of peace.

His shoulder-length black hair whipped about his face, obstructing his vision. In a practiced motion he tipped his hat forward, gathered his hair, tied it low to the base of his neck, and then settled his hat back into place. Long hair had never been something he had thought he would have. Ever since he had become captain of his own ship, he found it made him look more mature. One needed that when leading a group of hardened men into the hard seas.

The salty breeze blew in his face, causing his hat to gently tug upon his head, and the feather atop began to dance. The sky further darkened as it showed its last few traces of colorful sunlight. Soon, all would be dark, save for the lanterns aboard the ship.

The darkness about the ship didn't scare him. Only the darkness in his heart and memories could do that. There wasn't much he feared, but as soon as he closed his eyes, he could feel the shadows leaching into his soul, clouding his mind and his senses.

Growing up, he had been taught to believe in God. His father had taught him of Elohim and His love. He had said that Elohim knew him personally and would always be there for him. A lot of good that had done his father.

Ethan sighed heavily. So much had happened since his innocent childhood years. So many things that scarred his outlook on life and took the beauty out of his father's words. Even though he was only twenty-three, he had been hurt far deeper than many men twice his age.

If there really was a God who cared, surely He would have already pulled Ethan from the dark hole he felt enclosed by. No, He would have destroyed the darkness before it came. If He was real, then he must not care about him for still the darkness remained. Still, the nightmares pursued his mind, depriving him of his sleep and sanity.

"Captain?" A voice from behind caused him to stir from his thoughts. "Captain, the men are wondering what our next course of action will be." His first mate, Jonah, came up and stood next to him. He leaned his right arm on the rail and fixed his gaze towards the dimming light in the sky.

Jonah was a glimmer of light in Ethan's dark world. He was his oldest and often wisest friend. He had been with Ethan through the darkest and lightest times of his life. Jonah wore plain brown breeches with a white top. His black boots were laced up almost to his knees. His dark skin matched his short brown hair. Wise and ever-perceptive brown eyes looked over the water searching its waves.

"Can they ever just be patient and wait for me to tell them? We no sooner finish one raid than they are begging me to give them more." Ethan shook his head and gave a wry smile.

"Aw, come now, Captain. You know the men respect you in every way. They would jump into a lion's lair with you leading the way." Jonah clapped a hand on Ethan's shoulder. "You can't blame the men for going stir crazy, always being on the sea."

"I know, you're right. I could find no better or more honorable men if I had a thousand years to look." Ethan meant every word. The men aboard his ship had been with him for years, and he trusted them with his life.

Ethan sighed. "I just tire of people assuming I know what step to take. My thoughts seem so scattered and my soul so weary. I'm plagued by my own thoughts. So much so that it's hard to focus on what lies ahead."

"Are you still having nightmares, Ethan?" Jonah was one of the few permitted to be on a first name basis with him, at least when away from the crew. Jonah squeezed the hand he still had placed on his shoulder. "You know you can talk to me. Don't face those demons alone."

Ethan wanted so badly to share his thoughts with someone. To have someone take the dark from his heart and lift the weight on his shoulders. Alas, talking to Jonah would do no good. It would not change the past, and that's where the darkness had begun.

"I'm fine, my old friend. Think no further of the matter. I need only a few moments to collect my thoughts, and then I will address the crew."

"There a party up here that I wasn't invited to?" A voice, dripping with sarcasm, announced Jack's arrival. He was another of his most trusted crew mates and close friend. "I was feeling left out having to stay below." He leaned against the rail with them.

"Aw, quit your complaining. We have only been up here for a few moments." Jonah rolled his eyes and smirked at his friend.

"Well, the men grow more foul smelling by the moment. You missed the foulest of the stench by hiding away up here. My vote would be we dock somewhere and give these men and the boat a good scrubbing. I can't be a menacing pirate while smelling like a pig, and I don't smell half as bad as some." Jack scrunched up his nose, causing the other men to chuckle. He was always one to bring a smile to Ethan's face.

"Then you will like what I address the men with next." Ethan turned away from the dark horizon and faced the boat, imagining saying his words to the crew. "We will chart our course for the nearest accessible port. We will load up on supplies and do some much-needed cleaning." Jack's face lit up at the mention of it.

"Then what, Captain?" Jonah turned around with him.

"I have heard of another shipment of goods being delivered soon from the eastern kingdom straight to the king's own table."

"Please tell me we are going to steal it!" Jack fairly bounced next to him. "I do love to make that man angry." He rubbed his hands together in anticipation.

"My thoughts exactly. Anything we can do to cause the crown problems is something I'm interested in." Ethan gave a wry smile.

"We are behind you, Captain." Jonah and Jack crossed their arms and smiled.

"Well, let's go tell the crew." As they turned and started to go below, the stench assaulted his nose. "Let's hope we have strong winds to the next port."

CHAPTER TWO

The time of their departure finally came. She put on her sword belt; the cool steel felt comforting in her hands. She then removed a small dagger from under her mattress and attached it to her ankle. Annika remembered clearly the day her father gave her the sword and dagger.

The sword was made of plain steel; nothing was particularly special about it or Carter's. Her dagger, however, had a lion engraved above the hilt. It had to have cost a pretty penny. This was something she had always managed to keep hidden from Mr. Colburn, or it would have been taken from her.

Carter was fairly jumping out of his skin as he waited for Annika to finish saying her goodbyes.

It was only a couple hours walk to the sea, but they would need to get going quickly. The ship would be casting off soon.

Carter and Annika gave everyone one last hug. Tears were shed by them both, but it affected her the most. With one last look at the only home she'd had for the last five years, she waved one last time at the others. Annika and Carter donned their backpacks and began to walk up the winding pathway away from the orphanage.

When Annika turned around to wave, she could see Mr. Colburn through one of the open windows. He was reading a book, not even caring to see them off. Just wait, she thought, one day she and Carter would both make something of themselves. They would prove the words of Mr. Colburn wrong.

The children continued to wave, even as they became just dots on the horizon behind them. Soon they disappeared altogether, and the last remnants of the orphanage were out of sight.

Annika took a deep breath and let out a small sigh. This was the first step of their journey. Who knew what was coming next? One thing was for certain: this would be unlike anything she had ever done before and she relished the thought. She sent a quick prayer of thanks and safety for them as they ventured into the unknown.

The road to the port was quite the day's journey. By the time Annika and Carter reached their destination, they were both tired and hungry. Their boots were most likely filled with dust. There was even a fine layer on their tongues. There had been many horses and wagons going away from the port but none going towards it.

It had been weeks since their last rainfall. The pair had the evidence in their mouths to prove it.

They trudged the last few steps of dirt road until they reached the firm wooden platform. Annika smiled, the solid foundation beneath her feet felt like the next stepping stone towards her new life.

Carter's slumped shoulders straightened at the sight in front of them. His eyes grew large as he took in his surroundings. Annika followed his gaze and couldn't help the awe she felt as well.

A large wooden platform stretched out far into the sea. It stretched far enough into the sea that several large ships were anchored near the end. There had to be at least ten ships anchored next to the platform and at least a dozen more farther out. Several small rowboats were rowing away from the anchored ships to bring weary sailors onto Narine's shores.

Just then, a large salty breeze fanned Annika's face, eliciting memories of the days her family had gone to the beach. Her mother's smile and her father's belly laugh. Quickly the image faded again and left her feeling lonely. Lonely for the family she would never have again and hopeful for her future with all the family she had left.

"Stick close to me, Annika." Carter placed his hand on her shoulder and leaned towards her ear. "It seems there are some unsavory sorts around here."

Annika's eyes widened as she realized his meaning. The long platform that had brought her such pleasant memories was riddled with burly men. Several dozen occupied the space between them and the first docked ship.

She nodded. "I will follow your lead." Annika placed her hand on the crook of Carter's elbow and allowed him to lead her onward. Her instinct was for her to lead him and to put herself in the most dangerous position. She managed to restrain herself. It was good for the young man to feel sure of himself, and having him take the lead seemed to give him a great deal of pride.

Carter straightened his shoulders and did his best to put a fierce look on his face as they walked into the throng.

The men they passed were quite varied in their appearances. Some wore military uniforms, and their ships seemed to have the best spots on the dock. Those men were dressed finely in blue jackets with gold buttons. Their hair was slicked back and most had their faces shaven.

The rest of the men, perhaps fishermen or merchants, looked quite the opposite. Their boats lacked the finery of the previous ones, obviously not taking the time to keep up appearances like the military vessels.

Their faces were weathered, as were their clothes. Some of the men were missing teeth and others had gold ones in their place.

When they passed by, all around seemed to stop what they were doing and stare at them. Annika realized it must be her that they were staring at. Annika felt she was not the most attractive woman; her dull green eyes and plain brown hair were not unusual. Her clothing was not made of fine material either. If she had to guess, she would have said she was one of the first of the fairer sex they had seen in a while. It was uncommon for women to be seen at the docks, let alone to travel the seas. Unless you were quite rich and could afford the passage on one of the king's lines of passenger ships. He promised safe passage only for his own ships and charged an exorbitant amount for it.

As they neared the end of the platform, they came to a ship whose name matched their ticket. *Sailor's Journey* was inscribed on the side of the vessel in sprawling letters. What a fitting name for the boat that would take her on her own journey to a new life.

"I believe this is our ride, Carter." They both stopped to admire the ship. It wasn't as magnificent as some they had already seen, but it was well maintained and looked to be sturdy.

"I like the looks of it. The name is fitting too." Carter smiled a toothy grin at her. Annika smiled back and was, once again, thankful for his company.

"Are you ready for this journey? I do not wish for you to be halfway across the sea and decide you made the wrong decision."

"Are you kidding me?" Carter squeezed the hand that she had placed on his elbow. "There's no other place I'd rather be. I want to go wherever you go. Besides, this will be a grand adventure! Who knows, we may even see pirates!" He waggled his eyebrows teasingly.

"If only we aren't so lucky." Annika chuckled.

A man was standing near a skinny wooden ramp that led into the ship. He was tall, probably more than a head taller than Annika, who was five foot six. His wind-tussled hair was greying, as was his thick bushy beard. His kind brown eyes found Annika and a smile came over his weathered face.

"Are you Miss Harper?" His voice was deep but kind. He wore a clean blue jacket that gave him a level of authority, it seemed.

"I am. Are you the captain?" The pair walked closer.

"I am indeed, miss. Captain Samuel Grey is my name. Though I go by Captain Samuel to my crew. This fine vessel you see in front of you is mine. You won't find a more reliable ship on the seas." His smile was warm and helped to calm her nerves. He was far different than most of the men they had seen so far on the docks.

"I am glad to hear it, Captain. My brother spoke highly of you."

"That's right kind of him. He has long told me of his wish to bring you. We normally only carry goods, but I had to make an exception for the sister of my good friend." He held out a hand to her. She accepted his hand and gave him a small bow in greeting.

Annika gestured to Carter. "This here is my attendant and close friend. He will be traveling with us. I'm sorry for our appearance, we must look a fright. The way was unusually dusty and felt much longer than it should have." She chuckled.

"Goodness, did you walk here? The nearest town is at least five miles away!" He released her hand as his eyes gently took in her dusty clothing.

"I'm sad to say we did walk. Normally, I would enjoy a pleasant walk through the countryside. Today, however, was an exception. Nevertheless, we are tired and ready for this journey to continue. Thankfully the next leg of our journey will not require as much walking." She smiled pleasantly.

"Please do not worry, miss. You are quite striking with a bit of dust on you." He gave her a playful wink, the kind that a teasing father would give his daughter. She liked this captain already. No wonder her brother trusted him. "Have either of you ever sailed before?"

"I'm sad to say we have not. Though I've always dreamt of riding the waves aboard a fine vessel such as yours." She smiled, her excitement building.

Captain Samuel laughed as if she had made some joke. "Well, those waves are a might difficult to ride. Takes you a while to get your sea legs."

"Sea legs?"

"Yes, it takes a while for your body to get accustomed to the constant movement of the ship."

"The boat moves so much you have trouble walking?" Carter chimed in, his wide eyes full of curiosity.

"It's more so just adjusting to get your balance. Nothing a couple of days of practice won't fix. Soon, you will be walking on deck as if it was second nature. The movement won't even faze you." Captain Samuel turned his full attention to Carter. "Now, what is your name, lad?"

Carter straightened his back and spoke with pride. "My name is Carter Monroe, sir. It is my pleasure to accompany Annika on this journey."

"A pleasure to meet you, my boy. Please, come, let me show you both aboard." He held out his arm to Annika and she placed her hand on his elbow.

She willingly followed his lead up the thin ramp, all the while willing herself not to look down to the dark waters below. Thankfully, she could swim; that helped put her fears at ease.

On board there were at least a dozen men scurrying back and forth. The boat was a lot bigger than it had looked from below. It was a vast vessel that had to have enough room to house at least a hundred men.

Some of the sailors stopped their tasks and gave her a small bow. Others completely ignored her and seemed to mutter under their breath. Captain Samuel stopped walking and spoke in a commanding voice.

"Men, this here is Miss Harper. She will be under my care on this journey. You are to treat her with respect." He then placed his hand on Carter's shoulder. "And this is Mr. Monroe, who is accompanying her. They both have free rein aboard this ship. Carry on."

Some of the crew nodded their acknowledgments to her then resumed their endeavors in readying the ship for departure.

Although, this was a dangerous journey, Annika felt somehow safe and reassured knowing they were in Captain Samuel's care. Mathew had good judgment when it came to the people he trusted.

The next hour went by in a blur. Captain Samuel showed Annika and Carter their rooms, then directed them towards where they could relieve themselves. After the quick tour, he excused himself, saying he had many duties to attend to before they embarked.

Annika had a decent-sized room to herself. It was smaller than her room back at the orphanage but it was all hers, for the first time in many years. It would be a pleasant change.

Carter had a connecting room to hers with a door in-between to give them both privacy. They unpacked as much as they could in their small rooms and then went up to the deck.

Annika was surprised at the lack of movement that the ship had. She could feel the ship slightly move beneath her feet, but it was just a gentle sway. Carter and her seemed to have no trouble getting around.

At the end of the hour they cast off, starting the first leg of their long journey. The pair hung to the rail and watched as everything they knew faded into the distance. They watched until the land was just a small dot on the horizon.

The ship cut through the water, spraying sea foam into the air. Salty air penetrated their nostrils and gave Annika the sense of adventure she was looking for.

Her dream of riding the waves was finally a reality. Nothing lay beneath her feet now, just the ships deck and under it the dark water. Who knew what lay hidden in its depths. The thought thrilled and terrified her.

A couple of dolphins leaped alongside the boat as it sailed smoothly through the water. Annika leaned over the rail as far as was safe to watch their graceful movements. One could not help smiling at the sight below.

After a while, it became evident that a moving ship was much different than a docked one. The movement was a lot more noticeable. It was much harder to walk about, and her stomach had begun to feel queasy. One look at Carter showed he felt worse than she did.

The next few days, they were told, would be the most challenging part of getting adjusted to the movement of the ship. It turned out to be true. Annika had a queasy stomach for the first day, and it took her a few days to be able to walk and not feel dizzy.

Poor Carter, though, he had the worst of it. For two whole days he just stayed in bed and did his best to keep hydrated and fed.

Annika remained at his side, making sure he was cared for. On the rare occasion she went to the deck, she did not stay long. The crew had a way of making her feel uneasy with their stares. Hopefully, she would explore more of the ship when Carter was able to accompany her.

Food was brought to them as they recovered from their sickness. Annika struggled for a while to get food into Carter. After much convincing, he finally was able to eat some food and keep it down. On the third day of their journey, Carter was well enough to venture out of the cabins, which was a huge relief to Annika. It had been a lonely and miserable two days.

In the two weeks or so that the trip would take, they hoped to use it learning about the ship and the sea. They would have more than enough time to learn much of what was required for sailing. If only they could find someone willing to speak with them. They learned quickly who was kind and who was better to stay away from.

One of the friendliest and kindest of the crew was the cook. His name was Stew and, funny enough, he never made any of it. Since approachable characters were hard to find aboard the ship, they spent much of their spare time with Stew. They helped him in the kitchen as he prepared meals, all the while he told them thrilling tales of the sea.

The captain was the most enjoyable to be around, but he was often busy. When he had a few free moments, they loved to ask questions of the sea or to hear amusing stories of his time as captain. He was a walking and talking encyclopedia of tales and information. Captain Samuel took time to explain the basics of sailing to Carter.

There were other kind crew members but not too many seemed interested in taking time to talk with them. There were, however, many rather rude and unsavory members. Especially a man by the name of Maddock and his friend Simon. The two were as different as they could possibly be. Maddock's manners stunk almost as badly as his breath. His teeth looked to be rotting and yellow—not that you'd ever see them from a smile. Only a sneer would illuminate those yellow cavity-stricken teeth.

Annika did her best to stay out of his way, but she always seemed to feel his gaze.

Simon, on the other hand, was not unpleasant to look at. His teeth were white and straight, and his hair well groomed. It was the way he spoke to Annika that made her skin crawl. His gaze also made her feel uncomfortable, as if she were a fine piece of meat he wished to buy. He tried to be charming, but he reminded her of a snake.

Minus a few unpleasant people aboard the vessel, everyone seemed to be doing their roles. The ship sailed without delay and even a bit ahead of schedule. Carter seemed to grow stronger and braver every day away from the orphanage and the negative comments of Mr. Colburn.

Annika felt her new life growing closer and couldn't wait for the day they would reach Lookonia.

CHAPTER THREE

A week into their journey and things were still going smoothly. Carter had started spending a lot of his time doing the duties of a sailor. He now knew how to steer and even how to navigate using the stars.

Carter was very good at sketching, and being out on the open waves only seemed to strengthen it. He was constantly sketching things; the stars, the waves, and even sailors made it into his sketch book.

Annika was happy that Carter was enjoying the journey thus far. She also loved the sea and the feeling of the unknown over the horizon. The sea seemed to have a mind of its own. Some days it felt like a close friend and at other times felt as though it had a personal vendetta against you. Not knowing what each day would bring was hard but also part of the beauty of it. Thankfully, Elohim never left her. This long journey had definitely strengthened her faith. Each day was a test of faith and patience.

"Good morning, Miss Harper." Captain Samuel came alongside her. Annika had been leaning against the rail of the ship, looking down into the waves below.

"Good morning, Captain. How are you today?" She gave him a smile. He seemed tired lately. His eyes had dark bags beneath them, and his countenance seemed different. Perhaps the job of a captain was more taxing than she had realized.

"I'm well as can be." He looked as if he wished to say more but thought otherwise. "How is life at sea treating you? Does it agree with you?"

"Very much so. I love the waves and the adventure of it all. Carter is learning so much, I'd be very surprised if he is not disappointed when this trip comes to an end."

"I love having you two aboard. You both give a sense of peace and a carefree feeling." He sighed and looked at the billowing sails overhead. "The winds have been favorable for us. We should dock at our scheduled time, if not earlier." He leaned against the rail with her, the brim of his hat lightly flapping in the breeze.

"That's wonderful to hear. I had hoped we would be able to make it without running into a storm. I hear those can turn the friendly sea into a dark enemy." Annika had been praying they would not meet that enemy. She had heard many tales of men losing their lives to the ocean and its deadly embrace.

"Every sailor hopes for that very thing. Sometimes we are rewarded with favorable weather but oftentimes the sea is a deadly thing. You never know when she may up and turn on you." He shook his head, his thoughts far away for a moment. "Enough dark talk." He suddenly smiled, his eyes twinkling as he did. "I wanted to invite you and Carter to dine with me tonight."

"Oh, we would love to!"

"Wonderful, I will expect you there then. We will be having the last of the bread. Cook has been saving it for a special occasion. He swears there's very little mold on it." He made a wry expression.

Annika laughed. "We will be eating like kings tonight then."

Captain Samuel laughed with her and then excused himself, the duties of a captain seeking his attention once again.

Annika's eyes found the horizon, taking in the glistening water. The sun was starting its steady descent in the sky. Soon it would disappear, making it look like the sea had swallowed it up. She had thought sunsets were pretty back at the orphanage, but out here they were breathtaking. The colors in the sky all reflected into the water, filling the entire sea with color. She was always looking forward to the next sunset and what colors it would become. What painting was Elohim in the mood to create?

It was indeed a beauty to behold; that evening the sky was a beautiful display of purples and orange. The water reflected its brilliance. *Thank you, Elohim, for the beauty around us. You are truly magnificent.* Annika sighed in contentment. She and Carter both stood at the rail watching the display. After the sun made its decent into the waters below, it was time to meet the captain for supper.

The captain had a special table in his private chamber where he dined and had the most important crew members with him. Unfortunately, that meant Maddock and Simon would be there. As unsavory as their characters were, they were excellent seamen. Maddock was the first mate to Captain Samuel. How he ever managed that she would never understand.

Annika and Carter entered the small room and were happy to see the table already set and some bread on the table. Captain Samuel sat on the far end, his face illuminated by candles that were placed not so elegantly along the length of the table. He stood up at their entrance, as did a couple other men around the table.

Simon stood gallantly, as if they were there to see him. Maddock grumbled under his breath and reluctantly stood, his eyes never softening their intense gaze.

"How good of you to join us, Miss Harper and Mr. Monroe." Captain Samuel ushered them to seats near him.

They quickly passed the men and took their seats. There were a total of eight men already seated at the table.

"Thank you for inviting us." Annika smoothed her wrinkled skirt. It was one of the only two skirts she owned, and it was getting dirtier each day, despite her best attempts to clean it. However, on a ship like this, surrounded by dirty men, she felt over-dressed.

"Of course. Your presence is soothing, unlike my men here." He laughed and gestured to the men around the table. "Fine men and excellent sailors but soothing is not a word in their vocabulary." Everyone around the table chuckled, except for Maddock.

"Tell me, Miss Harper, how do you like sailing on the high seas?" Simon directed his full attention on her as he sat across the table from her. The look in his eyes and the way he smiled did not make her feel comfortable.

"We both love it. The sea can be quite soothing on its good days." She gave a small smile but could not look him in the eyes long.

She reached forward and took a piece of the crusty bread. It was stale and bland but at least it was bread, a rare commodity on the ship. The men around the table began conversing among one another. Carter, sitting closest to Captain Samuel, began discussing their route and what he had been learning on navigation.

"We sure are fortunate to have you onboard with us, Miss Harper. You are a welcome distraction from gruff sailors." Simon smiled over his glass of water. As if he had just paid her the highest of compliments.

"Do you tire of sailing?" She tried to turn the conversation away from herself.

"Yes, I yearn for the shore and all the pleasantries that come with it." The way his eyes raked over her spoke plainly of what he really enjoyed on land. She bit her lip to keep from gagging.

"Why do you continue sailing then? Surely there are jobs on land that would be appealing to you."

Simon looked to Maddock. "I'm currently under employment and it's good pay. Hopefully, someday soon I can stay on land permanently."

Maddock's normal scowling face twisted into an evil-looking grin. Somehow, his smile was even more menacing than his scowl. Annika turned to the man sitting at her right.

"What of you, Mr. Hall? Do you long for land or relish the sea?"

Doniphan Hall was one of the few men of whom she felt comfortable with. His shy exterior held a kindness within. He was the ship's doctor. He had been the one to give them advice on how to overcome their seasickness. Thick glasses rested on his pointy nose and sharp eyes peered through them. His thin frame was a rarity on the sea; all others seem to be brawny and rough. Doniphan, on the other hand, was kind and gentle. He did not seem the kind of person to fit in with a group of burly sailors, but everyone seemed to like him. None of the crew ever had anything negative to say about him.

"I am happy either way, honestly." He folded his napkin on his lap. "The land and sea each have their own benefits. I am happy for the land and the safety it ensures, but I can also appreciate the rolling sea and the adventure it invokes. As long as I'm somewhere that I can lend my services and help people, that is good enough for me."

Annika smiled widely at the man. "What a wonderful take on it all. I can most adamantly agree on your summary. I have not been on the sea long, but I can see the value in staying on land and sailing the seas."

Stew came in and delivered bowls of soup to everyone around the table. It was a simple broth, filled with some vegetables. Not quite stew but it was pretty close.

"Just wait 'til you see what the sea has to offer." Maddock's growling voice took her by surprise. Had she ever heard him talk? At least not directly at her before.

"Such as a storm or something of that sort?" She dared to ask him a question. He regarded her with glowering eyes. Simon's gaze made her grimace and want to hide in a corner. Maddock's gaze instilled pure terror in her heart.

"That, among other things," he said after a moment. "You have yet to see a storm invoke its full fury. Waves as high as the ship batter it from all sides. The wind howls, as if it were alive. Even the bright sky leaves in fright, leaving behind a thick darkness. If a sailor is lucky enough to survive such a storm, he thinks twice about going back on the sea."

Annika's heart sped up at the description of such a storm. The satisfied look on Maddock's face told her that's what he had wanted. He wanted her to feel fear and to cower in a corner. His smile was a triumphant one, as if he took pleasure in the fear he caused her.

"Maddock, stop trying to scare our guests," Captain Samuel reprimanded him, but Maddock looked like he couldn't care less what the captain thought. Thankfully he remained quiet. Captain Samuel glowered at Maddock and cleared his throat. "It's a rare time indeed to witness a storm such as that. Storms are common, but they do not often release their full fury. We have not long to go until our journey is over, and we are not in a time known for storms. Please, do not worry." His eyes looked to her apologetically.

Annika's mind was put at ease a little, but she did not wish for her obvious relief to show. She tried to keep a nonchalant look on her face. "I am quite confident in your skills and the skills of your men. Elohim has us all in His hands, after all. That's the safest place to be, especially on an unforgiving sea." She took a sip of soup.

"A figment of your imagination can't save you from any storms." Maddock's voice broke back into the conversation.

Annika mustered up her courage and looked Maddock square in the eyes. "If you wish to go through your life thinking that this magnificent world came to be without a creator, then you do so. I, on the other hand, know without a doubt that Elohim is the Creator. I'll put my full confidence in Him. He knows the winds and the waves. Even the hearts of men." He glowered at her, and she managed a small smile.

All conversation seemed to still around the table. Annika just hoped supper would be finished soon so she could escape the glares.

The rest of the evening passed uneventfully. They managed to make it through the rest of the meal without any more comments from Maddock. Although, Simon seemed as if he was unable to be quiet.

They went to bed and woke the next morning feeling quite rested. With the dawn came a bright new day full of new possibilities. The dawn was a wonderful sight to see after all the talk of storms. She just prayed they would not encounter the ugly side of the beautiful sea.

An uproar from the crew caused Annika to look up from a book she had been reading. She glanced over the top of her book and spied a handful of excited crewmen slapping each other on their backs and laughing together. Carter came running across the deck to her.

"Have you heard, Annika? The captain has given the crew time off to have a contest!" He jumped around in excitement.

"What kind of contest?" Annika asked as she closed her book, happy for any kind of excitement aboard the ship.

"A sword fighting contest! We will get to see the strongest on board fight each other! Come and watch with me!" Carter's excitement and enthusiasm were contagious. Annika allowed him to pull her forward.

Excitement filled Annika at the prospect of watching the swordsmanship contest. It had been a while since she had seen anyone outside of the orphanage practice.

Two men stood in the middle of the deck, and a crowd of sailors gathered around in anticipation. As she got closer, Annika realized it was Maddock fighting.

Maddock and the other man assumed their fighting stances and held their swords at the ready. A whistle from someone in the crowd signaled the start. Both men were strong and quick with their movements.

Annika found herself studying their strategies. Both seemed to know what they were doing, but Maddock had the advantage of size. She almost pitied the poor man that was battling Maddock, who seemed to be merciless. The two parried and blocked over and over again.

The pair backed away and turned in a circle while looking at each other up and down. Each seemed to be studying the other's technique.

Maddock slid his left foot forward and thrust his sword towards his opponent, who only just barely managed to block the blow, the weight of his opponent's blade almost knocking him down. They continued, with each one of them holding their own. All the while, the rest of the crew shouted out their excitement and disdain for how the match was going.

Annika's experienced eyes could tell that Maddock would be the victor. What he lacked in technique he made up for in strength. Sure enough, five minutes into the duel, Maddock had hit the other man's sword out of his hand. As he knocked him to the ground, he gave him a small gash in the arm, almost assuredly on purpose.

"Did you see that?" Carter hissed into her ear.

"I did. He really is quite ruthless." Her disgust for the man just grew daily.

The loser retrieved his sword and scurried away in shame. For the next hour, one by one, members of the crew challenged Maddock but no one could win. With each victory he gained, his pride seemed to swell even more. Pretty soon he looked so puffed up with pride he fairly flew about the deck.

"Anyone wish to challenge me?" he shouted to the crew. His greasy hair glinted with fresh sweat. His eyes seemed to glow with pride and what seemed to be pure disdain. The bravest and strongest had already tried. The rest of them were too afraid of losing to the beast.

"I can't believe no one else will try and beat the man. Why I could probably best him. It would only take one poke to pop him, he's so full of pride," Carter whispered into her ear. Annika stifled a snicker but not in time for Maddock to miss it.

"Did I hear something from someone over here?" Maddock walked to their edge of the circle of men. "Perhaps you, little lady, would like to challenge me." He ran the tip of his blade down her arm.

Anger flushed her face hot. Before she could respond, Carter stepped in front of her. "Leave her be, Maddock. It is I who said I could beat you."

"You?" The evil man thrust his head back and laughed. "You hear that? This twig thinks he could best me! No one has ever bested me, but go ahead. I would love to see you try." He leaned forward until his eyes were level with Carter's. "And how quickly I can squish you."

"Even a mere twig can cause a man to stumble. I accept your challenge." Carter had never looked so mature before. His eyes looked steady. The only giveaway was the slight shaking of his hands.

"Please don't. Carter, it's not worth it." Annika pulled on his hand and pleaded.

"No, I need to do this." Carter's eyes spoke volumes. He was looking to prove himself a man.

Annika nodded and sighed. "Fine, go fetch the swords. Both of them." Carter ran off to do her bidding and quickly returned with the swords.

Annika took her own sword from him and strapped the belt around her waist. The sword hung loosely at her side, the weight of it calming her nerves.

Carter faced Maddock, waiting for him to make his first move. All eyes locked on them, all voices silenced. Maddock's posture spoke of his pride and anger. Carter's seemed to show peace and composure, something Annika had taught him from their many lessons. No matter the enemy you face, the first and sometimes best first move is to show no fear.

Annika noticed Stew and Captain Samuel had joined the group now and were also watching.

"You just made a huge mistake, boy." Maddock cocked a crooked smile, exposing his yellow teeth.

He lunged towards Carter, aiming his blade for his head. Carter sprang into action and dodged the blade, at the same time coming up to the side and knocking it away. Surprise registered on the Maddock's face, but it quickly turned to anger.

He lunged several more times; each time his blows were avoided and blocked. Carter was smaller than Maddock and wiry. He could dodge pretty much any blow that was directed at him. It also helped that Maddock had been worn down considerably from his previous fights. Sweat slid down his face and dripped onto his shirt. His white shirt, if you could consider it white, was drenched in sweat.

Maddock aimed a weak thrust at his opponent. Carter dodged and was able to get behind Maddock and slap him on his backside with the flat side of his blade. That elicited hearty laughs and mocking towards Maddock.

"Perhaps you underestimated me?" Carter cast a sly smile to his opponent. Maddock looked ready to kill until he spotted something that turned his expression to pride again.

Annika looked and finally spotted the reason for his reaction. Simon stood at the edge of the circle of men with his foot outstretched and his blade at the ready. Carter had his back to him and would soon be tripped up and no doubt injured by Maddock.

"No, boy, you never stood a chance." He chuckled as Carter reached Simon, tripped over his leg and fell to the ground.

Annika sprang into action. Before Maddock was able to lower his blade to his opponent, she was there. She gave a quick block with her blade. As surprise registered on his face, she quickly parried and pushed him away from Carter.

"Only able to best a boy through trickery? That's low, even for you." She stood in front of the evil man. Anger coursed through her at the nerve of the man. She stood in front of him, looking every bit the expert swordsman she was.

Before Maddock could find any words to say, an urgent cry came from the outskirts of the circle.

"Pirates! Pirates, Captain! They are almost on top of us!"

That word struck fear into the hearts of the most hardened sailors. Pirates would steal your livelihood and sometimes even your life. Pirates had become a pretty big issue over the years to all. Every time you put yourself out on the sea, it was a possibility to run into them. You just hoped and prayed it doesn't happen to you. What were the odds, out of hundreds of ships that sailed through these waters, why did they have to pick theirs?

Annika was about to look towards the water and the cause of the ruckus when she caught the eyes of her would-be opponent. He hadn't been bothered by the chaos around him yet. His steely eyes were locked on her. Pure hatred and anger fairly seethed out of him. His mouth was drawn in a taught line, and his fists lay clenched at his sides.

She didn't have time to worry about him. There was a real threat out there, and it was much bigger than the sorry excuse for a man in front of her.

Annika grabbed Carter's hand. "Come, let's see how bad things are." The two of them raced for the rail. What they saw nearly brought them to their knees.

There was a ship so close to their own that you could see men scurrying aboard deck. A colorful flag flew atop the mast. You could even make out the writing on the side of the ship. The ship's name was *Redemption*. *An odd name for a pirate ship*, Annika thought.

There was a man standing on the bow of the ship, his full attention on them. He was too far away to see any details but, from the size of his hat and the feather atop it, he looked to be in charge.

Captain Samuel came up to Annika's side. "This could get messy. They have moved into a position that our cannons cannot hit. Soon they will be right alongside us and if we attempt a shot and miss, their ship will retaliate and we could get hit."

"Is there nothing we can do?" Carter leaned against the rail, squinting at the pirate ship.

"I do not want harm to my ship and my men. If at all possible, we will strive for peace. If we had caught them sooner that would be a different story. Just in case, though, I insist you wait in my quarters until this is all over. I have a place for you both to hide."

"Of course, please lead the way, Captain." Annika and Carter followed the captain as they exchanged worried looks to one another.

The captain sped them towards his quarters then showed them that there was a secret door in the closet.

He helped Annika and Carter into the small space behind the closet. "Whatever you hear, stay hidden until I come for you."

"We will be praying for your safety." Annika hated seeing the captain's kind face clouded with worry and maybe a little fear. He nodded then ran out the door. *Why Elohim? Why would you let this happen?* Annika franticly prayed for everyone's safety and for courage for herself for what may be ahead.

CHAPTER FOUR

Ethan stood with one leg on the rail of his ship and leaned on the arm he had propped on his knee. This was a large vessel compared to his but not nearly as fast.

He smirked. Whatever had been going on aboard the deck had distracted them all so thoroughly that he and his crew were able to just sail on in. That was the best situation he could think of. He didn't want to cause any bloodshed; that's one reason why he had overly large cannons on his deck and made all his men carry guns. The cannons were easier to catch sight of and instill fear in the hearts of their targets. If they were afraid, it was much more unlikely for them to attack.

From his position, he could see the crew onboard the other vessel, the *Sailor's Journey*. What a quaint name that was. They were all on deck with their weapons at the ready. Their guns were drawn, aimed at his men. The men aboard his ship had their weapons pointed as well, and he would bet they were far better shots.

They had connected the two ships with a long board. It was strong enough to hold several men at once.

On the other ship, standing in front of his men, was the merchant captain. He stood out above the rest with his jacket and captain's hat.

Ethan stepped back from the rail and readjusted his wide brimmed hat atop his head. The red feather stood high and gave him the proper look of a pirate.

"Ahoy there, men." His voice carried over the short distance between their ships. "How do you fare on this fine day?"

The merchant captain stood just opposite him on the other ship. "We were faring just fine until we happened upon you. What is it that you require of us? We don't have any treasures for you to plunder."

Ethan chuckled dramatically. "Ah, my good sir. I'm sure what you do have is enough treasure for us. I have it on good authority that you have a fine shipment on its way to the king of Lookonia himself. I like to say the king and I both enjoy the finer things in life. Would you permit us to take a browse through your merchandise?"

The man looked at him with a quizzical brow. "And what if I say no?"

"Well," Ethan withdrew his pistol and turned it so it glistened in the light. "We may have to strike a different sort of agreement." He grinned.

The men on the merchant ship shifted uncomfortably, their weapons beginning to quiver slightly.

"We have no wish to fight with you. Only to acquire the supplies you possess and be on our way." Ethan's voice carried over the water separating them.

"I have no guarantee that you will keep your word. Everyone knows pirates go back on their word. I will protect the lives of me and my crew." The older man stood tall and regal.

"It looks as if we want the same thing, then. I need your goods, and you wish to keep your lives. Surely both of these things can be accomplished. Does this not sound agreeable to you?" Ethan walked along the edge of the deck. "How about this? Myself and three other members of my crew will come aboard your ship. As long as you can guarantee my safety, my men will not attack. We will take the goods and be on our merry way."

The other man knew when he could not win. He had a larger ship but less skilled and armed men.

He sighed in resignation. "All right, you have my word."

That was enough for Ethan. He gathered up Jack and two other members of his crew and began to board the other vessel. He left Jonah aboard to look after the rest of his men.

"Come now, men, do not provoke any fights. If at all possible, we want to leave this ship with no bloodshed." He tried to show his crew and the merchants his confidence as he walked across the board his crew had placed down. He had long discovered the need of confidence in situations such as this. Many a battle had been won before starting because of it.

He tipped his hat to the older captain as he strode up to him. "The name is Captain Wolf. What might your name be, my good man?"

"Captain Samuel Grey," the man said through gritted teeth. He was handling this far better than most men did at this point.

"A pleasure, Captain. I'd appreciate looking at the merchandise now." He gave a sly smile and crossed his arms over his chest.

"Follow me." Although his words were civil, his eyes were shooting daggers.

Captain Grey led them to a room at the bottom of the ship. The boxes were filled with all sorts of things such as fine china, rich fabrics, and weapons.

"I have to say, Captain, I'm very pleased with all this. Seems as though the king and I have very similar tastes in many things." Ethan beckoned his men with a flick of his wrist. Jack and the other men started carrying loads of boxes back to his ship.

"My livelihood will be ruined. You pirate scum have no idea, nor do you care about the trouble you cause. The lives you destroy." Captain Grey gritted his teeth and stared coolly at Ethan.

Ethan sighed. "I know these circumstances are less than ideal, Captain. We don't wish to ruin anything for you. We have a different reason in mind." Ethan took his hat off and ran his fingers through his hair before replacing it. "Now that we are away from your crew, I would like to discuss the topic of payment. We will not take all your goods, and what we have taken we will compensate you for. What the buyer was paying you is what you will be paid in the like. Despite how this looks, I am an honorable man."

"Now you are just spouting nonsense to get me to drop my guard. If you think pretending to be nice will get me to tell you where the best goods are, it won't work. We have no great treasure aboard this ship." Captain Grey shook his head angrily and grumbled. "Men like you make me sick. Pirates have no honor, not when they can steal and keep for themselves everything that we have all worked long and hard for."

"Believe what you want of me. I only have my word and my coin to compensate you."

"Why don't you just stop this all right now and we can all go back on our way?" Captain Grey's eyes pleaded with him. This man reminded him so much of Ethan's own father.

"Now who's spouting nonsense?" Ethan chuckled. "Besides,"—he lowered his eyes to the floor—"I have good reason."

Captain Grey just stood in front of him, watching his merchandise leave in the hands of Ethan's crew. He looked so lost. Though he kept his feelings well masked, a spot of sorrow was still able to be seen in his eyes.

"Come, Captain, show me your books so we can get you paid. Surely you keep a log of it somewhere?"

The captain showed his first sign of fear as his head jerked back to Ethan. "No, that's quite all right."

"Please, I insist." He must still doubt his word that he wished to pay him. "I know we have met under unfortunate circumstances, but I give you my word. I wish to pay you fairly. A quick look into your books will give me the full price, will it not?"

They made their way to the captain's quarters. Captain Grey's hesitant footsteps were all too apparent. You could feel the tension mounting with every step they took. What could have caused such a drastic change in the strong captain? Ethan had to admit, he was more than a bit curious.

They reached the cabin and entered. "Let me just get the books here quick and we can rejoin the others." He scurried over to his desk and began rifling through its drawers. This captain could stand in front of a pirate and not bat an eye, and now something in this room was causing him to jump about the room like a scared rabbit. He seemed all too eager to leave.

Maybe the captain had something hidden in here he didn't want anyone to know about. Ethan began to walk about the room, his careful gaze not seeing anything of note. Nothing seemed out of place. It was not unlike his own quarters. In the far right corner was a small bed. Directly to the left of that was a large chest, probably holding the captain's personal items. In the middle of the room sat the desk and in the far left corner was a closet door.

As Ethan had begun circling the room, he could feel the other man's eyes following him. There was definitely something in this room he was hiding.

"In my experience there's only a few things that can cause a captain to fear." Ethan walked towards the bed and glanced at the captain. No peculiar reaction from him there. He continued on to the chest. "The largest I have found would be storms, and there's not a cloud in sight. Secondly would be pirates but you have already shown your fearlessness towards me." No reaction at the chest either.

"The other, and if not bigger reason..." Ethan opened the door of the closet. That action caused the captain to open his eyes wider. "...is if they are hiding something..."

Ethan groped the back of the closet. He found a latch and pulled it open.

"...precious." As the word left his mouth, dazzling green eyes locked with his. The young woman they belonged to blinked at the sudden bright light. Her eyes quickly adjusted to the bright exterior and they shone with anger. The fierceness in her gaze stopped him cold. No woman had dared to glare at him, not like this. Most were afraid of him, but no one could mistake the look in this woman's eyes. He had never before witnessed such a dazzling display of anger and beauty in one expression.

After recovering enough to look deeper into the closet, he found there was another person hidden behind the woman. A young lad who was squinting into the light to see him. He was largely and purposely blocked from Ethan's view by the young woman. Her brown hair was braided over her shoulder and framed an elegant face. Her pink lips were stretched taught in a deep frown. Dark lashes framed the eyes that looked on him with disdain. Ethan managed to find his words again as he yanked his eyes from her gaze.

"I see I was right, Captain. Do you make it a habit of keeping young children in your closet?" He turned away from the closet, as if they did not hold his interest.

"No, only out of fear for their lives and for the safety of the young lady. You spoke before of your honor, sir, I ask you to please keep it now." Captain Samuel went to help them out of closet.

"I'm not one to hurt children, let alone keep one for myself." Ethan tried to sound aloof. His heart raced now a woman and young boy were involved. He had not heard of this ship carrying any passengers. His word to the captain on not hurting them was true, of course. Ethan had never been with a woman and would never force himself on one. Pirates did have a bad reputation in that way, but for him and his crew it was unthinkable.

He turned to the desk and opened the book on top as the two hidden passengers came out from their hiding spot. Ethan glanced up at them. The young boy stood in front of the woman, showing bravery even though his limbs shook. His blond hair sat in a wavy mess atop his head.

The young woman stepped out from behind the boy and approached Ethan. She wore a simple brown skirt with a white top and a brown jacket over it. At her waist she had a sword, which confused him. What need did she have for it?

"I am no child, you ill-mannered pirate." She spat out the words. Even her voice was smooth and held no notes of fear. "You, sir, had best leave this ship now and not harm anyone." Her eyes sparked at her command, as if she actually believed he would do so. Her bravery and forwardness amused him.

Annika stood as straight as she could in front of the pirate, her arms crossed over her chest. The man dared to give her a cocky grin.

He didn't look intimidated by her in the least; he didn't even look mad. He wore brown breeches with a loose white shirt that was open, showing more of his chest than an honorable man would. He had black boots and wore a black wide-brimmed hat upon his head, which had a dark red feather sticking out of it.

"I don't make a habit of taking orders from women." He tipped his hat to her sarcastically. His straight white teeth seemed to gleam as he smiled. He had nice teeth for a pirate. Annika refocused her attention.

"That does not surprise me in the least. I've heard of men like you." She rested her left hand on the hilt of the sword, still attached to her waist.

"Men like me?" He seemed preoccupied as he leafed through the book on the desk. His tone seemed slightly annoyed, as if talking to a child who was a nuisance.

"Yes, men like you. Taking the hard-earned profits from respectable men to feed your money-hungry pockets. The thought disgusts me." She gave her best scowl.

The man had the audacity to laugh at her. He covered his face with a hand as he did.

"My lady." He wiped the hand down his face and his black eyes flashed at her. "You are quick to give your opinion. You know nothing of me and what brought me here. I do not have the want or the need to explain myself to you. Neither do I care what you think of me. I would like to conduct my business here with your captain, then we can all be on our merry way." He was unlike any man she had ever met. No one, not even Maddock, had treated her this way. He wasn't treating her harshly as some of the men had, but he seemed to almost mock her with his tone. She could sense no malice in his voice, however, quite unlike Maddock and Simon. "Don't worry yourself, I won't be here for long." He waved a hand at her and shifted his eyes to Captain Samuel. "I'm only here for the merchandise and then we will be on our way." He resumed his looking at the book on the desk. Whatever its contents were must be quite engaging.

Anger continued to rise in Annika. She took a few deep breaths to steady herself. In the closet she had been afraid for the crew and for their own lives. Now, after seeing the pirate, she just felt anger. *Elohim, how could You let this happen? This could ruin poor Captain Samuel. Please, Elohim, help us get out of this safely.*

The pirate had his back turned to her. He never had her out of his peripheral vision though. What could she do? She had her sword and even a hidden dagger wrapped around her ankle. A lot that would do to a boat full of pirates. Even if they were able to apprehend the scoundrel in front of them, what about the boat full of them outside? With their captain gone, they would either attack or run away. More than likely they would attack.

"Captain!" an urgent voice cried from outside of the room before she could decide what to do.

"Yes?" answered both the pirate and Captain Samuel.

A young man poked his head into the room. His jaw dropped upon seeing her. His vibrant ginger hair was messy and could rival the sunset with its hue. A bandana was wrapped around his forehead, and he had a hoop earring in one ear.

"Yes, Jack?" The pirate's prodding tore the young man's attention off her and to look at the annoyed pirate in front of him.

"Oh yes, Cap, there's a storm." The urgency returned to his voice. The shock was gone, replaced with something akin to fear. "It's right on top of us!" The boat began to sway, giving truth to his words. The words all sailors hated to hear, whether merchants or pirates.

"How did this happen? Did no one spot it from far out?"

"No, sir." Jack shook his head and walked into the room. "It just got dark all of a sudden and the wind picked up. It doesn't look good out there."

"Did you finish loading the merchandise into our ship?" The pirate captain walked away from the desk.

"Yes, sir, everything is ready to go."

"Good, let's finish up and leave immediately."

The ship lurched to one side and caused everyone to grab onto the nearest solid object to keep their footing. Carter held onto the edge of the closet they had just exited. Annika grabbed a wooden hook that was jutting out of the wall. The pirate captain, even with all the movement of the boat, never seemed to lose his balance or his cool.

"Come, Jack, our business is done here." With that, he lead the way out of the room and back to the deck. Annika followed behind him, afraid of what they would see. It was far worse than she could have imagined.

The sky was completely dark, even though it was midday. The wind howled as it whipped around them. The previously calm waters of the sea had turned into a raging monster. The waves were pounding the sides of the ship, causing it to sway violently, the motion spraying water into the air. Men were running around, securing the ship and trying to keep afloat. Gone was the fear of the pirates, replaced by something far more deadly.

The two ships were separated by a wide margin now. There was no way the pirates could make it back to their ship. The raging and uncontrollable sea would make any sort of steering impossible.

This would be an ideal situation if not for the storm. Having the pirate captain separated from his crew would have been an answer to her prayers. Because of the storm, though, no one was interested in his presence.

This isn't exactly what I meant, Elohim. I wanted deliverance, not a deadly storm intent on taking us all out. Annika looked around her as the crew franticly started tying the sails up. The pirate captain stood at the edge of the ship, surveying the distance between the two ships. He turned to look at Captain Samuel.

"I'm sure you are no happier with my presence here than I am. I shall look to change that as soon as the opportunity arises." The wind tried to take his words with it as he spoke. He had to fairly shout above it. Lightning flashed and hit one of the masts, causing it to ignite. Orange flames licked the mast and started to spread. "There will be time for more discussion on our situation later. Right now, I suggest you see to your crew."

Captain Samuel nodded in agreement and ran to help his men.

Both ships were in a mess. There were shouts all around and men scurrying every which way. Some were trying to put out the fire. Others just ran around, looking helpless as they tried to find what they could do.

Lightning struck again and this time hit one of the other remaining two poles. Now two of the three were on fire.

"Come, men." The pirate summoned his three crew members. "Let's do what we can to help." They ran forward into the fray.

That surprised Annika, but more than likely he was only helping to save his own skin.

"Annika, I'm going to help the captain!" Carter yelled to her. "You should get below deck before a wave gets you!"

"I'm not leaving you!" She grabbed his hand protectively. "Let's both go below deck!"

"No, Annika, I need to help them. Please, I need to know you are safe." His eyes pleaded with hers as he squeezed her hand. He pulled his hand free and ran forward to help the losing battle of putting the fires out.

Please protect him, Elohim, she sent an urgent plea and started to turn to go below deck.

A strangled cry reached her ears above the roar of the wind. She looked to the left and saw Maddock. He was stuck underneath a board that had fallen from a mast. The heavy board pinned him to the ground while he franticly tried to free himself.

Maddock was an awful man to say the least, but it was not in her nature to leave someone in need. Even if it was someone as unsavory as him. Annika ran forward and lifted the log with all her might. It barely budged. Maddock grunted and cried out with the pain it was causing to his middle.

Annika closed her eyes and tried again, using all the strength she could muster. The timber miraculously lifted, causing her to rejoice. She opened her eyes and saw that the pirate captain had been the reason for her success.

"Quickly, pull yourself out," he shouted to Maddock, who did so and scurried out from under the heavy burden. He stood and grimaced, holding his side. He glared at the two of them then rushed off.

She hadn't expected anything from him, but it annoyed her to see him act that way all the same.

"Get below deck, woman," the pirate yelled to her as he turned his back. She knew he was right, but it annoyed her just the same. If they were in different circumstances, she would have given him a piece of her mind.

As she began to once again go below deck, a massive wave jerked the boat around. Water washed aboard the deck and swept her off her feet. She was now thoroughly drenched and being pulled towards the edge of the boat by the receding water.

Annika screamed into the fierce wind as she was being pulled helplessly towards the edge of the ship. Just as she slipped off the edge, a strong hand reached out and grabbed hers. She hung in the air over the side of the ship and coughed water out of her lungs.

The dark-eyed pirate stood above her at the rail and held her hand with both of his. With a cry she frantically grabbed his hands, her body swaying with the movement. A wave breached the ship again, threatening her hold on his hands and dousing her further.

"I've got you! Hang on!" he shouted down to her.

"Trust me, I have no intention of letting go." She looked down to the darkness below and the cold water that looked all too eager to drag her into its depths.

Annika could feel the strength in the man's hands as he gripped hers. It would have been an easy task for him to pull her up if it hadn't been for the constant movement of the ship and the fierce wind.

With a few moments of struggle, he managed to pull her back onboard. She dragged her wet skirts back over the rail and planted her feet on the unsteady surface of the deck.

Her legs shook as adrenaline and fear coursed through her veins. "Thank you." She was surprised he was able to hear her words above the chaos.

"I'm not a heartless fiend, madam. I have morals and honor, just the same as everyone else." The look in his eyes was not unpleasant. She found herself staring and unable to drop his gaze. Somehow, she didn't see evil in his eyes. Kindness and sympathy radiated from his dark eyes for a brief moment. What kind of a man was this pirate captain really?

A loud crack split through the roaring wind and made the ship groan. Annika pulled her gaze from the pirate and was stricken to see that the ship was mostly engulfed in flames now. The loud noise had been a mast breaking. It was now balancing perilously in the air at an odd angle, threatening to tumble to the ship's deck.

With a loud crack, the beam splintered and fell to the deck and began to roll off the side. A half dozen men were pinned under it and cried as they, and the beam, fell off the boat and sank into the depths below.

Annika's mouth gaped open in horror. Their screams resounded in her mind. The roaring wind and the yelling around her seemed to fade in her mind. All she could hear was the screams of the men and her own labored breathing. Men had just lost their lives, and she had witnessed it. So much death and destruction lay all around her that it nearly crippled her. She sunk down to her knees.

Why? Why is this happening, Elohim? This isn't what I prayed for. Why did You even allow the pirates to board our ship? So many unanswered questions shouted in protest in her mind. She suddenly thought of Carter. The sounds around her began to filter back in as she came back to the present. The howling wind was a good alternative sound to the screams from before. Annika sprung to her feet to find the pirate still standing by her side. He was gaping at the mess in front of him.

"Carter!" Annika cried out franticly. *Oh, please let him not be injured—or worse, dragged off the boat.* Her heart lurched at the thought. Had his scream been one that was forever burned in her mind? She began to stumble about the ship, calling his name. The pirate followed closely behind.

Strange how mere moments ago she wanted nothing more than to be away from him, and now his presence was almost a comfort. In comparison to all the death and pain around her, at least.

Her frantic search was rewarded when she finally caught sight of Carter. He was trying to pull an injured crew member out from under a large smoldering board. He was covered in soot and was glistening with sweat.

Annika quickly came alongside of him and grasped his shoulders, which drew his attention towards her. His eyes registered a small amount of relief before turning back towards his task.

"His left leg is pinned under this beam. I can't lift it or pull him out."

The pirate came out from behind Annika and gripped one side of the sooty beam.

"Let us both give it a try." With both of the men helping lift, they were able to raise the board high enough for Annika to help the man out. They released their heavy load, and it fell with a thud to the deck.

"What should we do?" Annika turned towards Carter. "Where's the captain? Are there no plans in place in case this would happen?"

"No one has a plan in place for this," the pirate interjected solemnly, his eyes roving about the flame ridden deck.

All of a sudden Annika felt something hit her cheek. Then another on her arm. Was that rain?

"Did you feel that?"

"What?" Carter's tired eyes found hers. Suddenly, his eyes lit up. "Yes, I felt something!"

They both looked up just as the heavens released a torrent. The heavy rainfall caused the fires to crackle then fizzle out. Within moments the fires had all become nothing but smoldering piles of soot. With the rain, the wind stopped, causing the ship to sit eerily still. The lightning had also ceased and all that was heard was the pounding of the rain on the ship and water below.

All onboard were quiet, almost eerily so. Everyone just stayed frozen in place, as if afraid one wrong move and the rain would disappear and the fires would return.

Minutes later, the rain did stop but the fires were thoroughly drenched. The dark clouds broke open and the sun began to shine through. There was no sound now but the lapping of the water against the ship as it drifted.

Annika looked around to see everyone aboard the ship standing still. No one spoke, almost as if they feared this was a mirage. Soon a voice cried out in excitement. Then another. Soon the whole deck was cheering.

Men stood and hugged their neighbor. They stepped over fallen beams and raised their hands in happiness. Everyone but the pirate captain. He looked around the deck, searching. Soon he must have spotted what he was searching for and left.

"We made it, Annika! Elohim has pulled us through!" Carter threw up his arms with praise. Oh, to have the faith of a child. He hadn't questioned Elohim of why, just praised Him for His mercies.

Annika smiled and raised her hands in praise as well. She allowed the sunlight to warm her face and her chilled body. Soon the cries of excitement and praise died down, and other sounds reached their ears.

They could hear men all about them moaning. A stark reminder of the horror they had just gone through. Men lay scattered across the deck, crying out in pain.

"Come, men, everyone, help your neighbor. There are many in need of it." Captain Samuel's voice of reason brought a smile to Annika's lips. What a relief to hear his voice and know that he was well.

Everyone turned their attention to the injured sailors. Some began pulling boards up and off of sailors. Some men only needed help to stand and move to where they could be treated. Others were so badly injured they needed to be treated on the spot.

Annika spotted a man's hand sticking out from under one of the fallen sails.

"Carter! There's someone here." They both began to untangle the torn and twisted sail and found the sailor beneath. He was breathing but unconscious. Annika was just thankful he was alive. Hopefully, they would find more that way.

CHAPTER FIVE

E than stood with his crew mates at the rail of the ship. They looked out over the water towards their own vessel. He was going to lean on the rail, but the burnt appearance and its cracked exterior changed his mind.

Jack, who seemed to have suffered no injuries, had been the first to spot their ship. Now, as they were looking out to their magnificent vessel, it brought an air of sadness over them. Its once magnificent presence now looked as though it had been through a war. It was a sleek ship, built for speed, but now it looked like it could barely sail. The decks looked to have been burned but not to the degree that the merchant ship had. Two of the masts still stood straight and tall. A bit of movement on the deck showed that there were survivors.

"Looks to be in better shape than this ship, Cap." Jack nodded his head. "A bit of work and she will sail again, I would wager."

Ethan nodded his head and frowned. Repairs would most definitely be needed but that would be a problem. They were in the middle of the ocean. There was no land for miles. How would they get the much-needed repairs done?

The ship they were on started to lurch slightly, drawing his attention to the angle of the deck. A small barrel rolled slowly across the deck and bumped into the rail. He groaned inwardly. No doubt this boat had a leak and was sinking. What else could go wrong?

"Jack, go check below for leaks. I hope for the best, but I would wager there is hidden damage below. If you do find that is the case, check and see if it's repairable."

"On it, Cap."

Ethan looked about the deck at the men. Everyone was walking around looking for the injured. All but two men, who stood off to the side looking rather angry. One was clutching his stomach. Ethan recalled him being the one he and that woman had helped. That frown was a good reminder of who he was as well. The ungrateful face he had given them upon being rescued was easy to recall.

The woman had not been much help when they had saved the man, but it was impressive to see her try. Many would not have. Ethan would wager the man would not be returning the favor.

His eyes scanned the deck, ashamed to admit he was looking for the woman. He finally found her going from man to man. She must have found water and was distributing it to the injured sailors. He had to hand it to her; she had determination and a clear head in dangerous circumstances. Her ability to function, even after almost getting knocked overboard, was impressive enough.

A low moan dragged Ethan's thoughts away from the woman. Near Ethan, leaning against the rail, was a man. He was barely standing as he leaned forward, his hands clutching his head and face. His hands were over his eyes and there was noticeable blood seeping through his fingers.

"I know this is not our crew and we are not here under the best of circumstances, but I can't stand to see men in need. While Jack is gone, I suggest we do what we can and help." He looked at his two men.

"Aye, Cap." Chris, the strongest of the two, stepped forward. "I will check and see if I can lend my hands to clearing any debris left by the falling timbers."

Ethan nodded. "You do that. Marcus, you're with me." The other man nodded, and they set out to scour the deck. Ethan and Marcus helped several men in need of assistance out of the rubble. Within half an hour, Jack was back up on deck. He zeroed in on Ethan and hurried towards him.

"You were right, Cap. There is a sizable hole down there. We are taking on water quickly and it doesn't appear to be repairable. If we were at port and had the supplies at the ready, that would be a different story. Since we are in the middle of the ocean and hundreds of miles from the nearest port, there is no hope of repairing it. We would sink before we could get anywhere for help."

Ethan had been tying a bandage around an injured man's arm when he heard the news. He paused what he was doing and squeezed his eyes shut. Of all the things to happen, this had been a day for the record books. How many things could go wrong in one day? What had started out as a simple job had turned into a nightmare.

He opened his eyes and finished the wrapping on the sailor's arm. It looked crooked and sloppy, but he was decently satisfied with it. A quick tight knot later he was standing and facing his awaiting men.

"I will go and speak with the captain. I have a feeling he won't like what I'm about to suggest."

Jack nodded in understanding. "I know what you are thinking, and I don't like it either." He crossed his arms.

"Do you have a better alternative?"

"No, but that doesn't mean I have to like it." Jack smiled sarcastically. "Whatever happens, we are behind you, Cap."

Ethan squared his shoulders and put on a mask of feigned confidence. He found the captain at the bow of the ship talking with a crew member.

"Captain, how fare your men?"

Captain Grey jerked his attention to Ethan, as if he had forgotten all about him.

"With all that has happened, I had almost plumb forgotten about you and your men being here." He rubbed a hand down his weary face. "I did see you helping my men, so I owe you thanks for that."

"No thanks needed. We saw men in need and couldn't stand idle. We may not be in the same business, but neither of us want men to suffer."

"I can agree with you on that." Captain Grey nodded and sighed wearily, pain written on his expression. "To answer your question, we're not good. We lost at least a dozen men today. All three of our masts are down and the sails are unrepairable. Half the deck is burned and that's just the damage I can see."

"That's what I wanted to discuss with you. My men have discovered a sizable hole in your vessel. You are slowly but steadily taking on water." To punctuate his words, the ship tilted more.

"I will send my men down to look at it at once to see if it can be repaired." The captain quickly found men and ordered them down below. Ethan hoped they came up with a different answer than Jack had, but he doubted it.

"I sincerely hope your vessel can be fixed. In case it doesn't, however, I suggest we speak of your alternative option."

"And what would you suggest that would be?" Captain Grey crossed his arms and looked wary.

"My ship is close by and looks to be in better shape than yours. I do not wish any of you harm by leaving you here to drown." Ethan took off his hat, which surprisingly he still had, and ran a hand through his hair. "I suggest that we all board my ship. After a few repairs, she should be safe to sail."

"Board your ship? A pirate vessel?" The other man looked dumbfounded.

"Call it what you wish, but at least she floats." He gave a wry smile.

"Cap, is that land I see ahead?" Jack, who stood on the rail, pointed ahead.

Ethan looked to the faraway object and studied it. It was a small blur right now, but it was undoubtedly land.

"Aye, it is. Good spot, Jack." Ethan felt his first real smile start to form. This could be the one good thing to happen in this dreary day. Land meant they could rest and fix the ship.

"I suggest that we all board my ship and make our way to land. We can make necessary repairs and let the men rest on shore. What do you say, Captain?" The ship groaned and tilted more.

"I would like to hear what my men have to say on the damage sustained to my ship." He groaned and shook his head. "If it's as bad as I'm thinking it is, then we won't have much choice."

A short time later, Captain Grey's men came back and informed him of the situation. "I don't see that we have much choice right now." He gave a resigned sigh. "As much as I hate to do this, we humbly accept your offer of transportation." With that he sprang into action.

"Men, take the rest of the goods from below and whatever possessions you have and gather them up here. On the double. Our ship is sinking, and I don't think we will want to be here when it goes down. Prepare to board the pirate vessel."

"Captain, are you sure that is wise?" a stout man interjected.

"Right now, I would rather face a den of pirates than to sink to our watery graves." He turned to Ethan. "Can you signal your ship to come about so we can board?"

"Right away, Captain Grey." Ethan nodded and turned with his men. He gave them orders to get the attention of his ship and to get the board secured upon its arriving. Suddenly, the hair on the back of his neck lifted, a clear sign for him that someone was watching him. Further down on the deck stood the young woman; her sharp green eyes had found him and had locked in place.

She stared at him a moment and looked thoughtful. No anger or hate shone from her eyes, only a look of contemplation. After a moment, she turned back to her job of helping the wounded.

Once her eyes left him, Ethan realized he had stood trapped in her gaze for a few moments and was now behind his crew. He quickly walked away and rejoined his men. If he was not careful, she could prove to be quite dangerous indeed.

Ethan and his crew were able to signal their nearby ship. He was relieved to see Jonah's tall, broad form directing everyone. Hopefully, his crew had fared better than this one.

Within half an hour the ship was at their side, and they placed a board across the gap again. This time, instead of carrying stolen valuables, injured men were helped across. It looked to be over a dozen men were injured, and the remaining sailors were very shaken up.

They all hurried getting aboard the ship and moved the rest of their belongings onto it. The merchant ship was quickly starting to tilt. Soon it would be impossible to walk upright. Ethan had yet to spot the young woman, though. Where had she gone to? Her companion had been helping the injured across the platform.

The tapping of heels on the wooden deck drew Ethan's attention. There she was, one of the last aboard the sinking vessel. She was hauling two bags on her shoulders. One bag would be easy enough to hold but two made it a bit of a handful.

"Let me help you with that." He came up behind her and relieved the bags from her arms.

"I am perfectly capable of carrying my own things," she said, annoyed, though she sighed with relief as she stretched her back. He did his best to hide a smile.

"You just focus on keeping your balance while walking on the beam. I don't want your death on my head." He chuckled as he nimbly crossed the board. He had excellent balance as he walked across the wobbly plank due to years of practice. He dropped off the bags and turned to see if she needed help.

The young woman was already halfway across and walked with complete confidence. Even as the board wobbled her feet never wavered. Her head was held high as she confidently strode across the plank, almost as if she commanded it to stay still. Not afraid of heights and has excellent balance; Ethan added those attributes to his growing appreciation for her. She was feisty and had a killer scowl, but she was soft beneath that exterior. That was evident by the care she gave to the injured men on deck and the worry that had shown on her brow.

She landed nimbly on the deck and didn't cast a second look at Ethan. She found her young companion and stood with him.

Minutes later the last of the men were off the sinking ship. They made haste and lowered the sails that were still intact.

As they sailed away, they all watched in somber silence as the merchant ship lurched dangerously to one side. The groaning of the wood carried across the water. Loose debris fell off the side and into the ocean. With another large groan, the ship fell completely to its side. It only took a matter of minutes for the ship to disappear into the dark waters below, never to be seen again.

Ethan pulled his gaze away from the now empty sea behind them. He was not looking forward to having so many extra men with him, let alone ones that held no trust for him, for obvious reasons. That would make this already perilous situation even more difficult.

He looked ahead of them towards the island in the distance. Despite the broken mast and torn sail, they were making decent time. The blur of land was now unmistakable.

"Smith, my spyglass please," Ethan called to the nearest crew member. Smith was a short man, barely reaching Ethan's chest. His long dark blond hair was tied behind his head, and his face had evidence of stubble growing back from his most recent shave. He was the ship's navigator. He led them across the sea by looking at the stars and the ocean currents. Smith produced the object and quickly placed it onto Ethan's outstretched hand.

"Thank you." Ethan held the gold cylinder to his right eye and looked towards the island. "What island do you suppose that is? I wasn't aware that there was any land out this far into the sea." Through the spyglass he could see that it was a large island with a tall volcano rising from its center. The beach was white and had palm trees scattered about. Any other detail was too small to make out yet.

"There isn't, Captain," Smith's aged, gruff voice answered confused. "Well, at least, not to my knowledge. Though I know we were shaken off course by that storm, so I won't be able to know where we are exactly until nightfall. I find it doubtful that we traveled far enough to reach any land on the maps I have." His gold tooth glinted as he showed a small smile.

"So, what's your conclusion then?"

"Well, Captain..." Despite their dilemma, Smith looked gleeful. "I will double check for sure tonight, but I believe we are looking at an unknown island."

"You know that doesn't really help our situation, right, Smith? I don't see the reason for excitement. Doesn't an uncharted island mean our lives will be harder?" Jonah said as he joined them.

"Well, you haven't slaved away the day looking at maps wishing some-day your name would be on one." Smith gave a mock eye roll and grinned crookedly at Jonah.

"You and I have very different kinds of wishes, my friend." Jonah chuckled. Smith laughed in return then excused himself, probably to go and think of a name for this supposedly new island.

"Good to see you still standing, my friend." Ethan gave his friend a good pat on the back, making him grimace. "Did I speak too soon?" Jonah quickly bit back the pain and straightened again.

"I'm fine, Captain. During the worst of the storm, a large crate landed on my chest. I have some bumps and bruises but nothing serious." The man could have lost a leg, and he still would have just brushed it off and insisted he was fine. Who knew how much pain he was really in.

"I'm glad to hear you are safe and, for the most part, unharmed. It looks like our crew and ship had better luck than the *Sailor's Journey*."

"We have ten wounded, two seriously, but it could have been much worse, though. We came out much better than they did." He turned and looked Ethan in the eyes, his concern written on his face. "I'm not looking forward to having them onboard with us. I mean, we did just try to rob them."

"I didn't like the idea either." Ethan sighed and propped his leg on the rail of the ship. "However, there wasn't an alternative unless we were completely heartless and just left them to die. I wasn't willing to even think of that as an option. Just before the storm started, I was just about to pay the captain for the goods we were taking. I will still do so. That should help keep the peace around here, as well as help him get back on his feet."

"I agree. I believe it would help mend a bit of bridge between the merchants and us. Many of the captains we have encountered through the years don't believe you actually wish to pay them back. Once you do, you gain their respect in a way. You are known now as a gentleman pirate to many. Everyone but the king, of course. Those who have heard of you see you as a sort of hero."

"I don't care about my reputation. As long as the king knows I'm here, I don't aim to leave anytime soon. I will be a thorn in his side for as long as I can. Everyone else can see me as thief, I don't care."

Jonah placed a hand on his friend's arm. "But you do care." He spoke quietly, so the other men couldn't hear. "You hate what the king has done, but you care about the people. You have a heart that has been wounded, and you try to convince yourself that you are hardened because of it. The opposite is true. After suffering great loss, you began to care more. That is why you pay people back for what you steal."

Ethan sighed, knowing how the conversation always went. "Your high praise for me is undeserved, but I thank you all the same. I do care about the people, but right now my goal is making the crown suffer. That's all I want." He had to do something, or his own grief would cripple him.

"I'm with you in whatever you decide, Captain."

"Thank you, Jonah. Let us focus on more pressing matters, such as reaching the shore and what repairs are needed to get us sailing again. Right now, we seem to be more like limping."

"I agree." Jonah nodded. "If not for the strong current and the breeze at our backs, we wouldn't be going anywhere. Let's hope they can sustain us the rest of the way."

"That we can agree on. Would you mind showing me what kind of repairs need done? I need to see for myself the damage we have sustained."

"Sure thing, Cap. Unfortunately, we lost a lot of our supplies in the storm."

Ethan inwardly groaned. "What kind of supplies?"

"Well, we lost half our water supply. The barrels that contained water were cracked and we lost much of it."

"That's bad news indeed." With the crew they had just taken on, their water supply would be gone in a matter of days. They would have to hope the island could supply them with some water as well. So far, the island was like a mysterious beacon of hope.

It took the better part of the day to reach the island. By the time they entered the green bay, it was sundown. The sun began its quick decent behind the massive volcano. There was a beautiful orange and pink sky overhead, and it colored the water with its reflection. Even through the darkness they could see that the island was large and covered very densely with jungle. No sign of human life was visible, unfortunately.

Ethan stood, facing the mass of men aboard the ship. Captain Grey stood close to him. The men's gazes were torn between the captains and the island in the distance.

"It may be beautiful, but if we don't prepare ourselves and our crew correctly, it could be a bad situation." Ethan looked at Captain Grey. "I believe it wise to send a group onto the island to search for a place to camp. Perhaps they could also stumble upon inhabitants on the island. It would be preferable if we could find someone and could get supplies. I have taken a look at the damage, and while we fared better than your ship, we are still barely limping along."

Captain Grey sighed. "I haven't surveyed the damage so I can't speak on that. I do agree that it would prove beneficial to know if there is a settlement here and to have a place found where we can camp. Your ship is not large enough to house us all for long." He turned to Ethan, his eyebrows drawn together. "I know this is not my ship and I have no right to give orders to anyone. I have to say, though, I would like to still be included in decisions, seeing as how many of these men are my crew."

"Of course. Captain Grey, I'm sorry things turned out this way. I completely understand your concerns and I want you to be included in the decisions. Right now, there are two captains on board, and I wish for you to still be treated as such." He smiled at Captain Grey. "I would like to continue the conversation we were having aboard your ship at the earliest convenience." Captain Grey looked curious but said nothing as he nodded.

Ethan turned and nodded to Jack, who gave a loud whistle. All the men turned and looked to Ethan. "Men, there are no obvious signs that this island is inhabited. We still must take a look and see for ourselves. Our best hope is to find civilization. I would like to personally take a team of men onto the island tomorrow in search of people, or in the very least, something to help fix the ship. I won't lie to you all, the ship is not in good condition. Right now, we can't do much more than just drift. There is no possibility of us making it to the mainland in this state, especially with our shortage of supplies. Finding help or at least supplies is essential. What do you think, Captain Grey?" Ethan gestured to the older man. He hadn't looked the same since his ship had sunk to the depths.

Captain Grey nodded and addressed the men. "I agree with the decision. We may have met these men under less-than-ideal circumstances, but they have been generous enough to allow us aboard their ship. If any of you feel animosity towards anyone get it out of your system. Like it or not, we will be spending a lot of time together, and I think we would all find it more pleasurable if we could get along." His men grumbled under their breath but nodded in understanding. "If anyone has any concerns, please share them with me directly. I will be staying behind while Captain Wolf's group goes on to the mainland. I feel I should stay with our wounded men."

Ethan nodded his assent to the captain. "Now, my crew, please help our guests find their accommodations for the night. Show them where to sleep and anything else they may need. Ant, where are you, my man?" His ship's cook raised his hand and stepped forward.

"Are you able to prepare a small meal?"

"Of course, Captain." The man in question came forward. His slim figure giving him the nickname Ant. His graying beard was scraggly, and his eyes shone with purpose. "Always ready to do my duty. Besides, maybe it will cheer everyone's spirits some having a full belly." He smiled gleefully, happy to be able to do something with his hands.

"Might I be of some help to ya?" An older gentleman stepped forward. "I was the cook back on *Sailor's Journey*. If I ain't cookin, I ain't useful."

"I'd welcome the help." Ant nodded. The two were as different as they could possibly be. Ant's slim figure and height was a stark contrast to the other man, who looked like he sampled more than his fair share of the food.

"I know today has been a hard day for all." Ethan regained the attention of his crew and their guests. "No one could have foreseen it and none of us will forget it. The ocean may have unleashed its fury upon us, but we have survived. We will never forget the men we lost. Let's use the memory of our fallen friends as a drive to push forward and to survive. We will never forget them, but we will honor them by living."

He looked around at everyone's solemn expressions. Some looked at the ground while others looked at him with hope. Many men stood propped against a neighbor or lying on the floor.

"All right, let's get going, men." With that the men dispersed themselves about the ship. The young woman stood still with her companion.

She looked lost and unsure of where to go. Of course she would; she was on a strange ship and had no idea where she would be safe. Her long brown braid had dried, and now small pieces had escaped and blew about her face in the breeze.

Ethan approached the pair and plastered on his most dashing smile. "Well, it appears we will have to endure each other's company for a spell. I do believe formal introductions are in order. My name is Captain Wolf." He tipped the wide brim of his hat.

"My name is Annika Harper," she said after a moment's pause. "And this is Carter Monroe. He is accompanying me on my journey."

"Beautiful name that is, Annika." He grinned as her cheeks inadvertently took a slight shade of pink. She was very easy to tease. "Good to meet you, lad." Ethan stuck his hand out to shake Carter's hand but was met with only air.

"Wish I could say the same, sir." The boy's anger towards him remained. Not that Ethan could blame him.

"You mentioned taking a small group onto the island tomorrow?" Annika pointedly asked him.

"Yes, a small group of men, maybe fifteen of us, will go to the island tomorrow. Hopefully, we will find some people who can help us get repairs or find some much needed supplies. We lost some of ours in the storm."

The two looked at each other. "We would like to accompany you." Carter raised his chin confidently.

"I'm afraid that's not possible." Ethan shook his head. "The jungle is no place for a young boy, let alone a lady. Who knows what we will encounter out there." The boy's face fell in disappointment while Annika's glowed with determination.

"I refuse to be cooped up on a ship and not know what our futures will hold. Honestly, I would feel safer in the wilds of the jungle than cooped up on a pirate's ship. Besides, Carter really wants to get a look at it." Carter smiled sheepishly. "Where he goes, I go." Her green eyes dazzled in defiance.

Ethan chuckled. Though she was striking when mad, he was not swayed. "I think not. You two may remain here together, keeping each other company. That's an order." Ethan knew the journey ahead would be tasking and possibly dangerous. It was no journey for a woman.

"You will find bedding down below with the crew." Ethan, changing the subject, gestured to the door going down. "I believe your captain is down there already." Annika stood in front of him with her arms crossed, annoyance dripping from her scowling eyes.

"For both of us?" Carter squeaked out, apparently deciding to drop his demand to leave. He put a protective hand on Annika's shoulder.

"I have a different idea in mind for the lady, if she so chooses it." Carter eyed him warily. "Nothing nefarious up my sleeves, I promise." Ethan held his hands up playfully.

"Lead the way, Captain." Annika looked curious. No doubt wondering if he would be fair towards her or if he was leading her into a trap.

Ethan walked away with them close on his tail. It was only a short walk to his quarters. His boots thudded across the wooden planks of the deck. Annika's footsteps were so light and graceful compared to his.

"Here we are." He walked into the room and opened the trunk on the floor.

"Where are we?" Annika warily asked him as he pulled out a shirt and a pair of pants from the chest.

"My quarters, of course." He noticed her open mouth and red face. She looked at a loss for words. He chuckled. "Don't flatter yourself, I won't be staying here. I have no need to put up with a flighty female. It's for that reason I want you to stay here, well away from my men."

He, in truth, wanted to keep her and her reputation safe, but it would not help his pirate image if he admitted that. Ethan decided to stay an uncaring pirate in her eyes. Annika rolled her eyes and tried to appear unfazed as the cherry red color slowly faded from her cheeks. A small, almost imperceptible sigh and a relaxing of her shoulders told him that she had been rattled.

"This will be your room for the remainder of your stay on this ship. I'm sure it's not as fancy as what you are used to, but it should suffice. I hope I can trust you not to look at my private articles." He grinned and emphasized the word private, eliciting the cherry red look again. My, he would have a hard time not teasing her.

"I have no need to search through your private articles. I couldn't care less about what you do in your free time." With a huff she entered the room fully. "My, you do live a simple life don't you, Captain?" She referred to the drab interiors around her. "I half expected to see your quarters lined with the riches you have plundered from hardworking men."

"I'm sorry to disappoint you." He didn't even bother to defend himself.

"I left my things back on deck."

"I will send someone to fetch it for you. Come, Carter." He held his hand out and motioned him to exit the door before him. "Let's leave Annika to get settled. I will show you where you can stay." They both started to walk out the door.

"I'll be nearby if you need me," Carter called to her.

With that Ethan took Carter down below deck.

CHAPTER SIX

Annika walked about the cabin room, feeling weary and antsy. Every time she closed her eyes, the image of those poor sailors being crushed and then washed overboard would plague her mind. Not to mention the fear that had welled up her throat when she remembered almost falling to her death. At the time there was so much adrenaline coursing through her veins that she didn't even have time to stop and be afraid. Now, on her own in a dark room, she felt afraid and very much alone. The morning couldn't come quickly enough.

Sometime soon she would have to succumb to sleep. Her sore body needed the rest. Though that would mean she would have to sleep on the pirate's bed, and she was sure it would smell of him. She wrinkled her nose in disgust at the thought.

What nerve that man had thinking he could command her like she was some child. He may be used to commanding his crew, but she would not allow him to order her around. He even had the audacity to call her by her first name. It was how she preferred to have people address her, but it was very forward of him to just assume without her consent. Though she couldn't quite figure out why her heart had leaped when he had said her first name.

It had been several hours since she had seen anyone. After Carter and Captain Wolf had left her alone in the room, a young pirate brought her things to her and had quickly exited.

Since then, she had seen no one. Someone had even brought her food and left it just outside the door for her, which she had appreciated at the time as she enjoyed some much-needed time alone to pray. Now, she just felt left out and in need of something to take her mind off the terrible images that plagued her. Plus, she had so many questions about today and what was going to happen tomorrow.

She had every intention of going with them on the island. Contrary to Captain Wolf's belief, she was used to being outdoors. Her father used to take her and her brother hunting with him and they would sleep under the stars. She was probably better suited for it than many on his crew were. Besides, she wasn't part of his crew and wouldn't be so easy for him to command. She would broach the topic with him again in the morning.

Annika wished she were a fly on the wall where the two captains undoubtedly sat together, put aside their differences, and spoke of the future and what their plans would be. She had been impressed with the way Captain Samuel had been able to talk with Captain Wolf and the humility he had shown. Come to think of it, it had surprised her how kind Captain Wolf had been in return.

The wood on the wall brushed against her fingers as she traced the grain of it. It was so difficult for her to stay cooped up, not knowing what was being discussed and what would be happening. She hated not knowing. The fear of the unknown was enough to drive one insane if you dwelt on it. For that reason, she tried her best to push her questions down.

Annika suddenly felt the urgent need to leave the small quarters of the captain. Even if it was just to step out and feel the gentle breeze from the ocean. The captain's quarters were starting to feel stifling. She yearned to take a breath of fresh air and calm her shaky nerves. Surely no one would blame her if she went for a quick stroll about the deck, right? What if that blasted pirate was there to try to get a rise out of her again? After some thought, she realized she would rather brave seeing him again than to stay cooped up here a moment longer.

The cabin was so dark with just the one candle to illuminate the room. It cast the eeriest glow about the walls, making strange shadows as it flickered. Her vivid imagination worked on the double as she quickly found her cloak and stepped out the door before she could change her mind. From the doorway of the cabin, she could see most of the deck in front of her.

Annika found the rail to her right and looked out over the water. She inhaled the fresh salty air as she took in the silvery moonlight. The moon was full tonight and cast a beautiful silver shimmer across the water. The island ahead of them sat in complete darkness, as if to add to its mystery.

Despite the circumstances of the day, it was relaxing looking out over the water. With each lap of the waves against the ship, it felt like Elohim was just whispering words of reassurance and love to her. Her ship had been robbed by pirates today and she had witnessed people losing their lives to the unforgiving sea. Even with all of that going wrong, Elohim had used the pirate to save her from a watery grave. He had deemed her worthy of protection.

Annika began to slowly walk about the ship. Everything was silent save for the gentle waves and the occasional faint laughter from a sailor below deck.

All of a sudden a quiet melodious song reached her ear. There was a faint strumming of an instrument, and a soft and rich voice accompanied it. Annika was entranced. The voice had such a velvety tone to it and beckoned her to find its source. Just ahead, hidden behind the mast, sat a man. He sat against the rail, his hip propped on it. His head was cast down, looking at his instrument.

Annika stopped and stood behind a rather large crate. She was close enough she could listen but hopefully not to alert him of her presence.

She studied the figure shrouded in shadows. When he lifted his head and sang out again Annika nearly fell over backward. The face belonged to none other than Captain Wolf. His normally smug face was gone, left was a gentle look as he lightly sang the next verse of his song. Annika recovered from her surprise and leaned closer to listen.

His song was quite sad. It spoke of a sailor lost at sea, trying to find his way back home. There were no stars to guide his way; the moon was his only companion. He sat still on his drifting boat, waiting for the stars so he could find his way home. It was a beautiful song. She had never heard it before but imagined such a beautiful and sad song was sung often by a lonely sailor.

His song made her spirit feel soothed and her heart a little lighter. Despite the sad nature of the song, his soothing rich voice seemed to engulf her. Perhaps that's why he sang, and such a sad song too. Perhaps his mind was plagued with the same thoughts as hers.

The captain, upon finishing his song, hung his head once more and quietly strummed his instrument. His silhouette was all she could see now, his face shrouded in the darkness. Annika sank back into the shadows and went back into the cabin. How could such a soulful voice be held by such a horrid man? Could a kind soul be hidden down deep in him? She highly doubted it.

Annika quickly got prepared for bed and decided to finally give in to sleep. She sank down into the bed and covered herself up with the surprisingly soft blankets. She rested her head on the pillow and tried to get some sleep. The bed did smell of what she imagined was the captain's scent. It was a mixture of saltwater and some kind of wood. She didn't even mind it as she sank into a deep sleep.

The next day arrived and with it the harsh reality of their situation. The island was barely visible due to a thick veil of fog that blanketed the air around it. The sun even struggled to pierce its way through. It lent an air of mystery and a certain level of fear to the island. What surprises would be awaiting them? Would there be people living there, or would they be all alone?

Annika had heard rumors from the men standing around her saying that this was possibly a new and unexplored island. She greatly hoped that those rumors were proven false. They needed help. Annika prayed that they would encounter people, and they would be given help off the island. Maybe they would even find some authorities to get the supplies from the pirate ship and give them back to Captain Samuel.

She didn't have a burning hatred for the pirates anymore. She had been saved by their captain and had even glimpsed a gentle side to him. He was still a pirate, though. He had undoubtedly stolen from many a sailor and had ruined their livelihoods. He probably didn't even think about them once he had sailed away. Just took off with everything that they held dear and plundered it for himself. That's what she and the *Sailor's Journey* would have been to Captain Wolf. If not for the storm, they would have just been another stop on their stealing spree.

The crew was gathered on deck again to receive orders. Annika searched among the men until she found Captain Wolf.

"Good morning, Captain Wolf," Annika said as she stepped up to him. He looked at her in surprise, no doubt wondering why she had sought him out. Then his face changed from surprise to annoyance. Gone was the gentle look from the previous night, left in its place a frustrated grimace. His jet-black hair was once again pulled back and tied at the nape of his neck. His large black hat shaded his eyes from the sun. Why was it that today she noticed that he was quite handsome? Why had that thought not passed her mind yesterday?

"It would be a better morning if you would not broach the silly notion of you tagging along." He shook his head and turned to watch the island.

"I'm not going to back down on this. I have every right to go if I so wish it. I am not a member of your crew that you may order me around. I know you think of me as incapable and useless since I'm a woman. I will tell you now that you know nothing about me." She hardened her expression. He seemed to think about if for a minute and then his face changed.

"Fine, but I will tell you right now that I don't like it." It kind of worried her why he so quickly changed his mind, but she didn't dwell on it. She nodded her head and marched away, proud of herself for having stood up to the pirate.

It took a while to get everyone organized and ready for the quick rowboat journey to the island. They had set anchor about half a mile from the island and would need to take rowboats to get further.

Fifteen men went, plus Carter and Annika, and the rest of the crew stayed behind. They took two rowboats to carry everyone and their supplies. It didn't take long to get everyone loaded onto the boats and rowing towards land. Annika noticed that Stew was among the men coming. At least they would hopefully have decent meals on the trek.

The rowboat ride went quickly, the waters smooth and clear. Even the fog in the air was beginning to clear up. The sun began to peek through, and the dark and mysterious island took on a new side. The sparkling waters gave the island a more gentle feel than the fog had. The palm trees on the beach were gently swaying in the breeze. Even the sand was white and looked pristine.

After they pulled the boats onto the beach, Annika jumped out and planted her boots into the soft sand. Once her feet made contact with land, it was a shock. It felt so strange to not have the swaying of the ship and instead have solid ground. To stand on solid land again felt as foreign to her as it once was to be on the ship. Carter stepped down behind her.

"A strange sensation, isn't it?" Annika asked as she closed her eyes and took in the island breeze. It smelled of trees, and something sweet lingered in the air.

"Yes, it is indeed. It is nice to feel the solid ground after a day like yesterday. I have to admit, though, I like being on the water better." Carter kicked the sand with his boot, sending sand flying into the air. They walked a bit further up the beach, watching crew members arrange supplies.

"I have been surprised at how much I really do enjoy just being on the sea. The sunsets, the gentle swaying, all of it appeals to me." Annika sighed and breathed deeply. "I have to admit, though, I do enjoy the simple pleasures of being on solid ground."

"Such as?" Carter bent down and examined a shell in the sand.

"The simple pleasures of fresh fruit and bread. A soft bed to sleep on at night. Seeing animals scurry around underfoot."

"I see what you mean." Carter picked the shell up and stood to his feet. The men in front of them seemed to be readying themselves.

Annika was struck by the beauty of the island. Back home they had some sand and some palm trees, but this was completely different. A large beach with snow-white sand stretched as far to the left and to the right as could be seen. Large palm trees were jutting out of the sand further up the beach. Their wide leaves stretched out, casting shadows across the sand.

Seagulls cried faintly in the distance as the gentle breeze traveled through the trees. Annika had read in books about tropical paradises, and this must be what they had been describing. Many of the sailors aboard must have felt the same, for some just knelt down on their knees and looked around in awe.

"Ever seen anything of this sort before?" Captain Wolf asked from behind Annika, commanding her attention.

"Never before have I witnessed such beauty," Annika answered honestly. Sea gulls flew overhead, their wings gracefully beating the air. "I'm sure you must be used to this by now."

"I have seen many a beach and paradises before. This one is, by far, the most pristine."

"So what's the plan, Captain? I have been left a bit out of the loop. Have we any indication that this island is inhabited?"

"I believe we are on a new island. At least there isn't an island here on the maps aboard the *Sailor's Journey*," Carter surprised her by piping up.

"You studied navigation, lad?" The captain sounded surprised as he laid a hand on his hip.

"Only briefly, I'm afraid. I didn't get long to look at the map but from what I can remember, this island wasn't on it." Carter shrugged his shoulders.

"When did you get a look at a map?"

"I saw the map aboard our ship a few days ago."

"I'm very impressed. It takes an experienced sailor to read a map, let alone memorize it." Carter slightly flushed at the praise. The captain came up beside Carter and laid a hand on his shoulder. "Would you like me to introduce you to our navigator? He can show you more. I can guarantee he would show you all he knows. Even if you don't want him to." He gave a wry chuckle.

"I would love it, sir!" Carter's eyes were wide in excitement.

"Wonderful! He came along with us. Come, I'll introduce you." The two men walked off in search of the navigator, leaving Annika behind.

She smiled, proud to see Carter getting the praise he deserved. He was a smart boy with so much to offer the world. He had always had excellent memorization. Now he was getting recognized for it. It was actually quite thoughtful of Captain Wolf to have seen that Carter had a love for the sea and then to offer him a way to find guidance on it. Her opinion of the man shifted slightly, even without her really knowing it.

"Well, I'm pleased to see you could join us, Lady Harper." Shivers went up her spine at the sound of the voice. She turned and found Simon standing behind her. His blond hair was messy and it blew in the breeze. If it wasn't for the look in his eyes and the way he said her name, she would call him handsome.

"Hello, I was not aware you were coming along on the trek." If she had known he was coming, it would have tempered her resolve to come. "As am I. It's wonderful to be on solid ground again."

"My coming was somewhat of a last-minute decision. I have to say, I'm appalled at the pirate captain." He stepped closer to her, his eyes peering down at her. Fear coursed through her body and froze her in place. "If it were up to me, I would keep you somewhere safe. Somewhere that the elements couldn't hurt you or mar your beauty." He was standing far too close to her. She regained movement in her legs and stepped back from him.

"I'm quite thankful for the opportunity to come. I would hate to be treated like I could break at any moment. I'm capable of far more. Now if you'll excuse me, Carter said he needed to speak with me." She attempted to give him a smile and was angry to find herself shaking.

He grinned. "Not a problem. We will be seeing much of each other." The gleam in his eyes made her heart fill with dread. She scurried off to find Carter. She would have to watch her step from now on. The jungle may hold many dangers, but that man was more dangerous than a hundred snakes.

An hour later, they were all set for their trek through the jungle. With one last look at the open beach, they plunged into the unknowns of the overgrown jungle.

The interior of the island was far different than the beach. The trees were quite dense. Tree roots were snaking above ground, practically begging sailors to trip over them. There were palm trees as well as many other trees Annika didn't recognize. Vines and moss hung from the branches. The gentle chirping from birds echoed through the trees while mosquitoes enjoyed buzzing about looking for a meal.

It was wonderful to hear the pleasant sound of birds once again. Their song was very much like back in the kingdom of Narine. Their chirps and tweets were quite cheerful and excited, as if they were spurring the weary travelers onward with their music.

Annika walked behind Carter and Captain Wolf as they trudged through the forest. Other than the sound of the birds overhead, everything was new and completely different than anything she had ever seen before. Her head swiveled back and forth as she tried to capture every detail around her.

A howling from behind her caused her to jump in surprise and twirl her head around to find the culprit. There was a large animal with long arms and legs and an angry face hanging from its tail in the trees behind them. As she watched the strange creature, her foot caught a root and she wasn't able to catch herself. The ground came rushing to greet her as strong arms caught her under her arms.

She was righted on her feet and suddenly realized Captain Wolf had once again come to her rescue. He grinned but his eyes held gentle concern.

"Watch where you're going, Annika. What has taken your interest and sent you sprawling into my arms?" She stepped back from him and straightened her skirt, unnerved at how easily he used her first name.

"I'm sorry for 'sprawling' into you. I was mesmerized at the sight of that strange creature back there." She pointed it out and saw the captain struggle to hold back a laugh.

"Have you never seen a monkey before?"

"A monkey?" She had read about them in books before and even heard descriptions of them, but this was nothing like she had imagined.

"Yes, it is called a howler monkey. They do like to make their presence known."

"I can only imagine why it was given the name." Annika laughed at that. Had she just shared a joke with the pirate captain? No matter how small of a joke it was, she had felt comfortable enough with him to laugh.

"Are you able to continue on? You didn't hurt yourself?"

She shook her unnerving thoughts away and smiled. "No, I am quite well and ready to continue."

They had already fallen behind the others by now. They continued walking, enjoying a comfortable silence between them.

Other animals started showing their curiosity. Captain Wolf, to Annika's surprise, began pointing them out and naming them for her.

"There, on that branch about ten feet up, is a parrot." It was a beautiful bird with bright and colorful feathers. Annika thought it to be one of the most beautiful birds she had ever seen.

He next pointed out a strange creature that lived in a shell. It was about the size of a coconut and there were long heavily armored legs sticking out. He called it a coconut crab.

As they walked deeper into the island, Annika kept her eyes open for more. The hairs on the back of her neck pricked up; she felt the gaze of someone or something. What was it this time? Maybe another monkey had come to yell at her.

Hidden in the darkness, Annika caught sight of a dark figure. It stayed hidden for the most part in the shadows of the trees. All she could make out was a dark form and glowing yellow eyes. If her eyes hadn't been roving the jungle, looking intently for other signs of wildlife, she wouldn't have caught it.

Suddenly, it stepped out of the shadows and she was able to see it clearly. Seeing this particular animal sent shivers up her spine. It was large and looked to be some sort of cat. It was orange with black stripes and a long tail. It licked its lips as it watched her, drawing her attention to the two large fangs that extended from its top jaw. Each fang had to be at least six inches long and looked as sharp as a dagger. The sun gleamed off the sharp weapons. Then, as quickly as it had appeared, it shrank back and disappeared into the trees.

"What is orange and has black stripes?" she asked nervously.

Captain Wolf held a branch out of her way as she passed by. "Is this a guessing game now?" He chuckled and continued to lead her in the direction of the others.

"Well, it looks like some sort of cat. Does that help?" He stopped suddenly, causing Annika to almost bump into his back.

"Why do you ask?"

"There was one over there, watching us." She pointed in the direction.

His eyebrows drew together in worry as he looked all around them. Upon seeing nothing, he prodded her forward gently with his hand on her back.

"If it's what I think it is, then it's not something you want to meet. Let's catch up with the others." The others had just now disappeared into the brush ahead.

"Well, what is it? Why does it have you so spooked?" Annika managed to squeak the question out as they hurried along, though she felt like she already knew the answer. Any beast with fangs like that were best avoided in her book. They managed to catch up with the others, and Captain Wolf gripped the man's shoulder at the back of the group.

"Pass the message along that a tiger has been spotted." The sailor's eyes widened and he nodded.

"A tiger? Please tell me that it's a peaceful vegetarian that loves to be cuddled?" Annika knew from the look he held that it was far from the case.

"If you cuddle a tiger creature, you will never be heard from again. It's a ferocious hunter of the jungle, usually at the top of the food chain. A tiger is known for its strength and agility. Its razor-sharp claws and fangs have been known to kill a man instantly. One of my crew was mauled by a tiger before we could save him."

Annika drew in a sharp breath. "How horrible! That poor man." She looked down for a moment.

"It picked him off because he was at the back of our group." The amount of danger they had been in suddenly struck Annika. Thank Elohim they had not had a closer encounter with the beast.

"They sure have abnormally large fangs."

"What do you mean?" He glanced behind them, scanning the jungle.

"The two fangs in front reached past its jaws. I sure wouldn't want to be anywhere near that thing's mouth." She shivered.

"Are you sure?" he asked. Annika turned around and saw confusion in his eyes. "How long do you think they were?"

"I don't know. Maybe this long?" Annika spread her hands apart about six inches.

"That's very strange. I have only heard of a creature like that in stories."

"You mean an Ancient?" Annika's jaw dropped open. The term was one only used in stories told to young children. Normally the animals in the stories were ferocious and man eaters. They called those Ancients. Everyone knew they were not real, just scary monsters in stories. "How is that possible?"

"It's impossible, of course. I have never heard of any other animal like what you described, though. How big was it?"

Annika shrugged. "I didn't get a good look at it, so I can't be sure. From the looks of it, its shoulders would have been about here." She placed a level hand at her shoulders. The captain's eyes grew wide.

"That is far bigger than any tiger I have heard of. Now I'm even more curious. No offense, Annika, but I hope you are just not good at measurements." He hastened his steps and grabbed her hand. "To be on the safe side, let's stick with the others."

CHAPTER SEVEN

The next three hours were a grueling trek through the dense jungle. Ethan found it difficult, so he couldn't even imagine how Annika felt. They hiked through the jungle and saw no signs of the island being inhabited, by any human at least. There was an abundance of animals who made their home in this paradise. Animals of all sorts showed up to watch the band of travelers as they trekked through the jungle.

Some were easily recognizable, even to Annika. Others even Ethan struggled to discern. Some animals stared at the group of sailors with curious wide eyes. Others looked annoyed and did their best to ignore them. A few of the more unusual ones bared their teeth and hissed before running deeper into the jungle.

Sadly, they were not able to shoot anything they could have for supper. A few sailors tried but were unsuccessful. After a few miserable attempts the animals disappeared.

Eventually, after walking for so long and seeing no signs of people, they turned around and started back for the beach. They decided to take a slightly different route back hoping to find something, anything, or anyone that could help.

Ethan pulled his hat from his head and wiped his sweaty brow. He wouldn't be wearing the hat if not for its protection from the sun's beating rays. His clothes had long since become drenched in sweat. It had to be one of the hottest days of the summer, and everyone was feeling it.

The crew walked much slower now, their footsteps dragging the farther they walked. Their clothes looked no better than Ethan's and their faces showed defeat. Ethan refused to let a look of anything other than determination and leadership onto his face.

He had left Annika's side by now and had taken his place near the front, leaving her in the care of her friend. He glanced back and noticed she was feeling the heat as well. Her thick brown hair was tied up on her head and sweat still poured from her brow. Every inch of her skin was plastered in it. With all the layers a lady had to wear, she had to be more miserable than him. She didn't show it, however. She marched ahead with her lips taut and determination etched on her brow, though her dazzling green eyes showed the depth of her weariness as did her weakened step.

He couldn't believe he had let her come. At the time, he had really wanted to say no but had thought if she wanted to make a fool of herself, then he should just let her do it. Surely within hours she would be begging to return to the ship. After that she wouldn't be so quick to complain about his orders. He had to admit, though, she was doing much better than he had thought she would. She seemed to be handling the heat and walking better than some of his crew.

Ethan's thoughts went once again to the strange animal Annika had described. Surely, she had been mistaken. It was impossible for it to be an Ancient. If it was, then that meant that some of the stories could be true. How many of the other stories and myths were also real and memories of their existence had simply shrunk into myths? To find one here would be like one of those stories coming to life. One of the horrifying nightmare stories you would tell around a campfire.

Just behind Annika walked a sailor from Captain Grey's crew. Ethan had seen them standing close to one another on the beach. He had thought they might be interested in each other until he had caught a glimpse of Annika's fearful face. She had never been afraid of Ethan, a supposed fearsome pirate, but had been shook up by that sailor.

It was obvious that the sailor was interested in her, though, his feelings and efforts easily discerned. Captain Grey had taken on some rather unusual sailors. Ethan certainly would not have hired half the men he had.

"Might I offer a bit of protection from the sun?" He held his hat out to her. Although not ideal, as it had already been on his sweat-drenched head, she accepted it.

"At a time such as this, I would be happy to wear a pirate's sweaty hat." She tried to give a weary smile. All that appeared was a faint quirk of her lips.

"You, madam, have stooped to a new low." His comment elicited a genuine, albeit weak, laugh. Her eyes took on their sparkle again as she glanced at his eyes. Ethan was careful not to look at her eyes too long; instead, he looked at the hat upon her head. It was a strange sight, seeing his wide black hat on her much smaller head. It hung lower on her brow than it did on his. He had to admit, with the sword at her side, it looked good on her. He still didn't know why she would carry a sword at the ready. Could she even use it enough to defend herself or was it all for show? Most women he had encountered would frown upon seeing such a weapon, let alone to carry one. She was very much still a mystery to him.

A small wave of excitement ran through the men, and Ethan turned forward to see what had caused it. They had just broken through into a clearing, which in itself was cause for joy. What lay in the clearing, however, was cause for celebration. A small group of huts sat at the end of the clearing, no more than a mile away. That meant there were people living on this island. The sight of it brought a new purpose to everyone's footsteps. A new thrill ran through the men at the thought of seeing people and hopefully getting help.

The distance between them and the huts quickly closed. Upon reaching the group of huts, everyone quickly lost their enthusiasm. The dwellings, that had sparked their hope, looked to be falling apart. What once must have been crude dwellings looked like they would fall over with a heavy gust of wind. Some of the mud and straw huts had gaping holes in them. All of them had weeds all around them about waist high. Even vining weeds were now closing off some of the doorways and snaking onto the roofs. There wasn't much hope for them finding anyone still living here.

Ethan stood in front of the weary men and plastered on a look of confidence he didn't really have. They looked at him expectantly.

"Today has been a long day for all of us. The sun will be setting soon, and I suggest we stop here for the night. Let's take a look around these huts, in case there are still people living here. If they are no longer occupied, we can see if there's anything we can use here. Perhaps any supplies that have been left behind. In the very least, hopefully some drinking water."

The men dispersed among the huts and began looking around. There were thirty huts, from what Ethan could see, most of them looking uninhabitable now. Ethan turned to Smith, who was standing near him, a map open in his hands.

"Can you tell where we are?"

"I've marked our trek into the jungle. This is what I have so far." The older man gestured to his map.

Ethan was disappointed to see a very empty map devoid of all details.

"I only have been able to mark what we have seen," Smith continued, as if sensing Ethan's thoughts. "I don't even know the shape of the island. I would love to get to high ground and see if I can get a good look at what's around us." Despite the long trek, he didn't look tired. His love for mapmaking and the possibility of something new kept him from being weary.

"So, we aren't far from the beach then," Ethan remarked as he studied the map.

"Aye, you're correct there, Cap. Only a few minutes' walk, actually. If we had entered the jungle just a bit to the left, we would not have had to walk all through the jungle." Smith paused and looked off into the distance. "I'd like to request to journey on to that large rock structure just about half a mile away." Smith pointed in the direction. "I could get a much better idea of what this island looks like from there."

Ethan thought about it for a moment. It would be a good idea to get a layout of the island; maybe there were still people. These huts had to come from somewhere. Perhaps they had just moved their camp somewhere else.

"Very well. See if you can get a group of five men to accompany you. There are predators in the jungle, and I think its best if we travel in groups."

"Aye, Cap!" Smith spun away, in search of some willing victims that he could persuade to go with him. Ethan smiled as the man walked away, mumbling to himself about who would be willing to go. He had never seen Smith this excited about anything in the years he had known him.

"Cap." Jack came alongside him, breaking his thoughts. "I've done some checking, and it looks like fifteen of the cabins are in good enough condition to stay in."

"Good, at least we have found a place we can stay the night."

"Excuse me." A thin sailor came up alongside of Ethan. "I was a doctor aboard the *Sailor's Journey*. I have discovered some plants that would prove beneficial to the wounded still aboard your ship."

"What's your name, sailor?"

"My name is Doniphan Hall, sir." The skinny man gave a small bow. He didn't appear to be your average sailor. His lack of muscle and pale complexion seemed to suggest he stayed indoors a lot. Which is a difficult feat aboard a ship.

"I'm surprised. We have only been here a few moments, and you have already found medicinal herbs?"

"Yes, sir. This place seems rich with them. I found a good assortment of plants already, and that's just in the immediate vicinity. I have long studied plants and their healing abilities for the body. I take some sailing with me wherever I go. Unfortunately, many of my supplies are now at the bottom of the sea. On the trek so far, I've actually found some rare plants, some could cut healing time in half for the men. I believe it would be beneficial for the injured men to be brought here, where we could treat them easier."

Ethan rubbed his chin. "If you believe it to be necessary, then please go and tell the doctor of my ship, Saul, of your findings. You two may discuss it together." Ethan turned to Jack, who still stood nearby. "I think it would be wise for you and Doniphan to head back to the ship in the morning. Bring back the injured and we will set up base here. We won't be sailing for a while, so we may as well get comfortable."

"Yes, Cap." Jack gave a mock salute and grinned. Ever making light of a situation, even when it was dire. It did help keep the morale of the men up.

Ethan decided to inspect the closest hut to him. It looked like all the others, close to becoming a pile of mud and straw again. This hut was in better shape than many of the others, but the weeds were taking over. A vining plant grew up the side, having made its way over the roof, and hung right through the entrance. He pushed the flowering vine out of the way and glanced about inside.

It was a decent- sized room. Two straw beds were on the floor and a fire pit in the middle. The roof above the fireplace was cut out as a way for the smoke to escape. Ethan stepped further into the room; it would have been quite dark if not for the hole in the roof. He noticed there was a board hanging down that looked to be used to cover the hole when bad weather struck.

He stepped over to the bed on his left. It was flat and looked to be moldy from rainfall from the open roof. It wouldn't be something they would sleep on. Something white hung on the wall, grabbing his attention. Ethan reached forward and picked up the object. He was surprised to find that it was a tooth. It was not quite as large as Annika had described but it was close. If not from the animal she had described, he could not place the original owner of this particular tooth. Someone had drilled a hole onto one end of it and had a string pulled through the hole. At one point someone had worn this tooth around their neck.

He fingered the object and then placed it in his pocket. He would be on the lookout for the original owner of the tooth. The sheer size was enough to cause him pause, let alone how it was shaped to kill.

Ethan took one last look around the room before exiting, convinced that these would make a fine temporary dwelling for them. Many of the huts seemed to be weathered, but it would not take much work to make them habitable for a short time. Far better than what they could have made with their limited resources.

He stepped out of the dark room and into the fading rays of the evening. A small cry made his head swivel in the direction of the source. Annika came running out of a hut swatting at her arms and stomping her feet. She ran her hands over her head and her arms again as if searching for something, then she caught sight of him. She stopped moving and gave him a crooked smile.

"Are you all right?" Ethan stepped closer to her.

"Oh, I'm just fine," she said with false enthusiasm. She looked up and down her arms and dress. "Just looking for something."

A rather large spider crawled over her shoulder, peeking its head up at Ethan. He could tell from the markings that it wasn't poisonous.

"Could you possibly be looking"—he reached towards her shoulder, making her stiffen—"for this guy?"

He gently picked up the spider and held it in the palm of his hand. The creature nestled there calmly.

"How can you hold it like that? That's the largest and most disgusting spider I have ever seen." She stared wide-eyed at Ethan. "It was crawling all over me." She visibly shivered in disgust.

Ethan chuckled as he started to lower the creature to the ground.

"No, sir! You will not leave it here to come and attack me again. You go take it far away from here. Or better yet, squash it." She crossed her arms.

"I won't kill it, but I will move it out of the camp." He chuckled again and shook his head as he turned to leave.

When he was a few steps away from her, he whispered jokingly to the creature in his hands, "Women."

After releasing the spider at a safe distance, Ethan returned to camp and made a mental list of things to do. The first step was to find fresh drinking water. If they couldn't find fresh water, then at least they could hopefully find some water they could boil. There was a well in the village, but it was bone dry, causing them to search elsewhere. Right next to the village was a marsh land. It had a lot of water, muddy foul-smelling water. Still, it was water. They had brought some from the ship back with them but were quickly running out. Several men found some buckets and headed out for the marsh.

Ethan caught sight of Annika; she was looking far more composed as she stood near her friend. He was once again surprised with how well she was handling the journey. Most women would have scoffed about the notion of sleeping on the ground in a mud hut. Most of them wouldn't even have made it through the mosquitoes. She had surprised him at every turn. The one thing to break her composure had been a spider. He bit back a chuckle just thinking about it.

Ethan picked up a bucket and found two sticks laying next to it. He took those with him and tossed them towards Annika who surprising had pretty good reflexes and caught them. She looked quizzically at him.

"Since you insist you know what you were doing, why don't you get the fire started?"

"With just two sticks? Surely you have a better fire starter than that?" Her mouth twisted into a frown. She held the sticks out in front of her, studying them. Probably wondering how she could produce fire from them.

"If you think you are strong enough to stay out here, then we are going to need to you pull your weight. Starting a small fire should be no problem." He grinned and began to turn away. "We are going to need it to boil some water." He turned and joined the others as they headed for the marsh, leaving a glaring Annika behind.

He couldn't help but laugh as he walked away. Hopefully, he was far enough that she couldn't hear him. Sometimes, he found himself purposefully riling her. He didn't do it out of spite or to see her struggle. She was just so much fun to tease. So, in a way it was her fault, he reasoned.

The swamp land near the huts was very eerie during the daytime. He didn't want to imagine it at night. A low fog engulfed the whole area, making it darker. The only sounds he could hear were crickets and the occasional ribbit from a frog.

Three men had brought a bucket and were bending down to get them filled. Ethan joined them and lowered his bucket into the water. Muddy water slowly sloshed into the bucket. It looked horrible and smelled even worse. Small sticks and other debris were mixed in with the water. His stomach churned at the thought of needing to drink it. They had brought some water with the from the ship, but it wouldn't last them more than a day. Better to have another option just in case. Ethan vowed to look himself for more water as soon as he could, preferably some from a more reliable source.

Upon standing up, Ethan took another look around him at the swamp. The water was still but the harder he stared at it, somehow, it appeared to be alive. The trees that hung over the water added to the eerie feel of the place. Once the men were done gathering water, they turned to leave. A strange hiss came from behind them. Ethan looked back but saw nothing unusual. Though he did see a rather large bat taking wing and disappearing into the swamp. Yes, it would be best to find water somewhere else if possible—and soon.

CHAPTER EIGHT

When the men returned to camp, Annika had a blazing fire waiting for them. Her smiled broadened when she saw Captain Wolf catch sight of the roaring flames. His jaw dropped slightly and disbelief showed on his rugged face. He reined in his disbelief and tried to act nonchalant.

"Well, this is a surprise." He strode up alongside her and placed his bucket on the ground.

"Is it? Did you not ask me to get a fire going?" Annika picked at some dirt beneath her nail, doing her best to appear nonchalant.

"How did you start it? Did you use the sticks?" He sat down on the log she was occupying.

"I had a better way to get it started." She smiled at the curiosity that showed on his face. She sighed dramatically. "Oh, I could tell you about a rare mushroom I found on the bark of an aged tree in the jungle. I could then tell you about how I was able to use it to get a spark going and turn it into the blaze you see before you." Ethan's eyes showed disbelief and perhaps even a little shock. Annika laughed at him. "However, that would be lying, I'm afraid. I have a far less intriguing explanation. Doniphan lent me his flint and steel."

The captain sat in silence for a moment and then suddenly threw his head back and laughed. It was a deep and hearty laugh. The first real laugh she could remember him having. Several men around him started laughing as well.

"You have quite the imagination, my lady. Although you had outside help." He pointedly looked at Doniphan, who averted his eyes sheepishly. "I am grateful to you for starting it all the same." They shared a smile. His black eyes twinkled in the firelight just inches from her own. She was struck once again with how handsome he was and how enjoyable she sometimes found his company. *Only sometimes,* she reminded herself and pulled her gaze from his. He was still a pirate after all.

"You must show me this mushroom, though." His teasing voice brought her gaze back again.

Annika laughed anew. "Perhaps someday, Captain. Someday."

The men unloaded the water they had collected and poured it into the pot that was already placed on the fire. They soon had water boiling. At least they would have more water to drink. Although, upon smelling it, Annika wondered if dehydration would be a preferable option.

Captain Wolf had left her by now and sat on the other side of the fire. He had his pistol out and was cleaning it. The fire light gleamed off the smooth metal. His face was calm, almost reverent as he cleaned the weapon. Annika had never been taught how to use a gun, so the weapon was foreign to her. His eyes drifted up and found hers. He smiled and her ears grew warm. What a bad habit she had been developing, her gaze always falling upon him. She dropped her eyes and stared into the fire again.

Stew came around the fire and started passing around food to them. He had packed along some hard tack from the ship, and he also passed around some unusual looking fruit.

"I found these just over yonder. It has a sweet taste, and it fills yer belly too. There's plenty more where they came from."

"What are they?" Annika turned one over curiously. Its skin was a mixture of red and yellow.

"They are called mandaws." Stew took a juicy bite out of his. "Ah, that hits the spot."

Annika took a small bite and was hit by a delicious and foreign flavor. As she chewed, she noticed Carter was having a similar reaction, pleasure written on his face.

"They are delicious!" Annika exclaimed.

"Miss Harper, you've never had one before? They are quite a common fruit at many marketplaces," Doniphan quietly asked the question.

Memories of her days spent behind the confining walls in the orphanage sprang to her mind. "Well, I didn't frequent many markets back home. I have never seen, let alone tried, this before." Annika brushed off his question, and although her answer had been true, she had not wanted to explain the real reason.

The light was quickly fading, leaving a beautiful streak of orange to stretch across the sky. The towering cliff walls in the distance began to grow shadows upon them.

Several men, whom Annika had noticed leaving camp earlier, returned and found Captain Wolf. Simon had gone with them, giving her a few hours of relief from his gaze. The captain and one of the men conversed over a map before eating the meal that had been passed around. What could they have been doing? Annika decided to ask if she had the chance.

Simon's ever-alert eyes found her atop her log and smiled when he saw the space next to her was unoccupied. He was making his way towards her when Carter sank down into the seat. Simon looked angry at first, then he put on one of his charming smiles again and took a different seat.

"Thank you, Carter," Annika whispered under her breath.

"Anytime." Carter smiled then his face grew serious. "I don't like the way he looks at you."

She sighed. "Believe me, I don't either." The men around the fire began conversing, the air filled with laughter and conversation. "Unfortunately, I'm afraid we will have more encounters with him. I do not think I can avoid it altogether."

"Unfortunately, I know you are right. Please, don't hesitate to call for me. I'm here if you need me. You just say the word and I will be by your side." Annika looked lovingly into the young man's face.

"Thank you, Carter." He was the closest thing to family she had besides her brother. Even still, she was closer to him than her own brother because of the time they had been apart.

The darkness engulfed them and left them with a chill, even with the fire. With the night came sounds she had never heard before. Off in the distance a roar was heard along with the quick squeal of an animal. Annika's gaze shot to Captain Wolf. His eyes found hers and he nodded. The tiger-like animal she had caught a glimpse of before had found a kill. Annika shivered. Knowing predators were out there was bad enough but not knowing how close was disconcerting.

The thought of it being an Ancient felt like an impossibility. She had often heard stories from her parents when she was younger. Her father had spoken of Ancient creatures who were bloodthirsty beings, intent on hunting you down. They were stories that, when you went to bed, the only comfort you had was knowing they did not exist. Perhaps she had been mistaken and had just imagined the large teeth on the cat. The gleam on the edge of its razor-sharp teeth entered her mind's eye again, dispelling that theory.

They had started a fire outside but would soon be retiring to a hut. Two of the huts had been cleared out by the pirate who went by the name of Jack. He was one of the kindest of any of the sailors she had met, even though he was a pirate. Annika found it hard to let her guard down around men who were known criminals, let alone had robbed them.

"We had better turn in for the night." The captain slapped the hat he had retrieved from her earlier against his leg. "Who knows what tomorrow may bring. You all go get some sleep. I will keep watch out here. Jack, would you start fires in the two huts?"

"On it, Cap." He gestured to one of the nearby crew mates. "Hey, Chris, come give me a hand, would ya?" Jack left, accompanied by the man called Chris.

"I will keep the fires going while I keep watch. We will all take turns." He assigned the duty to several other young men, leaving Annika and Carter out from any of the night-watch. She could tell Carter felt left out, but she couldn't help but feel relieved. She would sleep better knowing he wasn't the first line of defense should something happen. Not that she did not trust his abilities; she just wanted to keep him protected. Annika was starting to understand exactly why Captain Wolf had wanted to leave her aboard the ship. Not that she would tell him that.

The night had a spooky feel about it, making the crew a little anxious. Perhaps it was just being in a strange and unknown place. With the little knowledge they had of the island, it caused an eerie feeling after the sun set. The shadows on the cliff face were even more eerie now. Almost as if they were alive and watched them. Soon the fires were started in the huts and were blazing strong, beckoning the crew to spread out.

"Miss?" Jack came alongside her.

Annika tore her gaze from the shadows about her and looked to the young man. "Yes?"

"I know you will be sleeping next to the men, which isn't ideal, but I set something up for you, just for tonight. If you'd like me to show you?" He smiled, and she allowed him to lead her and Carter to a hut. Inside was a blanket hanging down from the roof, giving her have as much privacy as possible.

"I know it's not much, but at least it gives you some privacy. Tomorrow, we will get another hut cleaned out for you."

"Are they really that bad?"

"Well, these huts have years of mold and damage to them. It takes a while to clean them out enough for us to be able to sleep safely in them. Not to mention all of the unwanted visitors. Spiders and scorpions or such."

Annika shivered. "This will be just fine for tonight. Thank you so much for thinking of me." She smiled at the man who couldn't be any older than her.

"I was happy to do it, miss. It wasn't my idea, though. Cap asked me to do it." Surprise must have shown on her face for he continued, "I know you don't trust him, and I can't blame you for that. I'm sure you won't believe me, but Cap is a good man. Give him the opportunity to show you." With that, he left her at the hut entrance.

Several men lay scattered over the floor already trying to get a bit of sleep. Carter chose a spot on the floor at the edge of the curtain. Far enough to give her privacy but close enough to help ensure her safety.

Annika looked back at the fire and noticed Captain Wolf alone, looking at the map he had held earlier. She walked towards him.

"Will you be up long?" she gently asked him as she sat down.

"Why? Will you miss me?" he teased and looked up. She gave him an annoyed eye roll. "Sorry, couldn't help myself. No, I will be up for a few hours, then Chris will replace me."

She gestured to the object he had been engrossed with all evening. "Doing some late-night reading?" He looked at the paper folded in his hands.

"It's as accurate of a map as we can get of this island. Everywhere we walked this morning and what Smith saw on the boulders." Captain Wolf pointed in the general direction of the rocks now shrouded in darkness. Smith must have been the man whom she had seen talking with him earlier.

"Brave man to climb those." She had seen it earlier in the light and it had been a formidable sight.

"Foolhardy is more like it." He smiled as he said it. "What he brought though is quite helpful. Would you like to see?"

"Please." She scooted closer to him on the log they sat on.

"This here is the beach we arrived on. We walked through the jungle here." He trailed his finger along the path they had taken. "This is where you saw the...strange animal. We then continued on until here then turned and went back." He looped his finger around and turned back towards the beach slightly to the left of their original route. "This is where we are now," There was a small area marked out with tiny miniature huts.

"What's this area?" Annika pointed to a spot that had lots of water drawn into it.

"That is the swamp. Smith said that it goes on for miles."

"And what is this?"

"That is the volcano. Smith reported it was the largest he had seen. Thankfully, it does not appear to be active."

"Well, that's a relief." Annika sighed. "It's not a lot of information but this map is quite beautiful. The markings are quite detailed." She stroked her fingers over the thin piece of leather.

"That's Smith for you, he is very detailed oriented. I want him to draw a secondary map, as it wouldn't hurt to have a spare." He sighed. "Smith can only draw what he sees. He doesn't know how large the island is or what's on the other side of the mountain."

"I will have to commend the man on his mapmaking skills."

He groaned. "Please don't. He has a big enough head already." Captain Wolf chuckled, his breath tickling her ear. Annika suddenly realized she had drawn quite close to him while she had been looking at the map.

She pulled away suddenly and retreated to a safe distance on the log. "I appreciate you showing me." For some reason she felt flustered. Not in the same way Simon made her feel. Something incredibly different that she could not put her finger on. She didn't trust this captain, of course. Something inside her felt comfortable in his presence, though. Even when he teased, she found herself enjoying it. Not a good combination of feelings to have around a pirate. She physically shook her head, hoping those feelings would disperse with the action. Still, they refused to leave.

"Well, it is getting late. I believe I will take my leave." She turned to leave but stopped after a couple of steps. "I hear I have you to thank for the privacy curtain. That was a surprisingly kind gesture. Thank you." She smiled and met his gaze.

A warm smile greeted her. "My pleasure, Annika."

With that she hurried to the hut she would be sharing with some of the crew. Annika was unsure of what the future would hold or even what the morning would bring. Despite her better judgment, something in her wanted to trust the mysterious captain.

The morning came too quickly for Annika. Her night had been spent swatting away mosquitoes and constantly feeling like something was crawling on her. Finally, she had drifted into a restless sleep.

With a small groan, she rolled over and struggled to her feet. The need to relieve herself far more urgent than to lay in the insect-infested hut. She stumbled to her feet and checked to make sure everything was in order with her dress. She had slept with all her clothes on, in contrast to when she would usually wear a thin night dress. As she had feared, her dress looked like how her night had felt. Her blue skirt had dirt stains all over and her white top looked more like a light brown. Everything she wore was crumpled and wrinkled. Hopefully, soon she could change.

She took a new top out and opted to use the same skirt since she had only brought three with her. Annika pulled open the curtain and peered around it. The sun was just starting to cast its warming rays outside, not yet awakening the crew. Carter lay closest to the curtain, her brave knight, ready to defend her honor if the need arose.

She was surprised to see Captain Wolf was the closest to the curtain on the other side of the circle of men. She was sure that spot had been taken by another sailor. Chris—yes, that was his name—he had been there before. If she was not mistaken, he had taken over some of the night watch, so perhaps the two had just switched places.

With careful steps she tiptoed out of the hut and made it safely into the sunshine. The early morning rays gently warmed her chilled skin. Jack was sitting close by and noticed her arrival.

"I need bit of privacy." She gestured to the nearby bushes. He instantly understood her meaning.

"I can escort you to the nearest bush if that would be of help. I will still be close enough to watch the huts." He gave her a tired smile. Who knew how long he had been up.

"That would be wonderful. Thank you." They walked to the bush she had been using as her spot to hide from the crew to relieve herself. "How did everything go last night? I would assume all went well since we did not hear anything?"

"You would be correct. I haven't spoken with Cap, but Chris said all went well. I only just now started my turn. Chris was up before me, but Cap took the brunt of the night watch. I knew I couldn't trust him to wake Chris up earlier." Jack shook his head in feigned annoyance. His care for his captain was evident. In fact, all of his crew seemed to follow him without a second thought. No one doubted him; they trusted him absolutely, even with their lives.

They approached the thick bushes, and Annika pushed her way through. They created a nice wall around her, enough to make her feel protected from outside eyes. "You seem to all think highly of your captain." She continued their conversation from behind the bush after relieving herself. She had already unfastened her blouse and was attempting to put the new one on.

"Aye, that we do. He's saved our backs dozens of times. He treats us all like family."

"I must say, I find it strange that a pirate captain would be able to invoke such feelings from his crew. Most pirates I have heard of are horrible to their crew and are only out to make easy money for themselves." Annika fastened the last button on her blouse and smoothed her skirt. She reached down and checked her stocking. Her dagger was still secularly held within.

Next, she checked her braid. It was horribly tangled and barely even a braid. She attempted to brush her fingers through her hair and braid it again.

"That's definitely not our captain." Jack chuckled. "Cap and I go way back. He's like a big brother to me. Jonah and Cap both are."

These men had a strange dynamic about them. The feeling she got from Captain Samuel's men was mere obedience because they were being paid. Not many of his men would follow him blindly out of honor and respect. Captain Wolf's men however, seemed to all be good friends. Always there to help and very loyal to him. How could men like this be pirates?

Annika stepped out from behind the bush and rejoined the man as they walked back to the huts. She draped her dusty blouse over her arm.

She glanced at the sailor on her right; his bright ginger hair shone in the early morning rays. In this sunlight his head looked like it was ablaze. A kind smile shone back at her. She liked this sailor; he spoke his mind, but he was pleasant to talk with. He was kind to her and Carter as well, nothing like she would have imagined a pirate. Neither was his captain, for that matter. The ones who scared her most were from her own ship.

Once they returned to camp, there was more movement among the men. Carter was just now coming out of the hut with several other men stretching their cramped arms and legs as they went. Stew was out of the huts already, as was Doniphan; they both sat at the main fire with a handful of other men.

Captain Wolf sat by the fire as well, stoking it with a large stick. His clothes were rumpled, but he looked fresh and alert. If he felt fatigued by his long night watch, he didn't show it. Jack left her side and walked up to him. He slapped him on the back.

"That's the last time I trust you to dish out the night watch fairly." He gave a teasing smile.

"You all just looked so peaceful, sleeping like wee babies. How could I wake you?" Captain Wolf teased him back. The two men didn't have the typical captain and sailor relationship. Their banter was amusing. Annika stifled a chuckle. Nothing about these pirates was typical.

"How did you fare through the night, Annika?" Captain Wolf turned his attention towards her. Her first name came easily from his lips now, shocking her slightly. She had forgotten that she stood so close to them, staring.

"It was not an easy night, I must say, but I survived." A sheepish grin slipped onto her face. "You should have seen me before I freshened up."

"I'm pretty sure the ground here is more rock than dirt." He chuckled. "Seems as though we will be here for a while. We should try to find some type of bedding."

"Perhaps we could make hammocks!" Carter had come up behind Annika and chimed in. His blond hair was a mess and his clothes were wrinkled. His eyes were wide and excited though, no trace of sleep left in them.

"Out of what?" Jack tapped his chin thoughtfully. "We can use the blankets that we brought with us! There were crates of them on *Sailor's Journey*. They are going to bring some men and more supplies from the ship today so they can replace the blankets we use." Excitement shone in his eyes.

"Great! I made a hammock back home. I could be of some help." Carter and Jack walked away, talking excitedly about their new plan. Although Jack was a few years older, it was good to see Carter making a new friend. If only they could bond over something that didn't include stolen goods.

"Is what Jack said true? Will we be having company soon?" She directed her attention to Captain Wolf, who had not taken his eyes off of her yet.

"Oh yes, it is true. Doniphan believes he has found some plants to help with healing the wounded. He wants to bring the men here to the huts to treat them."

"I believe that's a grand idea. Fresh air will help with that too. Will they be leaving soon?"

"After breakfast, four men will return to the beach and row to the boat." Captain Wolf stoked the fire again.

Sure enough, after they had a meager breakfast of crackers and fruit, four men set off for the beach. They would be gone for at least half the day. In the meantime, everyone set about making the huts more livable. True to his word, Captain Wolf himself cleaned a hut for Annika. He made sure to see to it that there were no creepy crawlies.

They made another hut their storehouse. They placed water and extra food, sealed in containers, in the hut. The main outside fire stayed stoked throughout the day, boiling water when necessary. Stew was able to find some wild herbs growing nearby. If they could get some meat soon, they would really have a good meal. Some men, including Stew, who were hungry for meat, decided to brave the swamp and go fishing.

Everyone else stayed at camp and got the place ready for all the new-comers they would soon be having. Jack and Carter were off making their hammocks and installing the ones they had finished.

Doniphan had left in the morning, in the company of three other sailors, for the beach. The rest of the men, those who were not fishing, lay around camp unsure of what to do. Simon seemed to be making friends very easily. He was quite close with many men in the group. Or perhaps they were old friends from Captain Samuel's ship; if they were she could not recognize them. Thankfully, he stayed out of her way all morning. It helped that she was out of sight for a good part of the day.

That left Captain Wolf. Annika hadn't seen him since he went off on his own into the jungle earlier. He carried a pistol with him, along with the sword he always had at his side.

Annika had been busying herself as best as she could. She would enter the huts and remove the debris that Jack had skipped over during his first round of cleaning. If this was a man's version of clean, she was afraid to see what it was like before. She cleared out sticks and leaves and even managed to remove years' worth of cobwebs. A large stick was her weapon of choice for this attack. The webs stuck to the end of it and well away from her hands. Her sword, hanging at her hip, was hindering her movement. She unstrapped the belt and leaned it against the wall, focusing on the next cobweb in the far corner. If they were stuck here for a while, she aimed to live in as much comfort as possible.

An all too familiar sensation overcame her, and it was time to visit her favorite bush again. A quick glance around the camp and she saw no one she knew well. Jack and Carter had been her companions to the bush lately, but they were nowhere to be seen. The urge was strong enough to push her towards the bush on her own. It was daylight and there were plenty of people nearby if she should need any assistance. Birds called out a cheery song from the trees on the outskirts of the field as a gentle breeze brushed her cheek.

Annika took her usual spot behind the bush and hurried as much as she could. For some reason her nerves were on high alert. She had just finished and had exited the bushes when she got the strange feeling that she was being watched. A quick cursory glance around proved futile. There was no one close to her; the only sounds were the men still around the fire a short distance away. Annika tried to shake the feeling, but it stayed. Her imagination was known to run wild.

Suddenly she realized why she was so alarmed. The bird call had changed drastically. Their cheery song had changed to one that made her feel tense. Their song came faster and made her feel like something was going to happen. She heard a rustling in the tall grass near, in the path that she needed to use to get back to camp. A branch cracked and the grass rustled. She had not imagined that.

Her eyes darted around as she held her breath in fear. Finally, her eyes settled on a familiar sight. Bright yellow eyes gleamed at her from in amongst the tall grass. Hungry eyes, the same ones that she had spotted on their trek the first day. The sunlight glinted on its dagger-like front teeth. Fear coursed anew through her veins, causing her hair to stand on end and her heart to race. A scream bubbled up in her throat, but her frozen muscles refused to let it out. Her eyes remained locked with the fierce predator in front of her. Her hand by instinct reached for her sword and was dismayed to find it missing. Of course, she had left it in the hut.

Suddenly the beast pounced at her. Annika's well-trained muscles broke from their fear and sprang into action. She just managed to jump out of the way of the agile beast. Annika started running as fast as she could; unfortunately, she was running away from camp. Her arms pumped and her legs took on a speed she had never known she had possessed. The pounding behind her told her the cat was fast at her heels. She knew that the beast would soon overtake her if she did nothing. Annika steeled her resolve and commanded her feet to move faster. She screamed, not so much out of fear but to hopefully draw the attention of someone nearby. The animal was so close now she could feel its breath.

Elohim, please, save me! Annika managed a quick and urgent prayer as her legs carried her further from camp. As she ran, she tried very hard not to think of the sharp teeth that were oh so close to her now, especially those sharp incisors.

Suddenly, a shot rang out of nowhere and the beast growled in anger and pain. Not wanting to lose her concentration and fall, Annika just kept running, her lungs about to burst. Suddenly a figure came out from the trees and ran towards her and the cat. The fearsome beast turned from her and decided to go for the other target. She slowed and saw Captain Wolf had come to her rescue once again. What could he do against such a beast? He tried to load his gun again. He was seconds away from being pounced upon when Annika remembered the small knife she kept on her ankle.

Annika withdrew the knife and ran after the charging beast. She was twenty feet behind the animal now and it was quickly approaching Captain Wolf. The animal lunged at Captain Wolf, and he went to shield his face. Annika threw the knife and hit the creature right in between the shoulders, causing the cat to overshoot its jump. It knocked the captain to the ground as it jumped clumsily into the air and skidded to a painful stop. There was now a bullet in the animal and a knife sticking out from between its shoulders. The wounded animal looked at them both, blood seeping from its wounds, then escaped into the jungle to find food that didn't fight back.

Annika breathed heavily and sighed in relief. Her aching muscles protested as she remembered the captain and ran towards him.

"Captain! Are you all right?" She knelt down at his side. He drew his eyebrows together and struggled to take a breath.

"I'm fine." He finally managed to say. "Just had the wind knocked out of me." His breathing was more normal now as he slowly sat up.

"How are you?" His words dripped with concern as his eyes examined her.

"I'm fine, thanks to you. If you hadn't been there to get its attention, I would probably have been mauled by that beast by now." The thought made her nauseous.

"When I saw it right behind you, I thought for sure you would be a goner." He shook his head in disbelief. "You can sure run for a woman—well for anyone actually. What did you throw at it?"

"My dagger."

"You had a dagger on you?" His eyes widened.

She laughed. "I always keep one tied to my ankle in case it's needed. Today, that paid off." She grinned at him.

"Remind me to never get on your bad side." He chuckled. "I owe you my life," he said more seriously. His eyes showed a pool of emotion that Annika couldn't even begin to decipher.

"You jumped in to save me from a rampaging Ancient tiger. It is I who owe you thanks."

"Well, I guess we are even then." His smiled warmed her insides.

"I guess you were right. That cat definitely had dagger-like teeth and was far too large to be a normal tiger." He brushed dirt and grass off his clothing. "I can't believe I'm saying this, but that has to be an Ancient."

"How is that even possible? Those stories weren't true, they couldn't be. Right?" She tried to give a shaky smile.

He sighed. "I always thought them just stories. Now, I can't be so sure."

Suddenly voices surrounded them on all sides. The crew had finally reached them.

"Is anyone hurt?" Jack worriedly asked.

"What happened?" asked Carter, as he came up behind Annika. "We heard you scream and saw the tiger." They all spoke at once, making it hard to understand them. So they all thought it to be just a tiger. How would she explain to them about it being a creature from legends?

"We are fine," Captain Wolf answered for her and chuckled at the crew. "Thankfully, I was close by to help. Where were the lot of you? Napping on the job, were you?" He sat, one leg propped up with his arm resting on it. He had retrieved his fallen hat and held it. His roguish grin was enough to make her breath quicken. One shouldn't have the right to be as handsome as he was.

"I was helping Carter set up the hammocks. We were close by but she had a head start. Did you see how fast they ran?" Jack moved his hand through the air in a straight line. Trying to use his hand to simulate how quick. "Lady Harper moved quicker than a bobcat with its tail on fire." A few men chuckled.

"Miss Harper, are you all right?" Simon's all too familiar voice drawled.

She stiffened and looked behind her. "Quite all right, thanks to Captain Wolf here." Simon's charming smile wavered for a moment then resumed.

"I am pleased to hear that." He helped her to her feet and stood close to her.

Annika stepped back towards Carter. "Oh no, I just realized I have lost my dagger, though." Tears threatened to surface at the loss.

"We can replace the one you lost from our armory of weapons."

No dagger would be able to replace the beauty of the one she had lost.

Captain Wolf stood to his feet, bringing him quite close to her. "I'm more curious as to why you keep one on you," he whispered in her ear. His breath causing shivers up her spine. The feeling of being close to him was quite the opposite from Simon. With Captain Wolf there was a mystery and a sense of protection. Which was strange, being he was a pirate.

"That is a story for a different day." She smiled and stepped away.

"Are you really ok, Annika?" Carter came up to her and gave her a fierce hug. She hugged him back. Right now, everything seemed surreal. The fact that she had just encountered such a fierce beast hadn't really sunk in yet.

"I'm fine." Annika gave him a quick squeeze. "I have to say, though, all that running really took a lot out of me. I would love a drink of water. Even if it is that despicable marsh water." She turned up her nose, not relishing the thought of drinking it.

"Let's go get you some." Carter smiled and held out his arm to her. She took it gratefully and allowed him to escort her. Most of the other crew joined them.

Annika stole another look at Captain Wolf. He was still standing and talking with Jack and Chris. His eyes found hers and he smiled. With each passing day, her feelings towards this man changed. She had started hating him and now she was confused by her emotions. One thing was for sure: she was relieved to have Captain Wolf around.

CHAPTER NINE

Later that afternoon, Doniphan returned with a large portion of the men from the ship. They found huts for everyone, and a couple huts that were specifically to house the wounded. They decided the wounded would have to sleep on the ground. It would be far too difficult to move them into a hammock. So, they spread leaves and blankets on the ground to cushion them.

Captain Grey arrived with them, and Ethan was happy to see Jonah had come as well. Ethan stepped forward to greet the captain and his old friend.

"Glad to see you both made it safely." He shook Captain Grey's hand. The man had an odd look on his face whenever he caught his eye. Ever since he paid him for the merchandise they had taken, plus some for the loss of his ship, he seemed to be confused. Ethan broke from his questioning eyes and gave Jonah a hug. The big man gave him a bear hug and hard pat on the back.

"Good to see you, Cap. Looks like you have all been partying here." His eyes danced with humor.

"Far from it, I'm afraid. Just this morning, Annika and I had a run in with a strange creature. Don't worry, we are both completely unharmed." He quelled the worry showing on their faces.

"Jonah, good to see you!" Jack came alongside him, grinning. "Did Cap tell you about this morning?"

"He was starting to before you rudely interrupted," Jonah chastised him, a grin betraying his harsh words.

"I'll continue the story for you, then." Jack, undeterred by the teasing, pushed forward. "Annika was ambushed by a tiger and took off running—which I will tell you now, that girl can run. Anyway, Cap shot the beast causing it to turn on him, undeterred by the bullet. Right as it was going to pounce on him, Annika threw a knife into its back and scared the beast away."

"What's more,"—Ethan leaned in closer—"I haven't told the other men yet, but it was unlike any tiger I have ever seen before. It was larger than any tiger I have ever seen, and it had the addition of two very—very—long teeth."

"How am I just hearing about this now?" Jack's voice was fringed in excitement.

"Curious. So, what do you think it could be?" Captain Grey tapped his bearded chin.

"I know this may sound crazy, but the only creature I've heard of that even resembles it is an Ancient." Their faces showed shock and disbelief. "I don't know how it could be, though. The story I heard was not exactly a very believable one."

"I've heard of stories about an animal like that!" Jack grinned from ear to ear. He was far too excited about this. "I remember a story about an Ancient cat that had teeth like daggers and a taste for human blood."

"Yes." Ethan inwardly shuddered. "That is what I have heard as well. It just makes me wonder...if an Ancient cat exists, how many of the other stories are true as well?"

They all stood in silence for a moment, looking thoughtful. Ethan could not get the image of the cat out of his mind. The gaping mouth full of teeth rampaging towards him would forever be etched in his mind.

"Until we know more, I suggest we keep an even closer watch out." Captain Grey frowned. "You said Annika outran the beast? That woman continues to surprise me." His tone had obvious admiration in it.

"Continues?" Ethan asked confused.

"Yes, before we met you all, Carter was challenged to a sword duel. He was unfairly tripped and would have been injured if Annika had not stepped forward. She blocked the blade and beat the attacker back. That's when we were fortunate enough to come upon you." A teasing look of his own passed the captain's face.

"Who would challenge a boy to a duel?" Jonah looked puzzled. Ethan was still stuck on the fact that Annika knew something about swordplay. Although it did make sense, seeing she always carried it with her. He had thought she probably knew some basic moves, but this new information made it sound like she had been trained at one point.

"A rather unsavory man I unfortunately hired on. Maddock is his name. He arrived with our group. There he is now." Captain Grey pointed to a man who was chatting with someone whom Ethan had come to recognize well. It was Simon, whom Annika always seemed to be wary of. It took just another moment for him to realize the identity of the other man. It was none other than the man that he and Annika had saved during the storm. He was a hulking man who looked like he hadn't seen the inside of a tub for many weeks. That wasn't the fact that struck him, though. Maddock and his companion were whispering intently, their eyes shifting from each other to Annika. She followed Doniphan around, awaiting his word on any care the wounded men may need.

Why were these men so interested in her? Losing a sword fight was definitely something that would bruise your pride, but Maddock seemed to look at her with hate. Simon, on the other hand, gazed at her with a look that made Ethan uncomfortable. He had seen Annika's reaction to being close to the man. Her obvious disdain for the man must not be noticeable to Simon, or maybe he didn't care.

Ethan kept his eyes on the men, studying them. "I suggest we keep a close eye on him. I don't like the way he and his companion look at her."

"I agree, Captain. I have only been in the big one's presence for a day, and I can already tell he is a difficult man. He never talks to authority without glaring." Jonah eyed the two men thoughtfully. "From my experience, sailors who don't respect authority are not to be trusted."

Captain Grey sighed. "He wasn't always that way. He showed up one day, and he played an excellent part. He was attentive and did his work well. He soon brought Simon on board and recommended him to me. I hired him on and gave Maddock a place of authority on the ship. Slowly he began to undermine me and became more unsavory. It's just this last trip that he has become unbearable."

"He got what he wanted and was able to show his true colors is what it sounds like to me." Jack crossed his arms. His cheerful face twisted into a scowl.

They all agreed. "Well, Captain Grey," Jack began, "would you and Jonah like to come with me? I can show you where you can stay. Carter and I have made accommodations for you both." Jack led the two men away from Ethan and into the huts to show them the hammocks he and Carter were still making.

The night before they had only used two huts for shelter, and tonight they would use ten. Jonah had only left ten men aboard ship, two of those being the ship's carpenters. That left the rest of them on land now and needing a place to rest their heads. Annika had her own private hut, save for Carter who would sleep behind a curtain. He refused to leave her side.

The remainder of the day passed by in a blurl soon it was already time for supper. Their group was now too big for the one fire, so they split up. The captains sat at the outside fire while the rest of the crew had the fires started in their respective huts. Stew passed out more hard tack and mandaws. He accompanied that with crackers.

"Sorry, Captains, I had hoped to have some fish to feed ya. This doesn't really show my skill," Stew grumbled as he found a spot on one of the logs around the fire. Ant had stayed on the ship to get food for the remaining men. So that left Stew to feed the large group on his own. If Ethan read the man correctly, however, he did not mind. He relished the work and always needed to keep his hands busy. All day he had been trying to catch fish, unfortunately to no avail.

Around the captains' fire sat Annika, and on her two sides sat Carter and Stew. They were directly opposite Ethan on the other side of the fire. Jack sat to his left followed by Jonah. To the right sat Captain Grey and Doniphan.

"Shame you weren't able to get a bite." Ethan's stomach agreed with him as he bit into the hard tack.

"Oh, we had plenty of bites, Captain, but each time we would pull it up, the line would break. Never seen that happen so often before. Plenty of bites but no fish to show for it." Stew rubbed his neck as he stared into the fire.

"Strange indeed." Captain Grey broke the silence. "I have to say I'm thankful for this food all the same. A bit of hard tack in the belly sits the same as a juicy fish." He bit into the hard dry lump. "It's just not as nice going down." He smiled, causing all around him to chuckle.

Ethan found himself frequently stealing glances across the fire to Annika. She laughed at something Carter told her and covered her beautiful smile with a hand. Her long brown hair remained braided down her back, but pieces had escaped and now framed her face. The fire seemed to dance in her dazzling green eyes. Those same eyes found their way to his and he looked away. When he dared to look up again, he thought he saw a faint smile on her lips as she looked away.

He wouldn't admit this to anyone, but he was growing to enjoy the young woman's company. She was unlike any woman he had ever met. She was fiery and strong-willed but had a passion to protect those she loved, even when the odds were against her.

Plus, she was just plain intriguing to him. She had many hidden talents, among those was her familiarity with weapons. Now he had a report telling him that she was indeed not a stranger to a sword. This woman gained more of his respect every day in everything she did.

Annika had a fire in her, but one look at her actions would show her gentle spirit. Ethan chided himself and placed the thoughts of Annika out of his head. He was a pirate, and she was a lady. Better to remember that now. Plus, he had a mission to complete, if they ever got off this island.

As tantalizing as her beauty was, and how kind a heart she possessed, he had to keep his focus. So for the remainder of the evening, he kept his eyes on everyone else but her. Well, mostly that is.

That night, there were many more men to split the night watch with. They could assign several men per night and have a fresh batch for the next night. Four men took turns that night and only had to do a few hours apiece. Ethan was given the night off, which he sorely needed. He had thought it a good idea the night before to stay awake longer than the others, let them get a good night's sleep. It had been fine until later in the day, after the whole incident with the Ancient cat had happened. Now, his aching muscles were screaming for rest. Although the ground was hard, Ethan was able to sleep soundly.

Ethan opened his eyes and suddenly realized he was in his old bed. His familiar room looked so much smaller than he remembered. He crawled out of his covers and looked around him. He could see all of his toys and games stacked in a corner.

The fresh smell of home was so distinct—pine, his father's favorite wood to carve. The strong smell instantly made him feel at home.

Ethan realized he was much smaller. His hands were small enough to tell him he had to be under ten years old. Suddenly his father entered the room, gently crossing the cobblestone floor. His all-too-familiar eyes were enough to cause Ethan to hitch his breath.

His father's strong arms lifted Ethan up and gave him a hug. Ethan's eyes watered as he grasped onto his father's arms. Tears fell from his eyes. Oh, how he had missed him. Suddenly his father pulled away and looked into Ethan's eyes. His voice was quiet, almost imperceptible. What was he saying? Whatever it was seemed important. The look in his eyes alone was enough for him to know his father was saying something he should be listening to. If only he could make out the words.

Ethan held his father's warm, loving hands. Suddenly a dark figure crept in behind his father. In one fatal blow, the figure struck him down. His father's smiling face turned to agony. Ethan could do nothing, his muscles frozen. The familiar face of his attacker coming into the light. The face started laughing an evil laugh; it reached clear down to Ethan's toes.

Why, Elohim? Why can't You save my father? Ethan started crying as the figure closed in on him, knife held high.

Ethan bolted upright, his arms held up in self-defense. A small cry escaped him. There he sat, on the hard ground in one of the huts, men all around him. He had his arm raised, knife in hand, ready to attack. Slowly, realization dawned on him. It had been another dream. Ethan lowered his hand, dropped the knife, and lowered his head into his shaking hands. Tears streamed down his face. Why must he continue to have nightmares?

The dreams often started out warm and wonderful, which made it so much harder to see the rest of it. Every time Ethan shut his eyes, he saw his father's pained face and the lifeless look in his eyes as his blood drained from his body.

He had not been a child when it had happened. Five years ago, Ethan had lost both his father and his brother. He had barely escaped with his life on that fateful day. Ethan's body shook all over, and he was drenched in sweat. He needed to get out of the hut and get some fresh air.

Carefully, hoping no one would see, he crept out of the hut. They had no doors to open. He had counted on that when he had laid down. From his spot on the floor, he had been able to see Annika's hut. Somehow it made him feel better if he was able to see the door. He would be more likely to be able to protect her that way.

Ethan snuck out of the hut and crept away from the night watchmen. The moon was still bright in the night sky overhead. It would not be long until morning, though.

Once he was a good distance away from camp, he sank to his knees. He was not an emotional person, and tears did not come easily to him. His heart so shut up and locked away from anything that could hurt.

When his nightmares came, it was a different story. That was the sure way to get through the fortress of walls around his heart. Tears came easy then, the raw pain exposed and hard to control. His father had meant everything to him and to have him taken away, especially in that manner, was hard. In one night, he had been robbed of his father and his only brother. He was no longer the same person inside. The main sources of his joy and love had been stripped away. Now he was plagued by the good and the bad memories from his father and brother. One night he would think of the times where they exchanged hurtful words with one another. Then the next he would remember the times when they laughed together. Each was painful in their own way. If only he could forget and never have to feel this pain.

Would his nights always be plagued like this? Many nightmares had been interrupting his sleep; he was almost used to it by now. The pain they brought would never lesson, however.

This dream was one he often had. One of several different scenarios. Many times, he had dreams of the actual incident that had occurred, digging deeper into the hole in his heart. Other times, like tonight, he had a pleasant memory of his father tainted by the harsh reality of what the future would hold. In each dream, however, Ethan always asked

Elohim why He would take his family. His questions were always met with silence. Ethan sighed and looked into the vast expanse above him. The stars twinkled overhead as the breeze caught his loose hair. If there was a god, he would not have taken the things that had meant the most to him. Without his family, he felt hopeless and completely lost. Like a sailor stuck at sea without the stars to guide him.

After a while Ethan rose to his feet and decided a short walk could help clear his head. He meandered around, not knowing what direction he was going.

The tall grass brushed against his pants as he walked past. The ground was wet with dew and clung to his boots. A couple of early birds called out, in hopes of being answered. Their cries faded in the night air. The moon lit the path before him, his eyes on the uneven ground.

Before long, he looked up and found he was in the swamp. He stopped walking and looked around. It was even more eerie at night, if that was even possible. The fog was even heavier now that there was no sunlight to brighten it. The fog slowly drifted in over the calm black water. Even the soothing sound of crickets only made the place more mysterious. A splashing sound and movement to the right caught his attention.

Stew stood on the bank of the swamp, fishing. Ethan couldn't help but chuckle quietly. The man was dedicated, Ethan had to give him that. Thoughts of fresh fish must be a powerful motivator for him.

Ethan was about to turn and walk away when he suddenly felt strange. As if something wasn't right. He looked at Stew again and tried to figure out what was bothering him.

Nothing was immediately catching his eyes. Stew was pulling his pole, the line taut.

"Yes, come to papa," Stew's excited voice cut through the still air. The water near the bank of the swamp was moving slowly. Suddenly Ethan realized that was not a natural occurrence. Something was in the water. It moved slowly for Stew, who was only a few feet away now. Before he could react, a large reptile shot out of the water, its giant jaws clamping onto Stew's leg.

The man yelled as he was thrown to the ground. He clawed the ground in a desperate attempt to pull himself away. The root of a tree was the only thing within his reach. It snapped and he was being pulled into the water, his leg at an odd angle.

"Stew! Hold on!" Ethan yelled and ran at a sprint to reach the man. He grabbed onto the frantic man's hands, trying to keep him out of the water. The animal was long, maybe eight feet, and had green almost leather-like skin. It was a crocodile, big enough to pull a full-grown man into the water. Its beady eyes were locked onto Stew. By the determined set of the creature's jaws, it didn't look like it would be letting go anytime soon.

It started shaking his whole body, causing Stew to flail out. Ethan lost hold on Stew for a moment as the man's body was jerked painfully from one side to the other. Ethan struggled to grab hold of the man again.

Their cries had caused the rest of the crew to come and investigate. Two more men came and helped Ethan hold onto Stew. Another took a sword and started stabbing the crocodile's leathery hide. The sword barely penetrated its thick hide, but it distracted the beast enough that it let go. It went to turn on its next victim when a dagger was suddenly shoved right in between the creature's eyes. It thrashed for a moment then lay motionless on the edge of the water. Its head and front legs were on the shore while its back legs and tail were floating on the surface.

All eyes swerved to see Doniphan poised over the animal, still gripping the dagger that was plunged into the creature's skull. This skinny and unassuming man before them had killed the beast.

Doniphan took in their surprised expressions. "What? I study animals too." He stammered sheepishly, withdrawing his knife. "They have a weak spot on the head right in between the eyes." He wiped the blood off on the ground then turned to Stew.

Ethan then remembered the injured man who lay on the ground next to him. "Are you all right, Stew?" The man rolled from his stomach to his back. He looked ready to respond when his eyes jumped to his abandoned pole. It jerked towards the water but was caught by Stew who had lunged for it. He raised his pole in triumph then pulled on the line. Suddenly a fish was pulled up onto the bank. A large one, it had to weigh at least thirty pounds.

"I am now!" Stew looked unbothered by his near-death experience.

"That's what you are worried about at a time like this? What of your leg?" Ethan glanced down, now noticing the holes in his pant leg and the lack of blood.

Stew laughed heartily. "This old thing?" He propped his leg and pulled the pant leg up. "I haven't felt anything there for quite some time." Underneath was a wooden leg, small holes dotting the length of it. A testament to the size of the crocodile's mouth and razor-sharp teeth. Ethan started laughing, all his pent-up adrenalin and sadness from the night slowly fading away. Men around him started laughing as well.

A hiss and a splash stopped their laughing short. The crocodile was being pulled into the water by an even bigger one. Its hungry eyes seemed to taunt them as it pulled its catch into the water. Soon the water was teeming with crocodiles as they fed on the carcass of the other. The water seemed to be alive with all the bodies.

Ethan suddenly remembered the tooth he had found upon their arrival at the huts. He found it in his pocket, completely forgotten until now. This was indeed the tooth of a crocodile but, by the looks of it, a much larger one. It had to be at least three times the size of the one that had grabbed Stew. Shock and fear coursed through him as he looked out over the murky water, still teeming with hungry crocodiles. Who knew what lay in all its depths? This island was starting to feel more and more deadly by the hour.

"I don't know about you all, but I think I'll celebrate back at camp." Jack backed away from the gruesome sight in the water and ran back to the huts. A couple of the beasts started to exit the water and hiss at the men, causing chaos as everyone scrambled away and back to the huts. Stew held tight to his prized fish.

They ran up the small hill and onto the open expanse of the field. The sun chose now to begin to spread its warm rays upon the island. The dew on the ground sparkled as they parted through the grass. The huts were only a short way away from the swamp. It felt even closer now that they knew of the dangers close by. Perhaps there had been a reason the huts had been abandoned.

Ethan spotted Annika who was quickly running towards them, her eyes awake and concerned. The men ran past her and towards the huts.

He slowed to a stop in front of her, unable to ignore the worry in her expression.

"What's going on?" Her frantic eyes begged him for answers. "Is everyone all right? Where's Carter?"

"He's fine." Ethan pointed to Jack and Carter, who were congregating around Stew.

"Oh, thank goodness. When I heard the screams, my mind jumped to the worst-case scenario. What happened?" Her worried face searched his then scanned his body for any injuries. The thought of her caring for him made him oddly happy.

"Stew had a very close run in with a crocodile."

Annika gasped. "Oh my, is he all right?"

Ethan began walking back to the huts with her, parting the tall grass as they walked. "I don't think anything could keep that man down. That croc had his jaws locked onto Stew's leg and was whipping him around. After he was out of the jaws of the beast, his first thought was of the fish on his line." He chuckled. "He managed to pull that fish in despite all that."

"That sounds like Stew." She smiled. "Does he need medical attention?"

"I don't believe so, I was afraid of that too. Seems the man has greater luck than any I have ever met." They stopped just behind the large group of men around the fire. "That croc managed to bite him on his wooden leg. Miraculously, he's got no wounds to show for his close encounter."

Stew was holding his prized fish up for all to see. Several men cheered and slapped him on the back. The fish was very large, but it still wouldn't satisfy all their aching bellies.

"Did you hear of the excitement, Miss Annika?" Simon walked towards them and gave his full attention to her. He stood quite close to Annika, causing her to ever so slightly inch closer to Ethan.

"I did. Seems as we have a very lucky and very blessed cook." She gave a small smile.

Simon sighed and shook his head. "So many close calls already. I'm afraid we could see much more of that during our stay here. I only wish you did not have to witness such atrocities."

Annika smiled a true smile. "I don't wish to be in the jaws of one of the beasts, but I would like to see one." She looked at Ethan. "It's another animal I have only read about."

Ethan chuckled. "Well, good for you, we have an entire swamp just teeming with them." He noticed that Simon's eyes followed every movement he made, the frown on his face only when Annika was not looking. It bothered Ethan that this man showed no respect for him. No fear and no respect for a captain was not a good combination for a sailor.

Annika seemed to be very uncomfortable with the presence of Simon. "I better go and get a look at this prized fish of Stew's." She quickly excused herself and entered the throng of men.

Simon didn't even bother to excuse himself, just turned and walked away. Ethan was growing to dislike the man more and more.

Captain Grey came up to Ethan, arms crossed and a smile playing on his lips.

Ethan cast him a sideways grin. "Looks like you missed all the excitement."

"The accounts of the tale seem to grow more extreme by the minute. I'm sad to say I missed everything." Captain Grey smiled at the joy on everyone's faces.

"It was definitely an experience I will always remember. Stew is quite the character." Ethan shook his head and smiled.

"We agree on that. Is he all right?"

"Oh, he's surprisingly uninjured. That man has no fear in him. If he had lost the fish, that would have been a different story." Ethan chuckled. He knew full well this morning could have gone much differently.

"Sounds like Stew." Captain Samuel chuckled and looked at Stew, as he sat cleaning his fish and telling the tale of his brush with death. "He has worked for me for a long time. He's a good man, one of the best actually. I'm just relieved to see he's ok. I don't want to have any more deaths." His gaze fell to the ground. Ethan realized the loss of Captain Grey's men weighed heavily on his mind. There weren't many captains that cared about the welfare of their crew, just the money they could make from them.

"That's another thing I wanted to talk with you about. Everywhere we turn there seems to be something deadly. Yesterday we had the encounter with the strange cat and today with the crocodiles. There were so many of them, and those are just the ones we have seen." Ethan leaned his head back and looked at the mountain wall in the distance. "I think it wise if we make our visit here as short as possible."

"What do you suggest, then?"

"We need to gather materials to fix what we can on the ship. I also think it would be wise to send out a few parties to explore the island. Maybe we missed something and there is civilization close by." Ethan could only hope. If they didn't figure out something soon, they would be stuck here for quite a while.

"Is the ship that bad? Could we not limp our way along?"

"No," Ethan shook his head. "I have looked at the damage and talked with our carpenter. It's a miracle it didn't sink as yours did. We need to get some wood cut and get the mast reinforced, or it would fall down with a strong gust of wind. There are many other repairs that need done. So, our next step would be to get some timber. I left my carpenter and some able-bodied men behind to work on what they can."

"If we need to get going on all that, what's the point of exploring the island?"

"First of all, it will take us a while to get wood and everything we need on our own. If we can find a town or something, there could be someone who could help. On the other hand, all our drinking water is coming from the swamp. We need to spread out and find more water and food. Stew's fish is big, but I don't think it will last for long." He smirked. Stew had finished cleaning the fish and admired his work as he held it up.

"I don't see as though we have any other options," Captain Grey said thoughtfully.

"I agree. Let us get repairs underway and send some men to explore the island, carefully."

They both watched Stew's animated expressions as he continued the story. He brought his wooden leg up and showed the deep holes in it to his surprised group of onlookers, which was growing by the minute.

Ethan found Annika watching him from the entryway of a hut. When his eyes found hers, a small blush crept up her face and she turned away, disappearing into the hut.

"You have me perplexed, I must say," Captain Grey quietly interjected, drawing Ethan's attention back to him. "I don't understand what you are. No pirate takes supplies and then pays for them, especially at a higher price than what they are worth." A small sigh escaped him. "At first, I hated you for taking my livelihood. Then you paid me for it, even after my ship sank. You even gave me money to help in the loss of my ship. Since then, I can see the love you have for your men and the respect they show you. I may not understand you and I may not trust you fully, but I'm beginning to respect you as a captain." His weathered face crinkled as he smiled. Captain Grey reminded Ethan so much of his father.

"I appreciate that, Captain Grey. Maybe, someday, you will understand." Ethan returned the smile. He hoped someday they could meet again, under different circumstances.

"Please, call me Samuel." The older man smiled. "It's what my crew and friends call me." Ethan realized what the man was saying. He was offering a branch of understanding to Ethan. A sign to say that he respected him, and that perhaps one day they could even be friends.

"I appreciate that. I would be happy to call you Samuel, but I will continue to give you the respect you deserve and keep the captain on there as well. I'm sorry but I have no name to give you other than Captain Wolf." Ethan felt sheepish. It's not that he did not trust the captain. He had his reasons for not saying his name.

"That's what everyone calls you, even your men. Do you not have a first name?" Captain Samuel joked with him and Ethan gave a weak smile.

"I do have a first name, though it's known only to a few."

"Cryptic. I see, perhaps one day I will know it." Captain Samuel smiled.

Ethan returned the smile. "Maybe, Captain Samuel." He then excused himself and walked towards the men.

"Hey, Stew!" He called out. "Are you going to cook up the fish or marry it?"

He left behind a confused but smiling Captain Samuel.

CHAPTER TEN

Annika entered the small hut and looked around the circle of wounded men. Some lay on blankets, sleeping. Others had developed fevers or were in intense pain from their wounds. Doniphan was kneeling down by the side of one of the injured men. She had found herself drawn to helping the men who were wounded. The anguish and sadness in their eyes drew her to help.

"How are they doing?" Her quiet voice brought his gaze momentarily to her.

He sighed. "Some have made quick recoveries and are not needing any attention. They would be the ones with sprains or cuts. Most of them are actually outside with the others." He stood to his feet and crossed his arms. A worried expression crossed his face. "These men are the worst of the bunch. They are not doing as well as I would like."

"What's wrong with them?" Annika's eyes skimmed over the men, taking in their bandages and wounds.

"A variety of things, I'm afraid. Over there we have a man with two broken legs." He pointed to a man who was lying flat on the ground, sleeping. "The only reason he isn't in more pain is because he managed to get some alcohol from friends. I have several men with gashes in their legs and abdomens. Infection looks to be setting in. This man was impaled by a beam." The young man in question had a large bandage on his shoulder and was sweating through his makeshift bedding. His lip quivered as he slept.

Annika was horrified by all the pain that surrounded her. "What can be done for them? Is there any way to heal them or even to alleviate their pain?"

Doniphan nodded. "That's why I wanted them on land. I have seen many herbal plants that I can use to help with the infection and with the pain. Nature is oftentimes the best medicine."

"So you have said." A large man entered the hut, his bearded face showing age and weariness. "I have not had much experience with plants helping men. I have yet to be convinced."

"Lady Harper, this is Saul, the doctor aboard Captain Wolf's ship."

Saul nodded briefly at her and spoke before she could utter a word. "Hello, miss. I have to say, I'm surprised to find you here. Most of the crew would cower anywhere near men in this condition."

"Why is that?"

"It's a reminder of what could happen to them." Saul's solemn expression quieted any of her comments. He walked forward and held a hand to one of the men on the floor. The man leaned into the touch in his sleep. "This man is burning up. Fevers are setting in."

"I was afraid it would come to this." Doniphan didn't sound surprised. "Are you all right to stay, Saul? I am going to collect some plants that I believe can help."

Saul nodded. "I'm willing to try anything at this point."

As Doniphan walked out of the tent, Annika followed. "Doniphan, may I come with you? I would be very interested to learn of what you find, and I want to do what I can to help."

He looked surprised and slowed his steps. "If you care to learn, I would be happy to show you. As for helping, it would help the men just to have interaction. Sometimes just being present can help alleviate their pain." She matched her steps to his long stride.

Doniphan smiled at her. "Captain Wolf has upped the amount of men to patrol the area. He even has assigned men to accompany me into the jungle." Annika did indeed see more men walking around the edge of camp.

"Into the jungle?" The dark trees loomed overhead.

"Yes, much of what I need should be in the jungle. I've already collected what I can around camp." He saw her worried expression. "I'm sorry, I forgot that you had a chilling encounter yesterday during my absence. I don't blame you if you wish to stay in the safety of camp."

Annika paused for a moment, the fear threatening to make her stay. "No." She pushed down her fear and thought of the wounded men. "I must face my fears, and I do wish to learn. Please lead the way." Doniphan nodded and found their escort.

Chris and Jack would be their protection when they trekked into the jungle. Annika knew of Chris but had yet to properly meet him. Jack's presence and easygoing nature would help alleviate her fears. His carefree smile was a good distraction.

The four of them set off into the trees. The jungle seemed to be teeming with wildlife. The insects were far more plentiful under the trees. Birds called greetings to one another in the treetops and made a beautiful and light-hearted song. It was nice to hear such carefree spirits; hopefully, that meant there was no danger nearby.

Hardly any light was able to make it through the dense trees, so it was quite darker than in the field. It was almost peaceful, if not for the knowledge that large predators hunted in its grounds.

"See here?" Doniphan pointed to a plant on the jungle floor. "This plant here is good for its numbing properties and for its benefits in reducing infection." He picked off a large portion of the plant. Its leaves were about the size of her palm.

"What's it called?" She fingered a leaf between her thumb and forefinger.

"It's called gerhaw. I can grind it up and make a salve out of it. This is an excellent find for the men." Doniphan stuffed the leaves in a large satchel he had slung around his shoulder.

An insect buzzed onto Annika's neck and she slapped it, missing her mark. By the time they were done out here, they would have more bite marks than clear skin.

Jack and Chris joked quietly as their eyes looked about the jungle. Every little noise seemed to attract their attention.

"I feel better having you men around." Annika smiled at them.

Jack grinned. "We are quite intimidating, I would say. No animal would dare attack us."

"I was thinking more along the lines of I could probably outrun you." Her comment elicited laughs from both of the men. Even Doniphan chuckled, though his eyes never left the ground. All joking aside, she did feel better knowing their attentive eyes were scanning the jungle.

Soon, they had collected a couple other plants. Doniphan said they would be good for healing and for their antibacterial properties. One was even good for lowering a fever. Which, unfortunately, was looking like it would be needed by many of the men.

It was already noon when they walked back to camp. They had not gone far, but the day's heat and humidity had worn them down considerably. Once they reached camp, they received water and a bit of fish soup from Stew. It tasted heavenly. Though it was mostly water, it had a wonderful flavor.

Stew had used the remainder of his morning catch to make the soup. The fish had just enough flavor to mask the swamp water it was made with. After a warm bowl of soup and a quick drink, Annika followed Doniphan back to the sick hut.

Doniphan spent the rest of the day showing Annika how to grind the herbs and how to apply them. She held cool towels to the men's fevered faces and helped clean wounds. This was all new to her, but it felt good to be of help. By evening, the men seemed to be doing better; at least they seemed to be relieved of some of the pain they were in.

"Good work, Doc." Saul came up beside Doniphan. Respect showed in his eyes. "Whatever you gave them at least helped them to sleep better."

"I just hope it also helps with the healing." Doniphan waved away the praise. Annika had come to really appreciate the work these men did. They had the most difficult job she had ever seen. Helping men through pain and suffering was a taxing job, physically and mentally. The fear of losing someone was always on their minds. The guilt after doing so probably weighed heavily on their shoulders.

"You did a wonderful job today, Lady Harper." Doniphan smiled weakly at her. He seemed exhausted; his eyes were even beginning to droop. "I really appreciated all your help."

"It was my pleasure. I really have a new appreciation for what you both do."

"It's our job," Saul interjected. "It's the least we can do as well. I hate to see men hurting and I never could just sit back idly."

"Have you seen a lot of injured men? I don't mean to pry, I was just curious."

"You mean because I work on a pirate ship?" Saul chuckled at her red face. "You're not prying. Honestly, the worst we have had would be some infections and food poisonings. All brought on by our own dumb mistakes. We have had few injuries, let alone fatalities, from anything Captain Wolf has asked us to do."

His words surprised her. "I find that hard to believe. We are not the first ship you have come upon, am I correct?"

"Yes, that is correct. Captain Wolf has been doing this for years, but we have managed to have very few injuries." He smiled at her. "You have a lot to learn of our captain."

"So I've heard." A wry smile twisted her lips. The sound of men snoring reached their ears.

"Doniphan, you take Lady Harper and go get some supper. Bring me some after, would ya?" Saul found a spot on the floor and got comfy. "I'll sit with the men."

Doniphan nodded solemnly, "I'll be back shortly."

"You do that." Saul grinned. "I'm mighty hungry."

Annika and Doniphan exited the tent and found the sun's rays beginning to dim. The captains and most of the men stood around the fire talking and laughing together. It looked as though none of the hardships they experienced had happened.

Doniphan and Annika walked towards Stew, who was handing out bowls of soup. His eyes lit up when he caught sight of her.

"Did you hear, Miss Harper? I caught myself another beauty." His toothy grin highlighted his missing teeth.

"I'm surprised you were brave enough to go back there after what happened." Annika accepted a bowl from Stew.

"I like to think I'm brave, but I ain't stupid." He laughed heartily. "I walked a little ways and found a different area of the swamp. Far more open, the water is even a bit clearer. I could see a croc if it decided to come close."

"That's wonderful." Annika grinned. The delicious smell in the bowl beckoned her. "Let me tell you, I will greatly enjoy the fruits of your labor."

"Does this mean the water will taste better if we get it from there?" Doniphan spoke up, sticking his tongue out slightly, remembering the stagnant water they had to endure.

"Right you are. Fact, my stew tonight is made with that water."

"You really are a wonderful cook, risking life and limb for us to eat. Now that's dedication." Annika smiled and looked down at the soup in her bowl. Chunks of fish floated in the mixture along with something new. "Did you say this was stew?"

"Yes, it is. I managed to find some edible root vegetables to bulk it up and some fresh herbs for flavor. It's a right proper meal this time." He smiled proudly.

"I'm so excited to try your stew, Stew." She grinned, remembering him telling her he never made stew.

"Well, I can tell you it's the best stew this side of the island." He grinned and handed another bowl to a sailor. "Here, take these as well." He handed her and Doniphan each a mandaw.

"I'm going to need two bowls and more fruit if you have it. I'm taking Saul his supper." Doniphan's hands were already full with his own food.

"Why don't you run that to Saul and come back and get one for yourself? I'll have one ready for ya." Doniphan nodded affirmably.

"Thanks again for your help, Miss Harper." Doniphan smiled and quickly walked away to deliver food to Saul.

Annika looked at Stew and smiled. "Thank you, Stew. Make sure you eat too." She stepped away and joined the others around the fire.

The sun was quickly fading, and the cold was beginning to set in. The sky was beginning to turn bright shades of orange and red. All too soon the sun would be set, and the island would be covered in darkness. Nighttime was admittedly her least favorite. No one knew what was lurking in the darkness beyond the light of the fire. How many eyes watched them, thinking about the most opportune time to strike?

Annika did not see anyone she knew well, so she found a seat on a log near the fire and indulged in the flavorful stew. The strong tastes of it hit her; the fish was smoky and there was some sort of herb as well. It was simple but after having several meals of just fruit and hard tack it tasted heavenly. It was even more flavorful than the one from lunch. Probably a different fish, and the addition of the new herb made a big difference.

Annika savored the stew with her eyes closed. The lively talk around her gave a pleasant atmosphere. The voice of Stew caught her attention. Upon opening her eyes, she saw Stew sitting to her left with the attention of several of the men.

"All right, lads. I'll tell you a tale, one that is sure to interest even the likes of you." His crooked teeth glinted in the fire light.

"I've heard that before, Stew." Annika realized Chris was sitting next to Stew. He rolled his eyes at the man. "Last time you told a story, it was the same one my mother told me when I was a lad." Men snickered behind their hands good-naturedly.

Stew laughed and shook his head. "Your mother told you strange stories when you were young. My own mother would turn over in her grave if I told the story of the leviathan of the deep to a youngin'. Now come closer, lads." He waved his hands to them. "Come closer as I spin you a tale full of treachery, royalty, and death." His eyes gleamed mischievously.

The men all hushed and listened closely, their eyes riveted to the big man. "Long ago, in a time full of peace and harmony, there was a king and a queen. The king was so strong and wise that it was said he had a deep connection with Elohim. Rumor had it that he was divinely favored and that no army could stand against him and his men.

"He fell in love with a young maiden from Nesher. They married, and she became queen and stood by his side. Their love for one another was as strong as the tides. She was the most beautiful lady in the land. Think of the most beautiful maiden you have ever seen, and you would not even come close to seeing one of her beauty. The goodness in her heart matched her husband's. They ruled the kingdom righteously and were loved by all their people.

"During their reign, all was perfect. Food was never scarce, and laughter was heard on every street. It was as if Elohim himself was present in every decision they made and, therefore, the land prospered. Their fields produced double what they normally would. Even their animals flourished and multiplied quickly. Their kingdom was the envy of all who witnessed its splendor. Their prosperity drew men from all regions of the world. One man in particular would change their lives forever." Stew's eyes glinted as his tale wove even deeper.

Annika found herself on the edge of her seat. The man did have a way of capturing an audience. Most of the men around the fire had now stopped their activities and were focused on his tale.

"On a bright and sunny day, a ship docked on the shores of this flourishing kingdom. A man, with eyes like darkness and a heart even darker, stepped foot onto the lush shores. It's said that even his footsteps caused the grass to blacken and die. He was a charmer, though, with one smile he could disarm even the wisest of men. His very words were like velvet and seeped unwarily into your very soul. That, unfortunately, would be the kingdom's downfall.

"The man befriended the king and became his closest friend. The king would even consult him before making any decisions. Once the king took his eyes off Elohim and turned instead to the man, the whole kingdom suffered. The crops began to die, and the animals no longer flourished. The once sunny skies became dark and filled with clouds. Those clouds never opened up and gave water, though. They just blanketed the kingdom in a shroud of darkness. Soon the kingdom was in complete turmoil, as was its king.

"In this time of need, it was far too easy for the newcomer to take what he wanted. One fateful day, after becoming the king's most trusted advisor, the man got the king alone and took his life. He gave the queen a choice: be his bride or join her husband. With a resolute look about her angelic face and a smile on her lips, she refused and was forthwith sent to the grave along with her husband. He did not stop until all the royal family was runout or killed. The evil man convinced the kingdom that it was in tatters because of the late king. Under his new reign, he promised peace and harmony. The desperate people accepted his help, and he took his place on his newly acquired throne. Never has a more wicked man sat upon the throne, and there he sits to this day, driving the country and its people into ruin."

Stew ended his tale, and the silence that followed after dragged on.

"That one was better than the last made up tale at least." One man finally broke the silence.

"No, my stories are all true. Sure as the sky is blue and your teeth are yellow." He winked at the men, causing a round of laughter. "What I tell you is all true. It's the story of the kingdom of Narine and its demise. If you like, I can tell you the tale of the kingdom of Lookonia someday." He grinned.

Annika had lived in Narine and had never heard of the tale before. Granted she had lived in an orphanage, and they had done their best to seclude the children from the outside world. What a sad story it had been. Such godly people being led astray and meeting their demise. If that was really how things had happened, it was tragic. Annika, of course, knew a little of the king in Narine. He did not have a good reputation at all. In fact, she had heard people use his name as the reason for the current state of the country.

The men laughed and begged for another story. Stew just laughed. "Not tonight, lads. Catch me tomorrow, though, and I will spin you the tale of the long-armed beast who took my leg clean off." Several men laughed and begged for him to tell it now. He just shook his head and smiled. The man did like to leave others in suspense.

Still thinking of the story Annika glanced around the fire. Men were beginning to start up conversation again. Across from her, she saw Carter and Jack talking to one another. They must have joined the group while she was engrossed in Stew's tale.

Jack looked to be only a few years older than Carter, so it was good to see them both getting along so well. Her eyes drifted over the men until she locked onto eyes already looking at her. Simon smiled when she caught his gaze, and she managed a small smile in return.

Maddock whispered something to Simon, making him smile wider. His gaze never left Annika's. Her cheeks grew warm. Were they talking about her? His gaze made her so uneasy. She lowered her eyes and looked instead at the forgotten bowl of stew in her hands. Even without looking up, she could tell Simon was still watching her.

The delicious stew had grown tasteless in her mouth. It could be a delicious pastry for all she knew, but her taste buds had lost the ability to function. Her very thoughts felt invaded, as if everything was just out for Simon's and Maddock's greedy eyes to take in.

"Men, can I have your attention?" Captain Samuel's calm voice rose above the voices of the men. Everyone's eyes sought out Captain Samuel, who stood straight and tall behind the fire. His grim face caused the men to silence. "As you all may have gathered, we will be here for a while.

Captain Wolf's ship is in need of major repairs. It's going to take a lot of hard work from us to be able to get her sailing again."

Captain Wolf, who had been reclining on a log next to Captain Samuel, stood and crossed his arms. His appearance seemed to demand everyone's attention even more than Captain Samuel's. Perhaps it was the fact that he was a pirate. Or perhaps it was the way he carried himself. His whole demeanor spoke of strength and authority.

His eyes shone in the firelight. "It's true, we have a lot to do to get back on the water. We need men gathering supplies and helping with the repairs. Tomorrow, we will have a schedule worked out and will explain it in depth. In other news, we have a completely unexplored island. For all we know, there could be a settlement on the other side. I believe it's in our best interest to send out teams to explore the island."

A murmur broke out amongst the men. "Who gets to go on these explorations?" Maddock's all-too-familiar voice broke through the silence. His ugly face was twisted into a scowl.

Captain Wolf settled his gaze upon the unpleasant man but did not falter. "We will choose the best men out of the ones who volunteer." He passed over Maddock, as if he was hardly worth his time. Maddock's face grew even more tight, but he remained quiet.

"We will talk more of it in the morning," Captain Wolf continued. "We will start repairs tomorrow, and we will also send out the exploration parties tomorrow. So be prepared either way and decide if you want to volunteer or not."

With a wave of his hand, he dismissed the men to continue on with their activities. Men finished up their food and sat in front of the blazing fire. The overall atmosphere of the men was more subdued now. They had just had a stark reminder of their current state.

Annika glanced across the fire and caught sight of Carter still smiling and talking with Jack. They seemed to be having quite the animated conversation. Her eyes wandered briefly to the two men who held her heart in a deadly vise. Maddock and Simon sat close together, speaking in hushed tones. The look on their faces was a mix of anger and excitement. At least they were not looking at her anymore.

A sudden thought occurred to her. If they volunteered to go on the exploration team, then perhaps she would be rid of one or both of them for a while. Or, if they did not volunteer, perhaps she would. The idea stuck with her, causing a smile to brighten her face. She would be away from unwelcome stares and have the added bonus of seeing new things on the island.

What of Carter, though? She could not leave him behind. She looked up and found him and Jack missing. Their log now sat unoccupied. Where had they gone? A quick glance around and Annika still could not see them.

She stood and quietly slipped away from the fire, intent on finding Carter. The air grew colder and the surroundings darker the further she got from the fire. Small fires were in the huts keeping their inhabitants warm. Light spilled out from the doorways, illuminating portions of her path. Voices drifted through as she walked past.

An ominous feeling overcame her, sending shivers down her spine. The hair on the back of her neck pricked up and she fearfully glanced over her shoulder. A familiar face was right behind her, his snake-like eyes glinting in the moonlight.

CHAPTER ELEVEN

Ethan sat around the fire listening to the men and sometimes inter-jecting. If this were just his crew, he would be speaking more and having fun. However, these men were not his and he did not trust them. Some of their eyes were shifty and their expressions dangerous; he had a hard time understanding why Captain Samuel hired them.

The fire crackled as he gazed about the men. Jonah sat conversing with Captain Samuel, something about sea currents. Jack had been sitting with Carter, but they were gone now. Perhaps off to continue making their hammocks or to invent some other contraption. The two seemed equally excited about inventing. They had many more men to supply with beds.

Ethan found his eyes wandering to the space Annika had been occu-pying. Her lovely presence made it a chore for any sailor to look away. He was surprised to find her gone, her spot on the log empty. Perhaps she had gone with Carter to their hut. They were most often in one another's company.

Something just didn't sit right with him. It was as if something was wrong, but he couldn't decipher where the feeling was coming from. He had oftentimes had feelings like this; he had ignored them once and had paid the consequences. Ever since then, he had listened to the warning in his head. It was the same feeling he would get when a hidden storm was about to pounce on his unsuspecting crew.

His eyes scanned the skies overhead and found nothing amiss. The stars overhead twinkled unheeded by any clouds. That did nothing to put his mind at ease. In fact, his heart rate began to speed up.

Finally, his eyes caught onto Maddock. He was glaring directly at Ethan. Any negative feelings he had felt towards the man earlier were tripled tonight. The way he had questioned him and showed obvious disdain for any authority. The way his eyes seemed to dare Ethan to provoke him. One thing was for sure: he was not to be trusted.

Ethan realized it wasn't Maddock that was inciting his unease. His companion, Simon, was missing from his spot by Maddock. The sight of the empty space on the log seemed to shout trouble. He had seen Simon watch Annika and had seen her obvious unease. Men like him seemed to only have one thing they wanted. Maddock's face twisted into an evil smile. His eyes seemed to convey a silent message to Ethan.

Warning bells sounding in his mind caused Ethan to get up and seek out Annika. As he walked around, his eyes frantically searched the swarm of men around camp. His heart was pounding uncontrollably now. Where was she?

A small cry drew Ethan attention away from the fire and towards the dark huts. Some of the huts were already occupied and had fires inside them. Small fractions of light shone through, as if lighting the trail he needed to take. Scuffling of feet was all he heard, but it was enough to guide him forward.

The sight before him infuriated him to his core. Upon rounding a corner, he found Annika pressed up against a wall. Simon was standing quite close to her, forcing her to back to the hut wall. He had one hand on the wall next to her head and the other he was using to capture her hand, which was currently trying to withdraw her sword. Her escape and form of protection cut off. The fear in her eyes was enough to make Ethan's blood boil.

He sprung forward and gripped Simon's wrist and yanked it back, causing the man to stumble backward. "Good evening, sailor." The kind words came out in a bite. His words dripped with anger and a heavy warning. "I do believe you are making the lady uncomfortable." He squeezed Simon's wrist, causing the man to grimace behind his trembling smile.

"I was only talking with her." He turned to Annika, who now stood next to Ethan. "Isn't that right? Just friendly conversation is all."

Annika huffed angrily. "If standing unwillingly within inches of your rank breath is considered friendly conversation. I assure you that is not how I interpreted it." Simon's smile dropped and became more of a sinister sneer. He attempted to step towards Annika. Ethan withdrew his sword with a swift movement and held it beneath the surprised man's chin.

"You would do wisely to leave this very moment. If I find out you have harmed the lady, or have any intent on doing so, you had better sleep with one eye open. You're lucky I don't slice you open right here." He glowered at the shorter man and straightened his spine. Thankfully, after another glare, Simon walked away.

Annika let out an audible sigh of relief. "You have my eternal gratitude, Captain. That man makes my skin crawl."

Ethan turned to her. Her eyes sparkled with the little light the moon shed. "Did he harm you?"

"No, but he was making me very uncomfortable. I believe it would not have been long before he would have tried. He was not listening to my refusals and became a bit too friendly. That's when you walked in." She gave him a shaky smile and rubbed her arms. The air now held a chill.

"Please, let me walk with you to your hut." He gestured her forward, in the opposite direction Simon had gone. As they walked, he couldn't help but notice how her fearful eyes darted left and right. She had not had this reaction even after an Ancient tiger had attacked.

"I'm sorry Simon is causing you problems. Would you like me to talk with Captain Samuel? It's within your rights to do so."

She shook her head and attempted a brighter smile. "No, it's all right. I'm sure your warning tonight was enough to keep him away."

Annika tripped over something, and Ethan instinctively caught hold of her elbow and held her steady. "Allow me." He placed her hand on the crook of his elbow and continued walking. "I have not spent much time with Simon or his companion, Maddock. I know enough to dislike the both of them. I've been at sea long enough to spot someone who will cause dissension and quarreling among a crew."

"Those are their best qualities, I am sure." Annika laughed, this time a real one. Her quiet laugh was contagious.

Ethan smiled in return. "Have they always caused you trouble?" They stepped around a small bend and walked down another row of huts. Her hut was just a few doors down.

"As soon as they laid eyes on us, I'm afraid." She gave a weary sigh. "I don't know how the two of them get along. Maddock seems to hate me and my presence with the crew because of my gender. Then there's Simon, and he seems to enjoy my gender far too much. They are complete opposites it seems."

They arrived in front of her hut and were happy to see a fire blazed inside. Carter and Jack were sitting around the fire and discussing something quite animatedly. "I want you to tell me if he gives you anymore problems."

She let go of his arm and stood in front of him. "That's actually something I wanted to speak to you about." She bit her lip, as if not sure she should continue speaking. "I know you didn't even want me to join the men who came early onto the island. So that makes me even more hesitant to ask this, but I assure you I do not do so to earn your ire." She took a deep breath. "I would like to request to join a team tomorrow, Carter and myself. Before you say anything, please know my reasons. My main reason being that if I were to be on an expedition, I would be free from the company of two certain sailors. The second, and not as important, reason being it sounds like an adventure."

Her words just seemed to spill out of her and after she was done, she stood in front of him quietly. Ethan thought for a moment. If he was to leave tomorrow and leave her behind, Simon may take that as a good time for him to make his move on Annika.

"I agree," he said at last.

Her jaw almost dropped open in disbelief. "Really?"

"Yes, I think it would be a good way for you to stay out of their way. Removing you completely from the situation for a few days may allow Simon to cool off."

"Thank you so much, Captain." The smile she gave him dispelled any trepidation he had. "I know you may not believe me, but I can be of help to you on the journey as well."

"I have not known you long, Annika, but I know you well enough to not underestimate you." He grinned and gave her a small bow. "Sleep well."

"You as well, Captain Wolf." She gave him another dazzling smile and entered the warm hut. Ethan walked away and found himself wishing he could hear his real name come from her lips.

Annika stood with Carter and listened to Captain Samuel speak of the repairs and supplies that were needed. Some men were assigned to cutting timber and hauling it to the beach. From there, they would need to be rowed to the ship which could be interesting.

Then Captain Wolf began speaking of plans for the expedition teams. There were to be two teams of men going out to explore the island. One team would be going to explore the interior of the island. The other team would explore the island via the beach. Both groups would look for food, water, and were hoping to find people.

Captain Wolf said he would be leading the team going into the island's interior, and Chris would take the other team. Annika's heart was beating rapidly. Would Captain Wolf keep his word and assign her and Carter a spot on one of the teams? She once again felt glares coming from the direction of Simon and Maddock, strengthening her hope and her fervent prayers.

"If you wish to go on the expedition, please raise your hands. I will pick a handful of you to go. The rest of you will need to stay behind and help with repairs." Captain Wolf stood with one hand on his hip and the other resting on the hilt of his sword.

He somehow looked even better today. How was it he seemed to be getting more handsome on this trip and every day she just looked more dirty? His dark hair was pulled back and tied at the base of his neck. His wide-brimmed hat sat upon his head and the feather moved in the wind. His white shirt was untied a little bit, showing the start of a muscular chest. Annika brought her eyes back up quickly to his face and could have sworn, by the small quirk of his lips, that he had caught her looking.

Men all around her raised their hands. A majority of the men gathered raised their hands enthusiastically. Shouts of excitement and men calling for their names to be called. Captain Wolf's eyes roved over them all, searching for the men he favored and trusted. He began calling out names for Chris's team. He chose six men to go with Chris, making sure to put both his crew and Captain Samuel's on it.

All the men whose names had been called gathered around Chris. Excitement shone on their faces as they talked amongst themselves.

Next, Captain Wolf began to search for members to take on his team. She and Carter raised their hands in the air. He assigned Jonah, whom Annika had come to know as Captain Wolf's right hand man. Then Jack's name was called out.

Annika was starting to become a bit afraid... Would he keep his word? He hadn't even glanced her way since he had begun to call out names.

Captain Wolf's eyes traveled over the expectant faces of the crew in front of him and came to rest on Annika.

"Annika and Carter will go with my team as well," he said the statement quickly and seemingly without much thought. He then quickly turned to address the other men. "Thank you all for volunteering. I know we are strong. We can get through this together. If we all put our best efforts in, we will be back on the water in no time."

"Now, Captain, I don't feel this was fair. I think you may be playing favoritism here," Maddock's familiar gravelly voice cut through the crowd. The men parted and allowed Maddock to step forward.

"You dare question me, sailor?" Captain Wolf's eyes narrowed as he purposefully did not address Maddock by name.

"I do. Seems to me you need people with you who are capable and strong, not women and children." His mouth twisted into a sneer. The men were unusually quiet, recognizing the disrespect Maddock was showing Captain Wolf. Their expectant eyes roved from Maddock to Captain Wolf.

"I have kept silent about your disrespect on many occasions. Know your place, sailor. I will not keep my mouth shut for much longer."

"With all due respect, Captain. I do know my place and it isn't here. I am a strong man and capable of beating out any of your men here if you wish for me to show you. I suggest you have the children try their luck against me. See for yourself if they are good enough to join your team."

Captain Wolf frowned. "You are skating on very thin ice. Stand down." His eyes flashed in warning, which Maddock completely ignored.

"Maddock." Captain Samuel stepped forward and glared at him. "You will show Captain Wolf respect."

"Why? He's a pirate who robbed us, remember? Am I to be told to respect the men who pillaged and plundered us?" Maddock spoke to the rest of the men. Some men nodded in quiet agreement; others shook their heads.

"I agree our situation is not ideal." Captain Samuel tried to regain control of the men. "Regardless, we are here now. Neither us nor the pirates are going anywhere. We can either fight amongst ourselves or fight to get out of here alive. Our best bet of doing that is working together. You don't have to like it, but as your captain I am ordering you to stand down."

Maddock glowered at his superiors before turning again to the crowd of men. "Are you going to let this pirate make all the decisions for us?" Captain Wolf's men looked angry at the treatment of their captain while Captain Samuel's men raised their hands in agreement and shouted.

What now? Annika shifted uncomfortably from one foot to the other. She was feeling extremely uncomfortable in this situation. In a way she had started this argument. Though she figured it would have been just a matter of time before Maddock spoke up to authority on his own. She only wished it had not been because of her.

She looked around at the men. Captain Wolf needed control of the situation. If he just pushed aside their feelings and put Maddock in his place, it would show he didn't care for their opinions. If he relented to Maddock's words, then he would seem cowardly. Annika bit her lip nervously. She had not expected this to get so out of hand.

"I think it only fair for them to show their necessity for being on your team." Maddock's eyes gleamed as a sneer crossed his face. Captain Wolf stared the man down, his eyes showing deep intensity. Any normal sailor would have fled just witnessing the anger in his eyes, but Maddock just looked him in the eyes, undeterred.

"I accept." Annika stepped forward, drawing the attention of both men. "If I win, then both Carter and I are to be allowed to go on the expedition. If you win, then we will step back and do what the captain says. Sound fair?" She crossed her arms and allowed a small cocky smile to cross her face. If she had guessed right, Maddock hated feeling inferior, especially towards a woman. The anger in his eyes showed her guess had been correct.

"I agree." He gritted the words out. His large arms crossed over his bulky chest.

"It must be a fair challenge, though." She tapped her forefinger on her chin and walked closer to the men. "We both know you are larger than me, so it must be something that requires skill, not brute strength." If it came to a fighting match she was guaranteed to lose. As much as she hated to admit it, the man was big and had muscles to spare. He indeed was a formidable opponent.

"What would you suggest?"

An idea popped into her head. "What of archery? Is that something you could do?" Nowadays men were obsessed with guns, and many were not well trained with a bow.

"Fine. We shall do archery, then." His lips curled up into an eerie smile. Her skin crawled but she shook off the feeling. His reaction made her stiffen. The look in his eyes told her that he was not unpracticed with a bow. Would she soon be regretting her decision?

"See that tree stump?" Maddock pointed a fat finger out over the field. Annika came up beside him and caught sight of the stump. It was at least one hundred yards away from the group. "There's a knob on the side of the stump." Annika squinted and caught sight of the knob. It was about the size of an apple and would not be an easy shot. Simon handed a bow and an arrow to Maddock.

He took the bow and notched an arrow. The line pulled taut, the muscles on his arms standing out as his hands steadied and he took aim. With a hiss, the arrow left his fingers and sank into the stump. Its sound caused Annika's heart to lurch. It was a solid hit, and the stump had shaken from impact. Jack ran forward to see how close the shot had come.

He came running back moments later. "An inch to the right of the mark." Maddock grinned smugly. His shot was a hard one to beat.

Annika called upon strength from above when her eyes caught sight of a tree. It was about fifteen yards further away than the log. It was a mandaw tree; large fruit hung from its branches. This far away, the fruit were just small dots. A sudden feeling of confidence overtook her. As if a divine hand were pointing her in this direction.

She took the bow from Maddock and received an arrow from Simon. The bows string was tighter than she was used to, but it would have to do.

The string pulled taut and she steadied her hands. "Hey, Stew, are you in need of more fruit?" She smiled as excited whispers ran through the men. "Top right, second fruit down." She released the arrow, and it sailed swiftly through the air. It raced past the log and towards the mandaw tree. It disappeared into the distance and a branch shook from impact.

Jack ran off to check how close she had gotten. Maddock pointed to Simon and growled. "Simon, you go too." The two men ran towards the tree and came back minutes later. Jack had an excited smile on his face.

"A perfect shot." He held the fruit in the air, an arrow cutting through the middle of it. Juice dripped down the side of it and fell to the ground. Annika's heart leaped at the sight of it. A grin tugged at her lips and a prayer of thanks spilled out in a whisper. Men shouted excitedly and gathered around Jack to inspect the fruit.

"That settles it, then." Captain Wolf stepped forward and once again commanded the attention of the men. "I believe we have proof now of the lady's expertise. If there are no further objections, let us get on with it. To those who are staying behind, you get your orders from Captain Samuel." He placed his hand on the man's shoulder. "I will leave them in your capable hands."

He clapped his hands together and dispersed the men.

Annika and Carter hurried to get their things packed. Annika had a small satchel she could hoist over her shoulder, so she packed the necessities in it. From behind his curtain, Annika could tell Carter was doing the same.

"Are you certain that was wise?" Carter stepped out from behind the curtain holding a bag.

"Whatever do you mean?" She knew he referred to her archery duel with Maddock but did not want to speak of it. She was already hating what she had done.

"You know what I mean. Was it a wise idea to outshoot him like that? Especially that thoroughly? Now there's an even bigger target on our heads."

She sighed. "I know what you mean. I don't know what happened. I had no intention of speaking up, but once I did I was committed. Perhaps they will forget all about us in our absence."

"We could hope, but I find that very unlikely." He grinned and slung his bag over his shoulder. "To be honest, though, I would rather meet that tiger than stay another minute with those men." Carter stuck out his tongue in mock disgust, eliciting a giggle from Annika.

CHAPTER TWELVE

They took their meager belongings out of the tent and met for breakfast. Stew served some of the fish he had caught just hours prior. He cooked it with mandaw and some kind of herb Annika couldn't distinguish. Once breakfast was over, they collected some hard tack and bottles of water. Stew also handed out some crackers to the explorers. Stew had always been kind to her, but over the course of the trip she had come to think of him as a close friend.

"You sure showed that unsavory character what for." He laughed under his breath. "I'm right proud of you, missy. I'll let you know if I need any more mandaws." He elbowed her lightly, winking. Annika laughed and continued packing the food into her bag.

Everyone had gathered into their assigned groups, and it was now time to go. Chris and his men took off for the beach, and within minutes their forms disappeared into the dense forest ahead.

Captain Wolf's team was assembling their gear now. Annika double-checked her bag, not wanting to leave anything behind.

"Got enough food?" Captain Wolf asked as he swung his bag onto his shoulder. After receiving affirmative answers, he looked at Annika. "Got a bow and arrow?" His teasing expression made her smile.

She adjusted the bow that was on her back. "Ready for action." She carried her sword, bow and arrows, and a dagger she had found to replace the old one. Though nothing could truly replace the value her dagger had. Memories could not be replaced, let alone its beauty.

"Then we will head off. Stick close to each other and share if you see anything of interest, good or bad." Captain Wolf turned and waved to Captain Samuel, who stood nearby. "I'll leave everyone else in your capable hands."

After addressing Captain Samuel, he walked confidently into the jungle. Was he as nervous as she was? She doubted it. Not once did he waver or shake. He was all confidence and strength.

Annika said a brief prayer for safety and noticed Carter's eyes were shut, his lips moving in a silent prayer. The way ahead was unknown, unexplored. For all they knew, they could be walking into death and misery. They could use all the prayers they could get.

The jungle ahead was even harder to walk through than she had remembered from their previous trek. They trudged onward, barely making headway it seemed. The tall trees were very dense and the terrain uneven. Vines hung from overhead and twisted around each other. With each step they took, they needed to swing a machete just to clear their path. Mosquitoes buzzed all around, biting them on any exposed skin.

They were heading east, away from the swamp, and veering slightly off from the mountain. They walked all morning and even into the early afternoon. Each step they took was painful and the progress was slow.

Soon it was unbearably hot and a good time to take a break and eat something. Their clothes were drenched, and they were breathing heavily.

They found a small clearing, barely big enough for them all to sit in. The trees were parted a little, showing the rays of the sun onto the jungle floor. The humidity was almost unbearable, and all of them were breathing heavily.

"It's another hot one today, Cap." Jack spread out onto his back and stretched his arms wide. His stomach rose and fell dramatically. Jonah sat on the ground next to him. His posture, usually straight and tall, seemed to be a bit droopy. Thankfully, for the most part, the sun was not able to penetrate the thick jungle canopy. Now it was the humidity in the jungle that stole their breath and soaked their clothing.

"Let's rest for a while before heading back out. I want to add a few things to this map." Captain Wolf took his map out and studied it. Then he placed a few marks on the leather.

Tentatively, Carter moved closer to the map. "I could do that for you, Captain. I enjoy drawing and feel I have learned a few things about navigation already." He looked longingly at the map in Captain Wolf's hands.

"Ahh, that's right. You did say you were interested in navigation. All right, it would be a big help if you wish to do it. Just be careful with it. We only have two maps. This one and the one Smith possesses as well."

"Understood, Captain. I will handle it with the utmost of care." Carter accepted the map into his awaiting hands. His eyes looked hungry for a challenge, his fingers fairly twitching with anticipation. He opened the map and studied it, adding marks and detail where he thought they were needed. Captain Wolf observed him but kept quiet.

The rest of the men pulled some hard tack and crackers out of their bags, as well as some water. They gulped water like their lives depended on it. Annika followed suit, although more ladylike than they were; she pulled her food out and began eating.

Birds called out friendly greetings in the trees, and every so often you would see a bright flash of color as they flew from branch to branch. The howls of monkeys sounded in the trees, probably warning others of the unwelcome visitors in the jungle.

"How far have we walked, Cap?" Jack took a bite of the hard tack and waited for him to respond.

"Not as far as you may think." Captain Wolf studied the map over Carter's shoulder. "I was keeping track as we went, and I think we have only traveled a little over two miles."

Jack groaned. "No way, I think your count is off. It's been at least twenty miles, I'm sure." His teasing pout brought a smile to their weary faces.

"'Fraid not. What's worse is it will be just as hard on the way back. You'd think we would have opened up a pathway through the jungle, but we seem to have been swallowed up by the foliage. There is no clear path back." Captain Wolf looked behind them and sure enough, the jungle looked just as thick as before they walked through it.

Jack sighed. "Can we ever get a break? It's like this jungle is out to get us." He popped the last bite of cracker into his mouth.

"It isn't the easiest place to live in, that's for sure." Jonah, having finished his food, lay down on his back and closed his eyes briefly.

Carter rolled up the map and gave it back to Captain Wolf, who studied his workmanship. "I'm impressed. This is far more detail than I would have done. Your measurements seem to be sound as well." He held the map for a moment then offered it back. "Would you like to hold onto it for me?"

Carter's eyes lit up. "Yes, Captain! Thank you!" He took the map and tied it to the outside of his pack, an easy place to get to while walking.

"It's so hot!" Jack moaned. Everyone knew he was joking but his words were true. Annika had never before sweat this much.

Jonah sat up and looked into the wall of trees. "I miss the wide-open sea. Here, all we can see is what's right in front of our faces. When I'm on the water, it's as if the whole world is there for me to see."

Carter smiled. "I haven't spent near as much time as you on the water, but I can see what you mean. The water has become a very special place for me now." Annika watched as a sad smile crossed his face. If she had to guess, the cause of it was his not being on the water for long. Even after they left this place, he would only have a week or so on a boat. Then they would be in the kingdom of Lookonia and have no reason to leave.

"At least on the water there's a breeze," Jack grumbled to himself. They all chuckled.

Annika looked up into the cloudless sky, her smile turning sad. After this adventure, Lookonia would seem so dull. How was one to go and have a normal life after something like this?

"What of you, Miss Harper?" Jonah's voice pulled her back to the present. "Despite our circumstances, have you enjoyed having a break from the sea?" His kind eyes looked back at her. How was it none of these men fit the common look of a pirate?

"On the contrary, I too have developed a sort of longing for the sea." She felt Captain Wolf's eyes on her. "Don't get me wrong, I love land and the reassuring presence of it. Though I can't help but love the feel of the unknown on the water. I'm not an experienced sailor, like the rest of you, but I love the mystery of what's just out of sight. What will come into view next, some unexplored island or a beautiful sunset. It's as if the sea is a wonderful friend and a powerful enemy, all wrapped into one. It's impossible to hate but easy to fear. I suppose that sounds silly to you all." Her eyes dropped to her lap.

"Not at all," Jack piped up, his grumbling forgotten. "Many men sail for need of money and others for adventure. The ones seeking money usually grow to hate the sea. It's the ones who are drawn to the sea and its mysteries who feel the way you do."

Annika smiled at him.

"How long have you been sailing?" Carter asked.

"We only started sailing a few years ago. We don't have much of a head start on you." Jack grinned until he caught sight of a warning glare from Captain Wolf. His smile quickly faded to an apologetic grimace. That was a strange reaction. They seemed to be great sailors for their short amount of time on the sea. It must not take long to become accustomed to the sea and its mysterious ways, especially if on it for years. But what had been the reason for such a warning from Captain Wolf?

They sat in silence for a few more minutes. The only sound to be heard was from the animals overhead and the buzzing of the ever-present mosquitoes.

"All right, that's enough rest." Captain Wolf finally broke the silence as he stood to his feet. "We have a few more hours to spare in the day. I suggest we make use of it and walk further before camping for the night."

It was mid-afternoon and everyone was already exhausted. Annika was not looking forward to more walking, but knew she could not complain. It would probably only make Captain Wolf regret bringing her along. She mustered all her energy and straightened her back. The trees ahead of them were thick and dark, adding to the hesitation they all felt about continuing.

The group trudged forward, somewhat energized by the small meal they had taken but still weary. Their sweat drenched clothes clung to their backs and made the way even more miserable. The air was getting even more thick with mosquitoes as well.

A sound suddenly found its way to Annika's ears. It was a low rumble, barely distinguishable.

"Do you hear that?" Everyone turned their attention to her as she listened.

"I don't hear anything," Jonah replied after a moment.

"I do!" Carter's eyes shone in excitement.

They walked further through the thick jungle as the sound grew louder. "I hear it now." Jonah smiled. They all knew now what the sound was.

Suddenly, they emerged from behind some trees and saw a beautiful flowing river. The water rushed past them and sparkled in the sun as it moved. Near the water was a small beach. White sand covered a wide area of embankment. Coincidently, it was the perfect site for a camp.

Annika laughed and ran towards the water. She knelt by the edge of the gushing river and splashed water into her face. Soon Carter joined her and sighed in contentment. The water was cool and clear, a wonderful feeling to a weary traveler.

"This is a welcome sight." Jonah joined them.

Soon they were all at the water's edge, enjoying the refreshing liquid on their hot skin. It was still not safe to drink it without boiling it first though. One look at it and Annika knew it would taste heavenly compared to the swamp water.

Annika looked around at her companions. Jonah and Jack were to her left and Carter and Captain Wolf to her right.

She had just lifted a handful of water when she caught sight of Captain Wolf, and her movement ceased. The water trailed through her fingers and fell to the ground. He had removed his hat and had dunked his head into the water. Upon pulling his head out of the water a sigh escaped his lips. He slicked back stray strands of ebony hair. The long silky strands dripped water onto his shoulders and down his face. A smile was set on his lips, his eyes closed. It was the most peaceful she had seen him since the night she had found him singing.

His handsomeness struck her once again. How was it that his appearance had changed so drastically since their first meeting? She had hated him upon sight then. No thoughts of his looks entered her mind, not until the first time she had caught a real smile from him and it had shaken her impression of him.

Ever since then, he had quickly become an ally, and it was impossible to ignore her feelings any longer. Somewhere along the way she had come to care for him.

He opened his eyes and caught her gaze. He quirked an eyebrow up and gave a questioning look. Annika's cheeks grew pink at being caught staring. Quickly she turned her attention to the water once again and debated on dousing her own head into the cool water, if only to hide her embarrassment.

"Let's camp here for the night." Captain Wolf stood to his feet and planted his hat firmly in place. "I know I talked of walking further but now we have a clean water source."

"You don't have to try and convince me, Cap." Jack's grinning face was dripping with water.

Captain Wolf laughed. "All right then, as long as we are all on the same page."

"I don't think you will hear any argument from us, Captain." Jonah smiled and took the handkerchief from his neck and doused it in the water.

Carter stood to his feet and retrieved the map from his pack. He smiled as he added the new detail of the river and the new camp they would soon set up at its edge.

The next couple of hours went quickly as they set up camp. A fire was started and firewood found to feed the blaze. The men buried some thin tree trunks in the sand and found a way to erect a small roof over their heads. It would not keep any animals out, but it at least offered some sort of protection from the elements.

As the men were setting up camp, Annika looked around for any fruit trees. She did not feel like venturing into the jungle for fear of meeting something far hungrier and less picky than she was. There were no mandaw trees in sight of camp. In fact, she had not seen any on their entire trek. The trees around them seemed quite barren. Defeated, Annika returned back to camp and found the men sitting around the small fire.

"Find any food?" Carter's hopeful eyes found hers.

She shook her head. "Nothing, but I did not go into the jungle. I'm hoping that there's something to pick further in. Would someone go with me?"

"I'll go with you." Jonah stood and stretched to his full height. He was at least two heads taller than she was.

"Thank you." She smiled and led the way to the trees. It surprised Annika that Jonah was the first to volunteer. Throughout their whole journey together, Annika could only recall a handful of times that he had even spoken to her. Perhaps he was hungrier than he had been letting on.

They wound their way around trees and beneath branches, barely dodging vines on the way. It was getting dark out and harder to make out the terrain.

"I find it hard to believe there is nothing here to gather. Although, I don't even remember seeing anything on the way here. Can you?" Annika attempted to start a conversation with the intimidating man. He had never been mean or rude to her. It was his size that made him appear intimidating.

"No. I can assure you, if I had seen something I would have picked it and brought it with us."

Annika peered up a particularly tall tree. Its branches seemed to reach up endlessly. No fruit was hanging from its limbs or any trees nearby. With the setting sun and the little light that could find its way through the branches, the area was growing quite dark.

"You outshooting Maddock was quite impressive." Jonah's blunt words surprised Annika.

"Thank you." She smiled and continued her search.

"How is it that a woman was taught archery? I hear that is not your only skill either." Jonah followed her, not focused on the trees anymore.

"My father taught me." Annika stepped over a large root and ducked under a large leafy plant. "His ideas on how a lady should act were far different than most others. He said that the world is not a safe place, and he wouldn't always be around to protect us. His obvious conclusion was to teach us all the necessary skills to survive and to protect ourselves."

"Us?"

"Yes, my brother and I. He's actually the one I was on my way to meet when we stumbled upon all of you." She imbued her words with a bit of sarcasm.

He smiled but otherwise ignored her tease and continued with his questions. "Is your father with him, or did you leave him behind in the kingdom of Narine?"

Annika's smile faltered and was relieved she was not facing him. "No, my father is not with us anymore." An uncomfortable silence fell over the two of them. "What of you? How did you find yourself to be in Captain Wolf's company?"

"Oh, my father and his were close friends. So we have known each other since we were kids." The amount of loyalty he felt towards his captain was commendable.

They passed a few more trees and still found nothing. "I heard Jack say you all have only been...seamen"—she tried to choose her words carefully—"for a few years. What did you do before then?"

Jonah was quiet for a moment, as if mulling over his response. "We were both still young and living with our families. Jack was as well. Our fathers are no longer with us, so we had nothing to keep us tied to land." It was a very vague answer but that was all she ever seemed to get out of these men. They were very secretive about their past. Though, every pirate was sure to have things to hide. She had to wonder, though, what sort of thing would drive one to become a pirate?

"I see. Well, Captain Wolf is a blessed man indeed to have a loyal friend such as you and the rest of his crew." She cast a smile over her shoulder and thought she saw a small one on his lips as well.

Finally, the pair found a small mandaw tree tucked away in the jungle. It was only a skinny little tree and had a couple skinny fruits hanging from its scraggly vines. Not exactly a meal for them, but at least it was something.

"This will have to be all we bring back. It's getting too dark for us to stay out here any longer." Jonah carried the small bunch of mandaws in one arm.

"I would have to agree." Annika could barely even make out the shapes of trees around them now. If she had been on her own, she doubted she would have made it back. Jonah, however, seemed to have night vision. He walked sure and steady over the uneven terrain while she stumbled.

He held an arm out to her, and she gladly took it. The rest of the way back she kept a firm hold on his arm. It only took a few moments to make it back to camp. Upon emerging from the trees, it was a little bit brighter. That was quickly changing, the sun was shedding its last few rays before sinking low on the horizon.

Annika thanked Jonah and left his side to step closer to the fire, a chill hanging in the air. Her eyes drifted up and found Captain Wolf looking at her with another one of his unreadable expressions. Would she ever be able to decipher the mystery that lay behind his troubled eyes?

CHAPTER THIRTEEN

Ethan anxiously awaited the return of Annika and Jonah. His eyes constantly scanned the trees as Jack and Carter talked around the fire. The sun was rapidly setting, and the temperature was cooling down too. He suddenly appreciated the fire more.

He absently listened to Jack and Carter as his eyes scanned the trees. They had been gone for maybe half an hour now. He had been ready to volunteer to join her when Jonah spoke up. Why his friend wanted to accompany her was a mystery to him. Jonah was never one for small talk, at least around people he did not know.

Finally, he caught sight of them exiting the trees and his heart was finally able to calm down. With danger behind every bend, he was constantly on alert. His eyes caught sight of Annika's hands, which were firmly wrapped around the crook of Jonah's elbow. A hot flame of annoyance shot through his body at the sight.

His annoyance was unexpected and perplexing. What had that been? There was no reason for that to spark his anger. He had no connection to Annika and therefore did not care who's arm she held. If that was indeed true, then why did he still have an uneasy feeling in his stomach?

Annika approached the fire and held her hands up to its warmth. Her gorgeous green eyes found his and he found himself unable to look away for a moment. What was it about her that had him so captivated? She seemed to study him for a moment, as if she was able to read his very thoughts.

A slow smile spread across her face, illuminating her white teeth. "We found some mandaws for supper at least. However, we were only able to find the skinniest of mandaw trees out there. No sight of any other fruit-bearing trees."

He smiled back. "Well, skinny fruit is better than none at all. A mandaw, even a small one, will help get the hard tack down and the dry crackers."

Jack groaned from his spot at the fire. Ethan had almost forgotten Carter and Jack were there. "Oh, I miss having food—real food I mean. Imagine a warm pastry and a hot cup of coffee." Jack closed his eyes and pulled up some distant memory of the food. "I miss having a full stomach. Don't you, Carter?"

A sad smile was on the boy's face. "I'm not bothered by the lack of food."

"How can you say that? I've seen you scarf down any food that's given to you, so you obviously enjoy it. Do you not miss eating to your heart's content?" Jack faced Carter fully now, looking perplexed. Annika seemed to have taken an interest in the conversation and sat listening.

Carter was silent for a moment and looked at Annika. They seemed to be sharing the same thought, their eyes conveying a silent message.

"I can't remember a time where I have been able to eat until my stomach stopped complaining."

"Does Miss Harper not feed her help enough?" Jack grinned in a teasing way. Ethan could read a note of sadness in the air though.

Carter sat up straighter, defiance in his eyes. "Not at all! Annika is the only good thing in my life. If it wasn't for her, the orphanage would have been a suffocating place." That knocked the grin off of Jack's face. The air was filled with silence as they all took in Carter's words.

Ethan had thought that Annika had been a wealthy woman traveling with a servant. He never would have guessed they had both come from an orphanage. Ethan looked at Annika, whose face was turning pink. She did not look angry, only embarrassed.

"It's true." She sighed and broke the silence. "We just left the orphanage a couple weeks ago. Carter and I have known each other for a long time. When my brother, in Lookonia, sent for me, I knew I had to bring Carter. The ticket allowed for me and a servant to go so that's what Carter became, though in name only." Her eyes had become sad.

Jonah, who had also found a seat around the fire, held a half-eaten mandaw in his still hands. Jack's normally bright face had become solemn.

Ethan thought back to the time the two of them had said they had never tasted a mandaw before. It made more sense now that he knew they were from an orphanage. It was a place known for feeding their children little and treating them as slaves. Orphanages had earned themselves a bad reputation; some people felt dirty even mentioning the place.

"It wasn't all bad, though." Carter smiled at Annika, the brotherly love on his face apparent. "I don't remember anything outside of the orphanage, but as soon as Annika came things weren't so bad. She taught us reading and mathematics. Why, she even taught us how to defend ourselves." His hand went to the sword on his side. "What's more is she brought us all together. We became more of a family."

Annika's eyes had begun to water as she smiled at Carter. Ethan had never seen a tear form on her face. The sight of her moved to tears for some reason caused Ethan to feel choked up. Had he really never seen her cry?

"I was considered an orphan too." Jack's quiet admission surprised Ethan. He knew it was true, but Jack was not known for bringing up his past. "My ma died when I was just a baby and when I was ten my pa up and left. With no family of my own, I was considered an orphan. I wandered the streets, looking for food. I met Jonah's pa and was taken in. I was lucky to find a family who cared for me." He looked up at Carter and Annika with a sad smile on his face.

A sense of camaraderie seemed to fall upon the three. Carter, Jack, and Annika all smiled at one another. In a way, Ethan supposed, everyone around this fire had suffered the same kind of loss. He was not arrogant enough to say his pain was worse than theirs, but he did know the feeling of loss and betrayal. He and Jonah had both lost their fathers, practically at the same time.

"Since we will be in each other's presence a lot from here on out, I would appreciate being called Annika. I don't believe we have the need for formality in this place." She smiled sheepishly at them. "Truth be told, I'm not used to formality anyways."

Jack chuckled. "We aren't either. It would be an honor to call you Annika. Our captain has already been bestowed that honor it seems." He threw a crooked smile at Ethan.

Annika turned her dazzling smile to him. "Well, he never did ask for my permission, but I feel as though he doesn't do that often."

Ethan shrugged his shoulders and smiled.

"You know what though? I've gotten used to it. I believe it would be weird to hear you call me anything else."

He stared into her green eyes and saw sincerity behind them. When he had first met her, he had thought to put her in her place by giving himself permission to call her whatever he liked. Plus, it had riled her so badly and he enjoyed that. Now he realized she hadn't complained about him calling her by her first name. It just came naturally to him and honestly it had felt good to know that he was the only one, other than Carter, who had that privilege.

The two exchanged smiles, a deeper emotion hidden just below the surface. Silence fell over the group again, save for the crackling of the fire and the chirping of crickets. An owl hooted in the distance.

"Well, I don't know about you all, but I could use some supper and entertainment." Jack replaced his smile and tried to lighten the mood.

They passed around some hard tack and crackers. There were just enough mandaws for them to have two apiece. The second one would be saved for breakfast.

"Would anyone like to hear a story?" Jack's eyes came alive again. They all nodded enthusiastically, eager to bring joy back into the dark night. "I will tell the tale I heard from Stew the other night."

"Is this the tale I heard the others mention as a story for babies?" Jonah's dry humor brought a smile to Ethan's face.

"Well, I thought it was a daring tale with a gripping ending. How about you just listen and tell me what you think after." Jack grinned and sat forward on his seat. "Have you ever heard the stories passed down from our ancestors that spoke of the Ancient creatures that used to walk the earth and swim the seas?"

Ethan knew the stories well, as his father would frequently tell them. The strange cat-like creature had been one of those stories. A shiver ran down his spine at the memory of their recent encounter with it. That story did not do the animal enough justice. It was far more terrifying in real life.

"Well, it's said that we used to share our earth with some of the most unusual creatures ever created. We call them the Ancients. At the height of man's climb to dominance over the earth, we got greedy and destroyed the Ancients. Soon they all died out and became just the stories we hear about today. Well, somewhere, in the murky waters of the kingdom of Lookonia, is said to be one of those creatures still living. Its reputation for sinking fishing boats and pulling men overboard caused panic to spread. It's said that this particular area of the sea has the best currents and the strongest winds, cutting the length of your journey in half if you dare to enter its waters. That is, if you survive the journey.

"A young man from Lookonia had precious cargo in the hold of his ship. It's said that the kingdom of Nesher, the northern kingdom, wished to buy his cargo. He was tasked by his father to make safe passage to Nesher. He knew the ocean was riddled with pirates and was terrified of his shipment being taken from him. This brave soul was not one to believe in stories of monsters. He thought them better told for children on their mothers' laps, as we know some who agree." Jack cast a teasing look at Jonah, who just shook his head and chuckled.

"If this sailor could just make his way through the unknown waters of legend, he would get to his destination in no time at all. The waters were rarely traveled, for fear of the legend. So there would be little chance of encountering any pirates on the journey. His boat laden with riches and his mind full of hope, he set out into the uncharted waters. If only he knew what dangers awaited him.

"The long journey ahead passed by without a problem. The skies were clear and the waters smooth. The young man had quite decidedly made up his mind about the false nature of the legends. The currents pulled his boat forward while the winds eagerly helped them on. It was indeed the fastest way and definitely the most deserted one as well.

"One evening, as day was turning to dusk, an ominous feeling fell over the crew. In the distance, a dark blanket seemed to cover the ocean. The bright daylight would soon disappear when they entered the darkness. There was no way around. They had to plunge forward. As darkness descended, the only light they had was from lanterns. With the darkness came the silence. It stretched on for hours as they all waited. For what, they did not know. No one could have prepared for the storm that hit them. It came out of nowhere and turned the calm into chaos. Men had to fight just to stand up on their own feet."

Ethan's thoughts raced their own experience onboard a vessel such as that. Images from the fateful night ran through his mind. Annika's sorrowful eyes met his; she was thinking of the same thing.

Jack continued on, unfazed. "The boat swayed from side to side violently. All feared that they would soon meet their ends in the dark depths. When suddenly"—Jack held his palms in the air dramatically, causing a wry smile to cross Ethan's face—"the storm stopped. All was calm, too calm. Behind them was a wall of storms and lightning. It stretched on for miles and encircled this area of complete calm. In the center was a large rock structure, its sharp edges jutting into the sky.

"Everyone held their breath, waiting. When suddenly they were attacked from below. *Bang!* Something hit the ship. Then again and again. With each hit, the ship jolted and groaned. Finally ,the attack stopped. The sight that greeted them next would strike fear into the hardest of hearts.

"A large head came up out of the water and stretched high into the sky. The creature's neck was as tall as a tree and much broader. The head was bigger than a man and the mouth gaped open, smoke billowing out. The eyes glowed a sinister yellow and its teeth glistened in the sun.

"That is the last time those sailors were ever seen. They sank below to their watery graves. Legends say that Nesher has not been seen or heard of since for no one braves the journey or lives to tell the tale." His voice had dropped low as he whispered the ending.

"If they all died, how do we know any of the story is true?" Carter crossed his arms and smiled.

"You don't. It's just a story, of course." Jack laughed.

"Well, I'd like to think someone did survive and lived to spread the tale."

"That is possible, Carter. Parts of the story are true. The legend of a monster is very true. I could point to you the exact spot between Lookonia and Nesher that is known for monster sightings. Everyone says it's just a legend, but they stay away all the same."

"My grandad said he saw something in its waters," Jonah piped up, smiling. "He said the sight of it drove him from being a sailor and he decided to take a job inland." Everyone laughed at that.

Ethan smiled. It was good to smile and feel at peace. Peace was something that he rarely found these days. Memories from his past always seemed to haunt him. Nights like tonight gave him hope.

The rest of the evening was spent sharing more stories and having a good laugh. It was surprising how well they all got along after such a short amount of time together. Jack volunteered to take first watch for the night then Jonah would take second. Ethan was to take the last watch of the night.

He used one of his shirts as a pillow and covered up with the blanket he had brought along. Surprisingly, it did not take long for him to fall asleep. All too soon Jonah was shaking him awake, signaling it was time for his turn to stand watch.

Ethan attempted to rub the sleep from his eyes as he walked around camp. The gentle breathing from his companions a welcome sound in the quiet night. The fire was beginning to dwindle, so he threw in some new branches. Annika groaned, capturing his attention. She rolled over, still sleeping, and stretched her arms above her head. It reminded him of something a young child would do. He smiled, finding her even more endearing and chastising himself for that.

She rolled from side to side a couple of times before she finally opened her eyes. Her green eyes found his and she smiled. The sweet smile brought a gentle tug on his heart.

"Can't sleep?" he asked quietly as she joined him at the fire.

She shook her head and stretched her arms. "No. Unfortunately, sleep seems to be escaping me. Actually, I have need to use...well, to be in private for a moment." A sheepish smile crossed her face.

"Of course. I'll walk with you to the nearest bushes. I'd really rather not have you going out on your own at night."

"Thank you. I have to admit, the jungle is a bit terrifying at night so I would greatly appreciate your company." Her smile was contagious. What was it about this girl that made him want to lower the walls around his heart?

They walked down the sandy beach a little ways to a small cluster of bushes. "This island may be dangerous, but it has its good moments, does it not?" Her gentle voice called for his attention. He suddenly realized that Annika had stopped walking. She stood about five feet behind him, her head tilted back.

Ethan looked up and saw just a normal night sky overhead. "To what do you refer?"

She turned and looked at him, incredulous. "Do your eyes not see the bright stars and the heavenly display? Why, it's something out of a book really. I've seen stars before, but they seem to shine brighter here."

Ethan turned his eyes again to the sky, trying to find the beauty she saw. He wanted to be as captivated as she was, but he only saw the same stars as normal. He was quite used to the sight.

"I suppose I am boring compared to you or perhaps just used to it. I don't see the display you are describing."

"When I look at Your heavens, the work of Your fingers, the moon and the stars, which You have set in place, what is man that you are mindful of him, and the son of man that You care for him?" The passage spilled from her lips easily. The verse sounded familiar. A distant memory beckoned him before he shook it away.

"Sorry." She smiled. "It's a verse my father loved. He used to take me outside late at night, when my mother and

brother were already asleep, and show me the stars. He used to tell me that verse all the time." Her eyes grew misty as she thought of her own distant memory.

"What would he show you?"

"He would teach us the constellations and their names. There are constellations that look like animals and almost anything else you can think of. I don't remember a lot of them now. It's been so long since he told us." Her eyes scanned the sky and excitement entered her face. "See those stars up there? There are three bright stars surrounded by a bunch of smaller ones."

Ethan looked but could not find the specific stars she spoke of. Annika came closer and gently touched his arm and pointed again. He was closer to her hand now and finally saw what she was referring to.

"Yes, yes I do see them."

"Good, those stars form a constellation my father told me about. It's a symbol that often is used to portray Elohim. It's a roaring lion. The bright stars are the lion's eyes and nose and mouth. The dimmer ones are the mane of the lion."

Ethan vaguely remembered his own father teaching him the very same thing years ago. His father's hands had held him and told him of stories from the scriptures as they studied the stars. Funny how that happy memory had remained hidden from him until now.

"Those three bright stars were always special to my father." A sad smile crossed her face. "He used to say that the star on the left was supposed to signify my mother and the one on the right was his star. In the middle, the brightest star, was Elohim. He held them both together and was the center of their relationship."

"Your father sounds like a good man."

"I had thought so too." A cloud of anger touched upon her face before she buried it beneath another smile. "My, I really need that bush now." She continued walking and Ethan followed. What had her father done that caused her such sorrow?

They came upon a hedge of bushes a short walk down the sandy beach. Both tall enough and thick enough to work.

"Is this suitable enough for you? I can still see camp from here."

Annika quickly took in the height of the bushes. "Yes, I believe they will work fine. Please, if you wouldn't mind, just turn your back."

"Of course." He turned his back to the bushes and heard her rustle through them.

As he waited for her, his eyes were drawn to the sky. Somehow, the stars seemed to twinkle more brightly to him. The sky, which he had gotten so used to, suddenly seemed alive and brighter than he had ever seen it. The stars themselves could not have changed. No, it had to be his perception of them had shifted. Strange how a few words from Annika had suddenly brought light back into the night for him.

Suddenly, he heard a fearful gasp followed by a thud in the sand. He turned around and saw nothing in the bushes. "Annika? Are you all right?"

"I think you should see this, Captain."

Ethan pushed through the bushes and found Annika sitting on the ground, staring at the sand. She did not look particularly frightened, just shocked and—was that sadness?

Her eyes met his. "Look at this."

Ethan bent down with her on the sand and saw what had startled her. A skull was laying in the sand. It was a human skull, and it was not alone. The two of them silently looked on, too shocked to speak. The beach was littered with skeletons, half buried in the sand. Some of them still had clothes on while others were bare. All of it had remained hidden from sight because of the bushes.

"What happened to them?" Annika's voice was barely a whisper.

"I don't know." Ethan held out a hand to help her stand up. Their eyes were still riveted on the grisly scene in front of them. A few long moments stretched on before Ethan realized he still held her hand. Surprisingly she had not let go and might have actually moved a little closer to his side.

"Perhaps you should go back to camp." Ethan looked back at camp and saw all was still well. Everyone remained sleeping around the fire. "I would like to take a closer look."

Annika shook her head. "No, I'd like to stay. I'm just as curious as you are."

Ethan nodded and walked into the mass grave, still holding Annika's hand. She willingly followed his lead and stuck close to his side.

Upon first sight, it looked like there was at least twenty men here. Skeletons lay in pristine condition. Some were complete, while others were missing a leg or some other extremity. In the middle of the throng of it all was a bright colored coat, the red faded from its time in the sun. A wide-brimmed hat, similar to Ethan's, lay in the sand. The skeleton of the man must lay beneath the sand.

"What could have caused such devastation?" Annika half hid behind his arm and looked at the bright coat. Her shaky breathing had steadied now. Her concerned eyes roved over the beach.

"I can't be certain. It could be a number of things. Disease, starvation, animal attack, that's just to name a few." He examined the bodies as well as he could with the moonlight. "All these skeletons here are exposed. The sand is not covering them. Yet, their lower halves are completely gone." He bent and examined them. Annika bent down with him. Having her so close was beginning to make it difficult to focus. The death surrounding him made it possible to shake most of those feelings off for the moment.

"The spines are completely severed." He was shocked, it would take a lot to sever a spine like this. "Something happened to these men. Something with enough brute force to completely slice the bone."

"Like an animal?"

"I don't know anything with enough power to do all this." The sheer amount of men who died struck him. So many lives had been lost. "This island is anything but ordinary, though, as we have already witnessed. Whatever it is, I'm not interested in sticking around to find out. At first light we will head out."

Annika nodded from behind him. He turned to face her and found his eyes only inches from her own. Bright green eyes looked back at him, surprised. Her eyes were the color of emeralds but richer, if that was even possible. They were filled with an emotion he couldn't quite understand. Did she feel what he was feeling? He was sure if he looked into them long enough he would fall for her completely. He cleared his throat and turned his face away, his face hot for some reason.

"Let's head back to camp and tell everyone about this."

"Yes, of course." Once they had gone through the bushes Annika let go of his hand. As soon as her soft hand slipped from his grasp, he missed the warmth.

She walked ahead of him, her steps quickening. Had he said something wrong?

The next hour was spent in a blur. Upon waking everyone up, they ate a quick breakfast and gathered their supplies. Jack and Jonah wanted to witness the mass grave before embarking. Ethan decided to stay back and let them take a look without him. He had already seen enough.

Soon, they were on their way. It was decided to go up river. If they went down river, they would eventually come to the beach. More than likely, Chris had made it this far on the beach. Which would make upriver a better spot for them to explore. When they were ready to head back to the others they would go down the river, just in case Chris had missed something.

The loud noise of the river diminished and left an eerie quiet in its place. With the rising of the sun, the heat was relentless. He couldn't complain too much, though. At least now they were walking out in the open, not cutting through the jungle. Plus, they had cool water nearby should they really need to cool off.

That did nothing to stop the relentless heat and humidity in the air. Soon, their clothing was soaked with sweat again. It seemed impossible to have dry clothing on this island.

Suddenly, a sound entered their ears. It was another roar from the river but all around them seemed calm. Upon rounding a bend in the river, they found the source, stopping them all in their tracks.

CHAPTER FOURTEEN

G listening water crashed gracefully into a pristine lake, causing a gentle roar. The mist from the falls almost made it sparkle. The scene in front of them felt like a dream. It was by far the prettiest spot Annika had seen thus far. Even the birds chirping ahead sounded more peaceful. The sun gleamed on the surface of the waters, as if it beckoned them to enter.

"It's beautiful." Annika was fairly breathless as she took in the sight before her. A large bird landed in the water and swam around. The sun shone through the mist of the falls, causing a beautiful rainbow of light.

Annika laughed and ran towards the water, pulling off her shoes and weapons. She entered the water and sank deep, up to her neck. The cool water tickled her skin and almost took her breath away. It was the most wonderful feeling. It was somehow different than the river yesterday. Perhaps it was the shorter walk, or maybe the otherworldly look of the place. The water had a bright green hue to it, but it looked incredibly clean.

Splashing near her took her attention; the men had splashed in behind her.

Jack dove into the water and came back up again, shaking his wet hair. Carter followed Jack and dove right in, laying on his back and swimming about. Jonah ran in and just sank under the water, bubbles appearing on the surface. After a few seconds he reappeared, smiling from ear to ear. Captain Wolf stood on the edge of the lake, watching them with a smile. His eyes scanned their surroundings, always on alert.

"Come on in, Captain," Annika called to him. His eyes swerved to hers. "Or are you afraid to have fun?" Her eyes teased his. A smile slowly spread across his handsome face. He took off his hat and shoes and left them on the beach. His weapons were also left behind in the sand. The whole time he never took his eyes off hers. She stood captivated by his gaze. He slowly entered the water, men splashing all around him, and walked towards her.

Captain Wolf stopped a few feet away from her, the water about his waist, and smiled as he dipped below the surface. Water engulfed his head and bubbles came to the surface of the water. Soon, he reemerged, his shoulder length black hair dripping with water and his black eyes sparkling. The pure joy on his face took her aback, as did his charming good looks. He ran a hand through his hair as he tilted his head back and looked at the sky, he sighed. Legs kicking, he pushed himself into deeper water. When his eyes opened and he found her staring, he smiled. His smile reached clear down to her toes. She gave a sheepish smile and went under the water as well.

Everyone enjoyed a few moments of bliss, cooling off in the water, then made their way to the bank. They found a spot in the shade of a large tree to set up camp. The tree was large. In fact, it could really only be described as massive. If they all linked arms, they would more than likely barely reach all the way around it. It was so tall and the branches so wide. The tree had vibrant green leaves and held an abundance of life. Birds called to one another, causing a beautiful song to fill the air.

Captain Wolf turned and put a hand on his hip. "I think it would be wise to make this our campsite for the day. If we use this place as our base to return to, we could get a lot of exploring done and still have a bed to return to. Does anyone have any objections to that?"

"Have you seen this place? We would have to be crazy to willingly leave here." Jack grinned and reclined on one of the large roots from the tree.

Everyone agreed with the plan, so they began setting up camp. They managed to get a fire started, despite the dampness all around them. Annika stood in front of the fire, hoping to dry her drenched clothes and hair.

Jack and Carter took some fishing poles and started fishing, hoping to catch something for supper. If they couldn't catch anything, it would be hard tack and crackers again.

Captain Wolf and Jonah worked on making a suitable shelter. Something that would stand strong for the few nights they would be here.

Annika was tasked with finding supplies needed for the shelter. Palm tree leaves and bamboo were the most needed and the easiest to find. The island seemed to be made of the things.

Annika explored the trees at the edge of their small camp, intent on discovering the much-needed supplies. It did not take her long to find some palm tree leaves. They were at least two feet across and strong. She gathered armfuls of the leaves and began transporting them to the men.

Several trips later, she found some good shoots of bamboo. Those would be a much bigger chore to move, as the sturdy stocks would take some effort to cut down. She focused on moving a few more batches of palm leaves.

The sight of a familiar tree shot joy into her heart and made her mouth water. A large mandaw tree was towering over her head, its branches laden with ripe fruit. Right next to the mandaw tree was another tree with a fruit she actually recognized from Narine. It was an angel fruit tree. The name had always been a mystery. Why would you name such a bland tasting fruit after an angel? Regardless, it was edible and tasted far better than hard tack.

The fruit was far too tempting to not pick an armful and take it back to camp. After she dropped the fruit off with the men she decided to tackle the task of cutting bamboo.

Suddenly the hair on the back of her neck pricked up. The same feeling she had felt when the tiger had ambushed her. A quick glance about her yielding no reason for concern. Still the feeling remained, leaving her uneasy.

"Is everything all right, Annika?" Captain Wolf came up behind her. Annika, startled, whirled around and ran straight into his chest. His hands caught her shoulders and helped steady her. "My, aren't we jumpy." He chuckled.

Annika attempted to smile but the heat on her face was hindering her.

Captain Wolf's face turned serious. "Are you all right?" His eyes scanned the trees, looking for signs of danger. All Annika could think of were the hands he still had on her arms and how close she stood to him.

"No, I'm fine." She stepped away from him and smoothed back some strands of hair that had come loose from her braid. "I'm sorry, I didn't see you there."

"Are you sure? You look rather flustered." The concern on his face was touching. Annika did not feel like telling him the reason for the warmth in her face. That would be an awkward conversation to be sure.

"No, I'm fine. Thank you. I was actually just about to go get some bamboo."

"Let me help you. I've got the machete for it." He grinned and held up the weapon. He deftly swung the machete a few times in the air in an impressive display.

"Most impressive. How long did you practice that?" She grinned teasingly.

He flexed his right arm dramatically. "It just comes naturally." They both laughed. She led him to the bamboo and with Captain Wolf's fast machete work and Annika hauling, it did not take long to collect enough for the shelter.

By the time evening came around, they had a wonderful shelter put up. Someone had hung a rope in the tree and had created a canopy over their heads with several strands of the rope. The ropes were tied to a bamboo frame and the roof was made from palm fronds. The walls were a mixture of both, protecting them from the outside to a certain degree. It had three walls, as the fourth side was left open to get heat from the fire which was nearby. It was impressive, actually, that they had been able to accomplish so much in such a short amount of time.

Captain Wolf had gone to check on Jack and Carter's progress with the fishing. That left Jonah and Annika to stay around the fire. She took a mandaw and bit into the sweet fruit. From her spot around the fire, she could still see the boys at the water's edge through the leaves on the shelter.

"You are all so close. You are more like a family I would say," she spoke out loud, breaking the silence. Jonah turned his attention off sharpening the blade of his knife momentarily. "For a pirate, Captain Wolf has a lot of good friends. Which is so unlike what I have heard a pirate is like."

"What have you heard of pirates?" A teasing smile lit Jonah's face.

"Oh, I don't know, mainly stories of their cruelty and viciousness. How they care only for themselves and lining their own pockets." She leaned forward and added quietly, "I have even heard stories of pirates making people walk the plank or swim with man-eating serpents."

Jonah chuckled and took a good look at his knife before replacing it back in its sheath. "So, you have heard of the exact opposite of us and our captain."

"I don't understand why he is different, though. May I speak frankly?" At Jonah's nod, she continued, "You started out as our enemies and since then have become what I would call friends. Your men seem to be more trustworthy than Captain Samuel's and your captain treats you like his own blood. What am I missing? How could you all take from hardworking men when everything I see suggests you could never do that?"

Jonah stayed quiet for a moment. Had she offended him? It was something she had been wondering about for a long time but had not possessed the courage to ask until now. Now that she had finally asked, she was almost afraid of the answer.

"There's a lot you don't know about the captain." He locked his serious eyes onto hers. "He's not your common pirate."

"I am becoming increasingly aware of that fact." Annika laid the mandaw aside for the moment.

"I can only imagine the confusion you must be in, for you know not the full story. Captain Wolf is the kind of man who prefers to leave his life a mystery to most. Though, I believe he will open up to someone someday. Someone that he can open his heart to and share the aching from within." He sighed and added another small log to the ever-growing blaze. "Sadly, I know I cannot help him with his grief, but I pray someday Elohim will send someone his way."

"I had no idea you were a believer, Jonah." Annika looked at him, incredulous.

He laughed. "No, I'm sure you thought the only god a pirate could worship would be treasure. Actually, Captain Wolf used to believe as well. His past haunts him too vividly at the moment for him to see clearly, however."

"What about his past haunts him so?" Annika leaned forward on her seat.

"That's all you're getting from me. That is for the captain to share if he so chooses. What I will tell you is Captain Wolf paid your captain back for everything he took. Plus extra for the loss of his ship."

His words shocked Annika. She sat frozen for a moment, her mind trying to make sense of what her ears had heard.

"Paid him back? What do you mean? Surely, you're jesting."

"No, it's true. Captain Wolf has his reasons for taking, but he would not do so at the expense of hurting others. The only one he wishes to hurt would be the crown." He looked quickly at the others, who still stood by the river. "Don't go spreading that around either. The captain wants to keep his fierce reputation known to all. But I believe, even if he doesn't know it yet, that he would want you to know. I want you to know, the captain is the most honorable man I have ever met." He turned back to the fire, gave it another poke, he seemed satisfied with his work and leaned over to grab a mandaw.

How could what he said be true? If it was true, then everything she knew about Captain Wolf was completely wrong. She had been basing her opinion of him greatly on his stealing from poor sailors. Other than his supposed thieving, she knew him to be an honorable man, albeit one that liked to rile her. Everything she knew of the man needed to be rewritten.

If he didn't steal and instead paid them for their goods, what did that make him? Why would he do it? He could make off with their things and not get caught.

"Why would he do that? Why does he care to pay them back? If he doesn't want to steal, then he could just buy the goods after they dock." Her question brought Jonah's attention back from the fire.

"There are many things only the captain could tell you. He has his secrets. I will tell you that he makes no profit on the goods." He finished off the mandaw and threw the core into the fire. "That's all I can tell you." He stood and looked at her with a serious expression. "Don't tell Cap that I told you any of this." Annika could only nod her head in response.

Jonah walked away, leaving Annika alone with her thoughts. None of this made any sense. You don't become a pirate just to pay people for what you take. Surely, Jonah had said it as a sort of joke. She couldn't even ask Captain Wolf if it were true. If it was, she was not meant to know it. If it was a lie he would laugh in her face.

"Annika!" Carter's excited cry reached her ears, pulling her back to the present. He came slowly towards her, holding a large fish. He could barely carry it. He was bent over with his burden. Jack walked behind Carter, a grin spreading across his face.

"Did you see me? I caught this beauty all on my own." Carter dropped the fish on the ground and stood taller, proud of his catch.

"My aching back and stinging fingers say otherwise." Jack laughed.

"Well," Carter said, kicking the dirt with the toe of his boot, "I may have had some help ,but it was my catch to begin with."

"That is quite the haul!" Annika smiled and looked the fish over. "Stew would be quite jealous."

"Do you mind moving this to the river again?" She pulled out her dagger and turned to the young men. Carter saluted and bent back over to carry his fish.

Once it was back at the river, the boys left her to do her work. She began gutting the fish, enjoying the familiarity. Her father had taught her from a young age, how to catch, kill, and cook the food she found. That included gutting which, although a grotesque and messy business, was second nature to her now.

"Wherever did you come from?"

A familiar voice broke into her thoughts. Annika glanced up to find Captain Wolf standing above her, watching, a charming grin on his rugged face.

"I don't know what you mean." She tried to turn her attention back to the fish. Her thoughts on the man before her hadn't become clear yet.

"You are quite efficient with a bow, dagger and from what I hear, swordplay as well. Now I find you gutting a fish. Most women wouldn't even watch, let alone do it themselves." He sat down on the ground next to her, his leg only inches from her skirt.

"If you must know." She finished up her work with the fish, cleaned her hands in the river and then sat back once again. "My father taught me. He said it was only right for a woman to know how to get along in the world that she was born into. He taught my brother and I all he knew." Annika tried to keep her eyes busy, looking everywhere but at the handsome man beside her.

"He sounds like a wise man."

A lump formed in her throat, what kind of wise man would do what her father had? She closed her eyes and scolded herself for allowing the pain to come to the surface again. It had been years since he had left. It should not bother her so badly now. Then why did it still ache as badly as the day he had turned his back and walked away?

"I'm sorry, was it something I said?" His concerned voice brought tears to her eyes.

"No, no it's nothing." She opened her eyes and blinked away her tears. "There's not much to tell. He taught us so much, and for that I will always be grateful to him. When it came down to it, though, he left us." Her voice was almost monotone, as she tried to hide her emotion. "We both wound up in an orphanage. My brother left to pursue his passion for ministry. Which is where I am heading now."

"I heard you speak of the orphanage last night. Had you really never left since you entered its walls?"

"I'm sad to say that is true. I was, of course, allowed into the courtyard but town was extremely off limits." Memories of the lonely days and what she and the children had faced flooded her mind.

"I'm terribly sorry. A father should never leave his children, let alone willingly. Perhaps he had good reason for it."

Her features hardened. "Perhaps, but I will never know." She shook her head and stood up.

"I lost my father too." His quiet submission surprised her.

Perhaps she could learn more about him now. Her mind was full of unanswered questions about the man before her. "I'm so sorry. Has it been long?"

"A few years now." His eyes were downcast. The pain evident on his face. "I just wanted you to know I'm not oblivious to the pain of losing someone you love." His smile was sad, something Annika had not seen from him before other than in those stolen moments. The sight of it now, here for her, was enough to make her own eyes water. Suddenly, he stood to his feet and brushed dirt and dried grass from his pants. "Well, enough of this sad talk. Let's get this fish to the fire, shall we?"

"Absolutely." They shared a smile.

"I hope we are able to get some meat off this fish. I have seen better cleaning jobs, but I suppose this will do." His tease brightened the mood, and she punched him lightly in the arm. They both laughed and headed for the fire.

If Annika had been unsure of her feelings before it was even worse now. This "pirate" or whatever he was, was a mystery to her. One thing she knew for certain was the more she knew of him, the harder it was going to be to leave him.

A short while later, the fish was cooked and ready to eat. The hungry group looked at it, their mouths watering. They had hung it on a stick suspended over the fire. Annika removed it from the fire and cut off a piece of the warm fish.

"Here's the first piece, for Carter, who caught it." She handed it to Carter then cut a second piece. "And a piece for Jack, the muscle behind the catch." Her eyes danced as she teased the two. They both laughed and sunk their teeth into their portions.

Everyone else took a piece and sat down to enjoy it. Sighs and words of delight were on everyone's lips. It had been a while since they had eaten so much, and the fish was delicious. After their bellies were full, they sat back to look at the stars, which were shining in the dark expanse above.

The smoke from the fire dissipated into the starry sky. It was a pleasant aroma of fresh wood and of the wonderful fish they had eaten.

"Cap, what shall we be doing from here on? Do you think we are safe here?" Jack's voice cut into the peaceful moment, bringing their minds back to the present. Annika's thoughts went to the skeletons they had found.

"I've wondered that myself. We found fresh water, but it won't do the crew any good. We carried as much water as we could and used it all up in the time we spent coming here. So we cannot bring back water for them." Captain Wolf reclined on his back, propped up with one arm. He twirled a twig between his fingers. "We set out to find people, which we still haven't accomplished. Perhaps we will find someone close by, this place is far too beautiful for the natives of this island, if there are any, not to know of it." Captain Wolf threw the twig and glanced around the group. "I'm open to suggestions."

"We could even bring the crew here, once they are healed." Jonah still stared at the sky as he spoke.

"I'm hoping to not be here that long." Captain Wolf shook his head. "But if we are then that might not be a bad idea."

Annika watched as a star twinkled overhead and shot across the sky. She had no ideas about what the correct path to take was. She knew nothing of the best path to take. Thank goodness she was not in a role of leadership. What a heavy burden it must be.

She wasn't even sure why Elohim had let this happen in the first place. Ever since they had become stranded here, she had felt so lost. It had been the right choice to leave but she didn't know what direction to take. Even the job Mathew wanted to give her didn't seem right. Helping children was definitely one of her passions, but her heart felt attached to the sea now.

She took a quick glance at Captain Wolf, the firelight casting shadows across his handsome face. Even her feelings for a certain pirate were uncertain but growing by the day.

The silence seemed to engulf the group as they sat around the fire. No one spoke for a while, their own thoughts overwhelming them.

Despite being stuck in a dangerous situation, Annika couldn't help but feel grateful. Because of all the problems they had faced, she had met some really great people. Regardless of their less than legal occupation, they had time and time again shown their honor. They could have left them stranded and sinking. That hadn't happened, and now Captain Wolf treated everyone as one of his own crew mates and respected Captain Samuel. Not just anyone would do that, Annika imagined, much less a pirate. Regardless, if the information Jonah had given her was true, these men were not your everyday pirates. Each one of them was becoming quite dear to her heart and, so she imagined, to Carter's as well.

Annika stole another look at the captain to find his eyes were already on her. She felt heat flood her cheeks, and she was sure this time that it was not the fire. There was no more denying her growing feelings for this man. What had started as hate had blossomed into something different, something warm and exciting. Was it growing friendship that she was feeling for him? That couldn't be it. She didn't feel this was about Jack or Jonah. Was it something deeper? If so, she would have to rein those feelings in. This was a man who belonged on the ocean, no fear of the unknown and no ties that would keep him from it. He surely would not accept or reciprocate her feelings.

"Did you, by chance, bring an instrument, Captain? Such as a guitar?" Annika's voice broke through the silence, surprising everyone who had grown accustomed to the quiet.

"How did you know?" His eyes shone with surprise.

"You just look the sort of man who would play." Annika shrugged her shoulders with the lie and gave him a smile to suggest she had a reason for knowing. "The guitar is also sticking out of your pack. Somewhat hard to miss that."

"I'm not that good at it." He actually looked shy. This man who had stared danger down with a cocky smile now looked shy and embarrassed.

"Sure you are, Cap," Jack chimed in. "You play for us all the time." He earned a glare from Captain Wolf.

"Yes, but you are stuck with me."

Was he nervous to play for her? Annika smiled at the thought.

"Well, I'm kind of stuck with you too," Her teasing voice called his attention back to her. "You could think of me as one of your men."

"Now that is impossible." His warm smile melted her insides. "I will play for you, if you insist." He pulled out a small instrument from his bag. "Any requests?"

"How about something upbeat?" Jonah leaned forward on his seat atop a log.

Captain Wolf obliged, playing a fun tune that Annika didn't recognize. Captain Wolf closed his eyes as he played, his fingers deftly strumming and creating a beautiful sound.

"May I have this dance?" Jack stood in front of her and held his hand out.

She stood and curtsied. "You may." She laughed with him as they danced in front of the fire. The dance was fast-paced to match the tune of the song. Jonah brought out two sticks and banged a log to the beat as Jack twirled her around. They jumped and moved about the place. Annika's braid whipped about her as she moved. She lifted their hands in the air and spun once again, looking up into the sky. As she turned, she caught sight of Captain Wolf playing, his eyes were now watching her as he played.

"May I have a turn?" Jonah came up to Jack and her. Jack grinned and gave an exaggerated bow. She began to dance with Jonah now. The song had changed slightly. The tune was different now, almost faster and Annika didn't recognize it. She danced at least three more songs, taking turns with Jack, Jonah and Carter. All the while she felt Captain Wolf's intense gaze on her.

Finally, Annika could dance no more. Her legs threatened to buckle, and her breathing was labored. Oh, but she had such fun. It was the most she had smiled in a long while. She turned, grinning at Captain Wolf. His piercing eyes cut through the fire and seized her heart. A small smile crossed his face as he played. He ended the song and the night seemed to echo the final note.

"You play beautifully!" Annika grinned at him.

"I'm glad you found it enjoyable."

"Oh, immensely! You are quite accomplished. Will you play another?" Her eager eyes begged his. His face transformed into a look she was growing accustomed to but couldn't quite name.

His smile was gentle and warm as he began to play another song. This one was slower but still upbeat. This time he accompanied his playing with some singing. Jack and Jonah seemed to know the song as well for they joined him. Their voices blended beautifully, creating a harmonious sound. Annika sat, enjoying every moment of it.

The song was about a group of sailors who loved nothing more than to sail. Each verse spoke of their trials and the joys of sailing. Jack's voice was higher than the others while Jonah's was very deep. They added a lot of depth to the song, but their voices just accompanied Captain Wolf's. His voice brought the whole song together. His was deep but not like Jonah's. His voice was smooth like silk and somehow sounded even better than when she had heard him on the ship.

Once she had gotten the lyrics memorized, which didn't take long because the lyrics were simple and repeated, Annika joined in. Carter joined soon after her. Annika was not a wonderful singer she thought, but she enjoyed it immensely. The group swayed as they sang. Soon the song ended, and Captain Wolf began playing another.

"He writes most of the songs he plays," Jonah leaned towards her and whispered. "This one must be new. I don't recognize it."

Annika was shocked to hear that Captain Wolf had written the songs. He continued to surprise her. The song that he played now was a slow tune. It spoke of beauty in the fading rays of the sun and the twinkling stars of the night. He then went on to sing about beauty in the eyes of a woman. Captain Wolf looked around the fire at them all, but his eyes wandered to hers the most. If he had written this song too, he had really outdone himself. The words and his voice made them all sit in silence, entranced.

The song continued to flow. The lyrics spoke of fiery green eyes and lovely hair. That detail struck her, for right as he said it, the captain's eyes had found hers. The lyrics and the way he looked at her gave her a sudden revelation. Had he written this song with her in mind? The words could have been anyone. They didn't speak of love just of beauty and admiration. She wouldn't even had thought it was meant for her if not for the fact that she knew he had written it. Maybe she was wrong, and he had met more fiery green eyes than hers. Maybe hers weren't even filled with fire. The way his black eyes sought hers during the song made her feel otherwise.

The song ended and he just continued playing the melody, without singing.

"I think it's time we turn in." He continued playing. "I'll keep first watch."

Everyone agreed, as it was getting late. They ducked under the roof of the shelter and found their spots for the night. Annika laid the closest to the fire with only Carter sleeping next to her.

Annika lay down on her blankets and looked at the canopy above her as she listened to the music. She lay for quite a while, not tiring of the sound. Her eyes began to grow heavy as she turned to the side. Her drooping eyes caught sight of Captain Wolf as he sat playing. Her eyes closed shut when she heard him change songs. He began to sing quietly, his words barely discernible. He now played the same sad ballad she had heard aboard his ship. Had he written this one too? The sadness in his voice spoke to her, and she opened her eyes again.

Captain Wolf sat on the log, his eyes closed as he sang. His voice was quiet and filled with emotion. Her eyes drooped closed again, and she fell asleep to the sad and beautiful song he played.

Maddock looked at the happy group with a foul taste in his mouth. The happiness they showed was enough to make him vomit. He watched as Annika twirled around the fire, laughing. The corners of his lips lifted into a tight smile. What was coming next was something she deserved. She had brought it upon herself the moment she stood up to him—her and the kid. No one made a fool out of him and lived to tell it. Once they all lay down for the night, Maddock left and walked further into the jungle. It wouldn't be long now, and everything would be made right by him.

CHAPTER FIFTEEN

Ethan woke to the sun spreading its golden rays through the trees overhead, warming his chilled skin. The fire had died down sometime during the night. Jack, who had the last watch of the night, was starting to rebuild the fire again.

Sometime during the night it had begun to rain, just a light drizzle. Ethan could hear it hitting the makeshift roof above their heads as he had tried to sleep. Thankfully, they had very few leaks in the roof.

Ethan sat up and looked around camp. Everyone seemed to be stirring from their sleep now. Everything glistened in the morning light. Droplets of water held onto the grass and sparkled in the sunlight.

His eyes automatically sought out Annika. It was merely reflex by now. Her face was so peaceful, her hair was still braided and laying over her shoulder. He had yet to see her hair undone.

Her breathing was steady and deep. The movement drawing his eyes to her lips. Her lips were pink and parted. Ethan shook his head and stood to his feet. What was he doing, looking at her lips?

She moved in her sleep and Ethan couldn't draw his gaze away. Her arms were raised over her head as she stretched them out. Even her eyes were scrunched up tight, the unguarded action made him smile.

"Cap? Cap, are you listening?" Jack was talking next to him. Ethan guiltily jerked his attention away from the awaking beauty and looked at his friend.

"Sorry, you said something?"

"Yes, I did. Several times." Jack looked in the direction of Annika and realized why Ethan had been so distracted. "If you hadn't been preoccupied taking in the sights, then you would have heard me. I thought I heard movement out there last night."

Ethan jerked his head around. "You did? Why didn't you wake me?"

Jonah pulled his large body out of his blankets and slowly rose to his feet. By the sound of it, Annika and Carter were also rising behind Ethan.

"I was going to, but it was only there for a second. I didn't hear anything the rest of the night." Jack rubbed his clean jaw. He hadn't quite gotten old enough to grow facial hair. "Whatever it was, it was big. Maybe the size of a deer. It cracked a couple of twigs as it walked. So, either good game to hunt or something was watching us."

"We will need to keep our eyes open even more now." Jonah stood with his arms crossed, his eyes sharp.

Ethan nodded. "Agreed, but more than likely it was only a rabbit or something harmless."

"I don't know, Cap, that would have been an awfully big rabbit." Jack shook his head.

"Good morning." Annika stepped into their circle, along with Carter.

"Good morning, Annika." Jack gave her a wide smile.

She covered her mouth and yawned. "Did I miss something?"

Jack shook his head. "No, nothing much. The night was quiet for the most part."

"Well, I am famished. Shall we get breakfast prepared?" Annika looked around the group expectantly.

Ethan clapped his hands together. "Yes, who's up for some hard tack?" His smile was greeted with groans.

"Carter and I are going to go fishing again after we eat something. Hopefully, we will have something for supper tonight at least." Jack looked expectantly at Carter, who nodded.

"Of course we will, as long as I'm the one fishing. As you know, I am quite good at it," he teased Jack, who rewarded him with a light punch to the shoulder.

"I know where there are some fruit trees. I can collect some and we can have that for breakfast," Annika interjected and showed them the direction.

Ethan looked in the direction she pointed. It was where Jack had heard the noise.

"I'll come and help you. Just lead the way." Ethan stepped towards her. Jonah and Jack exchanged knowing smiles.

"Thank you." Annika's sweet smile made him forget about their teasing. Teasing was a small price to pay to be close to her again.

They walked into the trees, careful to sidestep the muddy patches the rain had caused. After some expert maneuvering around the mud, they soon came across the fruit trees. They were still laden down with fruit, which was good news for them. Annika reached up and took a fruit down from one of the lower branches, her shorter stature limiting her pick of fruit.

"I should have brought something to put them in." She laughed as she continued picking.

"May I be of service, then? Think of me as your personal basket." His grin elicited a chuckle from her.

"Here then, hold these please."

"Gladly, my lady." She loaded his arms up with as much fruit as he could carry.

"What do you wish me to call you?" Annika's question gave him pause.

"What do you mean?"

Her back was to him, hiding her face from his. "Well, you know my name, but I've only ever called you Captain Wolf. Is that what you wish for me to continue calling you?" Her eyes peeked at him over her shoulder, as she reached up and picked a mandaw. She reached for another one, but it was just out of her reach, even when she rose up on her tiptoes.

Ethan juggled all the fruit into one arm and reached past her to get the mandaw. She turned around and was just inches from his face. Her breathing stopped and her eyes widened. His arm was still up in the tree, grasping the fruit.

The closeness of their faces and her breath fanning his face was a great distraction. "My name is Ethan." His words came out in a whisper. After saying his name out loud, his heart began to race. What had possessed him to tell her that? Many in his own crew did not even know his full name. He couldn't let just anyone know his name, in case they recognized his face and could place him. It would be disastrous if that were to happen. Although that was all true, he couldn't help but tell her his name. Ethan longed to hear his name on her lips. His eyes dropped to them.

"Ethan." Her lips formed his name and his heartbeat quickened. His attention went to her eyes, which were shining. "I like that name."

"My father said it stands for strength." Where did that come from? Was he just blabbering now? This woman was able to take his senses from him far more efficiently than an enemy could. Yet, somehow, he did not mind it.

"You live up to your name." A shy smile lit her face. Her cheeks were quickly turning a shade of pink.

"You think so?"

"Yes, you show great strength and wisdom to your men." Her face had turned red now and her eyes jumped from his face to his arms. His right arm was still in the tree, holding onto a mandaw. Her head was mere inches from it.

They stood frozen for a moment, neither one knowing what to do but not wanting to break the moment. A sudden longing to kiss her sprang to

Ethan's mind, scaring him. Why was he even entertaining these thoughts and feelings? She would not care for someone such as him. She saw him as a pirate, someone who robbed and stole from sailors.

He could open the walls he had so carefully erected around his heart and tell her the whole story. Why he stole and what compelled him to pay them back. Though, if he did that, he would be completely vulnerable. She would not believe him, of course, and that would let her a step closer to his own heart. Best to hold his own feelings at bay and not fall for her.

As he stepped away and looked into her face, he realized he already had. No matter what the future held, she would always hold a place in his heart.

"I'd appreciate if you didn't use my real name unless we are alone. I don't permit my crew to say my name around others. Only a select few even know it."

"So I'm now one of them." She smiled. "Thank you for trusting me."

He smiled back, realizing he did trust her. "Well, are you ready?" He started to head back to camp, his arms laden with fruit.

"I'm coming, Ethan." His name flowed so easily off her tongue. It made him like his given name more, actually. "Why do you hide your name? I believe Captain Ethan Wolf sounds just as menacing, if not more so."

"I have reasons for not wanting my name to be spread around."

"I understand. You have a past you would rather forget. We all do to some degree." She placed a hand on his arm, stilling his walking. "What I'm trying to say is, if you ever wish to talk about it, I'm here."

"Why do you even care to know? I'm a pirate. I've stolen from you, and you have every right to hate me for it."

"I don't hate you." She squeezed his arm lightly, making his stomach tie into knots. A light shone from her eyes. "I have to admit I didn't care for you when I first met you. Since then, however, you have shown me that you are no ordinary pirate. The love you have for your men and the respect they give you is a testament to your character. I have been confused as to why a selfish pirate would invoke such feelings in his men and show such kindness to strangers. I've come to the conclusion that you are a good man. I don't know why you steal, but I believe you have a good reason."

She removed her hand and continued walking. Ethan followed behind and mulled over her words. To hear her say that she believed him to be a good man meant so much to him. He had not heard that from anyone outside of his crew in a very long time.

"Well, that's a sweet sight." Jonah smiled wide as they approached him, his words meaning the fruit they carried. His eyes carried a veiled tease that only Ethan picked up on. He gave a mock frown to his old friend. He had always been able to read what he was thinking and how he was feeling.

"This is breakfast this morning and maybe lunch and supper." He chuckled as Ethan set the fruit down by the fire.

Breakfast was simple but far better than just plain hard tack. Ethan ate his food happily. The mandaws and angel fruit were perfectly ripe. It was rare to have such good fruit when traveling the seas, so this was wonderful. He couldn't help but hope for a little more protein soon, though.

So much had happened since he and his crew had first come across the *Sailor's Journey*. New friends and allies had been made. They had been made through necessity, though. Would they last once they found a way to leave the island?

Ethan tried not to think about how hard it would be to leave Annika, knowing that they would not likely meet again. He had grown accustomed to seeing her sweet face in the morning. Accustomed to hearing her fiery talk and the blush that crept up her face at his teases. He'd known from the beginning that nothing could come from a friendship with her, but he couldn't stop wanting to be near her. He had to constantly tell himself to stop dreaming of a future with her in it.

After everyone was done eating their fruit, Ethan cleared his throat. "I think it wise if some of us went out and explored the immediate area." He looked up into the tree that towered over their heads. "I would like to climb this tree and see if I can get an idea of what's around us."

"Who will go with you exploring?" Jack asked as he wiped his mouth.

"Well, I only need one other man to go. We could use some people to stay and look after camp. Hopefully have some warm food ready by the time we get back." He grinned at them.

"I'm up for some adventure. That is if Carter can still fish without me." Jack grinned at the boy.

"Don't worry about me. I can fish just fine on my own. Your fish pulling skills are easily replaced, while my skill is priceless." The two bickered teasingly with one another, causing the rest of them to chuckle.

"So, it's settled. Jack and I will head out. Just as soon as I climb this monster and scout the area."

"Perfect. While you do that, I'll help Carter with fishing. He needs some pointers on his cast." Jack laughed and Carter stuck his tongue out at him, grinning.

Ethan laughed to himself and began climbing the tree. The trunk was long, but the many knobs and holds made it easy to climb.

He placed one hand in front of the other, his eyes scoping out his next hand hold. Once he ran out of big enough branches to climb, Ethan was able to see miles away. The jungle seemed to stretch on forever. The island was much bigger than he had initially thought. How would they be able to find anyone if they did live here? The jungle canopy was too thick to see through, and the island was so large. Even if there was a village somewhere they would be very lucky to find it.

Off in the distance Ethan saw their ship, just a tiny dot now, floating in the ocean. The huts seemed to be hidden behind trees. Not even smoke from a fire was visible.

The small lake in front of him looked like a shimmering mirror of light. It sparkled and almost made his eyes hurt. He could see the boys fishing at the edge of the water and Annika kneeling down at its bank.

The sun went behind some clouds and made the mirror lake less reflective. The green water was hard to see through, but he was able to see shadows below the surface. Fish darted around Carter's fishing line. It was impossible to tell, but he imagined that the water had to be over twenty feet deep in the middle.

Schools of fish, large ones, moved in synchronization around the inlet. The surface of the water was being used by many different kinds of birds, all trying to get a taste of the fish from below. Suddenly, the fish darted away and the birds flew into the air, screeching. How curious, what would cause them to do that?

A dark object from the river drew his attention. Something was entering the inlet and whatever it was, it was huge. He couldn't be sure, but it had to be thirty feet at least. It was moving quickly, its shadow weaving from side to side. Whatever it was, it was now in the lake, where his friends were. Ethan scrambled down the branches as fast as he could. He shouted a few times, hoping someone would hear him. So far, his voice had been drowned out by the distance.

He finally reached the base of the tree and sprinted to Annika, who still sat by the water. He yanked her back from the edge, her protests falling on deaf ears. Seeing his serious manner must have caused her to quiet down.

"What is it? What's wrong?" Annika placed a hand on his arm. Ethan stood at attention, scanning the water. Jonah came running up to them, seeing something was wrong.

"There's something in the water and it's big." Ethan suddenly spotted the dark mass below, moving quickly towards Jack and Carter. Annika must have spotted it too.

"What in the world?"

"Jack! Carter! Get away from the water!" Ethan began running again, Annika at his heels.

"What is it, Cap? We are pulling in a whopper!" Jack's excitement caused him to not notice the seriousness in Ethan's tone. The two of them continued pulling, the line taut. Suddenly, the water near their line rippled violently and their line went slack, causing them to fall to the ground. Surprised, they pulled it out of the water and put it on the bank near them.

Ethan reached them and looked down at their catch. The fish they had been pulling in was quite large, at least forty pounds, if not for the missing lower half at least. The fish was sliced clean in two. Jonah came running up to the group and stared at the fish with wide eyes.

"It just lost all the fight in it at the end." Carter stared open-mouthed at the sad sight.

"Let's step away from the water everyone." Jonah pulled the boys away from the edge. "Who knows what's out there." All heads turned towards the water. The dark object moved out of the lake and back down the river. From now on, they would need to be more cautious about approaching the water, if they approached it at all.

"Well, we have part of a fish now for breakfast." Jack attempted a smile, which came out crooked.

"What will we do, Captain? Is it safe to fish now?" Carter still looked out over the lake, his eyes scanning for the shadow.

"For the moment, I don't see how it would hurt to continue fishing, as long as we stay well away from the water.

Let's have someone watching for it coming back constantly while the other fishes."

"Aye, Cap." Jack nodded in agreement, as did Carter. Their carefree demeanor had turned serious. No one would be comfortable knowing something of massive size and, from the looks of the battered fish, sharp teeth was lurking in the cool green waters.

"Let's take the fish that's left and cook it up. While it's cooking, we can talk." They all seemed in agreement with Ethan.

The fish was soon on a large stick, propped up over the fire. The smell coming off of it made it difficult to focus.

"It will be good to have a bit of meat before we head out. It'll give us some more energy." Ethan tore his attention from the mouthwatering fish. He asked Carter for the map and held it out for Jack to see. "Any ideas on where we should head out first?"

"You're still planning on leaving? Is it even safe for us to stay here?" Annika asked fearfully, breaking into their discussion. She fidgeted nervously on her log. "I mean, we have no idea what we are dealing with here. Is it strictly a water creature or could it come on land?"

"From the looks of it, we are dealing with something over thirty feet." Jonah shook his head in disbelief.

"I believe this place is still our best bet when it comes to everything we need. Water and food are plentiful here. We just need to get along with the wildlife." Ethan removed his hat and beat it against his leg, a nervous habit.

"What if that's what killed all those men down the river?" Annika's fearful eyes shot to his. He pondered that for a moment. She had a point. The severed fish bones reminded him of the spines they had seen cut. Those men were right along the river, though. The tree with their shelter was a good hundred feet away from the water's edge.

"Who knows what happened to them. Perhaps they were washed up on shore. I don't know what to say since we know virtually nothing about the creature. Would you all rather leave and find a different spot to camp?"

Everyone looked at each other, waiting for a response. Finally, Carter spoke up. "This is the most food we have found anywhere on the island. We have fruit, fish, and plenty of water. No matter where we go, we have encountered danger. Isn't that why we have a night watch? I, for one, vote that we stay here. Just remain careful and keep our eyes open."

"Are we all in agreement then?" Everyone around the fire nodded. Annika's nod was more uncertain, though. "All right, then, that's settled. What will you all do in our absence?"

"I will fish. I'm not afraid of the creature." Carter lifted his chin. Determination shone in his eyes. Annika, however, appeared to not like the idea.

"I will help you," Jonah spoke up, probably seeing Annika's fear. "I need to brush up on my fishing skills. Plus, I can be your lookout. If that thing enters the lake, I will know about it." Annika smiled in thanks, looking relieved.

"While you both are fishing, I will forage for food and help in any way that I can." Annika smiled.

"Sounds like a plan, then." Ethan clapped his hands and stood. "We have plenty of time to do some exploring today, but first, I would like some of this mouthwatering fish." His eyes hungrily found the fish again. He heard a stomach growling loudly and was surprised to find it had been Annika's. She stood next to him, cheeks beginning to flush when she realized he had heard.

"You're not the only one that's hungry." Her mouth widened into a smile, showing her perfect teeth. With that they dug in. The fish didn't last long. Even though it was only half a fish, it filled all their bellies.

Ethan finally felt satisfied and took a long drink of cool water. As the water slid down his throat, he wondered what they would find today. More than likely just more forest. His heart leaped in excitement at the prospect. He liked this part, exploring new lands, meeting new people. It was what he had dreamt of doing, before...well, before his father had died and everything had fallen apart. His thoughts threatened to go dark until he heard Annika's bright laugh. He found his eyes wandering to her, as if she were a magnet. Her smile erased his sad thoughts and put a smile back on his face.

CHAPTER SIXTEEN

It didn't take long for the two men to pack their necessities and head out. Annika watched until they could no longer be seen through the thick blanket of trees. She sent up a quick prayer for their safety. While she was at it, she sent a prayer of safety for herself, Jonah, and Carter. Who knew what was lurking in the water? The morning went quickly after saying goodbye to Ethan and Jack.

Jonah spent a good portion of the day with Carter. He was incredibly kind to him. He showed him how to start a fire and many other things a boy his age should know. It was something that Carter was missing in his life, male role models. On this trip he had met many positive role models, and for that Annika was grateful.

She smiled as she watched them fish. Carter actually had to teach Jonah a few things. It seems his rusty skills were in need of a lot of buffing out. Soon they were fishing in unison, not catching anything but they were having fun. As they fished, her eyes automatically searched the water. The water had seemed like an oasis at first, almost like a piece of heaven on this deadly island. It had far too quickly turned sour. It was hard to imagine the place as a piece of heaven when a water beast could attack and swallow you up at any minute.

The water was very deceptive, tranquil from the outside, but it held dangers beneath its glossy surface. They hadn't even seen the creature but the pure size of it and the fish severed in half was enough to spread fear in their hearts.

Annika walked around the outskirts of the camp, studying the plants she could see. She tried to recall what Doniphan had instructed her on. Which plants that were useful for herbal medications and ones that were a good food source. Soon she had exhausted all nearby options and stood bored. So far, she had not played a huge role on this expedition. She wasn't the one who caught the food or went out exploring. She hadn't even built the shelter. Ethan had even helped her with cutting down the bamboo. All she had done was pick fruit and cleaned a fish. Anyone with hands could do that.

The forest beyond seemed to beckon her towards it. Monkeys called in the distance and birds sang out friendly greetings. Their song was tranquil and made the jungle seem inviting. One thing she had learned of the jungle was that it was quite easy to be fooled into venturing into its depths. One wrong move and you would be gone.

The light came through the overhead trees in such a way it appeared to make the leaves sparkle. It was such a beautiful day out. Despite all that had happened earlier, it still felt peaceful here.

Would it hurt if she went further in? She would take her weapons and stay well within hearing of the camp. The thought of finding more food to help the group strengthened her resolve. She looked back at Jonah, who still sat with Carter, fishing. Their determination was commendable, as was their patience.

Annika cautiously entered the thick curtain of trees and stepped into the forest. Everywhere she looked there was movement and noise. Whether that was mosquitoes or a reptile of some kind, the jungle never stopped moving. She cautiously wove her way around trees. Her eyes searched for anything on the ground or in the branches above.

As she searched, her mind wandered to the men. How were Jack and Captain Wolf, Ethan, doing? It would take a long time for Annika to get used to the captain's face with this new name. It was a fine name, a strong one in fact. It was as if it were made for him. It meant a lot to her that he had told her his name. Somehow, it seemed to make her feel somewhat special that she was one of the select few who knew it.

How many people had he struck fear into? And yet she knew his God-given name. She smiled at the thought.

The smell of a nearby mandaw tree reminded her suddenly of her conversation with Ethan that morning. His face so close to her own. His face was so interesting to look at. Yes, he was handsome but that's not what struck her the most. When around his crew and when he needed to be a pirate, his face was a mask of fearlessness and confidence. His glare could strike fear into anyone, but she was coming to realize that it was a role for him. He adopted that look when he needed it. When he was around his friends, those he trusted, he was far more relaxed. He still teased and had a boyish grin, but he was kind and far from arrogant.

Around her, however, his face held emotions that she couldn't understand. Gone was the look of the fearsome pirate, and in its place was something gentle and deep. Her face heated up at the memory. She tried to focus harder on the wildlife around her, knowing she was in a losing battle.

So far, she had seen no herbs that she recognized. She only had a handful that she had been taught about. The jungle was littered with mandaw trees and angel fruit so that was comforting at least. If she could find something else to add to their daily menu, that would be wonderful. Upon looking up, she realized she had gone quite a distance away from camp.

She sighed. This was all Ethan's fault. If she hadn't been thinking about him, she wouldn't have gotten distracted.

A sudden cry reached her ears, cutting through the jungle. It was quiet but unmistakably human. She stood in one spot, frozen, listening intently for the sound. There it was again. Needing no more reason, she turned away from camp to find the cause of the cry. Annika had never been one to not help someone in need, but she knew she must be careful. If it wasn't an animal, then who was it?

She had a curtain of trees and leaves in front of her path. The cry came again It sounded as though it were just beyond the trees. Cautiously, Annika peered through the branches of a nearby tree.

Beyond the brush she saw a small open sandy area. The trees all around seemed to be creating a sort of wall that she was barely able to squeeze through. Even the light was mostly blocked, the trees being so incredibly thick. Her eyes looked for movement and at first saw nothing. Suddenly, she saw arms moving and flailing in the air.

A young man, possibly her age or younger, was reaching for something to grab onto. She realized half of his body was under the ground. A sudden story that some of the men had spoken about, back at the huts, sprang to her memory. They had spoken of quicksand and how a friend of theirs had met his unfortunate demise because of it.

The sudden seriousness of the situation came upon her. Annika sprang from the trees and ran to the young man. She dropped her bow and ran full speed to the edge of the sand pit. His frantic eyes locked onto her and even more fear registered. He tried even harder to pull himself out.

"It's all right," Annika put a hand out and spoke calmly. "I won't hurt you." She stopped a ways away, not knowing where the sinking sand started. The man held onto the end of a thick root. By the looks of it, that was all that was keeping him up. Unfortunately, the root looked taut, ready to break at any moment.

His fearful eyes found hers, propelling her to hurry and find a way to help him. She studied the situation around her. The sand pit was about ten feet wide by the looks of it. The grass under her feet went another foot or so, then it was sand. There were trees growing at the edge of the grass, but none close enough for him to get a good hold of. The root he clung to was not going to last long.

The young man sank deeper into the sand, another anguished cry escaping him. Annika ran to the closest tree and franticly searched. Her searching was rewarded when she spotted a long vine hanging on the limb of a tree. Upon testing it, she found it to be strong but pliable. She yanked it down from the tree, relieved to hear it snap overhead and fall at her feet. She carried it to the edge of the sand pit. One end stayed in her hand and the other she threw forward.

"Grab the vine!" she yelled at the man, hoping he could understand her. He must have understood, if not her words then her actions. He let go of the root and franticly grabbed the vine with both hands.

Annika pulled the rope taut and angled the vine against the trunk of a tree. She sat down, braced her feet against a root, and began pulling as hard as she was able. For a long while, she wasn't able to pull him an inch. Finally, she felt the pressure give, allowing her to start pulling him out. The rough vine began to cut at her palms, but she did not care. Her mind was focused intently on getting the young man safely out. With every inch, her hands screamed but she could not hear them over her resolve to put one hand in front of the other. Every inch she gained was a victory, spurring her to push forward.

She stole a look at the man. He was further out of the sand now. Finally, his legs were the only thing stuck. His upper half was on the grass, slowly getting closer to safety. A few more tugs, and he was able to fully escape from the sand. He rolled over onto the grass and lay on his back. His breathing was heavy, his chest rising and falling with each breath. Who knew how long he had been in there?

Annika caught her breath and approached him cautiously. His dark skin was covered in sand and sweat. He wore brown pants that appeared to be leather. He wore no shoes, or perhaps they had been lost in the sand. His upper body was unclothed.

"Are you all right?" Her words seemed to surprise him,. He sat up and looked at her warily. "Please, I won't hurt you." She held both her hands out to show she carried no weapons. His eyes searched her curiously and landed on the sword at her side.

She had forgotten it was on. Carefully, she unlatched the belt on her waist that held the sword on. His eyes watched her intently the whole time.

Annika dropped the sword on the grass next to her. "See? It's gone now. I don't want to hurt you."

He seemed somewhat satisfied and instead focused intently on her hands. His own hands opened a pouch that was tied onto his waist. He pulled out a small piece of pottery and cautiously approached her. She began to lower her hands when he grabbed one of them. She would have been afraid if she hadn't seen the look in his eyes. He didn't look like he meant any harm.

He took her hand and applied a cream from the pottery he had taken out of his bag. The cream stung sharply, causing Annika to look closely at her hands. She was surprised to find somewhat large cuts from the vine she had gripped. The young man applied the salve to both of her hands. After the stinging subsided, she was met with a cooling sensation on her burning hands.

"Thank you."

A slow smile spread across his face. *Who was he?* Annika wondered. If he was here, then surely that meant there were others close by as well. Had Annika been the first to find someone who could help them? She was about to ask him questions when she heard shouting behind her.

"Annika? Annika, where are you?" Jonah was calling for her, his voice carrying through the dense trees. The young man's eyes jerked in that direction, the fear coming back into his face.

"It's all right, he won't hurt you," Annika tried to reassure him. That didn't seem to work, for the man stood to his feet quickly.

He studied her once more and smiled before disappearing into the trees. As he was fleeing, Jonah and Carter came into the clearing and caught sight of the disappearing native.

"Annika! What happened? Are you all right?" Jonah rushed over to her side, concern in his voice. His eyes strayed from her to the trees.

Annika was kneeling down still, her hands covered in the sticky paste he had applied. "I'm fine."

"Who was that and what did he do to you?" Carter bent down in front of her, looking at her hands.

"He didn't do anything to me. I have no idea who he was. I heard a cry, and I followed it here. I found him stuck in sinking sand. I was able to pull him out just in time." The burning in her hands caused her to pause and examine them again. "He applied something to my hands. It's messy but it doesn't hurt at all. It actually kind of helped with the burning."

Jonah looked warily around the jungle growth. "It's time to go back. Come, let's hurry. I don't like not knowing who's out there."

Annika reached for her sword as the two helped her to stand, her hands stinging.

"I don't believe he meant any harm." Annika brushed twigs off of her skirt. "He seemed kind."

"So, there really are people on this island," Carter said excitedly.

"It appears so. The real question is, if they know we are here, why have they not approached us?"

"Maybe they were just as surprised to see us. We should be ready to meet them soon if that's the case."

"I guess we will soon see." Jonah's eyes continued scanning the jungle. "You need to be more careful. If he had been an enemy, this would have ended quite differently. In fact, he could still be the enemy. We have no idea what their intentions are towards us." He helped her over a large tree root. "I'm glad you are ok. Cap would have killed me if something had happened to you."

"Surely you can't be expected to be responsible for every man. He can't blame you. Especially when I'm the one at fault."

"Yes, but you are different." His words confused Annika. How could she be different?

"Because I'm a woman? So, he really doesn't trust me to take care of myself."

"The captain has learned not to underestimate your skills. That is not the reason I am referring to." He bent under a large branch in his path.

What could he be referring to then? Annika kept silent as they continued walking. A sudden possibility struck her. Could it be that Ethan cared about her? First, the song from the night before, the sweet moment picking fruit, and now Jonah's cryptic words. If it was anyone else, she would say absolutely, he definitely cared for her. Since it was her, however, it was hard to accept the fact that he might have the same feelings she had.

Annika definitely cared about Ethan, but how much had yet to be decided. If she allowed herself to fall even harder for the man, she would have her heart broken when he left her for the sea. Nonetheless, the possibility of him caring for her as more than a friend made her heart leap.

Upon arriving back at camp, Jonah turned to her. "Let's get your hands bandaged up. I want to take a look at them."

"All right, thank you."

Jonah led her to a log and took a roll of fabric out of his pack. He inspected her hands and examined the cream that had been applied. Her wounds were not serious and would heal quickly as long as they didn't get infected. He was going to clean the paste off, but she declined. Whatever was in it was helping the pain immensely.

As Jonah wrapped her hands with the cloth, her thoughts drifted to Ethan. What would he say upon finding out there were people on the island?

CHAPTER SEVENTEEN

Ethan wiped the sweat from his brow and looked towards the horizon. They were on a cliff that overlooked much of the island. They couldn't even see the ship anymore it was so far away. My, but it was a beautiful sight from here. The sky was a stunning blue, a nice contrast to the dark blue of the ocean and the vibrant green of the island. Birds rose from the trees below and soared into the sky.

"It looks mighty nice from up high, Cap. Quite deceiving, isn't it?" Jack stood to Ethan's left. He was a talkative companion. Which was fine with Ethan because Jack normally didn't even require him to answer, giving him time to think.

"That it is." They both stood in silence, watching the fantastic view ahead. The massive volcano was to their back, stretching impossibly high.

To their right, the way they had come from, the huts lay somewhere hidden. In front of them was their camp hidden in the jungle growth, and further than that was the sparkling ocean. To the left was a vast and unexplored section of the island. It looked like there was some sort of drop off and then a vast valley of trees and other foliage. They could see nothing that would aid them in their search. The jungle growth was too thick to get a clear view of anything.

Ethan thought the next best place to look would be where that drop off was. For all they knew, it could hold an entire town. Neither one of them could get a clear look of it.

Before starting the trek back to camp, they took the view in for a few more minutes. Birds soared up out of the trees and made a quick ascent into the sky.

"What are those, Cap?"

"Perhaps some kind of parrot?" Ethan shrugged and squinted, trying to get a better view.

"No." Jack shook his head. "They aren't parrots. I don't know if I've seen anything like them before."

They both watched the animals as they flew into the air. Jack was right. Even from this distance, you could tell they were not parrots. They looked somewhat familiar to Ethan. Suddenly he remembered the eerie swamp and the large bat-like creature that had flown out of it. This is exactly what he imagined the large bat-winged creature would have looked like if he had seen it during the day.

A dozen of them rose into the air in unison and flew over them into the large volcano at the center of the island.

"Did you see their skin? It was smooth. I even thought I saw a beak and a tail." Jack walked back and forth, trying to see if they were still visible. They did not return, unfortunately.

"This island is full of surprises." Ethan shook his head. "Remember the Ancient cat from a few days ago? After having seen that, I don't know if anything this island has to throw at me would be surprising."

"I know. So strange. Although, I didn't see it with my own two eyes. So I feel like I have plenty of room to be surprised. There's a lot of things here I haven't seen before, though. A lot of smaller animals I couldn't even begin to name." Jack stopped looking for the flying animals and turned to Ethan. "Ready to head back?"

"Yes, let's do that." They walked side by side as they made the long trek back to camp.

"Disappointing to find nothing again." Jack kicked a rock that was in his path.

"Indeed, but now we know where not to look." Ethan smiled at his friend. In truth, he did not feel as carefree as he seemed. He tried to put on a confident persona around others, even his close friends. On the inside, though, he felt weary and defeated.

"You can be honest with me, Cap. We ain't doin' so hot, are we?" Jack bent low to avoid a large limb. Ethan did the same as he followed.

"We will survive just fine, if that's what you mean. That's not the issue, though. I have no idea how long repairs will take or even if they can be fixed. The carpenter didn't seem very confident that he could repair it fully."

"So we could be here for a while then." Jack's voice sounded weary.

"It's not such a bad thing." Ethan tried to rouse his spirits. "There's food and we are among some good people."

"I'm aware of that. I know there's a certain someone who you think is exceptionally good." Jack cast a sideways look at him, grinning.

"I don't know what you're talking about." Ethan tried to deflect.

"Don't even try to deny it, Cap. Even a blind man would be able to tell you care for her." Jack laughed.

"Is it that obvious?"

Jack grimaced and cocked a teasing eyebrow. "Painfully so." A growl came from his stomach.

"Was that you?" Ethan laughed.

"Aye, Cap." A sheepish grin stole over Jack's face when he looked back. "I've been dreaming of fish all day. No more of this tough hard tack." He stuck out his tongue. Ethan chuckled.

"Let's get a move on, then. I'd like to make it back before dark. I've had my mind on food as well."

"Yeah, right," Jack scoffed. "I know where your mind has been, and it hasn't been on fish."

"What makes you think I have my mind on Annika?"

"I think anyone would have figured that out from the song you played last night."

"The song?"

"Yeah, you sang a song about a young woman. She had fiery green eyes and beautiful hair." He stole a look behind him again. "You stared at her the entire time you sang it. That's one of the more obvious reasons, though. There's far more to be seen in between the lines." He turned to look at his feet, having to step over some overgrown roots.

"What do you mean?"

"I've known you for years, Cap. We grew up together. In all my time of knowing you, I've seen many beautiful women vie for your attention. Not once did you appear interested. Your thoughts weigh too heavily in the past. Then Annika came along and everything changed." Ethan walked silently for a while after hearing Jack's words. He must be very obvious to everyone in his feelings for her.

"I'm ashamed to say it, but you are right. I have grown far too attached to her."

"Why should you be ashamed?" Jack slowed to a stop and turned to face him.

"I'm a pirate, and she's a lady. She would never look twice at someone like me. Besides, once we leave this place, she will go find her brother and never look back." His gaze fell to the ground.

"You and I both know that you are no ordinary pirate." Jack gripped his shoulder firmly. "You may don the title 'pirate' but you couldn't be further from it. You are good, just, and fair. You're letting your fear of the past determine the happiness of your future. Besides,"—he turned back around and continued walking—"that's not how Annika sees you."

"How do you know that?" Ethan followed closely behind, trying his best not to stumble on the uneven terrain.

"I catch her looking at you just as much as you look at her. She used to look at you in disdain. I myself remember those fiery green eyes. Lately, however, she looks at you completely differently. She definitely doesn't look at Jonah or me that way."

Could that be true? Did Annika look his way just as much as he was drawn to look towards her? Surely that could not be the case. Even if so, why would she want to live the life of a pirate with him. He was not able to settle down and put away his pirating ways yet. His thoughts were too plagued for him to give it up and forget. His hopeful thinking of Annika would get him nowhere. At some point they would get the ship repaired, and once they reached the mainland, she would be gone for good. If he wasn't careful, she would take a big piece of his heart with her.

The rest of the journey back was filled with Jack's chattering. He spoke of their homeland in Lookonia. He was telling the story of Jonah's father and how he pulled in the biggest fish you ever did see. Ethan's eyes were roving over the grass when he saw something that stopped him in his tracks.

"Hold on a minute, Jack. You're the tracker, what do you make of this?" Jack came closer and peered down.

"Interesting," he finally said after studying it for a moment, "It's a boot print, but it's not one of ours. We didn't come this way. We are also too far away from camp for this to be any of theirs."

"So, there are others on this island." Ethan's thoughts raced with the hope of getting help. "I wonder why we haven't seen them yet. It's not like we have tried to keep quiet."

Jack remained kneeling on the ground and felt the inside of the footprint with his forefinger. "The print is old, at least a day old, or I would suggest to follow it."

"Right, we should continue to keep our eyes open. If we missed that, perhaps there's more." They continued towards camp, their eyes glued to the ground. Ethan's eyes scanned the uneven terrain. His eyes looked past the grass and rocks, looking for the unusual and the unnatural.

Finally, they found some more tracks. This time they were more fresh. They followed the prints, since they were going in the same direction as camp.

"Cap, you're going to want to see this." Jack stood at a tree, peering past it. The tracks led up to the tree and stopped, then they went in a completely different direction afterwards.

"Looks like they went off that way." Ethan's eyes followed the tracks.

"No, Cap, look at this." Ethan came up alongside his friend and instantly knew the cause for concern. From the tree they had a very direct and excellent view of their camp. "Whoever this was stopped and watched, then walked away. The prints here are deeper, suggesting that he stopped for a while."

"Are we sure it's not one of ours?" Dread filled his stomach.

"I will check the length of these with everyone's boots. Hopefully one of us is a match."

"If not,"—Ethan looked to Jack, who gave him a knowing look—"then we had someone spying on us." He looked through the trees again and saw Annika. His stomach churned. Hopefully, it was one of their own footprints. If not, they could be in even more danger. Who knew who was out there, friend or foe?

They entered camp with a new sense of dread. This was different than any danger they had faced as of yet. If their suspicions were correct, they had a completely new kind of enemy to be wary of. This potential danger was more mysterious, completely unknown.

Jonah saw them first and came to greet them. His stride was purposeful. He had a smile on his face but something in his demeanor looked troubled.

"Glad to see you two back. Did you find anything?"

"Not really. Saw some more animals we could not identify. We found some tracks nearby. We need to check and see who's they are. Did something happen here?" Ethan knew it took a lot to shake Jonah and cause concern.

"We had an incident."

"What do you mean 'incident'?" Had the water beast come back?

"Annika had an interesting encounter today with a native."

"What? So we aren't alone. That's great news! That would explain the tracks we found in the jungle," Jack mused. Ethan's eyes frantically sought Annika out, to reassure himself that she was all right.

"How did it happen?"

"I think she should explain. She tells me that he wasn't dangerous, but I didn't get a good look at him. You said you found tracks?"

"Yeah, deeper in the jungle and some just on the outskirts of camp here. Someone has been watching us." Jack's eyes grew round as he explained it again.

"Well, that's enough to give anyone the willies." Jonah gave a mock shiver, which was a rather funny sight coming from his large frame.

This pretty much all but confirmed that the prints they saw were not their own. They would need to double-check, but Ethan's gut told him that it wasn't theirs. Someone had been watching them, and that someone had approached Annika.

He had a strong need to talk with Annika and make sure himself that she was all right. She was adding some more wood to the fire.

As he approached, she looked up at him, her beauty striking him once again. His heart calmed upon seeing her unharmed.

She smiled widely. "Captain, good to see you all back. Did you find anything?"

"Not really, I'm afraid. I hear you found something, though."

"That I did." She absently ran a hand down her tight braid, drawing his attention to her bandaged hands.

"What happened?" He captured her hand and cradled it in his larger ones.

"I'm fine. It's just a couple small cuts." She smiled, her face growing pink.

"Annika," Jack said as he approached the pair at the fire, "Jonah said you had an encounter with someone today, but he didn't give us any specifics. Would you care to fill us in?"

Annika pulled her hand from Ethan's grasp and shifted on the log to find a comfortable position. Everyone found a spot around the fire, waiting to hear.

"Yes, of course." She began by brushing a lock of hair behind her ear. "I wanted to see if there was any more food nearby or even any herbs to pick. I wasn't planning on going far but I got distracted." Her eyes sheepishly found his. "And I went too far. That's when I heard a noise. It was a small cry, but it sounded like someone was in trouble. I ran towards the noise to see what it was."

She adjusted on her seat again, pausing her story. She looked uncomfortable having them all look at her so intently.

"I found a young man stuck in quicksand. He was barely holding on, so I didn't have time to go for help. I got a vine and helped pull him out. He didn't seem dangerous at all. I got cut from the vine as I helped him out. He even put something on them that really helped with the burning." She kept her hands closed and away from prying eyes.

"He didn't speak my language it seemed—at least, he didn't say anything to me. As soon as he heard Jonah coming, he got scared."

"Yeah, he hightailed it out of there before we could get a good look at him." Carter frowned.

"Thank goodness you are safe, Annika. Hopefully, this means they aren't dangerous. It also explains the tracks we found in the jungle." Jack nodded his head. "Good thing too. It was worrying at first seeing boot tracks so close to camp. Hopefully, you are right and they are friendly."

"Boot tracks? Boots like yours?" Annika's brows drew together in confusion.

Jack nodded. "Yes, not exactly, but I would say very similar to mine."

"I wouldn't think that would be from the boy I met and probably not from his people. At least if they dressed the same as him. He wore some kind of leather pants and carried a bag around his waist. That was it, though."

"You mean—?" Ethan found her meaning quickly.

"Yes, he had no shoes on, and I don't believe he ever had. I can't imagine him wearing boots like yours. Leather shoes of some sort maybe, but not boots."

"That means there may be more people out there," Carter piped up, saying what they were all thinking. They all sat in silence. That meant they had no idea about the owners of the mystery tracks. That was not a pleasant feeling at all.

"I'm going to go measure the tracks and see if it's any of ours." Jack jumped up and ran off into the trees. Leaving behind a quiet group, still deep in thought.

This place was steadily making him more and more uneasy. Was it even safe to stay on their own at the lake?

Jack came back shortly. He walked around and measured everyone's shoes. To no one's surprise, none of their shoes matched.

"I believe it's apparent that we need to do something about this. I'm just not sure what yet." Ethan rubbed his chin thoughtfully. "We don't know yet who is out there. Are they friend or foe? Is it safe to stay? We don't even know if it's safe to go back. What if they haven't found the main group yet and we lead them there?"

"It's too late to leave, even if we wanted to." Jonah watched the sun make its evening decent. "I suggest for the night we be even more diligent on lookout duty."

"Agreed." Ethan nodded. No one spoke for a while, adding to the anxiety of the group. A low grumble broke into the silence. All eyes went to Jack who looked around sheepishly.

"Any chance you got some fish to cook for supper? I am famished." Jack's dramatic flair elicited a chuckle from Annika, dissipating some of the fear in the air.

"Carter will have to show you his catch of the day." Her carefree smile calmed Ethan's erratic heartbeat. She looked about the group. "I don't know much about matters such as this, and I don't know what the next step should be. All I can suggest is that tonight we fortify the area, find some large branches and such, so we won't be as visible. In the morning, perhaps we will have clearer heads and a better look on the situation."

She was surprisingly calm, surprising everyone. With no other options in sight, they got to work cooking the fish and fortifying the area. They already had set up camp near the tree, giving them a shield to their back. Then the makeshift walls they had set up were partially enclosed. Only a few holes remained to be blocked off.

The night passed quickly. Everyone's minds weighed heavily with the thoughts of someone watching them. The walls they had created helped calm their thoughts. Ethan was to take first watch that night. If he had believed in Elohim he would have prayed for safety. Since he didn't, he sat and hoped they all would be safe.

CHAPTER EIGHTEEN

Annika awoke the next morning to the sun shining, its welcoming rays peeking through the leaves of their shelter. She thanked the Elohim for keeping them safe for another night. Yesterday's events still weighed heavily on her mind, but she was thankful for a new day. A new day to figure out a plan and maybe even leave this place. She had thought it to be an oasis, but the longer they stayed the worse it got.

Others around her were awaking as well. She doubted any of them had slept well, but hopefully they were rested enough to think straight today. Ethan rose from his blanket. He stretched his arms and opened groggy eyes at her. Where he was and realization of the decisions that needed to be made today drove the sleep from his eyes.

How heavy of a weight must he carry and Captain Samuel as well, having the lives of the men you care about in your hands. Every decision they both made would in some way affect others. Perhaps that was why she could see weariness in Ethan's eyes. He hid it well, but she could still glimpse a deep sadness in him.

They all awoke and fed the dying fire, bringing it to life once again. Things were quieter this morning; no one had a definite answer on what to do. On one hand, they now knew there were natives on this island. It was doubtful that they could help repair the ship, though. They also had found the possibility of more people, someone apart from the natives. If they stayed, they had the possibility to find help or at least supplies, but they were vulnerable to attack out on their own. On the other hand, if they left and there were enemies out there, they didn't want the crew to be found.

They all sat around the fire, eating some freshly picked fruit. It seemed rather tasteless this morning to Annika. The usually delicious juice of the mandaw seemed dull today. Even the sky seemed to show evidence of the group's mood. The sky was dark grey and a mist hung in the air, chilling them all.

"Is there time for me to go fishing now?" Carter interrupted everyone's thoughts. His face had looked glum all morning. Now he cast a small and hopeful smile about the group. Annika felt bad for not seeing the silence was affecting him too.

"If it's all right, I will accompany him."

Ethan's face found hers and he smiled. "Please do. Perhaps we will have reached a decision by the time you are done." He waved them onward. Annika and Carter walked towards the lake. It was crazy to think about how her thoughts had changed. When they first arrived, she had hated asking Ethan permission about anything. Now she trusted him and sought for his opinion.

Annika followed close behind Carter, who was walking along the shore of the lake. They walked over fallen logs and through tall grass. Finally, they had found a good spot, and he sat down to bait his line. Annika made sure that they were still within sight of the group. Although far away, they were still visible.

"How are you doing, Carter?" Annika sat down next to the youth, her eyes on the lake. She looked closely for any movement.

"I'm doing good actually. I miss the carefree feeling we had yesterday, though. I finally felt some peace but that was quickly shattered. Now, today feels heavy and gloomy." He threw his baited hook into the water and leaned back with Annika.

"I know what you mean. The tension is so thick you could cut it with a knife."

"A very dull knife." Carter grinned at her, making her laugh. She had missed times like this with Carter. He was always in such a positive mood.

"I'm sorry all of this has happened to us. I had wanted an adventure, but this is more than I bargained for. I never wanted to put you in this position." She sighed and glanced at his face.

"Are you kidding? I've been having the time of my life." His happiness surprised Annika.

"What on earth do you mean? You have been running from dangers we have only read about in books. We've almost sunk in a ship and barely escaped the jaws of an Ancient cat."

"Well, I didn't much care for the sinking of our ship. I would have preferred never to have seen that." His eyes clouded for a moment remembering that day. "When we lived in Narine, I never got to do anything. My highlights were reading books and taking lessons from you. Since then, I have learned how to navigate and I've discovered my love for the sea."

"I'm happy you are able to see the positives in all this. I just wish you could have learned of it without all the danger."

"I thank Elohim for everything that has happened," he said quietly. Annika looked at Carter, shocked. "Don't get me wrong, I am not happy that people died and are now still suffering. However, if our ship had never been attacked by pirates, we would never have met our new friends. The experiences I have had here are priceless, and so are the new friends. Elohim was able to take a bad situation and change it into something beautiful."

Annika was stunned by Carter's level of maturity. He had always been mature for his age, but since coming on the island he had become even more so. How had she missed that?

"I'm so happy you feel that way. I have to admit, despite our situation, I'm amazed at how much Elohim has given us." Her thoughts flit to Jack, Jonah, and Ethan. Her thoughts seemed to focus largely on Ethan. What would her life have been like had he not happened into it?

A tug at Carter's line pulled their attention back to the water. Carter tested the line and began pulling.

"I've got a fish!" He used all his weight to pull the fish in. Annika was just as excited as he was, She hadn't had a lot of fishing experience.

An odd feeling broke into her excitement, giving her pause. Something didn't feel right. The hair on her arms stood on end. Annika scanned the water, trying to find the source of the feeling. Suddenly, she spotted something poking out of the water. Two eyes were out of the water, staring at them. It was the eyes of some sort of crocodile, and a big one. She had no idea of the size since most of it remained submerged. The head alone looked to be as long as she was tall. The eyes alone were enough to strike fear into her heart and cause her breathing to pause.

The creature was slowly advancing towards the fish on the end of Carter's pole. Annika turned to warn Carter of the danger in the water. Carter's attention was not on the fish, however. He wasn't even looking at the water. His eyes were locked on something behind them.

Annika turned around to find another pair of eyes locked on them. These eyes caused her far more fear than the beast in the water.

Ethan watched Annika and Carter walk towards the water and along its edge, finding a spot near some trees. His mind was so jumbled this morning, maybe even more than last night.

"Did you get any sleep, Cap?" Jack interrupted Ethan's thoughts.

"Some." Ethan stared into the fire. A sound in the trees drew his attention.

All three of them stood to their feet in seconds and grabbed for their weapons. All eyes locked onto the trees as the sounds grew closer. Someone was walking through the heavy undergrowth and not bothering to keep quiet. A figure stumbled out of the trees and into the clearing. Jack sheathed his sword and ran for the figure.

"It's Chris!"

Jonah and Ethan replaced their weapons and sprang to help. Chris was struggling to stand when Jack came up and helped him to his feet. As Ethan approached, he could see that Chris was not in good shape. His right eye was bloody and bruised. His head was bleeding, and he seemed to be limping. His clothing was torn and sullied. Even his hands were cut and bleeding.

"Let's take him to the fire." Jack motioned for their help in moving Chris forward. Jonah stood on the other side of Chris and they both helped him towards the fire.

"What happened, Chris?" Ethan asked as they walked. The man seemed to be drifting in and out of consciousness. They managed to get him to the fire and laid him on Ethan's mat.

"Cap." Chris's voice was raspy.

"Give him some water." Ethan handed his water flask to Jack, who gave it to Chris. He managed to get a few mouthfuls and looked slightly more alert.

"What happened?" Jonah asked the question this time. Chris focused his groggy eyes on the man.

"Ambushed," he rasped out.

"By natives?" Jack tried to finish the injured man's thought.

"No, it was mutiny."

That word struck fear into the most hardened of sailors. That one word could bring the strongest and most feared pirate down to nothing. Ethan's mind went into overdrive at the thought.

"Mutiny?" Jack managed to whisper. "How? Who?"

"It was just shortly after we all left to explore. My group walked a ways on the beach and had to turn back. There was an impassable cliff."

Chris sat up, his strength returning. "When we returned, we found the camp had been attacked. Our first thought was natives. We soon found out how wrong we were. A group of men, from Captain Samuel's ship, had joined together and had taken control of the group. Anyone who disagreed was bound up."

"Why? Why would they do this?" Ethan couldn't think straight.

"Maddock." Chris leveled his gaze on the men, his one good eye filling with anger. "I managed to escape with minimal injuries." He held a hand to his head. "I stumbled about in the forest until I found your prints."

Ethan knew that Maddock had given him a bad feeling. Why hadn't he done something about him the first time he showed defiance? Their situation had gone from bad to worse.

"I left just after Maddock did."

"What do you mean?" Ethan's eyes swerved to the man again.

"He left to find you guys. I wouldn't have been surprised if he had gotten here before I did. Guess I was luckier than he."

The footprints near camp suddenly made sense. Someone had indeed been watching them. All the fears they had been feeling previously seemed like nothing compared to the truth. Maddock had been watching them all.

"Why would Maddock do this?" Jonah shook his head, confused.

"I know his type," Jack said with gritted teeth. "They don't care for others, only for what they can gain. More than likely he would have done something like this without being marooned on an island. This just sped up his mutinous ways."

"Yes, I can attest to that." Chris tried to sit more upright but winced in pain. "Maddock and his pal Simon were hard to get along with from the start. I also overheard something about Annika and Carter. I don't think he much likes them."

Ethan jerked his head back. Annika and Carter! Chris's presence had distracted him from the fact that Maddock hated the two of them. He had to warn them, now. Who knew where Maddock was hiding and if he was watching now. The faces of Jonah and Jack showed they were thinking the same thing.

Ethan took off running, He had to find them before Maddock. If Maddock had been waiting for a good time to strike, this would be an ideal moment. Especially if he saw Chris stumble into their camp. Ethan just hoped he wasn't too late.

He took off running for the water, hearing Jonah and Jack's footsteps pounding behind him as they ran. Ethan's eyes frantically looked for Annika and Carter. Finally, he saw her standing near the edge of the water, Carter next to her. Was that Carter? He looked too tall to be Carter. Ethan's heart dropped when he realized that was not Carter but the vile man in question, Maddock.

The man's sinister eyes looked up at him as he approached. Maddock held Annika in front of him as a shield. His left hand was gripping her upper arm while his right hand held a knife to her throat. If Ethan's heart had been beating fast before, it now galloped at a reckless pace.

"Good day to you, Captain." Maddock snarled the words at him.

"What's gotten into you? Let her go this instant." Ethan took a step closer to them.

"You come any closer and I push this knife into her lovely neck." His grip on the knife tightened, causing Annika to take a sharp breath. Annika looked so small and fragile at this moment. Her usual fiery eyes were filled with fear.

"What is it that you want?" Ethan took a deep breath and steadied his gaze on the man. He had to stay calm and collected, even if it was just on the outside. It would not help Annika if he lost his cool. Maddock would use it to his advantage if he didn't keep calm.

"How kind of you to ask." A wicked grin crossed the man's face. "I want your ship and everything in it."

"If you promise to leave my men and Captain Samuel's alone then take it, it's all yours." Ethan knew that nothing was worth the price of losing his men and the new friends he had made.

"Oh, I will take it. In fact, it's already mine. Lastly, we will be keeping this one." Maddock lowered his face and breathed deeply into Annika's hair. Her eyes opened wide with fear. "I know someone who has been dying to get to know you."

"No, that's not an option. You keep the ship, but all my people stay with me." Ethan crossed his arms to keep the enemy from seeing the shaking in his limbs.

"I don't think you understand the predicament you are in right now. You are not the captain anymore, I am."

An evil glint was in his eyes. All of a sudden, men came out of the woods and surrounded them. Ethan could feel a blade at his back.

"We will keep the girl." Maddock continued calmly. "We have unsettled business, and it will be nice to have a female around." He spoke with his head resting against hers. "I will also keep the boy." He looked over to the trees and Ethan saw Simon standing, hidden.

Simon stepped forward. He was holding Carter by the neck. A knife was also placed on his throat. The boy looked surprisingly calm, other than his fear-filled eyes which were locked on Annika. Ethan hated being so helpless. He could do nothing.

"I will keep the boy and use him as sparring practice."

Annika's body stilled from its shaking. Her fearful eyes filled with anger as they locked onto Carter. The two shared a look and something visibly shifted in Annika. As Maddock laughed, Annika brought the heel of her foot down upon his boot and crushed his toes. He yelped. The knife loosened its position on her neck as Maddock's hand fell downwards. As soon as the knife shifted, Annika brought her head back and crushed his nose. The knife fell from his hands as he brought them up to his face.

"You devil woman," Maddock yelled and cursed at her.

Ethan's gaze flew to the woman he had grown to care so much for. Her eyes blazed with new fire as she stared the man down. She had picked up his knife and held it at the ready.

"I knew you were stupid, but I didn't know how much so until now." Maddock wiped his nose with his arm. Blood continued to trail down his face. His face already had looked disfigured but now it was much worse. His nose stuck out at an odd angle from the blow he had taken. His face was streaked with blood as his eyes took on a hardened look.

"Now your face matches your personality." Annika had her feet planted firmly to the ground, her eyes never straying from the man.

"Simon, care to remind her of our upper hand?"

Annika whirled to see Carter, her face full of worry. As she turned Maddock, grabbed the hand of hers that held the knife. He yanked her over the edge of embankment. The only thing below her was water. Her feet dangled in the air as she tried to gain footing but failed. A sound in the water drew everyone's attention. All eyes dropped to the water, which was a couple feet below Annika's dangling feet. The largest crocodile Ethan had ever seen was below, looking up at her with hungry eyes.

"No! Stop! Please! Do whatever you want with us, just let her and the boy go!" Ethan tried to step forward but was stopped by a punch to his stomach. He doubled over but caught himself before he fell to the ground.

"No!" Annika's frenzied cry came to his ears as pain overcame his body.

"Oh, I already will do that. I've decided I have no use for the wench anymore. Too feisty for my blood." Maddock took her hand and flung her into the water below.

"Annika!" Ethan and Carter shouted in unison.

"No!" Simon shouted as well.

She splashed into the water, disappearing for a couple long seconds. Finally, she came up, gasping for breath. The crocodile quickly zeroed in on its prey.

Ethan scrambled to his feet, intent on jumping in and getting her out. Hands grabbed at his shoulders and stopped his progress forward.

"This wasn't part of the plan.," Simon hissed, his brows drawn together in anger.

"Don't question me. You have seen what I am capable of," Maddock growled. He turned to Ethan with an evil smile. "Why don't you stay and watch?" He roughly grabbed his chin and forced Ethan to watch the gruesome sight.

Annikasaw the crocodile coming at her and turned back. Her eyes locked onto Ethan's. The fear in her eyes was evident, but a calm suddenly seemed to descend upon her. How or why it happened he could not comprehend.

"You may think you are in control, but you are not. Someday your sins are going to catch up to you, Maddock. I know where I'm going, and it'll be a lot nicer than where you will be," Annika said loud enough for them all to hear.

Just then the crocodile lunged, latched on to her shoulder and dragged her down below the surface. Her scream was drowned out by the water as they both disappeared. The last trace of her were some bubbles and wisps of dark red blood that colored the water.

Ethan's body shook violently with grief as he fell to the ground. No, this couldn't be. His mind kept replayed the horrifying images over and over again. Tears came to his eyes and a deep pain formed in his heart.

A wail burst out from Carter, He crumpled in the arms of Simon as he cried over the loss of his friend. Simon appeared in distress as well, not for pain of losing a friend but for losing the item of his lustful thoughts.

"Could it be that the fierce Captain Wolf had a soft spot for the pretty lady?" Maddock laughed and started to walk away from him. Ethan stood and punched the man in the gut before anyone could stop him. Maddock doubled over in pain, sputtering.

"No." Tears fell down Ethan's cheeks. All the light that had been seeping into his life was diminished in an instant. "You won't get away with this." Anger began building in his heart, drying his tears.

"I already have," Maddock said after recovering his breath. He rammed his own fist into Ethan's face. He couldn't even feel the kicks that followed as he was too numb with grief. Everything he ever loved was always taken from him.

CHAPTER NINETEEN

Annika's world went dark as she was forcefully pulled below the surface of the water. A piercing red-hot pain shot through her shoulder. It couldn't compare to the pain in her heart as she remembered the look on Ethan's face. His eyes screamed to her what he had never said. In that moment she had no doubt—he really did care for her.

Her lungs begged for air, leaving a burning ache in her chest. The pain built and the panic set in. No amount of swimming and thrashing was helping her get to the surface. Soon she had no fight left in her.

She floated lifeless in her new dark and cold world. *Elohim, where are You? Why did You let this happen? Everyone I care about is in danger and I can't help them.* Fear and doubt began to consume her body as the darkness around her began to close in on her.

"Ye, though I walk through the valley of the shadow of death, I will fear no evil," a voice whispered in her head.

The strength of David as he had written those words was incomprehensible. His fear must have been overwhelming in those days, but he was able to rely fully on Elohim. In the midst of all the fear and pain he went through, he was able to write words that would encourage others for thousands of years.

A light began to flicker in her heart.

Annika.

A voice called through the darkness and wrapped its way around her heart. It was not something she could describe as an earthly audible voice. More like a feeling and a presence in her heart.

Annika felt warm and loved. This was the presence of her Creator. If everyone could only feel what she felt at this very moment, there would be no doubt of His existence. Despite the all-surrounding darkness, she felt no fear. For a long while she just basked in the presence of Elohim. If she had to die, at least this was what was awaiting her.

A realization suddenly came over her as feeling began to come back into her body. She wasn't going to die. Suddenly, the numbness in her body faded, replaced by a deep shiver and a piercing pain in her chest. Her weak lungs took in one shaky breath and then another. It was ragged at first but soon she was breathing evenly.

Annika slowly blinked and found herself in the darkness still. Only a small amount of light was able to penetrate. She realized she was in water up to her waist. A roaring sound to her left seemed to bring back her senses. She had just been attacked by a crocodile. A searing pain in her shoulder affirmed that. There was a wall of falling water to her left; a faint stream of light was able to penetrate through. The light caused the water to shimmer around her and reflect on rock walls. She was in some sort of cave.

Something hissed in the darkness, causing her heart to jolt. Her eyes sought out the cause of the noise and she finally settled upon the dark silhouette of the crocodile. Its gleaming eyes looked at her from its position in the water. Its presence was a stark reminder of her situation. She remembered the words that had just been spoken to her. According to Elohim, she would not die here today.

Glowing eyes stared at her from the water, but she felt no hostility in its gaze. Its size alone was enough to show its strength. It was a deadly hunter that would not have thought anything of eating her. She would just be a snack to him.

The only explanation for her still being alive was Elohim. He had deemed her worthy of saving from the jaws of death. She refused to believe He would abandon her now.

Annika backed up and found the ground sloped up and the water receded. She continued until her back hit the wall of the cave. With something solid supporting her, it made the darkness not quite as intimidating. In front of her the beast had not moved. It continued to watch her, its yellow eyes almost glowing in the dark.

The pain in her shoulder suddenly caused her breath to hitch. She placed a probing hand up and discovered deep holes in her left shoulder. It would need pressure. Who knew how heavily she was bleeding? As she sat in the dark, the warm and peaceful presence stayed with her. The pain was still present in her body, but her mind felt at rest.

What had happened after the creature had sunk its jaws into her? Undoubtedly, everyone thought she was dead.

Annika rested her head against the wall of the cave and looked up. A story in the scriptures came to her mind: Daniel and the lion's den. It was a wonderful story speaking of one man's awe-inspiring faith to his Creator. His faith in Elohim was enough to save him from the jaws of the starving lions.

In many ways she felt much like Daniel. The mouth of her own beast had been shut up. Daniel had even been cast into a dark pit and what Annika was in now reminded her very much of the same thing.

The crocodile hissed again, its attention off of her now. It turned and looked to Annika's left. Then Annika heard what had the beast's attention. There were footsteps approaching and voices yelling. The sounds echoed through the cave. Had the others found her? Her heart leaped at the thought of seeing them all again. Perhaps they had overpowered Maddock.

She leaned forward from the wall, looking in the direction of the noise. She saw the faint glow of a light, bouncing off the wall of the cave and the sounds grew louder, more distinct. Soon several torches came into view. Annika strained to catch sight of the bearers of the light. Was it Ethan and the others?

Men came and surrounded the beast with spears, warding off any attack it might instigate. A familiar person was coming towards her, but it wasn't who she had expected. The young man she had saved from the sinking sand came running to her. His running was quite loud as he splashed through the water. He reached her side and knelt down, placing a hand on her shoulder. She grimaced as he accidentally placed a hand on her injured shoulder.

"Sorry, come. We help." He helped her stand to her feet. She swayed as she stood next to him. He said something in a different language, hoisted her off the ground and into his arms. If this had been any other time, she would have protested quite loudly but she was having problems even forming words.

The crocodile hissed as they passed by but didn't attack. As Annika was being hauled out, she took one last look at the beast. She had felt the closest she had ever felt to her Creator in this cave alongside an enemy.

The young man carried her through dark tunnels. Some of the men carried torches, causing the flickering light to bounce off their bare chests and the walls. Her mind began to grow fuzzy on details as her vision began to fade. She must be losing more blood than she had first thought. The aching in her shoulder intensified and came in waves. Each new wave of pain made her world darker.

In contrast, the tunnels appeared to be getting brighter now. Where were they taking her? Annika strained to keep her heavy eyes open, but soon the pain was too much to bear and she succumbed to the darkness.

There was a warm sensation on her face. It was pleasant. It would have felt nice to just lie there and enjoy it if not for the searing pain in her shoulder. Annika jerked awake and was startled to see a woman sitting next to her. She scrambled away and instantly regretted it as a wave of pain overcame her.

The woman, a beautiful dark-skinned woman, leaned forward to gently help her lie back down. The woman's lips curved upward, showing a sweet smile and laugh wrinkles around her lips.

"What's going on? Where am I?" Annika frantically looked about the room. The room was small and reminded her of the huts they first stayed in. The bed she was currently on , a small table, and a chair were the only things in the room.

"Do not worry, you are safe. No harm will come to you here." The woman's voice was smooth but tinged with a strange accent. She smoothed back the hair from Annika's face with a gentle hand. She held a glass of water to Annika and helped her drink.

The sweet liquid poured down her parched throat. It was much better than any of the water they had tasted on the island.

"How did I get here?" So many questions were itching to burst forth. Her head was pounding, and her dry throat was begging for more water.

"We found you injured and in the lair of the Maveth. That was two days ago now." The woman's dark brown hair was straight and fell down to her waist. She filled the small water glass from a pitcher on the table. "As for your other question, you are now safe in the heart of Avigdor."

"Avigdor?" Annika shook her head, still trying to clear her thoughts. "I don't understand, where is that?"

"You need to speak with my husband and also Chief Tuviah. Can you stand?" Annika allowed the woman to help her up from the bed and take another sip of water. She was surprised to find herself so shaky. How badly had she been hurt?

"My shoulder really hurts," Annika said through gritted teeth as the woman helped her pull a pretty blouse over her head.

"Sorry." The woman offered a gentle smile as her fingers deftly moved. The outfit she had helped Annika into was a pretty white top and the skirt was a leaf green color. What struck her as strange was the woman had helped her put leather pants on first. Though they were comfortable, it was strange to wear them under her skirt.

A sudden realization came over her. "Wait, did you say it's been two days?" They must all think she was dead. She didn't even know if they were all right.

"Yes, you were in bad shape for the first two days. You slept the entire time and had a fever. Last night, the fever finally broke." The kind woman smoothed out some wrinkles on Annika's dress.

"Who are you?" Annika leaned against the bed frame. Her legs were feeling stronger but not completely reliable.

"My name is Rivkah. I'm the healer on Avigdor. What is your name?" Rivkah was a head shorter than Annika but seemed to be well built. Her arms looked strong, and she carried herself with confidence, though Annika noticed that she had a slight limp as she walked around the room.

"I'm Annika." She sighed, partially out of frustration. "I have so many questions."

"Come with me. It will be easier for you to talk with my husband." Rivkah opened the door and gestured for Annika to exit with her. They walked out of the small room, and Annika was instantly greeted with the warm rays of the sun. She squinted as her eyes adjusted to the light. Upon regaining her vision, the sight she saw nearly took her breath away.

A bustling village lay before her. Children ran by laughing. People stood outside, some gardening and others selling things in stalls. That wasn't what caught her eye so much as the animals. There was an animal that she had never seen before. Its back towered above people's heads and its tail dragged behind it. Its shiny green skin appeared to be scaled. It walked on four legs and had a saddle on its back. A man came next to it and patted its head. A happy sound came from the animal's mouth. The three horns on its head shimmered in the light. The man loaded some sacks on the animals back and guided it away from the crowd.

Annika turned her awestricken face to Rivkah, who was looking at her with a knowing smile.

"Where am I?" Annika asked the woman as she studied the rest of the village. She suddenly noticed that many of the people had large bat-like creatures perched on their shoulders.

Rivkah chuckled. She whistled and suddenly a creature flew out from the nearby trees and flew to Rivkah's side.

"Avigdor is a special place." She reached out and scratched the animal under its chin and it squawked happily. It was about four feet tall, but its wings had to be more than double that. It had green scaly skin and a long shiny beak. Its glowing yellow eyes studied her with great intensity.

Rivkah laughed at Annika's dumbfounded expression. "He said you would be surprised. Please, come with me. You will get your answers." She clicked her tongue, and the large animal flew off her shoulders and back into the trees.

Rivkah took her hand and gently guided her through the throng of people. She was grateful for the guidance as she was having a hard time looking where she was going. Words would not form in her mouth, and she stared at the unusual sights before her.

Everywhere she looked she was confused and in awe. Large lizard-like animals were in the fields helping with the heavy lifting. Others ran with children as they played a game with coconuts.

Some walked on two legs and others on four. There were tall animals and some just barely bigger than a house cat. Perhaps she was still asleep and had yet to wake up, although this all felt quite real to her.

As they walked, Annika noticed how pronounced Rivkah's limp was but somehow it did not slow her down. It took all she had to keep up with the woman.

Rivkah led Annika past several different huts and to a large fire. There were men sitting around the fire conversing with one another.

Rivkah approached a tall man who was dressed quite unlike the natives. His clothing wasn't as primitive as theirs. He wore black pants and a white shirt. His long blond hair was tied at the base of his neck. A thick beard covered a large portion of his face. His lips curved into a smile at the sight of Rivkah. He reached out and took her hand. Rivkah accepted his hand, and a smile graced her lips as her cheeks pinked up.

"This is my husband." Rivkah's twinkling eyes found hers.

"Ah, our guest is awake. How are you feeling?" He smiled warmly.

"My shoulder hurts a bit, but honestly I'm mostly confused."

"I can imagine why." He chuckled softly. He gestured to a log nearby. Annika was still not yet steady on her feet, so she accepted.

"I can see introductions are in order,." the man said as soon as he was seated. "My name is Gabriel, Gabriel Hoffman."

"Pleased to meet you." Annika attempted a shaky smile. "My name is Annika Harper. I was told by your wife that you are the man to talk to if I want answers. Please, won't you tell me where I am and where my friends are?"

"Of course. First, we have not left the island. Your friends are still close by. Our scouts are tracking them as we speak. Here, let me show you on a map." He smiled and leaned forward on the log that he sat on. He took a small stick that was laying on the ground and began drawing something in the dirt. "This is our island here." He drew a large oblong circle as Annika leaned forward and looked more intently.

He then proceeded to add some details that Annika recognized, the parts of it from the map Ethan had shown her.

"This here is where you and your friends entered the island." He pointed to a spot on the beach near the left side of the island. "These are the huts you stayed in for a while and this is the waterfall where you just left." He pointed out each spot to her as he drew them. Annika's curious eyes traveled across the map.

"What's this place?" She pointed to the middle of the island. In the center, where the volcano should be, he had drawn a large circle.

"That is where you are now. This is the heart of Avigdor. You see this here—this is the island's volcano. Its walls surround us." He pointed out the circle on the map. "These protect us from outsiders, giving us safety within their borders."

"So, all this time we have been on your island, Avigdor?" Annika tried pronouncing the strange word. "How long have you known that we were here?"

"Since you first came to our shores. The scouts reported your coming. You see, these people have long had visitors to their shores. Many have heard tales of the riches of this island and come to take it for themselves. Hidden within the volcano, they are kept safe from outsiders. Or the island's wildlife itself scares them off."

"We probably would have been scared off if we hadn't been stuck here." Annika smiled sheepishly. Gabriel seemed kind and was easy to talk to.

"We gathered that much from our scouting. The island is not easy to live on, is it?" As he spoke, Rivkah sat on the log next to him.

"No, that much is certainly true. Have you been watching us closely this whole time?"

"Yes, not me personally, but we have men who venture beyond these walls. They keep tabs on the island and its visitors."

"How are my friends? Last they saw of me I was in the jaws of that thing." She couldn't stop thinking of the pain on their faces and fearing for their safety.

"A few days ago, they were taken back to the huts. Now they are being held hostage. Kept out of sight in the huts while other men walk freely and eat food from the island. The others are fed little, but they are alive." Gabriel looked pained to tell her all this. For good reason. It was hard news to swallow. Her heart plummeted upon hearing it.

"I can't believe this. Maddock is such a twisted man to betray us like this." She frowned.

"Who's Maddock?"

"He's the definition of the word vile. He incited a mutiny and is now holding my friends hostage. Carter, my friend, and I are not in his good books. We hurt his pride, and he took an instant disliking to us. Not that it's difficult to incite his anger. He and his friend, Simon, have been bothering us since we first met. Mostly just angry stares but things started to escalate. I'm honestly not surprised someone like him would start a mutiny, but to see him actually go through with it..." She shook her head. "He threw me to the crocodile in the lake and made my friends watch as I was pulled under."

"Our men saw it happen. Sadly, they were too far away to intervene. They saw Maveth enter its cave behind the falls. They hurried, hoping they could help you, but were certain they would find you dead. Imagine their surprise when you were not only alive but had only minor injuries." He looked at her bandaged shoulder and grimaced. "Well, minor to some extent. We still don't know what happened. Why did Maveth let you go?"

"Maveth is the name for the crocodile, correct?" She remembered Rivkah saying the same thing but hadn't actually connected the name with the animal yet. At both Gabriel and Rivkah's nod, she continued. "I honestly am not sure. I thought for sure I was a goner. I can't explain it any other way than to say Elohim shut the mouth of Maveth."

Gabriel and Rivkah smiled widely. "He does perform miracles." He reached for his wife's hand and squeezed it. "We too know of Elohim and His power. It would not take much from Him to shut the jaws of Maveth."

The very mention of the animal caused Annika's shoulder to flare up with new pain. She winced. Suddenly, she realized what Gabriel had just said.

"You two believe in Elohim?" Annika's mouth fell open. Since Narine's decree, it was rare for her to meet other believers.

"With all our hearts." Rivkah smiled and stood. She came around to Annika and fidgeted with the bandage on her arm. No doubt her keen eyes had seen the small wince from earlier.

"The whole village does." Gabriel gestured all around him.

Annika laughed in astonishment. "That's amazing! It's so rare for me to find others who believe the same. I know it sounds crazy, but I was the most at peace in my life while in the jaws of death."

"Really?" Rivkah leaned forward, her eyes alight with curiosity. She pulled the bandage back and applied some salve to the wound. It stung for a moment but soon felt cooling.

"Yes, I heard a voice call my name right as I thought it was the end. I was suddenly enveloped in peace. It's really hard to describe, actually."

"Sounds like He still has plans for you," Rivkah said quietly as she finished putting the salve on. She once again wrapped Annika's shoulder and then sat by her husband.

"I hope He does." Annika smiled.

"Who are these people you are traveling with? Are they merchants?" Gabriel brought her attention back.

"Well…" This was going to be confusing. "It's a very long story. I'll tell the short version. The merchant ship we were traveling on got attacked by pirates. We both got caught in a storm and our ship sunk. Surprisingly, the pirates took us in. They have actually treated us kindly. Even going so far as to pay our captain back for the merchandise they took. Since arriving here, we have all become quite close. Ethan—Captain Wolf I mean—is a good man."

Gabriel's face was unreadable. "I don't have good experiences with pirates. I find it difficult to believe any could act honorably, such as you have described." Rivkah put a gentle hand on his knee. He grasped it and held on.

"I know it's hard to believe. I myself had a hard time trusting them at first. Captain Wolf has shown time and time again that he cares for his men and for us. Jonah told me of Captain Wolf's paying our captain back for what he took. He said he does that for everyone that they rob."

Curiosity filled his eyes. "Who's this Jonah?"

"Captain Wolf's first mate. His word is very trustworthy. I've never known him to speak falsely or even harshly."

"I see." His face had become puzzled now. "In my experience no pirate is trustworthy. I assume, like all pirates, they are horrible men with evil intentions."

"No, Captain Wolf and his men are not like that. They are more well behaved than Captain Samuel's men. Maddock was one of his. Everyone on Captain Wolf's crew is kind. We have all become friends, actually. Captain Wolf, Jonah, Jack, Carter, and myself. We were all camped at the lake, hoping to find help."

"I see. Very interesting." Gabriel rubbed his bearded chin, an unreadable expression on his face. He was silent for a few moments before continuing. "I will speak of this all to the chief. See what he has to say about all this."

"Will he help us?"

"I'm not sure, honestly. Give me some time to talk with him." He smiled reassuringly.

The creature that Rivkah had shown Annika earlier flew out of the trees and landed next to the couple. It gave a satisfied squawk and eyed Annika up and down.

"What is that thing?" Annika's wide eyes still couldn't really believe what they were seeing.

Gabriel laughed. "I said the same thing when I first came here. I'm sure you've noticed this place is far different than anything you have ever seen." Annika nodded, her eyes not leaving the strange creature. "Have you heard the stories of the Ancients that walked our lands and swam in our waters? Perhaps your parents told you stories of them?"

"My father once told me stories of Ancients that could breathe fire and others that could fly."

"Yes, my father had told me the same thing. He had written accounts, though, from people who had recorded what they had seen. The accounts spoke of large lizard-like animals, or Ancients so they called them. In the stories that you hear as children these creatures were always portrayed as evil. Burning villages and carrying off babies, that sort of thing. In the accounts I read, however, none of these so-called Ancients were destructive like that. Sure, they defended themselves and their young but, what animal doesn't do that? What's more is, these animals were not the scary fire-breathing monsters from the stories. Some have wings, like Talon here. There are even ones that live in the oceans and rivers, as you yourself experienced." He glanced at her bandaged arm.

"That was an Ancient?" Her eyes had to be bulging by now. So much information was being thrown her way it was hard to keep up.

"Yes." He smiled. "The animals that have been mistaken as blood-thirsty monsters are little more than extinct animals. The one you encountered seems to be some sort of ancestor to our modern-day crocodile. Perhaps triple the length and the strength as well."

The scar that was sure to be left on her arm would bear new meaning now. She had been in the jaws of one of the Ancients of legend.

"That's amazing! Why have they disappeared everywhere but on this island?"

"I've wondered that myself. In the accounts I read there are many times these animals were mistakenly thought to be dangerous and because of that many were killed. With much more of the land having been explored, it's much harder for them to stay hidden. Here? That's a different story. I believe Rivkah can explain to you more about the island itself." He stood to his feet. "I will go and speak with the chief now. Soon, he will call to speak with you as well."

"Yes, of course. Thank you. I await word from you."

With that Gabriel excused himself and walked swiftly away, leaving Annika and Rivkah around the fire.

Rivkah leaned forward on the log. "Would you like to see the island on the eastern side?" Her eyes glinted with excitement.

"What if the chief wishes to speak with me soon?"

"Not to worry, they will talk for hours. We will be back before long."

"Well, all right. I must say this place is very intriguing." Annika eyed Talon, who tilted his head and stared at her quizzically.

"Wonderful, come with me." Rivkah jumped to her feet. Talon took to the skies as Rivkah hurriedly limped away and Annika scrambled to catch up. They walked into a field that was close by, and Rivkah whistled shrilly.

"What was that for?" Annika looked around confused.

"You'll see." Rivkah looked back at her, her eyes dancing. The grass around them was tall and waved rhythmically in the slight breeze.

Suddenly the ground began to shake. Annika looked around wildly for the cause. It wasn't strong enough to be an earthquake or the awaking of a volcano. It felt like a whole herd of horses were running this way. Suddenly, two beasts came out of the tall grass and sped for them. The tall lizards ran on their hind legs, their long tails swishing behind them. They ran up to Rivkah and she stroked their smooth snouts.

"These are our rides." Rivkah summoned Annika closer. Annika's jaw hung open. She was expected to ride on one of those things?

"Why don't we just walk?"

"Not if you wish to be back soon to speak with the chief." Rivkah seemed to be enjoying the look on Annika's face. Her joy was quite apparent. "Do not worry, they are herbivores. They are ridden on all the time and are quite used to it."

Annika suddenly noticed the saddles attached to their backs. It looked somewhat like a saddle a horse would wear but looked completely foreign on such a strange animal.

"As long as your shoulder does not pain you badly?" Rivkah's eyes dropped their excitement and turned to concern.

Annika shrugged her shoulder, testing the level of pain. "It actually hasn't much since you put the salve on it."

"Wonderful!" The excitement returned. "Swifts have a very smooth gate, once you get used to it. We can start out slow and see how it goes?"

The large animals looked Annika up and down. Her unease rose at the thought of climbing onto its back.

"Swifts?"

"Yes, that is what we call them. You will understand why we gave them that name soon." Rivkah grinned.

"If you are sure it's ok." Annika sidled closer to the animal she was expected to ride.

"They are completely safe to ride. They would not hurt a fly. As for your shoulder, it only has a few stitches. With the salve, you should be feeling completely normal within a day or so. The salve works very fast. Come, I'll help you." Annika did as was requested and walked closer to the creatures. Their backs rose to Annika's head and their necks stretched another three feet. The animal's yellow eyes looked at her curiously. There was no fear or anger in its gaze, just avid curiosity.

Rivkah patted the animal's hindquarters, and it knelt down to the ground, exposing the saddle. "Grab onto the leather strap at the top." Annika was very clumsy, however, and struggled to get a good grip. Finally, with a bit of help from Rivkah, she got a hold of the strap and hoisted herself onto the saddle. Her skirts bunched up around her, exposing her legs.

"How do you deal with this?" Annika saw Rivkah was also wearing a skirt.

"Ahh, yes. I forgot to tell you." She pulled a strap from behind her back at her waist. The material fell forward and the front of the skirt opened up. Rivkah wore the same kind of leather pants she had given Annika earlier.

Annika found the strap and was able to untie it. The skirt opened in the front, allowing her to sit much more comfortably in the saddle. Now the addition of pants made sense.

Rivkah laughed and swung into her own saddle. "You look tense. Here, lean forward on its back and neck." She demonstrated.

Annika attempted to lean forward in the saddle as well. She was surprised to find the stirrups seemed to sit better in this position. There were even leather straps tied around the animal's neck for her to hold onto.

"That's better. Don't worry about steering, he will follow my lead. Just hang on!" With that Rivkah nudged her animal onward and made a clicking sound with her tongue. Off she went and Annika followed. Talon flew overhead and followed his master. No doubt he was puzzled at the newcomer's inability to balance atop her mount.

Annika tried to mimic the movements she saw Rivkah doing. She seemed to move in unison with the animal. She looked comfortable and graceful atop the large lizard.

Annika was surprised to find that even with the movement of the swift, her shoulder barely hurt. It took a few tries, but she was able to mimic the movements of the seasoned rider ahead of her. Soon she was no longer bouncing in the saddle. Instead, it felt as if she were gliding across the hills. It was a rather exhilarating feeling. One she could quite easily get used to.

CHAPTER TWENTY

Ethan leaned back against the rough wall of the hut he was tied to. Rain drizzled lazily on the rooftop overhead. At least they were indoors. That was the one positive he had found in the last couple of days.

He shut his eyes, trying to get some sleep. His anger had carried him through the last couple of days, but now he was just too tired. His strength felt completely depleted.

Now, with all the anger seeped out of him, all that was left was grief. Everything he knew and owned was at the hands of evil men once again. Sadness that his friends had been hurt and no one knew if they would even see the next sunrise.

Lastly, a deep aching grief for the life of a truly precious woman. She had indeed begun to take a firm place in his heart only to be ripped brutally out. Left in her place was now a big gaping hole. If his life had seemed dark before she came, now it was pitch black.

Every time he shut his eyes, all he could see was her beautiful face as she was taken down to her death. He had stared at the water until they had forcefully dragged him away and hauled him back to the huts. His anger had kept him from thinking of anything too deeply until just recently. Now his mind was plagued with thoughts of why? She was such a good and pure person.

"Hey, Captain, how you holding up?" Carter was on his knees next to him, his arms tied behind him and attached to the wall. Carter had been distraught and had grieved for Annika the whole journey back to the huts. Upon reaching their fellow prisoners, something in him had shifted. He still seemed sad but not overcome with grief as Ethan was.

"Evidently, not as good as you. Why are you still smiling? If you secretly have a reason, I wish you would tell me. I could use a bit of hope or humor." His heart ached too much for him to even attempt a smile.

"I'm struggling, just as the rest of you. The only difference is I have my faith to keep me going." The youth smiled a weary smile.

"How can you have faith in a god who could just take someone away, like he took Annika?" He closed his eyes, determined not to shed anymore tears in front of his men. Ever since the night he had lost both his father and brother, he had never cried for someone else. Over the last couple of days, he had definitely shed his fair share of tears.

"I thought the same thing for a while. I'm ashamed to admit it, but I struggled with her death and why Elohim would take her from me. She was the only family I had." Carter blinked moisture from his eyes. "But, Captain, Elohim didn't throw her into the water to that beast. Sinful men threw her in. Did you see her face before she disappeared? She looked in the eyes of that evil and had no fear. Elohim may not have saved her from death, but He did give her peace in the eye of it. I want to have that kind of faith someday."

Ethan and Carter both looked at the wooden ceiling above their heads, listening to the rain. Had Elohim really given her peace in her final moments? Ethan could vividly remember her face. Her beautiful face had love and peace etched into it. Even in the eyes of death, she had believed in Elohim.

Why had he behaved the complete opposite? Something tragic had happened to him, and he ran from Elohim.

Was Elohim out there, just waiting for him to call upon His name? It was hard to believe that someone out there could care enough about him to want him. Especially if they saw the anger and resentment he carried.

Carter's stomach growled in hunger, reminding Ethan of his own hungry stomach. They had been fed next to nothing over the last couple of days.

"Carter, would you tell your stomach to pipe down? Mine finally forgot about food." Jack's stomach began growling and he groaned. "Never mind, too late." His words were teasing as he gave them a small smile from his spot against the wall to Ethan's left. The room was filled with men, their arms tied behind their backs, attached to the walls of the hut.

"You've never been able to forget about food. Even in this kind of circumstance that's all you can think about." Jonah's big form was propped against the wall to Jack's left. He looked at his friend with his brow quirked up. Jack gave him a playful kick, if the feeble attempt could even be called that. Ethan was so thankful for his crew. Their smiles and laughter even in difficult situations was like medicine to his soul.

As the morning rays began to show over the horizon, he wondered what else the day would bring.

The field passed by in a blur. Soon they were riding through groves of trees. The fresh smell of fruit lingered in the air. In no time at all, they were past the fruit tree groves and were quickly approaching the volcano's edge. Rivkah slowed her animal and Annika's followed suit. They walked slowly for a few feet before Rivkah dismounted. Annika joined her on the ground and stared at the massive wall in front of them.

"This is what I wanted to show you." Rivkah walked ahead.

"It is impressive, I have to admit, but could I not have seen this from the village?"

"We are not here to see the wall."Rivkah laughed and limped to the base of the wall. She beckoned Annika to follow her. Near the wall was a wooden platform and ropes rigged over the top, stretching clear up the wall. Talon came swooping down and walked on all fours with them.

"What's this?" Annika ran a finger along the firm wooden rails of the platform and turned just in time to see Rivkah pull a lever. Suddenly, the platform jolted and started to rise. Annika gripped onto the rail wildly.

"Do not worry, this is completely safe," Rivkah said reassuringly. As the ground shrank below her, Annika really did not feel like it was.

"Is your goal for the day to terrify me beyond comprehension? If it is, you are doing a marvelous job." Annika was jesting, partially.

Rivkah laughed, which seemed to soothe Annika's nerves. "How are we going up?"

"It's something my people have developed. It's a pulley system." Rivkah beamed with pride.

The ground was now so far down it threatened to make Annika dizzy. She instead raised her eyes to the horizon and saw the sun was beginning to make its decent in the sky. It would set in a matter of hours.

The village lay in the distance, nestled between some hills and a stream. Even from this distance, you could see several of the larger Ancients moving about.

They jerked to a stop, the action causing Annika to rudely awaken from her thoughts. Surprise coursed through her as she realized they were already at the top. The platform was now level with the top of the wall. Rivkah turned around to the wall and opened a small latch on the rail.

She led the way onto the top of the rock wall. This section was smooth and flat. It must be used often, for there were rails and another pulley system on the other side. Another platform was sitting at the top, awaiting its next passengers. Rivkah did not take her on it but instead to the rail overlooking the other side of the wall.

"This top portion of the volcano is the smoothest. We just did a bit of work to level it out and create an area for us to use."

"Are you not afraid to live in the center of a volcano?"

Rivkah chuckled. "It's been dormant for hundreds of years. All that's left are the walls that you see now. We have smoothedout small portions at the tops."

"I see. Why is this spot so important?" She joined Rivkah at the rail and looked out at the jungle below.

"Just watch."

Movement below attracted her eye. As soon as she registered what her eyes were seeing, her mouth went slack. Big animals walked below, drinking in a small lake or grazing in the fields. The largest ones had very long necks and walked on four legs. Their large bodies appeared to move in slow motion, their footsteps heavy enough to shake the ground., Its body had to be over sixty feet in length and over thirty feet tall. Smaller ones walked nearby, grazing on bushes and bellowing peacefully to one another.

"What is this place? It's beautiful." Her voice was merely a whisper.

"This is the eastern side of the island. The herbivores are able to roam freely here. No carnivores are around to bother them. Well, very few at least."

"Why did we not see any of this before?"

"You all entered our island on the shores on the southern side. This is all out of sight, hidden in a valley."

"It's remarkable." Annika couldn't take her eyes off the sight before her. A different type of Ancient with plates atop its back approached the water. "Why are there no carnivores here but we have encountered more than our fair share of them?"

Rivkah sighed. "That's where our history gets a bit more complicated. At first, our people did not live within the safety of the volcano. We lived in small huts in the wilds of the jungles. We shared the island with a vast amount of animals, both herbivore and carnivore. Our people once saw these creatures as a threat and began killing any that they could. We would use their pelts for clothing and their bones for weapons. Soon we had hunted them into near extinction. Until one day a new chief came into power. He saw the value in all of the animals, both herbivore and carnivore, and did not wish to cause further destruction to them.

"We stopped killing the animals and tried to preserve the ones that were still on the island. But we had already upset the balance, causing the carnivores to run rampant and the herbivores to dwindle even further. The situation became so bad that we needed to move our people. Soon, we found this valley." Rivkah gestured to the valley below them. "It's at the bottom of a sheer drop off. After finding that, we eventually found a way past the walls and to our new home. We placed the herbivores in the valley below and have started a new ecosystem for them. Now, they thrive here and the carnivores on the rest of the island double as protection from outsiders."

"Would the carnivores not die off now that the herbivores reside here?" Annika watched a long-necked animal lean back on two legs to reach the branches of a tall tree.

"Somehow, a new ecosystem was created. They hunt things like monkey and deer, which are able to reproduce quickly now. Elohim's creation is rather resilient, is it not?" Rivkah smiled. "It's really taught us how to be better stewards to our environment. We only kill animals that we eat, and everything thrives."

"This is all so amazing. It's far different from anything back home." Annika shook her head and chuckled. "The biggest animal I had ever seen was a horse."

"Tell me of your home." Rivkah turned her attention to Annika.

"There's not much to tell. My friend Carter and I come from an orphanage. The animals there are not exotic like the ones here. We have fields and trees but nothing as magnificent as what I've seen here. I'd say home was pretty bland compared to this. Even the colors seem brighter here."

"What of your father and mother?"

"My mother died five years ago, and shortly after that, our father left us in the orphanage." Annika tried not to dwell on it. How could something from so long ago still hurt like this?

"I'm so sorry. My mother died as well. She died just a few years ago. Thankfully, she had met Gabriel and had learned of Elohim before she passed." She placed a tender hand on Annika's shoulder. "What was your mother like?"

Sweet memories started to play in her mind. "Actually, you remind me of her a lot. Your energy and your love of life. My mother was kind and generous. If anyone was ever in need, she was right there to help. If you messed with her kids, though, she was a force to be reckoned with." Annika laughed. "She used to tell us stories before bed and sing us to sleep when we were sad."

"She sounds like a wonderful woman. My mother did much of the same. Sounds like they could have been good friends if they had met." The two shared a smile.

Silence settled between the two. The only sound was the peaceful bellows from the large animals below.

"So, tell me, I have been meaning to ask... how did your husband find his way here? He seems to know much of the outside world."

Rivkah chuckled. "Yes, my husband does indeed have a vast amount of knowledge, though he is very humble about it. He actually used to live in the kingdom of Lookonia. He was close friends with the king. During the assassination of the king, Gabriel was abducted by pirates. They soon after brought him here to find the riches of the island."

"Really? He was abducted? How awful!" Annika turned and found a smile on Rivkah's face.

"Yes, he did have a rough couple weeks on the island with the pirates. They encountered Ancient cats and fierce crocodiles. They stumbled upon stinging ant nests and scoured caves full of giant beetles. Through it all, the pirates suffered immensely, but one thing that stuck out to us was the way Gabriel behaved. Through all of it he stayed calm and collected. Even as his hands were bound, he would still pray to his God, who was quite foreign to us at the time." Rivkah scratched Talon under the beak and the animal rubbed its head against her arm affectionately.

"We kept an eye on the pirates and had scouts listening in, trying to understand what they were saying. In fact, I was one of the scouts keeping an eye on him. The way he behaved and acted towards his captors intrigued me. Something about him was just different. The day his eyes caught mine from in the trees was the day my life was forever changed."

She paused long enough that Annika wondered if she would continue. Rivkah's face was serene, as if recalling a beautiful memory.

"I know he remembers those days differently," she continued. "But for me it was like finding a light in a dark world. After he came, Gabriel brought teachings of Elohim and His word. He taught us of the outside world. He brought light to everything he touched. That's why the people adore him so. Very quickly he became dear to me. I knew from the moment we locked eyes that he would forever hold my heart."

Annika sighed. "That's so sweet. You two really had quite the first meeting, I must say. How did Gabriel get away from the pirates though? Surely, they did not just let him go and sail away peacefully."

Rivkah's eyes darkened and the smile disappeared from her face. "Indeed not. The pirates tired of their unsuccessful search for riches. They camped along the river and the weather turned sour. The night became pitch black, and rain poured down. The darkness was only breached by the flashes of lightning and the burst of light from gunpowder. They turned on one another and shot whomever they felt like. It was as if their greed had blinded them so completely that they didn't notice the death all around. It was a horrific sight to behold.

"In the midst of the death and destruction I saw Gabriel, still bound. I ran into the skirmish and pulled him out. As we were about to enter the trees, we heard a great cry. We turned and saw Maveth had come from the water. In no time at all, he had killed whoever was left on that beach. No man escaped from the aftermath of that day, save for Gabriel. Even I barely escaped." She stretched her bad leg.

Annika's thoughts went to the stretch of river where they had found all the skeletons, the severed spines, and the scattered bodies. She shivered. The depth of the destruction from that day was indeed devastating.

"You were injured during the fight?"

Rivkah nodded her head. "A stray bullet got me while I was freeing Gabriel."

"I'm sorry, I can't even imagine what that must have been like."

Rivkah nodded. "Neither would you want to, but if it had not happened and if Gabriel had not been abducted, I never would have met him. We never would have wed, and I would still be living in darkness, without Elohim to light my way. Elohim is able to bring good from the worst of situations."

"I'm beginning to see that." Annika thought of the anger she had possessed towards Ethan when she had first met him. "I know I did not ask for us to be robbed by pirates, and I most certainly did not ask to be brought here either. If none of it had happened, I never would have met Captain Wolf and I would not have even known of the existence of you all."

"Are you and this captain close?" Rivkah smiled knowingly at Annika.

"We are friends. I'm sure he does not wish for anything more." Annika chuckled sadly and sighed. "I have to admit, I do care for him, but he holds such anger for Elohim and pain from his past."

Rivkah placed a gentle hand on her shoulder. "I understand. Matters of the heart are often complicated. I will be praying for you both." She lightly squeezed her shoulder. "Now, come with me. We have time for a quick ride around the lake before supper and meeting with the chief."

Ethan slowly walked outside, enjoying the few minutes of freedom they were allowed in the day. They were given a few minutes a day to go relieve themselves. Those who couldn't wait ended up going in the huts, making their already difficult situation even harder.

He hadn't found a way of escape as of yet. It had been a long two days since they had been captured, and his resolve and strength were beginning to fade. In that time, he had eaten next to nothing, as had the rest of the loyal men, while Maddock and his men feasted on wild game they had managed to catch.

The only people that Maddock had kept free were the ones fixing the ship. Some continued work on gathering materials, and the builders stayed on the ship and repaired damages. All this under constant supervision, of course.

It didn't take Ethan long to finish his business in the bushes. He spent the remainder of his time in the sun, soaking in its warm rays. The nights had been much colder lately since they weren't allowed a fire. The heat was not enough to warm his empty heart, though.

If he was a praying man, he would have used this opportunity to ask for deliverance from their oppressors. Since he wasn't, he could only draw on hope that the island's dangerous predators would find Maddock and his minions before the ship was fixed. It was surprising how quickly the repairs were getting done. Within days, the ship would be repaired enough for travel, at least until they reached a port where they could repair it fully. If they left this island, he would more than likely become a slave. Sold to the highest bidder at the next port, as would most of his men and Captain Samuel's loyal men.

Captain Samuel was kept close to Maddock for the most part. The evil man seemed bent on breaking the poor man's spirit, berating him with taunts and ridicule, and sometimes just plain beating him. The captain surprised even Ethan with his unwavering ability to remain strong and withstand their words and the physical pain. He would sit and take the taunts with a stoic look on his face, and the beating he would endure with a smile.

Ethan couldn't help but hope he would one day be as strong a leader as him, if they got out of this situation alive.

He sighed and opened his eyes again to the hopeless situation around him. Men were being rounded up, corralled back to the cramped huts. Ethan walked along beside them, their hopeless faces echoing how he felt inside.

Even Jack's normally perky attitude had shrunk to just a fraction of what it had once been. Everyone just sat and waited, for their impending death or their future as slaves. Who knew what the traitors had in store for them.

If only they had never boarded Captain Samuel's ship, they would not be in this mess. They would never have set foot on this island and would never even had met Maddock. Ethan would still be captain of his own ship and not bound in a dark and damp hut.

The decision to board Captain Samuel's ship had brought so many hardships to his crew. Though, he had to admit, there had been some surprisingly good moments as well.

He had met a good and honest captain, someone he could look to and strive to be more like. He had met Carter, who was a constant stream of kindness and compassion.

Above all, he had met a woman, one with the most spunk and kindness he had ever met. He had allowed himself to begin dreaming of the future instead of dwelling in his past. She had been a beacon of light in his dark and painful world. For a short time, he had entertained thoughts of love and a future.

His heart dropped upon thinking of her again, his mind constantly reminding him of her loss and the tragic last moments leading to her death. If anything, it was a consolation. He was glad she did not have to endure the pain of what their hopeless future would hold. It would have broken his heart and spirit even further to see her auctioned off as a slave or tormented by Maddock and his men.

The memory of her was bittersweet. There had been so many moments of peace around her. He suddenly realized that the last few weeks had been a soothing balm to his injured soul. Whether it was the new comrades he had met or the beautiful warrior he had fallen for. His world had gone from a dark and fearful place to one of light and love. For that he would always be thankful, even if it had just been for a few weeks.

Carter came and sat next to Ethan again as they were all being tied back to the wall. His eyes sparkled, and he was almost hopping with excitement.

"What has you in such a good mood today?" His own voice was almost unrecognizable to him after days of limited conversation and little water. Maddock's men finished binding them to the walls again and left.

Carter waited until they were out of the room. "I had a dream, Captain. I believe Elohim is trying to tell me something." He leaned forward and whispered in Ethan's ear, "I believe He is trying to tell me about Annika. She could still be alive." Ethan's heart wanted to believe that were possible, but his mind knew better.

He sighed. "You don't know how much I wish that were true, but it is impossible. You saw the blood, and she never came up. There's no earthly way of escaping the jaws of a beast like that. Best get those thoughts out of your head. They will only lead to disappointment."

"I don't think so, Captain. Remember, Elohim is not earthly." The young boy shook his head.

"In any case, don't speak of them to me. I see her demise every time I close my eyes and don't wish to be reminded unnecessarily." He turned away from the boy, hoping he understood to leave him alone. All was quiet for a moment.

"I know what I saw. You don't have to believe me, but be ready. Something is going to happen very soon, and we all need to be ready." Carter finally grew quiet. After a few moments, Ethan stole a look at the young man. He had fallen asleep and was breathing deeply, a smile upon his face.

CHAPTER
TWENTY-ONE

Annika and Rivkah entered the bustling village on their mounts. Their ride had been thrilling and incredibly beautiful. The heart of Avigdor was full of new sights and things that caused her to gape in awe. The lake had glistened in the sunlight as the trees swayed gently in the breeze. She had gotten used to the rhythm of the Ancient creature beneath her. She and the animal now moved as one.

The animal Annika rode on was called Ember, for the orange streak across his head. They were surprisingly gentle creatures, nothing like the Ancients in the stories.

After an enjoyable ride, they rode into town. Their height atop the animals' backs brought them a few feet above the crowd. The people seemed just as used to the animals as they were to them. The lizards walked calmly through the throng and to a gathering of huts.

Talon flew ahead and landed gracefully in a tree near one of the huts. The hut was slightly larger than the others she had seen. Rivkah led the way to the hut and stopped.

She slid off her mount. "This is my home here. You can stay here for the time being, if that's all right with you?"

Annika dismounted from the animal's back and slid somewhat gracefully down. "Yes, of course, thank you. Will we be speaking with the chief soon?"

"Soon. We will get supper ready and speak with him there." Rivkah rubbed her mount's head, and the animal nuzzled her cheek. "Thank you, dear friend. Go back to your herd now." She gave a gentle pat to the animal's neck, and it turned and looked impatiently at Ember.

Annika turned to her mount and found the animal had stuck its head quite close to hers. Eyes as dark as coal blinked curiously at her. "Thank you for a glorious ride. I can safely say you were the fastest and most gentle animal I have ever ridden." She ran her hand along the top of its head. Ember made a strange sound, almost like a purr. Then he left and joined his friend. It did not take them long to maneuver out of the busy city and into the fields.

"Do you ride them often?" Annika asked as she joined Rivkah in front of the hut. They wrapped the front of their dresses back on again and tied them at the back.

"As often as I can. With my bum leg I have to ride if I want to go any distance."

Rivkah brushed aside a curtain of colorful beads and entered the hut. Annika followed behind and found a quaint but functional home. It was much nicer than the huts Annika had stayed in just a short time ago with the crew. The ceiling was higher, and this home had several rooms. There was a small kitchen to the left and what looked like a sitting room. Two more doorways led somewhere else to the right.

The walls were made of wood and were held together by dirt and grass. The wooden ceiling peaked in the center of the building, making the ceiling feel quite high. Several windows were scattered across the home, giving it an open and airy feeling. The dirt floor had several soft and colorful rugs on it.

"Your home is lovely."

"Thank you." Rivkah smiled and got a large pot out of the corner of the room. She got to work making a fire in the middle of the room and placed the pot on a metal rack above it.

"Have you any experience in the kitchen?" she asked, fanning the small flame she had created.

Annika joined her by the fire. "I've worked my way around a kitchen a few times before." She smiled as she remembered the many days she spent in the kitchen at the orphanage.

"Wonderful, why don't you come and cut these carrots and throw them in the pot? I'm going next door to get some meat." Rivkah showed her a basket of vegetables and a knife with which to cut them.

Annika took the knife from Rivkah and assumed her spot at the counter. She had almost cut half the basket by the time Rivkah returned.

"Looks like you know how to handle a knife." She smiled and held out her arms. A giant cleaned bird was in her hands. "I've brought chicken."

"Wonderful, it's been so long since I've had any meat other than fish." Annika continued chopping carrots.

"Thank goodness you only ate fish. The animals beyond the walls are not good to eat." Rivkah prepared the chicken for the pot.

Annika's hand paused its rhythm of cutting. "How so?"

"They are full of parasites and disease. If you eat of any meat beyond our walls, you can get very sick and possibly even die. The symptoms take a while to show up, though, long enough for you to be too sick to recover."

"Thank Elohim we had not been able to catch anything other than fish." Annika sent a thankful prayer heavenward. Another thing to add to the list of the blessings in disguise they had been receiving all along.

"Yes, He definitely was looking out for you. We have herds of animals we raise here to eat. Here, they eat clean foods and are kept from any of the contamination outside our walls. That's where I got this chicken." Rivkah threw the last of the cut up meat into the pot and washed her hands. "There's a man next door who raises chickens. He supplies Gabriel, my father, and me with meat when we need it."

She gave a handful of some sort of peppers and strange mushrooms for Annika to cut next. "I haven't met your father yet."

"That will soon be remedied. He is the chief, after all."

Annika turned her surprised eyes to Rivkah. "I didn't know that. So, you are a princess of sorts?"

"Well, technically I suppose you could say that." Rivkah laughed. "My people haven't been held back by titles like that in years. Everyone respects my father and I. They look to my father for leadership and guidance. He is loved by all, but he does not ask to be treated any differently for his title."

"That is a rare thing to find, someone who cares more for the people than himself. I am looking forward to meeting your father. Hopefully, he can help me." Annika's thoughts turned to her friends once again. She could not stop thinking about them. Was Carter doing all right? He had always looked to her for leadership, even back in the orphanage. Now, he was alone, and what's worse was he thought her gone for good.

"I'm sorry your friends are in danger. I know my father and his beliefs. When he hears of your friend's predicament, he will not be able to stand idly by. He hates injustice. Ever since he met Gabriel and heard of what they did to him, he has had a strong viewpoint to help others."

"I'm happy to hear that." Annika blinked back tears. "I just hate to ask him to risk his life and the lives of your people when you have no ties to my friends. I hate being safe while they are hurting, but it's hard to ask for help when I know it will be dangerous."

"Don't worry, your friends are in Elohim's hands. Trust me, that's the safest place for them to be right now." The wisdom in the older woman's eyes was inspiring.

"You're right." She smiled and focused on the mushrooms she was cutting.

The rest of the preparation went quickly and smoothly. Annika finished cutting the vegetables and stirred the pot with a large spoon. Rivkah threw some dried herbs into the pot and the smell from the pot was intoxicating.

"Mmm...it smells so good! There's so much of it, though! Are we feeding an army?" Annika laughed.

"Well, my father and some of his warriors. So, yes, a small army." Rivkah grabbed a bowl from the counter. "We need some fruit to go with supper. Care to join me while the pot stews for a while?"

"Of course." Annika followed Rivkah out of the hut and into the backyard.

Talon sat at the top of the tallest tree, watching every move they made.

There were a handful of trees in the yard, each one laden with fruit. "What's this kind?" Annika approached the tree and held one of the large oblong fruits in her hand. A delicious tangy smell came from the fruit.

"That is a 'sour sweet'. Go ahead and pick some of those. They will go great in the fruit salad I'm making."

Annika picked a few of the large fruits and put them in the basket on her arm.

She moved on to the tree Rivkah was at and offered the basket for her to put the fruit she had collected in it. Rivkah emptied her arms of the fruit.

"These are 'charists', they have a beautiful, sweet taste. Perfect for bringing the sour sweet's flavor out more fully. Now, let's get one more kind." Rivkah moved onto the tree Talon was sitting in. "These will do wonderfully." She grabbed the fruit Annika had grown accustomed to eating on the island. The mandaw.

"Oh, I have grown quite the appreciation for those." Annika took a piece and raised it to her nose to smell.

"As have I. They are my favorite." Rivkah smelled one as well and gave a satisfied sigh. "This should be enough. Let's get these cut up and ready for supper. The men should be gathering soon."

They headed back in the house and finished the final preparations for supper. Rivkah had fruit and stew to serve, as well as some bread she had made earlier. The smell of food tickled Annika's nose and caused her stomach to grumble.

The sun had long since disappeared behind the towering rocky cliffs. The sky was beginning to show bright vivid colors, signaling the approaching sunset. With the sun's light quickly disappearing, shadows began to roll over the hidden valley, snaking their way over fields and around trees. It was then that Annika realized there was still some light from somewhere other than the fire. There were poles all along the street and throughout the village. Atop those poles was some sort of gemstone. With the fading light, the gems gave off a new glow. Blue light bathed all those within its reach.

What could they be? Annika had seen nothing like it. The glow was almost hypnotizing. Women had begun to show up at Rivkah's door to help take things out to the awaiting men. Annika hadn't even realized it, but while she had been staring at the gems, men had started fires and were mingling in the front yard.

Annika tore her eyes away from the glow and helped the women carry things out of the house and around the large fires outside. The women tried their best not to stare at her, but the men were quite open in their curiosity. Their eyes followed Annika wherever she went. She felt no malice in their gazes, only curiosity.

Rivkah pulled her off to the side. "I should have warned you ahead of time. Gabriel was the first person with light skin we had seen other than the pirates. The people are used to him now, but you will incite some more stares. Please forgive them, curiosity can get the better of some of them."

"No, I don't mind. I'm just as curious about them and your village. I'm sure I've given them my fair share of stares already." Annika chuckled nervously. She could still feel the eyes of many upon her. "I'm curious, what are those glowing blue gems? I've never seen anything of the like." Annika's eyes once again found the closest gem. Its blue color and glow was easy to find in the dark night.

"I see you have found the other hidden secret of our island. Not that it is so hidden right now." Rivkah smiled. "They are called amaris, meaning

'Given by God'. My people have been using them for centuries. As you can see, one of their uses is light."

"They are remarkable. What can they be used for other than light?" Annika tore her eyes off of it and looked to Rivkah.

"They are incredibly strong, practically indestructible. That makes them perfect for weapons. The smaller pieces are also used in jewelry. This is mine." Rivkah pulled on a string that was around her neck and a glowing gem appeared from under her blouse. "Around here, these are plentiful. We use them for decoration and sometimes even tools. As we understand now from Gabriel, these are quite rare and could possibly be why he was brought here in the first place."

Rivkah allowed Annika to study the gem and hold it in the palm of her hand. Up close she could see the glow from the gem was a mixture of blue and purple.

"It's beautiful." Annika said as she gave it back.

"I'll have to show you some of the things we use them for some time." She smiled. "Oh, yes, what I wanted to tell you was my father is sitting at the fire with Gabriel right now. He is waiting for you. Before you go, I just wanted to warn you. Before Gabriel came, we did not speak your language. Gabriel says I am a very quick learner, but not everyone here will understand everything you say or be able to communicate back. That includes my father."

Annika nodded in thanks and Rivkah scurried off to help the women. After she left, Annika found her eyes drawn to the fire and the men around it.

She spotted Gabriel at the fireside talking to a large and rather intimidating man. The man had leather pants on, and colorful feathers hung from a necklace around his neck. The feathers were so long and broad that they covered a large portion of his chest. This had to be the chief. The way he held his head high and the confidence in his gaze was enough to speak of his leadership.

A body suddenly stood in her way, blocking her view. A familiar face smiled at her.

"Hello." His voice was low for his age but something in his demeanor reminded her of Carter.

"Hello, we meet again. I'm Annika, what is your name?" She offered him a smile.

"Achim." He patted his chest then looked at her in concern. "How shoulder? Hands?" His words were thickly tangled in an accent. His accent was much thicker, which reminded her of what Rivkah had told her about the others and communication.

"It's all right. Thank you. How are you? You were not injured from the sand, were you?" He shook his head and looked to her hands. He picked her empty hands up with his one free hand and looked at her palms. Dried scabs were still present from when she had pulled him out of the sand. Although they were still present, they were not hurting; his salve had done wonders.

"Not bad." He nodded.

"Not at all. Whatever you put on them really helped. Thank you."

"No, thank you." He smiled at her. "Learned lesson about sand."

"Good, as have I." She chuckled. "Thank you for helping me get out of Maveth's cave."

He nodded his head and smiled. "Miracle. Lost many to Maveth. You must taste—" He stuck his tongue out, a teasing look on his face.

Annika laughed. "I'm glad he thought so." Achim grinned and gave her a wave as he went and got soup from the women.

"Annika, would you come here please?" She quickly brought her gaze back to the fire and saw Gabriel ushering her forward. The chief's eyes locked onto hers, studying her. This was her chance to gain his approval and the help of his people.

She straightened and smiled as she moved towards them. The chief's eyes watched her intently, making her slightly uncomfortable. Though she was determined not to let him see it.

Upon approaching them, they stood to their feet. Annika bowed. "I am pleased to meet you, Chief Tuviah."

He nodded to her. "Yes," was his only answer. She tried not to let it get to her. Rivkah had warned her ahead of time that he might have a hard time communicating.

"Please, join us. Rivkah was about to bring us some soup. We can eat and discuss." Gabriel motioned to a log near the fire and Annika sat down.

"Thank you. Has Gabriel caught you up on all of the details, Chief Tuviah?" As soon as she spoke, she hoped she hadn't gone out of line. Was it all right for her to address the chief without being spoken to first? Perhaps she should keep her mouth shut unless she was spoken to.

Chief Tuviah nodded. "Yes. I not sure. Why I should help?" He sat cross-legged with his arms folded over his chest. He was a very intimidating man to be sitting so near to.

Rivkah brought the soup and gave Annika an encouraging smile. "I understand what I'm asking you for is a lot." Gabriel began translating what she said into the chief's native language. "You have no ties to these men and no reason to risk the lives of your own. I honestly have no right to ask for help from you, especially since we are trespassing on your island." Annika sighed and bit her lip before continuing. "As much as I don't have the right, I must still ask. Please will you help us? These men are my friends, some as close as family."

An image of Carter came into her mind. A dark image of him beaten and bruised, target practice for Maddock and his merciless tactics. It was enough to make her queasy and cause the delicious stew to look unappealing.

She shook the image away and tried to focus on the task in front of her. "We have weathered storms and outrun beasts together. These men have earned my utmost trust, and I care a great deal for them." Ethan's image suddenly jumped into her mind. His dashing smile transformed into a look of pure agonyupon seeing her in the water with Maveth.

After a moment, Gabriel finished relaying her words to the chief. The man said something back and Gabriel turned to her.

"He wishes to know what you will do if they do not help?"

Annika thought for a moment. She had been wondering that same thing for a good part of the day. The possibility of not receiving help was becoming more and more probable.

"I know I am but one person, not intimidating in the slightest, but I have the most powerful ally of all backing me up. If Elohim is for me, then who can be against me? If I must go and free them myself, then that is what I will do. Or I will die trying."

Annika waited for Gabriel to relay her statement to the chief. The chief's piercing eyes found hers again. He was silent for quite some time. What was he thinking? Did he see her as pitiful and wishful in thinking she could do anything on her own?

"We help." Chief Tuviah smiled and nodded his head. His words brought a flood of emotion over Annika. Tears she had been holding back threatened to burst forward.

"Thank you so much." Annika smiled, hoping it would be able to cross the communication barrier and show her appreciation. He nodded, his lips slightly tilting upwards. That was enough for her.

"Wonderful!" Gabriel clapped his hands together. "Shall we speak of what happens next? Our greatest strength is we know about Maddock and his men. They are oblivious to even our existence here on the island. A surprise attack would be the best way to go, in my opinion. Maddock and his men have guns, we do not. We do, however, have a few tricks up our sleeves." The mischievous glint in his eyes caused her to smile.

"What kind of tricks?" Annika leaned forward, her soup all but forgotten in her hands.

"It's hard to explain, but we can show you tomorrow when it's light. Time is also an issue. Our scouts say that the men are getting antsy. As if they are finishing preparations on the ship and will perhaps leave soon. I believe we need to make a move as soon as possible." Gabriel looked to the chief.

He nodded and looked to the sky. "Next moon."

"Tomorrow night?" Annika looked to Gabriel who nodded in affirmation. Her heart was beginning to feel hope again.

"Yes, we have much to prepare before then. Tomorrow we will instruct the men. Let's discuss our strategy now."

Gabriel, Chief Tuviah, and Annika sat together and spoke of the future plans of attack. The more they spoke, the more confidence Annika gained. This was a risky move for all involved, but these people had already shown their ingenuity and some of their resources. With Elohim leading these people into battle, no one could stand against them.

CHAPTER
TWENTY-TWO

Annika stepped out of the hut the next morning and took a deep breath of the cool morning air. The sun was beginning to light up the sky overhead. Soon, it would shine its rays into the hidden valley and warm them all. She shivered, ready for the chill to leave her bones.

She sighed. Her body felt restless with anticipation. The day had come to finally liberate the others. This day would be one of restlessness and nerves. She had many hours left to wait and pray about the evening, which she had not stopped doing since they had formed the plan last night.

Noises in a field off to the right caught her attention. Men stood in a field nearby, practicing archery and their skills with spears. Their precision and strength both surprised and impressed her. Annika found herself walking in their direction, drawn to the activity.

Everyone seemed comfortable with their weapons and worked to-gether well. The ones with spears and swords sparred with each other, doing complicated moves. Some would use their neighbors as a stepping stool to get a flying leap into the air before crashing down on their would-be opponent—in this case, it was a bag of straw. Others whipped their spears around and whirled them in the air as they did some deft movements with their feet. In the blink of an eye, they would jump forward and thrust into the air. If anyone had been in their way, it would have delivered a fatal blow.

Then she noticed the lizards on the field as well. Once again, the presence of Ancients surprised and intrigued her. What were they doing in this environment? Some, like Talon, flew overhead, while others followed on foot. Either way, they were training with their masters.

The flying ones swooped in and practiced attacking the straw targets. Their claws tore mercilessly into the fabric and left behind deep gashes in the bags.

The ones without wings were jumping and attacking the bags with their human partners. They were perfectly timing their attacks with the thrust of their human partners' spears. While a warrior would thrust his opponent with incredible agility, the Ancient would circle around and attack viciously from the rear.

Annika felt some of her concern melt away. The strength of these men was enough to boost her confidence. She was surprised to see a good amount of women in the group as well. Many of them were archers, while a handful of them were sparring with the spears. They appeared every bit as well trained as the men. What they lacked in size they made up for in speed.

She suddenly realized what was at the tips of their spears and arrows. Sparkling blue gems shone in the light. It was amaris. Rivkah had said they used it for weapons. The gem was much less brilliantly lit up during the day, but it still surged with a purple blue hue.

Annika thought back to the night before. Chief Tuviah, Gabriel, and herself had sat around the fire for some time. As they had discussed plans, she had been thinking of what her role in them would be. She had managed to convince the two into letting her go with them, though they wished to test her skill level to see what she could do. She knew her way around a few weapons, but she surely was not as skilled as these warriors.

"Good morning, Annika," Gabriel said as he and Rivkah came and stood next to her. He smiled. "Are you ready for today?"

"Yes, I am beyond ready to get my friends out." She sighed and tried to calm her nerves.

Gabriel laughed. "I meant, are you ready to show the chief your worth on the battlefield? It takes a lot to impress him." He had a good-natured smile on his face.

Rivkah slapped him on the arm teasingly. "Oh, don't scare her. My father only wants to make sure you can handle yourself out there. He expects his warriors to have the best training in order to go outside of the walls. He wants to see if you can be safe out there. He has seen his warriors in action, but you he has not. As long as you are capable of defending yourself, he should be fine with you going." Rivkah smiled at Annika.

Chief Tuviah had every right to question her. Annika wouldn't want to get in the way of the chief and his warriors, who obviously knew what they were doing.

"I understand. As much as I wish to be right there, rescuing my friends, I don't want to hinder things. I will leave it up to the chief."

Chief Tuviah suddenly entered the field. The warriors stopped their practice and stood in silence, awaiting the word of their leader.

The chief's eyes wandered over his warriors. His face was stoic, as always, but his eyes seemed to show such deep love for his people it was heartwarming. He began speaking in a language Annika did not understand. Gabriel spoke quietly next to her, relaying the message.

"My people, as you all know our shores have been darkened once more by evil. We have long been plagued by those who wish to exploit our island for its riches. This time, however, we are faced with a different kind of evil. These men have hurt and imprisoned their own. If nothing is done by us, they will leave our shores, and we will have to live with the burden of knowing we could have helped innocent men escape a life of torture."

The chief paused and sighed. "I do not wish to lead any of you into battle and risk losing you. Our village and its people are so important to me. I, however, cannot stand back idly and watch evil reign on our island. I will be going to their aid whether anyone else joins me or not. This is not a requirement in the least. If any of you wish to not go, I will not force it. If you, however, cannot stand letting evil prevail, join me. Together with Elohim we can face anything."

Gabriel fell quiet, as did Chief Tuviah. Annika thought of the great strength the chief portrayed. He did not command these people to risk their lives but, instead, left it up to them to decide what they deemed was right. It was very much unlike the kingdom of Narine, who would take young men from their homes if its army was dwindling in numbers.

Achim stepped forward first, his arm raised in the air with his spear. The rest of the warriors came and stood next to him.

Achim spoke something and Gabriel translated for Annika. "We are with you until the end." The warriors gave a battle cry.

Chief Tuviah smiled at his men and nodded. "Let us prepare, then. We attack at dark."

They all dispersed and began practicing again. This time, however, you could see purpose on their faces.

The thought of freeing her friends soon was a wonderful one, as well as terrifying. She hated bloodshed and didn't relish the thought of having any of it on either side. The possibility of her causing harm to another was too much to think of. However, if the need arose in order to protect her friends, she would not hesitate.

"Annika. Come." Chief Tuviah called her forward. Her shaky legs carried her slowly towards the man. She willed them to stop quaking. She must show she was not afraid.

He led her to a spot in the field that had tree stumps and sacks of straw spread out across it. Some were just a couple yards away and others were hundreds of yards.

Chief Tuviah handed her a bow and a quiver of arrows. "Shoot many."

Annika looked at Gabriel in confusion. "He wants you to shoot as many targets as you can in a minute."

Annika nodded and swallowed, hoping her dry tongue would be able to form words. Her nervousness had to be visible to others. The quaking in her fingers as she held the weapon was too obvious to miss. Everyone on the field stepped back and waited in breathless anticipation.

It was not important in the grand scheme of things for her to join the others in freeing her friends. It's not as though she thought herself to be stronger or more capable than them. In fact, she would probably only slow them down. Though, she could not dispel the feeling of needing to be there. Whether that was loyalty or guilt for sending others in her place to save her friends, she did not know.

She raised her bow and notched at arrow, its tip glowing radiantly. She took aim at a straw sack that was about a hundred yards away. "Ready," she was able to call out.

"Go!" Gabriel shouted.

She released her first arrow. It sped forward and missed the sack by a wide margin. It did not have the power to even reach the target, instead sinking into the grass in front of it.

Her heart plummeted. She had not put enough strength behind arrow. This was not off to a good start. With every wrong move she made, it was all the more unlikely that she would be allowed to join them.

Her breathing was coming in ragged and painful. Annika squeezed her eyes shut. *Please, Elohim, calm my heart and steady my hands.* As the prayer formed in her mind, a calm settled over her body. Her fingers stopped quaking and her breathing came normally.

She opened her eyes and lifted her bow in the air. She pulled and aimed. Her next shot hit the closest target of five yards away. She took aim and released in rapid procession. Arrows went zooming from her hands and sank firmly into their targets. Arrows were imbedded in the closest targets and ones from hundreds of yards away.

Time had to be running out and Annika only had one arrow left. This last one would need to count. From over a hundred yards away she saw a lone stump. Was that one even used for target practice? Her bow was nocked and aimed out of reflex.

The arrow left her fingers and was followed by Chief Tuviah telling her time was up.

A collective gasp resounded amongst the people as her arrow sank into its target. Some had to step closer to get a better look. Seconds seemed to tick by before anyone said anything.

Finally, Achim looked at her with a grin upon his face. "Good shot." Others began smiling and gave her a small cheer. Annika's cheeks heated but her heart was happy.

"Good." Chief Tuviah stood next to her, and she held out the bow to him. "Keep. For tonight." He smiled then turned and focused on the training of his warriors.

"Great job!" Rivkah came along beside her and gave her a side hug. "I had no idea you were so accomplished with a bow. I know my father was impressed too, and that's saying a lot. He even gave you one of his bows." She fingered the bow in Annika's hands.

"It's an exquisite piece of craftsmanship." Annika slid her fingers down the soft wooden bow, taking in the gold detailing and the words on it. "What does it say?"

"It says, 'In Elohim the battle is already won.'" Rivkah smiled. "My mother made it for him before she passed."

"Then I cannot possibly accept it!" Annika pushed the bow to Rivkah. "It's far too precious for me to take into battle."

"No, please, you keep it. Mother made many weapons for my father. This is just one of many in his collection. Besides, my father wanted you to have it. It's an honor that everyone around will see." Rivkah placed the bow lovingly into Annika's hands.

Annika's heart warmed at the honor the chief had bestowed upon her. She was starting to see that his stoic exterior hid a gentle heart within.

Only a truly kind man would give a prized possession to someone he had just met.

"I've got to say, I'm impressed. Where did you learn to shoot?" Gabriel came and stood next to his wife.

"My father taught me." She smiled. "He thought it wise for my brother and I to know how to defend ourselves if the need should arrive, so he taught us all manner of defense." Sometimes, it was hard to speak of how she learned. When she did, her thoughts brought up the image of her father.

She owed much to him and his teaching. If not for him, she would not know Elohim. It was not easy for her to say that, though. His absence had made her doubt much of what she had learned. Thankfully, she had found strength through Elohim to get through his abandonment.

"Smart man. It's not common to teach women but, I dare say, a lot of good would come from others doing it as well." He smiled. "I'm going to go see if word has come back from our warriors who are watching Maddock and his men. I won't be gone long, but be sure you are ready for tonight. It'll be here before you know it." He squeezed his wife's hand and gave her a kiss on the cheek.

As his form retreated off the field, Rivkah leaned closer. "Come, I have something to show you."

Annika nodded and allowed Rivkah to lead her off the field and into the village. Where could Rivkah be taking her? They went down a street Annika had not seen yet. The huts here didn't seem to be inhabited. No gardens lay in the front or back and no children played in the yards.

Rivkah stopped in front of one particularly large hut and beckoned Annika inside. As she entered, the smell of dust and sweat wafted into her face. Thankfully, it was not strong enough to make her grimace, but it was quite noticeable.

Once her eyes had adjusted, she saw the whole room was full of weapons. Bows and arrows lined one wall while spears and other sharp objects lined the other. This must be the armory. Annika walked over to a spear and tested its weight in her hands.

"Am I to pick out a weapon?"

Rivkah shook her head, still smiling. "No, I have something for you." She walked over to the corner of the room and picked up something. She turned around and Annika was shocked to see the most beautiful sword she had ever seen. It was made of amaris. Its blade was glowing brightly, and the polished steel of the hilt looked like silver.

"It's beautiful!"

"It used to be mine. I want you to have it."

Annika's jaw dropped open in disbelief. "No, I cannot take it."

"Yes, you will. I have no need for it now." Rivkah patted her injured leg. "Do you know how to use one?"

Annika nodded. "Good." Rivkah smiled and placed the weapon in her hands. "I had special care put into making this sword. It takes incredible pressure and heat to forge amaris, and it must be chipped away with another piece of it. This sword is the perfect weight and is sharper than you can imagine."

"Thank you." Annika managed to breathe out the words. "I will take care of it."

Rivkah grinned. "I know. Come, I also wanted to give you this." She bent over a large box covered in dust. Rivkah opened it and revealed its contents. Inside was unusual clothing made of some kind of leather.

"What's all this?"

"It was mine." A sad smile crossed Rivkah's face momentarily. "This box is full of my armor and weapons. At one point, I wouldn't be caught anywhere without these." She picked up the top piece of clothing and fingered the material. It was deep green, like the jungle foliage. "Now, this is the first time I've looked at it since my accident." Her hand instinctively went to her hip. As if the pain was stronger with the memory.

"I'm sorry."

"Don't be." Rivkah smiled. "I have so much to be thankful for now. This armor carried me through many tough situations and saved me on several occasions. I was wearing it the day I got Gabriel, and we escaped the jaws of Maveth." She turned to Annika with tears in her eyes. "I want you to use it tonight."

"No, I couldn't do that. It's precious to you." Annika held the woman's hand.

"Do not mistake my tears as love for the armor. It's the love I gained that I am happy for." Rivkah smiled. "My memories of that day are hard to think of, but I also remember that day as being the first day I talked with my love. This armor holds memories both good and bad for me. If I had not walked through the veil of pain in my path, I would not have found the joy Elohim had on the other side." Rivkah held the fabric up again for Annika. "Now, I want you to use it and save your own love."

Tears threatened to fall from Annika's eyes. This woman showed kindness at every turn. She had not needed to take Annika into her home, but she had happily done so. She had treated her like a friend and a confidant. Because of Rivkah, she felt at home here already, as if she had known her forever. Now, she was giving her an important piece of her past.

Annika accepted the green leather into her hands and fingered it. It was as soft as velvet and as thick as chain mail. Somehow this didn't feel like ordinary armor, both physically and figuratively.

"Thank you so much." Annika hugged Rivkah tightly.

"Well,"—Rivkah smiled as she pulled back—"let's see if it fits, shall we?" She had Annika step behind a curtain and helped her get dressed into the armor. Upon finishing, Annika stepped back out into the light outside of the hut.

The fabric was surprisingly comfortable. The top was made of a soft and moveable leather. Tt was tight around her top and fell loosely past her hips. It was like a dress, but it was higher in the front, allowing easier movement in battle or moving through the jungle. There were also soft leather pants that went under it.

"It's leather made from the hide of Ancients. We treat it so it's soft and easy to put on but not easy for anything to penetrate it." Rivkah smiled with pride as she took in the sight of the armor.

"I thought you didn't kill Ancients anymore?"

"The Ancient lizards still die of old age, and we just make sure that they don't go to waste."

On top of the leather in certain places was bony green plating of some sort. It covered her chest and specific parts of her legs and arms.

"The plating is from them as well. There's this kind with giant bony plates on its back. When it dies, we use the plates and add them to our armor." Rivkah nodded her head. "It fits you perfectly, just as I thought it would."

The boots were made of leather as well but covered with intricate designs made from golden thread. Her hair was loose, and it flowed thickly around her face. The feeling of her hair being free from any ties was foreign to her. Although unusual to her, it was not uncomfortable. Her long brown hair was kept out of her face by a band of gold.

"What does this mean?" Annika pointed to the band on her head.

"It made me stand out as royalty."

"This is definitely not something I shall wear, then. It is one thing to wear your royal armor, but I cannot in good conscience wear your crown."

Rivkah smiled. "I thought you would say that. So, I got you this." She removed the golden band on Annika's head and replaced it with a leather one. Attached to it were colorful feathers and they hung down behind Annika's head and trailed down her hair. On the band was intricate detailing in gold and shards of amaris.

Rivkah smiled and tenderly adjusted a feather behind Annika's head. "There we go, it's perfect."

Annika looked down at herself and smiled. The chief's bow was attached to her back, and the amaris sword was on her hip. She truly did feel like a warrior now. If only she still had her dagger at her ankle. Then she would truly feel completely ready.

"Thank you so much, Rivkah." They shared a smile.

"I have one last thing. I'm not giving him to you, but I want you to take him with you."

"Him?" Annika's eyes opened wide.

Rivkah whistled and Talon swooped in and landed on the ground near her. Annika's heart sped up as she understood Rivkah's meaning. The animal still made her nervous.

"No, I couldn't."

"You can." Rivkah scratched the animal under his chin. "He has been my companion for a long time. We grew up together. He has been through battles and heartbreak with me."

"What could I do with him? It's clear he does not like me." Annika eyed the animal as it stared at her.

Rivkah laughed. "He's just studying you. If you take him, he can watch your back and even fight alongside you."

Annika was running out of excuses. "But I haven't practiced with him like the others."

"I know, but he is older and more experienced than most. He knows what you need before you even ask. You won't have to do anything if you don't wish to." A corner of Rivkah's mouth dipped down. "If you are really uncomfortable, you do not have to take him."

Annika thought for a moment. The animal was indeed terrifying to her but so were the swifts they had ridden yesterday, and she had loved it by the end.

"If you think he will go with me, then I'll give it a try."

"Wonderful." Rivkah turned to the winged animal. She whispered words to it and clicked her tongue. Talon turned his piercing eyes to Annika and screeched. Rivkah smiled calmly at her. "I have just given him the command to watch over you. He is fiercely loyal and will look after you like family now." Rivkah smiled. "You call him, and he will come to you. Otherwise, he will hang back and watch you from a higher vantage point. With his ever-watchful eyes it will be near impossible for anyone to surprise you on the battlefield."

"Thank you." Annika was nervous but could not deny it would be nice to have him by her side in battle.

They walked back to the field to check on the others. Talon walked along with them, somewhat clumsily.

"All you have to do is give him the signal and he will hang back and keep watch over you." She clicked her tongue, and Talon flew into the trees overhead.

They walked the rest of the way to the field with Talon sitting high in the trees. He was indeed watching them closely, his sharp eyes picking out anything unusual.

The hot sun wasn't as unbearable in the armor. Probably due to the people of Avigdor experimenting and finding something that would work perfect for the environment. Even walking in it felt unusual but surprisingly comfortable.

Perhaps Gabriel had come back by now with news. Upon their arrival, everyone stopped and stared at the two of them. They bowed their heads in respect. The sight of the armor and the one who originally bore it must be a grand thing for them to remember. They were giving respect to a great warrior.

Rivkah stood straight and tall. Annika didn't have to imagine hard to see the warrior she had been and likely still was. Rivkah smiled warmly and bowed her head to everyone before her. At her acknowledgement, they all returned to their training.

As they watched the warriors, Annika thought back to the discussion with Gabriel and Chief Tuviah the night before. The plan was to hit right before nightfall. The scouts had reported previously that the bound men were given a few moments of relief before dark. That would be the easiest time to strike and, hopefully, the one that required the least amount of bloodshed.

Once the men were liberated, that just left Maddock and his men to deal with. Purposefully killing people was not on the table for anyone. No one wished death upon Maddock or anyone he was associated with. To avoid any unnecessary killing, the best option was to take out their leader. Once Maddock was detained, the rest of his men would have no other option but to give up. That was the plan, at least.

"This is a change." Gabriel came up from behind. He smiled and took in Annika's appearance. "Avigdor armor suits you well."

"Thank you." Annika smiled as he turned to his wife and kissed her on the cheek. The look in his eyes told Annika that he knew what the armor meant and the memories it held for his wife.

Chief Tuviah approached from the side, a look of disbelief on his face. He said something in a different language as he walked to his daughter. He hugged her and gazed into her eyes, his love for her apparent.

Annika stood next to Gabriel and whispered, "What did he say to her?"

"He said he thought he would never see that sight again. He speaks of the armor you wear. I'm sure you already know the last time Rivkah wore it she got severely injured."

"Yes, she told me. Is it really all right for me to wear this? I tried to talk her out of it, but she would not hear of it."

"It's more than all right. It shows just how much Rivkah is healing as well. Not many times has she had to relive the past. I'm proud of her." He smiled at his wife, tears in his eyes.

The chief looked to Annika. "You look like daughter, when she first wore it." His small smile was contagious. His eyes looked wet from tears. Strange how this strong and fierce man could change so quickly to a caring and loving father.

"Your daughter is an amazing woman."

"She is." He smiled once again at Rivkah, his gaze full of warmth and love.

"Sorry to bring an end to this beautiful moment." Gabriel looked at them apologetically. "But the scouts have come back saying that something is going on at the beach. They have begun moving things onto the ship, including some captive men. It looks like they might be leaving soon."

"Oh no. What does this do to the plan?" Annika looked from the chief to Gabriel.

"It means that we improvise." Gabriel grinned.

CHAPTER
TWENTY-THREE

Ethan was beginning to grow weary of feeling hopeless. He was tired of seeing his men with downcast faces. The last few days had been hard on him as well as his crew. Would any of them ever be free again?

They all sat on the floor with their arms behind their backs, bound to the wall. Another night had gone by and with it their fear mounted. Some men quietly cried, while others sat in silence. The wounded were still healing, and the lack of food was not helping their progress. If everything went the way Maddock wanted, it would be a life of misery for all of Ethan's loyal men. Sadly, it was quite likely they would never feel free again. They would be passed from one owner to another. Slave trading had at one point been outlawed but it was very prevalent now, especially in the kingdom of Narine.

Jonah seemed to spend much of his time sleeping, propped up against the wall. Jack slept and fidgeted; he was not one who liked sitting idle. Carter still seemed content, which was beginning to irritate Ethan. It was difficult seeing happiness when you were in such pain.

"I know you may not believe me," Carter's quiet voice broke the silence, "but I just have this feeling. I know in my heart something will happen tonight. We need to be ready."

Ethan chuckled ruefully. "Not this again."

Strength shone in Carter's eyes. Unlike the others, his spirit was not broken.

"I am not ready to just give up to these evil men. Despite what they think, they do not own me and they never will. Even if I get sold off as a slave, I will never truly be theirs. I feel like I have been given a sign of hope from Elohim but even without a sign, it is an inconceivable thought to give in to these men. I will fight their plans with everything I have in me."

Ethan was humbled by the strength of character this young boy displayed. All the time Ethan had been sitting in anguish Carter had been alert and helping others. Spreading hope and joy to the men Ethan should still be leading.

"These are your men, Captain. They would follow you blindly into battle. Right now, they see their fearless leader afraid and hopeless. When the great Captain Wolf shows defeat, it causes fear to spread. Show them courage and hope, even if you do not exactly feel it at this moment. Having hope is better than a life of fear and darkness."

Jack and Jonah seemed to be strengthened by the words, for they sat up straighter, fire beginning to burn in their eyes again.

"He's right, Cap. We gotta show these men that not all is hopeless. We may be bound, but our spirits are not broken." Jack's excited eyes swerved to his.

The strength in his men, and the courage of the boy to return it to them, gave Ethan the strength he needed. His men would not want to sit idly by as they became slaves. They would want to rise and fight with every last fiber of strength they possessed. They were feeling this way because of his lack of leadership.

A spark of light began to fill Ethan's empty heart. He had been feeling his lowest, and it had taken a wise boy to fuel his fire again.

All the anger and hopelessness began to fade from his heart. In its place grew a strength he could not explain. His heart still hurt at the loss of Annika, but he was surprised that he no longer felt consumed by it. Was this how Carter had felt the whole time?

He looked gratefully at the young boy at his side. The strength in spirit that Carter possessed was so apparent to Ethan now. He had grown from a boy to a man in just a couple short weeks.

No matter what the outcome may be, Ethan knew Carter was right. He needed to show strength to his crew.

"Men," Ethan sat with his back straight. Over a dozen men's eyes swerved to focus on him. Their lifeless expressions caused him sorrow and guilt. "I know things have seemed bleak. I admit I have not been there for you all when I should have. I will forever be ashamed of that. I know our situation looks dire at the moment. I don't know about you, but I will not go down without a fight. If they wish to imprison us and take all that we have, let's show them we won't go down easily." He looked at Carter as he spoke. "A wise man has reminded me that as soon as we give up, we have let the enemy win." Carter's smile deepened.

The men in the hut began to raise their heads, their eyes picking up the light of hope.

"I don't know what the next step is, but I will promise you that I will not give up. I will fight for you and for our freedom with everything in me."

"I'm with you, Cap!" Jonah raised his voice so the men could hear.

"Here! Here!" Doniphan said and the others echoed. The men now looked to have a new resolve, a purpose.

"What do you have in mind, Captain?" Carter looked to him, determination in his gaze.

Before Ethan could reply, one of Maddock's men entered the hut. His eyes adjusted to the darkness, and he bent to untie Doniphan's binds from the wall.

"What's going on?" Doniphan's glasses had long since fallen off, and he sat, squinting at the man in front of him.

"Maddock wants to see all of you on the beach." The burly man dragged Doniphan to his feet. "Be ready." The way he said it was menacing. Ethan kept his gaze level and was surprised by his lack of fear. The man hauled Doniphan roughly out of the hut.

"Looks like you were right, Carter. Something is going on." Ethan lowered his voice so they all had to strain to hear. "We can't plan when we have no idea what's going on. Keep your eyes and ears open. We must seize any opportunity we can to get out of this."

Just as he finished speaking, another man came in and untied Jack's wrists. He nodded to the men as he was pushed out of the hut. Ethan's heart sank to see him leave. For all they knew Maddock could have a firing squad at the ready.

One by one they were all led out of the hut and waited outside under constant watch from the guards.

Soon the hut was emptied of its bound occupants. They were all lined up and held at gun point. Not much opportunity for escape yet. There were over a dozen men aiming their guns at Ethan and the others.

Ethan stood amongst the men and studied their captors. He knew that if Jonah, Jack, and himself teamed up that they could take out a handful of men without difficulty. Unfortunately, there were a lot of guards, far too many for them to fight, especially while bound.

They finished taking out the last of the men from the huts and began to push them forward.

"Get a move on, all of you." An angry man with two missing front teeth shouted at them.

Ethan began moving forward with the others. The men near him all shared a look. What was going on now? Would they all be leaving soon? Surely, the repairs could not be finished on the boat by now.

"Where are you taking us?" Ethan directed his attention to the man walking behind him. The man was tall and looked quite lethal, even without the gun he held in his hands.

"You'll find out soon enough." He sneered, his lips curled upwards in a way that made Ethan sick. The men Maddock had recruited had not been a part of Ethan's crew. So, how had Captain Samuel hired these men? On that hand, how could Ethan not have noticed the insurrection that was starting amongst the men?

The sun was still high in the sky, telling Ethan that it was probably shortly after the noon hour. The birds sang a soft, almost sad tune in the trees above. As if they could pick up the pain and the fear of the men walking on the jungle floor below.

They walked the short distance to the beach, about a ten-minute walk. Their path was not the easiest to traverse. The jungle overgrowth had been stomped down from multiple treks through it, but the ground was very uneven. Jack stumbled a few times, as did Carter. Jonah managed to stand and walk as straight as a board.

Finally, the ocean came into view, a beautiful sight for someone who had been kept indoors for days. It would normally have brought a smile to Ethan's face to see his ship in the distance, gently floating atop the water. Now his stomach churned with dread. His very own ship was going to be used to transport them into bondage.

Ethan and his men were told to stand together on the beach, baking in the hot sun. His hat had disappeared since their encounter with Maddock at the falls. What he wouldn't give to wear it again. Not only to protect him from the sun's warm rays, but it was also a symbol of being a captain.

The beach was littered with freshly cut wood and other supplies for fixing the ship. On the far end of the beach was a big lean-to, though it was basically just a roof with legs. Under it was a fire with a handful of men around it. That had to be where Maddock was, probably eating to his heart's content while they all starved.

Shortly after, a man approached Ethan. The stranger eyed him up and down in annoyance. "Maddock wishes to speak to you." A rough tug on Ethan's arm jerked him forward, away from the rest of the crew.

"Does he now?" Ethan grinned slyly. "Well, I'm a bit preoccupied at the moment. Maybe he could try back later. I'll make some tea and biscuits. Or maybe some cake, Maddock seems like a cake guy." A punch to his stomach caused him to fall forward onto the ground. Since his arms were still tied behind his back, he was unable to stop himself from falling. His face was rammed into the coarse sand. He groaned and rolled onto his back. Pain was causing his vision to be blurry. The sun whirled above his head. Had there always been three of them? Soon the image stabilized, and the sun returned to its steadfast position in the sky.

As he began a slow attempt to stand up, he realized something was pressing him hard in the backside. As he attempted to get upright, his fingers found that the object was in his back pocket. It was long and sharp. It was the crocodile tooth necklace he had pocketed so long ago. It had been forgotten until now. He had just closed his fingers around the tooth when he was jerked to his feet.

The man put his face right next to Ethan's and covered him with his foul breath. "I am not in the mood to hear your back talk. Maddock wants to speak to you, so shut your mouth and come with me." He jerked Ethan forward, causing him to stumble. Thankfully, he was able to right himself and ignore the pain.

Ethan turned his head around and saw Jack was bound a few feet from him. If looks could kill, Jack could have killed a hundred men with the glare he pinned on the big man before them.

"You ok, Cap?" He whispered, not taking his eyes off the man.

Ethan chuckled, causing more pain in his stomach. "Yeah, I'm fine. Looks like Maddock wishes to speak with me. Seems as though he isn't in the mood for pleasantries."

Ethan was being pushed forward, away from the others. His fingers were still closed around the tooth. The man who was dragging him was side by side with Ethan. As they walked, Ethan began to slowly work the tooth over his binds.

A gruff hand yanked Ethan forward. "Get your rear in motion. I don't have all day."

"What's got you in such a hurry? Do you have more people's lives to ruin or perhaps a village to burn?"

"Actually, I was just about to sit down and eat my lunch. So yes, I do have plans." A snarl came from his mouth.

"A shame that is. I haven't eaten either, maybe your boss will have food ready for us, hmm? Perhaps a grand feast in my honor?" Ethan smiled again, hoping to portray more confidence than he actually held.

"Don't hold your breath. You aren't exactly his favorite person right now. Also, don't call him my boss."

"Isn't that what he is?" Ethan didn't recognize the man. He must be from Captain Samuel's ship.

"He is not my boss. I'm not obedient to him because I have to. It works out best for me if I help out. I'm not one to take orders unless I get something out of it." The man's grip on Ethan's arm tightened painfully.

The soft sand made walking difficult. Their boots slipped as they made their way to the fire Maddock sat in front of. "I see, now who did you say is the one who is not eating because of orders?"

The man grabbed Ethan's hair and yanked his head back. "You talk too much." He pushed Ethan's head forward, causing him to stumble and have to desperately find his footing. He found himself standing in front of the man who had made all of this possible. Maddock's eyes glinted as they took in Ethan's vulnerable state.

"How good of you to join us, Wolf." The familiar rough voice of the mutinous man assaulted Ethan's ears. He pushed any fear he had down and replaced it with a cocky grin.

Maddock sat around a large fire with several other men. No doubt they were the most trusted of his followers. Strangely, Ethan did not see Simon. A large animal was skinned and hanging over the fire, cooking and sizzling as its fragrant juices dripped into the fire. The aroma was wonderful and caused his mouth to water.

Suddenly, Ethan noticed a hunched figure near the fire. It was Captain Samuel. He sat cross-legged off to the side of the men, his head bowed low. As Ethan sat down on a log near Maddock, Captain Samuel brought his gaze up. His face was bruised, and one eye was swollen shut. His good eye locked with Ethan's, a fire of righteous anger permeating from his gaze. Even after what looked like multiple beatings, the older man was not broken. His body may be bruised and failing, but his spirit was very much alive.

Ethan brought his attention back to Maddock. Suddenly, Ethan noticed the hat upon Maddock's head was his own. The red feather was broken, and the hat looked to have been trampled on. At one point it was a symbol of his leadership. but it now looked like it had come from the trash.

"Thanks for having me, not that I had much of a choice. You might want to let Mr. Cheery go back to his lunch. He was sure complaining about having to miss it."

Maddock barely even acknowledged the sailor. "You're dismissed. I have no need for you at the moment." Maddock waved his hand dismissively. The man looked like he was biting his tongue, probably about to say an angry retort. He finally turned away and headed for the group of Maddock's men who were congregating nearby, kicking sand angrily as he went.

"So, how have you found the accommodations thus far? I hope you haven't found our hospitality to be lacking." Maddock placed his chin in his hand, his elbow propped on one leg. A wicked grin was upon his face, enjoying the sight of Ethan tied up.

Anger burned deep in Ethan's heart. He knew what the sight of pure evil looked like. This man held all of the signs. Enjoyment of seeing others in pain and suffering was at the top of the list.

"Actually, we are faring rather poorly. I wonder if you forgot to tell us where the mess hall is?"

"No, I don't believe I forgot." His lips curled at the words, showing his yellowing teeth. The men around the fire smiled as well.

"Tell me, are you planning on leaving us without food and water to kill us off or just as a means of torture?"

Maddock laughed. "Torture is more up my alley, although I would not mind seeing the death of the great Captain Wolf."

"Do what you will with me but leave the others out of this." Ethan's anger mounted, but he kept a cool face. His hands still worked slowly at the rope around his wrists. As his wrists began to cramp and burn, he felt the rope beginning to give.

"It's too late for that, Wolf. Your men are far too loyal, I gave them the option to join me, and they all blatantly refused. I have to say, I'm impressed with the loyalty you inspire, however foolhardy it may be."

"That's what happens when you treat people with kindness and actually care about their wellbeing. Something you seem incapable of doing. Have you no heart or is it completely turned to stone now?"

"Heart has nothing to do with it. This world is not fair, plain as that. I have lived my life at the bottom of the social chain. It's just my turn to sample the finer things in life." Maddock took his hat off and scratched his balding head. "Though, I have to say I would have preferred a ship that wasn't half gone already."

"You were planning on a mutiny whether we had intercepted the ship or not?"

"Not at first." Maddock pulled a piece of meat from a stick over the fire. He took a big mouthful and spoke around the juicy meat. "The idea had crossed my mind, though. The events that happened after we met you just settled my mind."

"All this because you wanted to be captain? Could you not just have put in the hard work and become one yourself?"

Maddock glared at Ethan as he took another bite of meat. "I have worked hard all my life." He spoke with his mouth full, his words more of a mumble until he swallowed.

"One day, as I was denied a role of leadership once again, I realized something. I was never going to be a captain and that it had nothing to do with my skill level. I could sail circles around anyone if I wanted to. No, I would never become captain because of the way I look and my lack of title." Maddock's angry gaze locked onto the fire, intensity and anger heating his words.

"I was not born to a noble man, not even to a respected member of the community. My ma sold me off to pay for her debts and I worked for years with no pay. Finally, when I had paid back the debt, I was set free. I had no friends and no family I wished to return to. I was all alone. I had to work my way up the ladder from the very bottom. For someone like me the ladder is only able to be climbed part way. Once I became a sailor that's where I stayed. I never once was given the chance to show my leadership qualities. One look at my appearance and my background and I was turned away."

"Were you not the first mate aboard Captain Samuel's ship? That's a very big place of honor. I would not trust just anyone to that position."

Maddock scoffed. "After all my work for that man and that's all he could give me. Years of hard work and I got stopped at being a first mate. I deserved my own ship and he knew it. He wanted to keep me down because he feels threatened by me." He glowered at Captain Samuel.

"I never felt threatened by you." Captain Samuel croaked out the words, his injuries and lack of water probably making any movement or speech difficult. "I would have advanced you if I had not seen the anger you possess. That is a deadly thing for a captain to have." HIs face looked sad, the loss for all of the men he once cared for probably weighing heavily on his mind. The men whose lives had been lost, the mutiny of most of them, and Maddock's utter betrayal.

"Oh, just shut your mouth, old man." Maddock rolled his eyes and turned from him. "You're just like all the others, trying to keep me from what I rightfully deserve. Everything is going to start changing for me." His smile was unnerving.

"Can you not do that without captives? Just leave us here. You have no need for us."

"Oh, but you all will put a nice amount of coin in my pocket." Maddock's sneer showed his yellowing teeth again.

Why was everything about this man unhygienic? It wasn't even that his teeth were yellow. He smelled like he had taken a bath maybe twice in his life and his clothing was right up there with him. That was probably the main reason why he hadn't been advanced to captain. In fact, it was a surprise that he had made it to first mate. You could have the brightest mind, but if you did not present yourself as an authoritative figure, then it was highly unlikely for anyone to promote you to captain.

"I feel sorry for all of your men. They will always need to sleep with one eye open, never knowing when it will suit you to be rid of them."

"My men are just fine." Even as Maddock said the words, the men around the fire shifted fearfully in their seats. Now that Ethan thought about it, there had been a completely different feel to this atmosphere than the one he had grown accustomed to with his men. There was an air of fear drifting among all of Maddock's men.

"You should be worrying about your own men," Maddock continued. He waved his hand and Ethan watched helplessly as some men rounded up Carter, Jack, Doniphan, and a handful of other men.

They were taken to the boats and forced inside. Ethan tried to cut the ropes around his wrists harder but to no avail. He could only look on as his men and his closest friends were taken to the ship.

"What are you doing with them?" He turned his fiery gaze to Maddock.

"Just loading everyone up for the journey. We have a long way to go before we dock, especially with the poor repairs we made."

Ethan sighed. "Where will you be taking us?"

"Oh, did I fail to mention this? You and Captain Samuel will be staying here. I can't have you around, inciting your men. No, they will be far more complacent without you both."

Ethan gritted his teeth together in anger. The bounds around his wrists were beginning to fray. Just as he was about to cut the final bit of the rope, Maddock punched him in the stomach, doubling him over. With a quick movement Maddock took a new rope and tied his wrists even tighter.

"Didn't think you would get away with that, did you?" Maddock whispered the words in his ear, his hot putrid breath assaulting his nose. He gave Ethan a push and knocked him off his log. Ethan lay there, wondering what he could do. If he did nothing, his men would soon be sailing off in the arms of an evil dictator and he would be powerless to do anything about it.

Chapter
Twenty-Four

Annika followed the stealthy warriors as quietly as she could. Their footsteps made no sound as they made their way through the forest, practically making them appear as ghosts, silently making their way over tree roots and thick grass. Her breathing was heavy and her heart was racing, causing her steps to be slightly clumsy.

A twig cracked under her foot. In the quiet of the jungle, it seemed to be as loud as a gunshot to her.

Talon flew overhead through the jungle trees along with the others whose masters were below. They made no sound, save for the faint brushing of their wings through the leaves overhead. Even from here, Annika could feel the watchful eyes of Talon upon her. Right now, it was surprising, but she felt comforted by the feeling.

They continued on, and Annika tried to keep a closer watch on where she placed her feet. The chief was walking at the front of the group, leading his warriors into battle. Gabriel stood next to her, an amaris sword in his hands and a bow on his back. He walked differently than the warriors, who had been trained for stealth. Everything about him, his posture and the way he held his sword, seemed to portray power and skill. What had he been before coming to this island?

Achim came up beside Annika and pointed at his feet, showing her how he walked. She picked her feet up and laid them down slowly, her heel placing first. At first it was uncomfortable to walk and hard to do it each time, but soon enough she got the hang of it and was able to walk much more quietly. She smiled in gratitude to Achim, who nodded and smiled in return.

With a few shortcuts and guides who knew the way, they made good time to the small clearing where the huts were. What would normally have taken days was cut to just a few hours. Chief Tuviah signaled for all to stop. They crouched and walked slowly forward, peering through the greenery. The huts were about one hundred feet from their position. Something was not right. There was no one to be seen. The place looked abandoned. Where was everyone?

A man came running quickly towards them through the jungle, one of Chief Tuviah's scouts. He spoke quickly to the chief, who thought for a moment. Chief Tuviah then nodded and signaled for his men.

"What's going on?" Annika whispered to Gabriel. They all followed the chief and the scout, their footsteps not as quiet or thoughtful anymore.

"Seems much has happened since the last update. The men were rounded up and are already on the ship."

Annika's heart plummeted. Had they been taken from her completely? Tears threatened to escape her eyes when Gabriel placed a comforting hand on her shoulder.

"Fear not. They are still close to shore. There may still be something we can do. The scout also said that they left behind two men on the beach."

"Who could that be?" Annika's heart was beating wildly. Every moment they were idle was more time for the ship to leave and never return. What would she do if Carter was taken from her? She could not lose him.

What of her other friends? Her thoughts leaped to Ethan. Her footsteps quickened and matched the long strides of the warriors.

Soon, they broke through the trees and onto the sandy beach. The ship was indeed sailing away, but they must have only missed them by minutes.

"What can we do?" Annika's heart felt like it was being torn in two. "Is there nothing that can be done?" Tears were threatening to fall.

"Annika." Gabriel placed a hand on her shoulder and turned her around. Through her tears, a familiar form emerged.

"Ethan?" She whispered and blinked. He was indeed standing before her, being escorted by the warriors. His face registered shock and his eyes grew glossy.

Annika ran towards him and into his open arms. He held her tightly as she shook with tears. Something wet touched her head. Was he crying?

"How is this possible? Are you an angel?" Ethan pulled away and touched her face as his eyes examined her.

"No, I'm no angel." Annika laughed and wiped the tears from her eyes. "I have so much to tell you, as I'm sure you do as well." She attempted to step back from his arms, but he didn't seem ready to let her go.

"What about me? Did you miss me too?" Annika's eyes shot to the other familiar face. Captain Samuel, although he did not look at all like she remembered.

"Oh, Captain Samuel!" She broke from Ethan and gave him a gentle hug. "What have they done to you?"

"Nothing I cannot handle, dear." He smiled warmly at her.

Gabriel cleared his throat, a reminder that they were not alone. They had quite an audience surrounding them all. "These are my friends." She pointed to Gabriel and the chief. "This is Chief Tuviah and this is—"

"Someone who is happy to meet you." Gabriel stepped forward and shook Ethan's hand. "Are you two ok?"

"Physically I'm fine, but Captain Samuel on the other hand has been beaten repeatedly. I'm surprised he is still standing. Our men though—" Ethan pointed to the ship that was slowly sailing out of the cove.

"Don't worry about that. Chief Tuviah and I have a plan." Gabriel smiled but something in his eyes looked different to Annika. Curiosity and a hint of sadness seemed to be beneath the surface.

"Tell me, Annika, can you swim?" Gabriel looked to her.

Annika smiled. "Like a fish."

"Good to hear. We have to act fast." Gabriel and Chief Tuviah stood to the side and addressed the warriors.

Ethan came up and stood next to Annika. He gently took her hand in his larger one. Her eyes turned to his, which were full of emotion.

"I thought you were gone."

"As did I for a bit." She chuckled nervously and gripped his hand. "I'm fine, really. Maveth only left behind a parting gift." She pointed to her shoulder, which was bandaged.

"How? How can you still be alive? You never came up and there was so much blood." He shut his eyes, trying to block out the memories that seemed to haunt him.

Annika stepped forward and gave him another hug. His arms seemed to wrap around her so easily as if they were meant to be there. In his arms she felt safe and protected.

"I will tell you the whole story soon. Just know that Elohim saved me and sent these people to me, or rather me to them." Her words were muffled against his shirt.

Ethan chuckled causing Annika to look into his face in confusion. "What's so funny? Does the thought of my near-death experience strike your funny bone?"

He shook his head. "No, not at all. I'll have you know I have been very distraught over the whole ordeal. There hasn't been a minute where your face didn't pop into my mind and fill me with grief." He pulled her closer and tucked her beneath his chin. "No, I was chuckling because I find it amazing what Carter said now."

"What did he say?"

"He said that Elohim had told him that you were still alive. I don't know if I can believe that fully, but even I know that it is a miracle to have you back."

Annika was amazed that Carter had known. "How is he? I've been so worried about him."

"You would be amazed at the strength that young man possesses. He kept a smile on his face and encouraged others, even when I gave him a hard time for it. He was able to rouse me from my grief and rally us together again."

Annika smiled. Sweet Carter, always trying to help others. "My heart aches knowing he is sailing away." She looked over the water, willing the ship to return.

"If I may interrupt," Gabriel's calm voice interjected. They pulled away to see everyone was done talking. "We have a plan, but we must act fast."

"What plan could you possibly have? They are sailing away. Unless you have a ship handy?" Ethan didn't know these people like she did. Annika had no doubt about their ability. Whatever their plan was, she was all in.

Gabriel smiled. "I'm glad you asked. How do you feel about flying?"

Ethan watched as Captain Samuel was assisted by several men into the jungle. Evidently, they were taking him to the heart of Avigdor, whatever that meant.

His eyes strayed to Annika's fair face once again. He could not stop looking at her. His heart hadn't fully accepted that she was still alive. It's as if it was all a dream and he would awaken at any moment to find her gone.

The clothing she wore was completely foreign to him. The material was unfamiliar as was the shape of the skirt. He was astonished to see she wore pants. He knew it was some sort of armor just by looking at it. She looked far more prepared for battle than he was.

Perhaps this was all real. He would not be able to imagine that detail. Her hair was loose for the first time, her long brown hair waving in the wind. Her hair was thick and hung around her head like a lion's mane. Colorful feathers hung loosely in her hair.

Even her weapons were strange. The sword at her side was shining with an unearthly glow. She would have much to explain when they were not in a rush.

"What's going on?" Ethan leaned towards Annika and whispered. "Who are all these people?"

"These are Chief Tuviah's warriors. They protect Avigdor," she said as she anxiously watched the group of men converse in a different language.

"Avigdor?"

She laughed. "Sorry, that's what this island is called. I have much to tell you."

The blond man with a sword broke from the group and approached them.

"What are we doing? The ship is quickly leaving the cove. Even with the repairs slowing it down, it will disappear soon." Ethan felt very much out of the loop, which was something he did not like very much.

"We would prefer to do this under a blanket of darkness, but I guess we will have to make do," the man said casually. He handed Ethan a glowing sword. What had they said his name was? Something about him seemed familiar, but he had no time to dwell on it.

Ethan studied the sword, still perplexed as to what it could be made out of.

"Darkness? How does a storm sound?" Annika asked as she looked at the sky.

Suddenly, a flash of lightning erupted across the sky. The wind began to howl over the water. Waves appeared, pulling the ship back into the harbor as a darkness settled around them.

"Well, that is mighty convenient." Ethan raised a brow.

"Elohim's actions often are." Annika grinned. "What's next, Chief Tuviah?"

The tall man whom Annika had pointed out as the chief had a regal air about him. His posture was straight, and his eyes were steely. Ethan would hate to be on this man's bad side. How had Annika met these people and who were they for that matter?

Chief Tuviah looked at them both and signaled to the trees. "Fly."

Annika seemed to understand what he meant, for she turned with the other warriors and whistled. Suddenly, large bat-like creatures swooped out of the trees and landed gracefully on the beach. Ethan's eyes grew as wide as saucers.

"Ethan, meet Talon." She grinned at the shock and confusion on his face.

"What are they?" Ethan couldn't stop staring at the leathery creatures. The one by Annika stood close, as if protecting her. A flash of lightning erupted, causing the creature's eyes to flash as they studied him.

"They are just some of the mysteries and beauty on this island. I am anxious to share it all with you once we get our friends back. One thing I'm unsure of is how we will fly to the ship with them."

"I can help with that." The blond man with a sword interjected again. Should he ask for his name? Maybe for the time being he would refer to him as Blondie. Even though he did have some white hair appearing amongst the blond. "Talon and the other leather birds are not large enough for us to ride. They can, however, lift us off the ground for a short amount of time. If we hurry, they can carry us to the ship."

"Do we have enough for everyone to ride?" Annika looked anxiously at the ship struggling to get over the tall waves.

"We already sent a leather bird back to call for reinforcements. They should be here anytime." Several loud squawks came from behind, drawing their attention. "Right on time. And we don't have much of that to spare. Let's mount up."

Blondie spent a few quick moments explaining to Annika and Ethan how to hold onto the animals as they carried them over the water. Ethan then met his ride, a large leathery bird with black eyes. It was not quite as intimidating as Talon, Annika's ride.

Soon men began clicking their tongues and the animals flapped their strong wings, lifting into the air. Their talon-like feet gently grabbed the warriors and hoisted them into the air. They moved surprisingly quickly over the choppy water ahead.

Annika put a hand on his shoulder. "Are you ready?"

"Do we have a choice?" His legs shook and his fingers trembled. Could he really do this?

Annika turned to him with a shaky smile. "I don't think so." She clicked her tongue. Quickly, Talon and Ethan's mount picked them off the ground and carried them swiftly over the water.

Ethan sucked in a breath, his stomach complaining about the movement. The waves in the ocean made flying difficult, but with the power in the animals' wings they were still moving quickly. Ethan felt the trembling in his limbs quell, replaced by awe. This was something he had never experienced before, moving at these speeds and in this manner. He was flying. Even if it was just barely over the water, it was such a new sensation. With each beat of the animals' wings, they were that much closer to the ship.

Waves bashed the side of the ship, causing the vessel to sway dangerously onto its side before righting itself. With each wave, the ship was pushed closer to the high cliffs. Despite the crashing waves, Chief Tuviah's people were gathering above the water level, just below the ship's rails. Ethan slowed to a stop just behind Annika, bobbing up and down to the beating of the animal's wings.

"How important is this ship to you?" Blondie shot him a quizzical look. Thankfully he was close as he had to strain to be heard over the storm.

"The men are the first priority. I can replace the ship, my men I cannot."

The man's eyes lit up, as if pleased with the answer. Something about the laugh wrinkles around his eyes started to jog a memory that was hidden in the depth of Ethan's mind.

"Let's do this with little bloodshed then, shall we?" He grinned at Annika and Ethan. "Our first priority is the men. We will need to fly them back to shore in shifts. Let's try for stealth first and fight as little as possible."

Ethan and Annika both nodded their heads. Ethan's shoulder was beginning to cramp from the tight hold of the animal above him. Whatever they did, hopefully they did it soon.

The chief made a whistle sound, and he was carried closer to the ship where he was able to grab onto a rope hanging from the side. Once he had a hold of the rope, he signaled for the animal to let go and began making his way up the rope. His warriors followed closely behind, no sign of fear in their faces.

"Are you ready to see Maddock again?" Ethan asked near Annika's ear. She nodded, a firm expression set on her face.

"Let's get our friends back." With that they joined the others in climbing up the ship. The swaying of the vessel beneath their feet made it difficult, but they were making progress. The strange birds flew to the top and clung to the sides of the ship, out of sight.

Lightning continued to flash, and the waves rose higher. The ship was quickly approaching the jagged cliffs. If they didn't act fast, it would soon run aground.

Ethan gripped the rail with his cold hands and hoisted himself over the side. The sight of his ship should have brought him relief, but the chaos aboard gave him a sinking feeling. They had come over the rail near the back of the ship, hidden from sight somewhat by the deck and the masts.

He crouched down behind some barrels with the others, watching men run frantically around, trying to keep the ship afloat. Maddock was by the wheel of the ship, shouting orders and profanities.

This man was not made to be a captain. No one would look up to him and follow him unless they were forced or coerced.

"Am I right to assume that is him?" Blondie crouched next to Ethan. At Ethan's nod he continued, "Not exactly leadership material, is he?"

"You are right about that." Ethan looked up and down the deck, unsure as to why they had not been spotted yet. Ten or so warriors were crouched on the deck. The others must be waiting on the side of the ship.

Blondie scanned the deck in front of them. "We need to get moving. Those cliffs are coming too close for comfort. I'm unsure as to why they got this close, but we need to get everyone off." He turned and addressed the men around him. He then turned to Ethan and Annika to relay the message. "We don't want any unnecessary bloodshed so we will fight to subdue, not to kill. Also, our leather birds will stay out of this. If they were to join the fight, there would be few survivors. They will only be used as a final resort. We attack on my mark."

Everyone readied themselves for the chaos that was soon to grow even worse. Blondie glanced over his shoulder. "Annika, you take some men and go below deck and find the men."

She nodded. Ethan was about to protest when he thought better of it. He hated to see her walk away again. The reality of her being alive still had not quite sunk in.

"Go!" Blondie held his sword aloft and charged onto the deck, drawing stares and confusion from the weary sailors. Men swarmed up from all sides of the ship and worked on subduing the enemy.

As Ethan ran into the fray, he caught a glimpse of Annika leading a small team of warriors below deck and out of sight. Thankfully, the fight onboard was distracting all from the small group.

Many men were too stunned to even fight back. They raised their hands immediately in surrender. Unfortunately, there were still some men who didn't look quite ready to give up.

Ethan approached the first man, who held a sword out and assumed a fighting pose. The man took one look at the glowing sword in his hands and cowered. It only took one quick deft movement to disarm the man and knock him to the ground.

"You'll stay down if you know what's good for you. If you want out of Maddock's control, then surrender now. We are getting out of here." He left the confused sailor on the deck and used his sword to fight his next opponent.

The fighting around him intensified as the native warriors quickly took down one man after another. The men who were true followers of Maddock were the strongest fighters. Their hate and anger were enough to give a purpose in their steps. The sailors Maddock had threatened or coerced gave up rather quickly.

"I don't know how you got here but I can't say I'm pleased." Lightning flashed and Ethan whirled just in time to block Maddock's blade before it slashed his head.

"You wouldn't believe me if I told you." Ethan pushed Maddock's sword away. He and Maddock walked in a circle, sizing each other up. Maddock's greedy eyes watched Ethan's sword. His interest in Ethan's sword wasn't enough of a distraction. It might have actually made him attack with more vigor.

He yelled and lunged forward. Ethan sidestepped and knocked the blade out of the way. He was well accomplished with a blade, a testament to his many years of training. Maddock was not as accomplished as him. It only took a few minutes of fighting to see that. He was, however, much bigger and stronger. Any blow that Ethan would be unable to block would land a serious injury.

With each strike of his sword, Ethan felt like he was releasing the anger he had been storing up for the man. With Maddock's betrayal Ethan had seen his men suffer and could do nothing to stop it. Maddock had done everything he could to belittle Ethan and to strip him of his captain's title. With each successful blow he felt like his status of captain was returning.

"Captain Wolf, do you require assistance?" Blondie's voice broke through Ethan's concentration.

Ethan shook his head and continued the battle. The fighting aboard deck had subsided, all of Maddock's men having been overcome. Now the warriors all stood, watching the fight.

What Ethan had in skill Maddock seemed to make up for in strength. The repeated movements and blocks were beginning to weaken Ethan. Hopefully, Annika was doing better than he was.

CHAPTER TWENTY-FIVE

Annika descended the dark stairs. The only light was coming from a few lonely lanterns hanging on the walls. The ship rocked from side to side with the waves. As she carefully descended the steps, they creaked and groaned. Achim was behind her, followed by a handful of others. He gave her a reassuring smile.

She took a deep breath when she reached the bottom of the stairs. Nothing looked unusual yet, just boxes and crates. If the layout was anything like *Sailor's Journey,* then the kitchen would be to the right. Where would they be keeping the men?

A familiar voice cut through the creaks of the ship. It was Carter. Annika smiled and turned to find the voice. Her footsteps seemed loud on the wooden floorboards, regardless of the leather soles.

"Who goes there?" Another familiar voice reached her ears, but this one was not pleasant. She groaned inwardly; it was Simon. She had one more corner to round to where she assumed he was. "I thought I heard swords clashing."

Annika cautiously rounded the corner. Simon stood a few feet in front of her. His smile stilled and was replaced with shock.

"Hello, Simon. Long time no see." She gritted out the words. This was one man she had not been missing.

"How–how is this possible?" His words stumbled out.

"Annika?" A trembling voice came from behind Simon. Her eyes were still adjusting to the darkness. Finally, she saw there were bars behind Simon and beyond those bars the faces she had been worrying about. Carter, Jack, and Jonah were at the bars, looking at her in shock.

"It's me." She almost cried again at the sight of Carter.

"But how are you alive?"

Annika glowered as she turned her attention back to Simon. "I escaped the jaws of Maveth, no thanks to your captain either."

He held up his hands, the smile he was known for returning. "I'll have you know that I was very angry with Maddock for doing that to you. That is why I have been banished down here watching the prisoners. I had no idea he was going to throw you to the beast, or I would have protected you." His smile sent shivers down her spine as he stepped forward.

Annika pulled her sword out of its protective sheath; it lit up the dark room. Everyone's eyes grew wide with surprise.

"What is that?" Simon's greedy eyes had yet to leave her sword.

"A sword, genius. Now, don't take another step. I never asked for your protection or your attention. We both know you never had my well-being in mind."

He managed to look away from her sword. "I'm a gentleman, my lady." Simon's smile slipped a little as he attempted a small bow.

"A snake can put on gentleman's clothes but that cannot hide its venomous nature."

Achim and the others stood behind her in the crowded hallway. Simon's eyes caught their movement behind her. "I see you brought friends."

Annika's heart was filling with righteous anger. How long had she been feeling his gaze upon her? Since the start of her journey way back in the kingdom of Narine. Moreover, he was a key player in the mutiny against Captain Samuel and Ethan.

"Yes, I did. Lay down your sword and step back. Your captain and his men are most assuredly captured already."

His stance was cocky. Even in this situation he tried to use his charms on her. Though, charm was a strong word for the theatrics he attempted.

"Annika, please, I thought we were friends."

"You were gravely mistaken." Her eyes never left his.

"You wound me, madam. I defended you in front of Maddock. I even argued with him over his dropping you into the beast's mouth." He placed a hand over his heart, looking like he was hurt and had missed her.

Annika scoffed. "We both know you would not have defended just anyone and the only reason you would defend me was if you wanted something. I'll tell you right now, the moment I set eyes on you I knew you were fake. Your smile and demeanor are all an act to better yourself in the eyes of others. All just to get what you want."

Simon was no longer smiling. His eyes had become like steel. "So, you think you're too good for me, is that it? I know I'm running with a rough crowd right now, but it's only temporary." He sighed and ran a hand over his face. "You know, I'm starting to think dropping you into the jaws of a beast was the right decision."

Simon whisked his sword out and lunged for Annika. She threw her own sword up and parried his blow. Bright sparks sprayed into the air as her sword connected with his.

They parried and thrusted. She dove and ducked from his blade. She felt at a disadvantage; the close quarters hindered her movements considerably. That did not stop her from using her skills wisely. Her feet nimbly found their footing and very quickly began gaining ground. Simon was very different than Maddock in his skill level. Maddock was very strong and had some skill with a blade. Simon, on the other hand, was only decently skilled. His smaller form could not hold anywhere near the amount of strength that Maddock's had.

Annika was quickly pushed into the corner as she blocked the oncoming blows. If she did not get the upper hand soon, she would be trapped. Out of the corner of her eye, she saw a table to her left. That would have to do.

After Simon's next swing, she blocked his blow and turned to the wall. She braced her boot on the wall, found her footing, and leaped from the wall to the table. After landing securely on the table, she whirled around and jumped just in time to miss another swing of Simon's blade. Annika managed to step on the flat edge of his blade and pinned his sword beneath her feet. His surprised face sought hers. Before he could recover and retrieve his sword, she kicked and connected a blow to his face.

Simon stumbled backward, managing to pull his sword with him. Blood trickled from his nose and down his face. With Simon now injured and on the defense, Annika used it to her advantage.

She began to go on the offense, pushing him back. His blocks became hasty and sloppy. Her movements were straight and true as she attacked her opponent. She lunged to the left and slid her blade across his arm. He looked at the blood trickling down his arm for a moment. She used his pain to her advantage and stabbed him in his right shoulder. The sword fell from his grasp as his fearful eyes flew to hers.

Annika stood over him, sword poised to strike. She smiled and lowered her blade until the tip was skimming his face. "Achim, would you happen to have a bit of rope on you?" As the young man came from behind and bound Simon's hands, Annika leaned forward. "What's on the inside is what makes a true gentleman. Despite all your pleasant words and appearances, you were as trustworthy as a serpent."

Simon's face was growing red with anger. His eyes were wide, and his normally slicked back hair was in disarray. All attempt at kindness was gone.

"Annika?" She jerked her attention around to the men behind bars. She quickly grabbed the key off the wall and unlocked the door. Carter came leaping into her arms, and she enveloped him in a fierce hug. Tears were streaming freely down her face now.

"I knew you were not dead." Carter's voice was muffled in her shoulder.

Annika drew her head back and looked into his gentle eyes. "I heard of you and your courage. I am so proud of you and of the man you have become." New tears sprang to his eyes, and she hugged him tightly again.

"What about us? Are you proud of us too?" Jack came up alongside her with a wide grin on his face.

"Oh, immensely!" She laughed joyfully. "It's so good to see all of you!" Annika gave Jack and Jonah quick hugs. They all seemed in one piece, perhaps thinner and tired, but alive.

"I don't understand." Jonah for the first time looked flustered and in awe.

Annika laughed. "I will explain later. Right now, we need to get everyone off the ship."

"Why? We can take them now." Jack crossed his arms, a cocky grin set on his face.

"I have no doubt of that, but the ship will hit the cliffs soon. We don't have much time. Captain Wolf is up with the others buying us what time he can, so we must hurry."

"Cap is up there? Why didn't you say so? What are we doing standing around here for?" Jonah smiled and nodded to the warriors. That was all the prodding the men behind bars needed. Jonah and Jack led everyone, including Simon, out of the cramped room and up the stairs.

Annika followed along and was assaulted by the angry wind that met them upon reaching the deck. Her loose hair flew all around her face, causing her to have to hold it back.

Before she could look around and search for Ethan, something gave her pause. Her eyes skimmed the area, trying to find the cause. Ethan's captain's quarters was the only thing near her. A strange feeling came over her, and she felt compelled to enter it.

She slowly creaked the door open and was instantly brought back to her first night on the ship. She'd had so much anger and fear at that time. Crazy how things had drastically changed since then.

Inside looked basically the same, other than a mess left behind by Maddock's careless men as they searched for riches. She was about to leave when she felt the pull again. What was it about this room that was giving her such pause? She walked slowly around the small room, looking for anything that could be the cause.

Her fingers skimmed over the rough wooden planks on the wall. A knob in the wood caught her attention, her forefinger stopping on it. She pressed it in, and a small door opened up. How had she not seen this the night she stayed here? Or maybe the better question was, why she had seen it today?

The inside of the crevice was small but was completely stuffed. There was a leather book, its cover worn from use and age. She pulled it out and fingered the soft material. A leather band rapped around the book, keeping it shut.

A glimmer from inside the crevice got her attention. There was an intricate dagger hidden in the back. Above the hilt was the head of a wolf, its fur littered intricately with glimmering jewels. Right next to it was a golden necklace with what looked to be a wolf crest. Were these family heirlooms of Ethan's?

It felt wrong looking through his private things, but something told her that she needed to take them out. If the ship was going to sink, he would want these items. She tucked the knife into the book and placed the book into the belt around her waist. The necklace she placed around her neck and tucked beneath her blouse. Hopefully Ethan would agree with her decision to take them.

"Annika, you coming?" Carter came to the door of the room and looked in.

"Coming!" She closed the door in the wall quickly and raced out of the room. The sound of metal clashing against metal reached her ears. "What's going on?"

Gabriel approached her. "We are starting to send the men back in shifts. Maddock's men went first and now we're starting with Captain Wolf's. They put up a fuss at first, but they are on their way now." He pointed behind him. "Captain Wolf and Maddock are engaged in a heated battle over there."

Swords clashed again, drawing her attention. Maddock and Ethan were circling one another, determination set on their faces.

"He's holding his own, but Maddock is not going down easy. We don't have long until we hit the cliffs. I wouldn't be surprised if it's minutes away. With all this fog it's hard to tell for certain."

Annika was surprised to see there was indeed a thick fog blanketing the ocean around them. *Elohim, please help us.*

Ethan blocked another blow from Maddock, his arms burning. His opponent seemed to have a never-ending amount of energy. Where was he drawing it from?

"Maddock, please, we must turn the ship around. If we do not, it will hit the cliffs!" Ethan shouted, his voice barely traveling over the fury of the wind.

"You are just saying that to confuse us. I see no cliffs!"

Ethan turned his attention quickly and saw that a thick fog had encompassed the ship. Nothing was visible beyond the rails, but dread filled his stomach. They were close, he could feel it.

"In minutes we will be upon them." Ethan dodged and rolled away from a slice meant for his head. He swung his own blade and caught

Maddock on the arm. The man cried out in pain and lashed out in new fury.

"We must abandon ship now or we will never make it!" Ethan parried another back breaking blow. Maddock's eyes glimmered angrily, and his teeth clenched.

"I will not abandon my ship! You are trying to take what is now rightfully mine!" Maddock sliced down with his sword, barely missing Ethan and imbedding his blade into the wood of the deck. He yanked it out and faced Ethan again.

"I'm not looking to take anything. I'm trying to save your life!"

"A likely story." Maddock thrust again.

What could be done at this point? It was entirely possible for Ethan to beat him, but it would take time. Which they were sorely short on.

"It's over now, Maddock. Look around you. How many of your men do you see?"

Maddock looked around and fear began to cloud his eyes. All of his men, save Simon, were off the ship.

"Surrender now and we will leave. No matter what you have done, I don't wish for your death."

Maddock looked contemplative for a moment before the dark glimmer returned to his eyes. "Never," he seethed.

Maddock made one last attempt to plunge his blade into Ethan. With his large size and momentum, he was barreling towards Ethan. Expertly, he avoided Maddock's blade and tripped him. Unable to catch himself, he fell to the ground with a thud.

Maddock groaned and attempted to rise, only to find Ethan at his back with a sword at his throat.

"Captain, we must leave now." Blondie's voice was sounding quite urgent.

"What do you say, Maddock? Are you coming with us?"

Silence was the only reply he received. He slowly stood and moved away from Ethan, blade clenched uselessly at his side. The look on his face was full of pure hatred.

"Captain," Blondie pleaded.

"Are you coming?" Ethan asked one more time.

"No." Maddock spit out the words.."

"Let's go, Captain." Annika approached and put a hand on his arm.

"You're supposed to be dead." Maddock frowned.

"You'd be surprised by how much I've heard that today." Annika smiled and her eyes sought Ethan's.

"Let's go." He took her hand and walked to the edge of the ship. The chief leaped over the rail with the blond man. It was now just himself and Annika left on deck.

Maddock stood defiantly. Simon, hands bound behind his back, stood with him.

"Come with us. If you want to live, you must leave," Ethan pleaded once more.

Maddock shook his head. "I don't believe a word you say. You go ahead and leave, save me the trouble of having to clean up your bodies."

A sudden deep urge to leave the ship filled Ethan's senses. "Annika, we need to jump. Now!" They leaped from the railing at the same time and fell into the churning waters below. Ethan found his way to the surface and gasped in his breath. He frantically searched for Annika and found her sputtering close to him.

Before he could even move to her side, a strong clamp around his shoulders pulled him out of the water. He looked up and was actually happy to see the leather bird above him. Annika was being lifted along with him over the choppy water. A groaning from behind them drew their attention; the ship had reached the cliff. A large wave took the ship and rammed it into the side of the cliff. Within minutes, the ship was not even recognizable. All that was left was boards and crates.

If only Maddock had been less stubborn, or perhaps Ethan had not said the right things. He had a great dislike for the man, but he hadn't wished his death.

Ethan and Annika reached the beach and were dropped gently onto the white sands. Everyone was gathered on the beach in shock of the destruction they had barely missed.

"We will check to see if they survived," the blond man said. "Though I don't have much hope." Everyone was quiet, the near-death experience and the events of the past few days still weighing on their minds.

"Now what?" Ethan looked to Annika and held his hand out. To his delight, she eagerly clasped his hand in her own.

"I have much to tell you." The smile on her face warmed his heart.

The storm had quickly let up and the last rays of the day warmed their chilled bodies. Annika felt her first moment of peace as she held Ethan's hand. They traipsed through the jungle, making their way to the village. A couple hours later, they entered through a gateway in the volcano's wall. Upon arriving at the other side, all the sailors looked around in awe. The walls surrounding the village were enough to draw their eyes, let alone the animals within. Even though it was dark, they could still see some of the Ancients. Plus, the glow from the amaris was another sight to behold.

Annika took time to point out the animals she knew and laughed at the confusion and wonder on the grown men's faces. The whole time Ethan had not let go of her hand. What could that mean? He could have let go or not even reach for her in the first place. The look in his eyes made her think that he felt the same way about her as she did him.

"Annika!" Rivkah raced towards her, and Annika let go of Ethan's hand to embrace her friend. "You're well, aren't you? You are not injured?"

Annika chuckled. "I'm fine, really. Your armor held up beautifully and Talon was wonderful. Thank you so much for all your help and kindness."

"Of course!" Rivkah smiled and leaned in so only Annika could hear. "I already spoke briefly with Gabriel. He says you found your captain, and I can see he was right." She waggled her eyebrows at Annika, who barely stifled in a laugh.

"Don't get too excited. Nothing has happened."

"That's not what it looks like to me." Rivkah grinned and looked her over once more. She peeled back the bandage on Annika's shoulder. "Doesn't look like you reopened your wound."

"It doesn't even hurt. There are others here who are not doing well, though. You already met Captain Samuel, I'm assuming?"

"Oh, yes." Rivkah nodded, her face solemn. "He is resting. That man received quite the beating. He has broken ribs, a broken arm, and bruises everywhere. He's in remarkably good spirits despite all his injuries."

"I'm happy to hear that." Annika sighed in relief.

"What happened to your arm?" Rivkah gently prodded the wound on Annika's arm.

"Oh, nothing serious. It's just a small cut." Annika smiled.

Rivkah examined it and nodded. "Get it washed up and I'll apply something to it later."

"Thank you, Rivkah." Annika hugged her again. "These men have not eaten in a few days or even had a drink. Jack's stomach has not stopped growling the whole way here. Would you happen to have something they could eat or drink?"

"Hey, you try not eating for a few days and tell me how you feel." Jack crossed his arms and grinned. He nodded at Rivkah. "My name's Jack, ma'am."

"It's a pleasure to meet Annika's friends." Rivkah turned her attention to the men behind Annika. "I do believe you will be happy to hear I have water now for you all and supper is being prepared."

Rivkah led the men away like a mother goose with her obedient children walking behind. Carter followed the group as well, no doubt his own stomach calling for sustenance. Annika laughed at the sight and was surprised to see Ethan still standing by her.

"Shall we join the others?" He held his arm out for her, and she took it. His steps were slower than the men ahead of them. "I have so many questions."

"That's understandable. Much has happened in the past few hours." Annika smiled. Her left hand was placed on his arm; it was a comfortable place to be.

"You haven't really explained what happened to you." She could feel his warm gaze upon her. They were approaching a small stream that flowed through the village. Tree branches hung over it and the water sparkled in the moonlight. Reminding her very much of the water in the cove right before she had been taken under.

She sighed, forcing herself to remember. "It happened so fast, which is good because I was not given much time to be fearful. I was pulled below the water and dragged deep. I was so cold, and I couldn't breathe. I could feel myself slipping away. My whole body became numb, and I lost all track of time." She paused, hoping he would not laugh at her. Should she tell him about the words she heard from Elohim? Perhaps he would laugh at her. "I know it sounds crazy, but I know Elohim saved me, I could feel His presence. Next thing I knew, Maveth had carried me behind the waterfall and just sat watching me until help arrived. Despite the terrible ordeal, I had never felt so close to my Creator."

"This whole talk of Elohim really confuses me. I'm so happy you are safe and sound now, but I can't wrap my head around it all. I was taught about Elohim from my mother and father at a young age. I believed in Him because my parents did. After they were both taken from me, I felt betrayed. How could the loving God whom I had learned about let such evil prevail? In the last day alone, I have witnessed some things that some would describe as miracles, but I still don't understand. Why would He not stop all the pain before it happens? If He made a storm appear for us today, why not take away the one that brought us here? Or even stop it before it started?"

Annika thought for a moment. These very questions were some of the hardest ones to explain and even confused her at times. What could she say to explain it? She let go of Ethan's arm and leaned against a tree that was on the bank of the stream.

"I don't know why bad things happen in this world. I'll never understand why my mom had to die and why my father left us." Annika bent down and picked up a stick and twirled it in her fingers. "I do know that Elohim is not evil. He cannot even stand the presence of sin. Which is what our ancestors did, they sinned and disobeyed Him. With that sin came the destruction and suffering that is now so prevalent today."

Ethan joined her at the water's edge. "That makes it seem like we all have no hope, no chance of ever finding happiness. What's the point of living a life knowing that we blew our chances of ever having happiness? Will we just fade into sin and forever be in the dark?"

"That's where Elohim's love and kindness comes into play. He loves us so much that He deemed us worthy of a second chance. He intervened and sent His only son to die in our place. Now, we have to the option to turn from sin. Unfortunately, that does not mean everyone will. Even with all the sin in this world, you can still see the power of Elohim. Despite our sin, He has not abandoned us." She threw the stick into the water and faced Ethan. "Elohim promises that if we repent and turn from our wicked ways that we will live with Him in paradise one day. Everyone who believes and calls on His name will be there. Which means you will see your parents again, as will I."

Ethan's eyes glistened, and he rapidly blinked and turned his face slightly. "You sound like my father." The corner of his mouth tilted into a slow smile.

"I'll take that as a compliment." She smiled back. "You know Elohim has protected us the entire time we've been on the island? After arriving here, I heard that the animals beyond the cliffs are harmful to eat. Everything but the fish carry parasites and disease. We only were able to catch fish."

Ethan's eyes grew wide. "That's true. Maddock and his men were eating a deer they had shot but didn't give us any. We were starved while they ate fresh game."

"So, you all being starved had an advantage to it I suppose."

"Yes, I suppose you could look at it that way. How deadly is the meat?"

"I've heard it's very deadly. By the time symptoms start coming, you could be too far gone to save." Annika shivered, then her eyes grew wide. "Some of Maddock's men turned from him. If they ate the meat, they could be in trouble. I will have to tell Rivkah of this."

"I guess we should be grateful that we were such poor hunters." He chuckled.

The others were now out of sight, no doubt taking refreshing sips of water. Annika's mouth watered thinking of it. Surely, Ethan needed it more than her.

Annika ran her hand over her neck and felt a hard object. "Oh, I almost forgot. I have something for you." Annika withdrew the necklace from beneath her armor. The gold reflected the moonlight as Ethan's trembling fingers clasped it.

"Where did you get this?" He squeezed the necklace in his hand.

"Same place I got these." She withdrew the book and the knife that was placed inside. "I don't know what lead me to finding them, so the only explanation I can give is Elohim. I hope you aren't angry with me for having them."

Ethan held the items in his hands and cleared his throat. "Not at all. If I hadn't been so preoccupied, I would have gone to get them. These items were the most valuable things on that ship to me. Thank you," he whispered the words, his eyes filled with emotion. His arms enveloped her in a gentle hug, and her arms naturally wound behind his back.

Her cheek was resting against his chest, his heartbeat pounding against her ear. "You're welcome." Had something changed between them? Annika couldn't help but wonder. She had never hugged him before today, and now this was beginning to feel normal.

"I have one more question for now." Ethan chuckled and pulled away. Annika looked up at him expectantly. "What are you wearing?"

Annika laughed and buried her head in his chest again before looking into his face. "It's Rivkah's old armor. I know I probably look silly in it."

"Not at all, it suits you." He reached up and touched her cheek. "You are stunning." He leaned forward and gently kissed her forehead. Annika's body stilled as her heart rate sped up. Her skin tingled where his lips had touched. That definitely was not something one would do to just a friend.

He chuckled at her shocked expression. "Shall we join the others now? I have to admit I am mighty hungry as well." Annika attempted a shaky smile, her heart still racing.

As they walked, hand in hand, she wondered what the future would hold for them next. Her life had changed drastically since she had decided to set out for the kingdom of Lookonia. Elohim had brought them to this island and had put Ethan into her life. Surely, that had to be for a reason. She stole a quick look at his face and found him already looking at her. Could Elohim wish for her future to be hand in hand with Ethan's? She could only hope and pray it would be.

CHAPTER TWENTY-SIX

A short while later, Annika sat around Chief Tuviah's fire, along with many of her friends. Carter, Jack, Jonah, Captain Samuel, and Ethan all sat around the fire as well, eating some stew that the women had helped prepare.

The chief suddenly held up his hand, and all around the fire grew silent. His calculating eyes scanned the group. He spoke in his foreign tongue and Gabriel translated. "The chief is happy to have met all of you. Annika had told us of you and pleaded to us on your behalf. At first, we doubted the need for our interference, but tonight we are proud to know you all. We have witnessed many of Elohim's miracles today, and everyone on this island will remember this day." Gabriel paused and waited again for Chief Tuviah before continuing to translate. "You are welcome to stay in our borders as long as you wish. You will always be welcome here on Avigdor."

"We are beyond grateful for your assistance and for your hospitality, Chief Tuviah." Gabriel translated Ethan's words to the chief quietly, as the big man watched Ethan with intense eyes. "None of us would be standing here if not for your compassion and kindness. I believe we will have to ask for your kindness for a while longer. Our ride out of here was thoroughly smashed into the cliff."

Chief Tuviah looked to Gabriel, who nodded. "Chief Tuviah has a gift for you all. The ship that brought me here is still on this island. A few repairs and it will be seaworthy, if you wish to take it."

"No, that's too much. We are already indebted to you." Ethan held his hands up, shock written on his features.

The chief shook his head a small smile on his face. "Not need. You take."

"Yes," Gabriel picked up where the chief left off. "We have no need for it. If you want it, then it's yours."

Ethan shook his head in wonder. "I don't know what to say."

Gabriel grinned. "I suggest you accept. It's not polite to refuse his kindness." He shared a smile with Chief Tuviah.

"If that's the case," Ethan chuckled, "then we wholeheartedly accept."

Gabriel clapped his hands together. "Wonderful! She needs a few minor repairs done before she sets sail but that won't take long."

Annika's excitement grew until she looked around and realized that meant they would be leaving soon. All these wonderful new people she met, would she ever see them again? A frown found its way onto her face. In such a short time these people had found a special place in her heart.

"Annika?" Chief Tuviah's eyes searched her face. There was no hiding anything from the perceptive man's eyes.

"I just realized this place has quickly grown on me. The people, the land, everything here is so different from beyond your borders. I know we must leave, but I will miss you all." She managed a sad smile.

Chief Tuviah nodded his head slowly, smiling wide. He spoke and Gabriel quickly translated.

"He said, 'You will always have a place here.'"

"Thank you." She managed to say and put a real smile on her lips. He looked at her in a way that reminded her of her own father. It would be hard to leave these people. Their kindness and acceptance was a rare thing to find. "So, where have you been hiding this ship? I have yet to lay eyes on it."

"We have hidden the ship in a small cove on the island. It's not a far distance from here. If you'd like, I could take you to it tomorrow?" Gabriel looked to Ethan and Captain Samuel. They both nodded.

"That would be much appreciated. Though I might just wait here." Captain Samuel smiled. He was bandaged in many areas and indeed did not look up to a hike in the jungle.

The rest of the evening went by quickly, excited talk of the new ship dominating the conversation. Annika just sat and listened, her thoughts straying to what would meet her in Lookonia. She had begun to hope for a future with Ethan, but would he even be interested now that they had a way to escape? She had made commitments to her brother, but now all she wanted to do was to stay here on this island with Ethan. Sadly, that was now not going to happen. Would he rush off the island and to Lookonia to get her out of his way as soon as possible?

After supper, it was time to turn in. People began saying their good-nights and making their way to their assigned huts. Carter was offered a bunk in Achim's hut. He agreed to it, which surprised Annika. He must feel safe here, otherwise he would never have left her side.

"May I walk you to your hut?" Ethan's low voice came from behind her. Jumping, she turned to find him standing quite close to her. Close enough she could feel his breath on her hair.

"I would love that." She smiled and willed her heart to stop beating so erratically. He held out his arm for her, which she gladly took. They walked side by side down the short lane to Rivkah and Gabriel's hut. Would they have many more moments like this? Soon, they would be off this island and back on a crowded ship. Would he still make time for her then?

The stars twinkled overhead, their brightness a sharp contrast to the pitch-black sky. The whole area was blanketed in silence, save for quiet talk around the fire and crickets chirping in the distance. The moon shone brightly overhead, and the glow of the amaris on the streets lit their path.

"This place is full of surprises. Everywhere I turn there's something that catches my eye. Do you have any idea what these are?"

"I was also intrigued by them. From what I have heard, these gems are called amaris. They are quite rare everywhere but on this island."

"I know I have not seen the like of them before." Ethan held a hand up to the nearest one. His fingers grazed its smooth surface. A moment of silence enveloped the two as they continued walking slowly down the path.

Ethan broke the silence again with a sigh. "I wish I had been able to talk to Maddock more. Perhaps I could have saved him." Annika saw the sadness in his eyes.

"Yes, but you gave him every opportunity to come with us. Maddock chose poorly and ended up paying the consequences." Annika sighed. "Regardless, any death is a painful thing to think of."

"I agree."

"What the chief did was quite the surprise, I never would have thought they had a ship. Let alone that they would give it to us."

"Yes, it was a surprise. Chief Tuviah has shown us much kindness. In fact, everyone here has. Rivkah has made me feel like one of the family."

They stopped walking upon reaching the hut. They both looked up at the glittering stars overhead. "Are you not happy to leave?" Ethan asked quietly.

Annika sighed, keeping her eyes on the stars. "I'm happy for the opportunity to leave. It's something I hadn't even thought possible after seeing the wreckage of the ship. It's just—" She paused, about to say she would miss him. She would miss this island and the distance from all the destruction in the kingdoms.

"Just?" He prodded her on.

Annika bit her lip. "I've come to care much about the people here. It's going to be hard to leave. This place feels like a paradise compared to what I have become accustomed to."

"I know what you mean. I haven't known them as long as you, but they have a certain way about them. In just the short amount of time I have been in this village I can sense a peace unlike any I have ever felt."

She nodded and bit her lip. "It's going to be hard to leave all of you."

"We've grown accustomed to having you and Carter around." He gave a crooked smile.

"And we have become quite used to being around you all." She tried to give him a convincing smile.

"We've all come to care about you two." His voice was hushed, barely even a whisper. Her heart sped up.

"As have we." Their faces were only inches away now. His breath tickled her nose. She had to be careful, as of right now he was not a believer. On top of that he was a pirate, sort of. He had given no indication of ever settling down.

"I suppose you will sail onto your next adventure once dropping us off?" Her gaze fell to the ground as she put some distance between them.

He was silent for a moment. "I have been living my life in a state of constant sorrow. My past always seeming to direct my future." Her heart sunk at his answer. "Since meeting you, though, I have felt true happiness on many occasions. It's as if you are a bright light in my dark world. I've grown accustomed to your smile and your laugh, which are enough to pull me from the darkness."

"Elohim is the only one who can do that for you." Annika held her breath as he spoke.

"I am starting to see that, thanks to you. I can't believe the things I have seen and what I have felt. I don't know how to cope with everything other than to admit Elohim is real. What that means for me I don't know yet."

"I could tell you more about Him sometime, if you wish."

"I would like that." He smiled. "I don't want to stop seeing you once we leave this island, but I don't know how to make that happen."

"I understand." Tears threatened to fall from her eyes.

"Do you?" His fingers cupped her chin and brought her gaze up to his. He frowned at her tears and gently wiped them away with his thumb. He sighed softly. "I want so badly to share my past with you, but I have buried it so deep it's hard to pull it back out."

"I hope one day you can share it with me. I have also become accustomed to seeing your face every day."

"Someday soon, I will share it all with you."

"I look forward to that someday, then. With all my heart." A quiet understanding passed between the two of them. Hopefully, one day, he would be able to free himself from the chains of his past and think of the future.

Annika stood up on her tip toes and planted a quick peck on his cheek. His eyes shot open in surprise and his mouth opened slightly. "Thank you for everything." She smiled and walked into the hut. He may not be ready to commit to anything with her, but she wasn't either. So many unknowns lay ahead in their future. One thing was for certain: she was excited to see what tomorrow would hold.

Ethan smiled and watched Annika retreat into the simple hut. Her thank you had caught him off guard. His skin felt warm where her lips had touched. He had to admit, laying down his burdens and opening his heart up to love again was very tempting. How could he do that when every time he closed his eyes he saw the same image over and over again? When would his nightmares subside so he could think of a future?

Ethan turned away and almost ran into the blond man, who was walking up the path to the hut.

"Pardon me, I was just walking Annika home."

He waved his hand nonchalantly. "Young love." He chuckled. Ethan could feel his face begin to redden.

"I don't believe I caught your name."

"My name is Gabriel."

The name hit him hard. What memory was trying to knock its way into his subconscious? Something about this man was too familiar for his liking.

"If you'll excuse me, I better get going to my own hut." He began to retreat into the darkness.

"You've changed so much, Ethan." Gabriel's soft voice ground him to a halt. He had said his name. How did he know his name? Ethan turned slowly and looked at the man's all-too-familiar eyes.

"How do you know my name?"

Gabriel smiled. "I'm not surprised that you don't recognize me. I heard of your name from Annika, and then I heard of the last name you adopted. Ethan Wolf has a nice ring to it. Something about you made me wonder, and when I saw you on the beach, I knew I was right. The necklace you wear only confirms it." He pointed to the chain around Ethan's neck. The golden wolf glimmered in the moonlight. "I know that crest well, seeing as I stamped it on many documents. Your father was a very close friend of mine."

Ethan inhaled sharply. This was hitting too close to home. "You knew my father?"

Gabriel nodded, his eyes sparkling in the moonlight. "Perhaps I should formally introduce myself. I am Gabriel, advisor to the late King Joel of the kingdom of Lookonia. Your father."

ABOUT THE AUTHOR

C haney Hobson is a passionate and gifted author who crafts Christian fantasy books. Her love for writing books can be traced back to her childhood. She spent most of her spare time writing short stories that she could proudly share with her friends and family members.

Chaney has always enjoyed epic stories of love, hatred, revenge, forgiveness, and spirituality. Apart from books, she is a loving mother to three wonderful kids. When she is not busy working on her next story, you'll find her baking, reading, crafting, and spending time with her family. She is enthusiastic, fun, creative, devoted, and a go-getter with a great desire to make a difference in the world. It is the same determination that motivates her to create unique stories.

If you enjoyed Chaney's books, please consider leaving a review on Amazon/Goodreads. Reviews help an author's work get seen and is a wonderful way to support them.